RAVEN STRIKE

DALE BROWN
AND JIM DeFELICE

RAVEN STRIKE

A DREAMLAND THRILLER

An Imprint of HarperCollins*Publishers*

This is a work of fiction. Names, characters, places, and incidents are products of the authors' imagination or are used fictitiously and are not to be construed as real. Any resemblance to actual events, locales, organizations, or persons, living or dead, is entirely coincidental.

HARPER

An Imprint of HarperCollins*Publishers*
10 East 53rd Street
New York, New York 10022-5299

First Harper premium printing: December 2011

10 9 8 7 6 5 4 3 2 1

PRAISE FOR THE NOVELS OF *NEW YORK TIMES* BESTSELLING AUTHOR
DALE BROWN

"Dale Brown is a superb storyteller."
W.E.B. Griffin, *Washington Post*

"[Brown] gives us quite a ride."
New York Times Book Review

"The novels of Dale Brown brim with violent action, detailed descriptions of sophisticated weaponry, and political intrigue. . . . His ability to bring technical weaponry to life is amazing."
San Francisco Chronicle

"A master at creating a sweeping epic and making it seem real."
Clive Cussler

"His knowledge of world politics and possible military alliances is stunning. . . . He writes about weapons beyond a mere mortal's imagination."
Tulsa World

"Nobody does it better."
Kirkus Reviews

"Brown puts readers right into the middle of the inferno."
Larry Bond

Also in the Dreamland Series

Titles by Dale Brown

Whiplash: Duty Roster

Lieutenant General (Ret.) Harold Magnus

Magnus once supervised Dreamland from afar. With Colonel Tecumseh "Dog" Bastian as its on-the-scene commander, the organization succeeded beyond his wildest dreams. Now as deputy secretary of defense, Magnus hopes to repeat those successes with Whiplash. His handpicked commander: Bastian's daughter, Breanna Stockard.

Breanna Stockard

After retiring from the U.S. Air Force to raise her daughter and help her husband's political career, Breanna found herself bored with home life. She was lured back to a job supervising the development of high-tech wizardry under a combined CIA and Pentagon program. But will she be happy behind a desk when her agents are in trouble?

Jeff "Zen" Stockard

Now a U.S. Senator, Zen still keeps a close eye on national security matters—and his wife.

Jonathon Reid

Reid's official title is Special Assistant to the Deputy Director Operations, CIA. Unofficially, he's the go-to-guy for all black projects, the dirtier the better. He knows how to get around agency politics. More important, he knows where all the agency's bodies are buried—he buried half of them himself.

Colonel Danny Freah

Fifteen years ago Danny Freah won the Medal of Honor for service far beyond the call of duty. Thrust back into action as the head of a reconstituted and reshaped Whiplash team, he wonders if he still has what it takes to lead men and women into battle.

Nuri Abaajmed Lupo

Top CIA operative Nuri Lupo is used to working on his own. Now the young CIA officer has to adjust to working with a quasi-military team—at least half of whom he can't stand.

Chief Master Sergeant Ben "Boston" Rockland

Boston finds himself shepherding a group of young CIA officers and special operations warriors across three continents. To do it successfully, he has to be part crusty old dog and part father figure.

Captain Turk Mako

An Air Force pilot on special assignment to the Pentagon, Turk Mako thinks of himself as the last of a breed. Real live fighter jocks are being rapidly replaced by "back home boys"—pilots who control unmanned aircraft from hangars in the States. Mako is out to prove neither he nor his profession is obsolete.

Al "Greasy Hands" Parsons

Once responsible for the teams that kept Dreamland's top aircraft in shape, the former chief master sergeant is now Breanna Stockard's right-hand graybeard and fixer.

RAVEN STRIKE

RAVEN

———

1

Southeastern Sudan, Africa

IT FELT AS IF GOD HIMSELF WERE HUNTING HIM, circling beyond the clouds, watching every movement. An angry, vengeful god, a god obsessed with obliterating him. It felt as if God had singled him out above all to be the focus of his persecution, the modern-day Job. Except that this Job must die, and die harshly, in bloody fire and unimaginable pain. To survive, this Job must do nothing less than outwit God.

Such thoughts would have been blasphemous to a believer, but Li Han did not believe in the Christian god, let alone the vengeful, twisted Allah his paymasters had created from their own misinterpretations of scripture. To Li Han, all conceptions of god were superstition, tales told to children to get them to bed at night. Li Han had no religion except survival, and no ambition beyond that.

Once, he had dreams. Once, he'd even had desires beyond staying alive.

He was going to be rich. He desired this so badly that he would do anything for it. And he had. Like a fool.

Too late, he learned that wealth and comfort were illusions. The simplest facts had taken so long to understand.

The pilotless aircraft droned above. Li Han could hear it above as he rested at the side of the mine shaft. He had constructed a passive radar device to tell him where the aircraft was, but it wasn't necessary now. All he needed were his ears.

Li Han waited as the engines grew louder. He saw it in his mind's eye as it came overhead. It was the shape of a dagger, sleeker than the UAVs he'd seen farther south, different than the one in Pakistan that had fired at his car but missed.

It was a special UAV. He flattered himself that the Americans had built it just for him.

The noise grew to its loudest—God's angry voice, calling him out.

He laughed.

The drone banked. The sound began to dim.

"You will go when I tell you," he said to the man standing near him.

The man nodded. He knew he was a decoy, knew even that he was very likely to die. And yet he stood there willingly, prepared to run, prepared to take the drone away.

Fool!

The sound lessened as the UAV banked toward the farthest edge of its track above.

"Now," whispered Li Han.

The man pulled the scarf over his head, pitched forward and left the cave.

2

Ethiopia, Africa

MELISSA ILSE FELT HER BREATH CATCH AS THE FIGURE emerged from the shadow of the hillside.

Mao Man, or an imposter?

Not for her to decide—Raven would make the call.

She watched the video feed change as the UAV's sensors locked onto the figure. His back was turned to the aircraft. The plane changed course slightly, angling so it could get a look at the man's face.

Melissa folded her arms to keep herself from interfering. This was the hardest part of the mission—to let Raven do its job on its own.

"Here we go," said Major Krock. The Air Force officer headed the team piloting the Predator UAV, which was flying with and helping monitor Raven. "Here he comes."

Melissa folded her arms. Even on good days she found Krock barely tolerable.

Four vehicles were parked along the hillside below. The figure kept his head down as he reached the dirt road where they were parked. Raven took data from its sensors, comparing what they gathered to its known profiles of the criminal the CIA had nicknamed Mao Man. The system began with the most basic measurements—gender, height, weight—then moved on to the more esoteric, measuring the figure's gait, the arc of his head movements. The computer could identify and sort over twelve hundred features, weighing each one according to a complicated algorithm. Using these data points, it then determined a "target match probability"; it would not strike unless that probability went over 98.875 percent.

It currently stood at 95.6.

Melissa watched the man on the ground reaching for the door handle of the vehicle. She could see the computer's calculations in real time if she wanted, pulling it up on her main monitor.

She didn't. What she wanted was for the operation to be over, to be successful—for Raven to prove itself. They'd been at this for over a month.

Nail him, she thought. *Let's go.*

Suddenly, the main video feed changed. Melissa looked over at the computer screen—target match probability had dropped below fifty percent.

A decoy?

There was another figure moving from the mine, scrambling down the hill.

Mao Man?

Raven wasn't sure. The computer learned from its mistakes, and having been hoodwinked just a few moments before, it would be doubly cautious now.

It was 87.4 percent.

Then 88.6.

It has to be him, she thought.

Nail him!

Come on, come on—kill the son of a bitch already!

3

Southeastern Sudan

Li Han heard the aircraft changing direction, its engines straining. He had counted on more time than this.

The motorcycle was twenty yards away. There was no sense running for it.

He stopped and turned, looking at the UAV tracking him. Its black skin stood out clearly in the blue sky. Barely a thousand feet away, it looked like a vulture, coming for its prey.

There was another nearby. This one was more common, a Predator.

Two aircraft. There was some consolation in that, he thought. He warranted more than the usual effort.

4

Western Ethiopia

A warning buzzer sounded as the computer confirmed Mao Man's identity. A missile had been launched from the interior of the mine he'd been using as cover.

The Raven immediately broke contact with its

target. Flares fired from rear of the aircraft. The UAV shut off its engine and fell on its wing, sailing to the right to avoid the missile. Still without power, the UAV twisted on its back and folded into a three-quarter turn, clearing the area so quickly that the shoulder-launched SAM tracking it had no chance to react.

Instead, it locked on the heat signature of the flares. In a few moments it was past them, and realizing it was about to miss, detonated its warhead. Shrapnel sprayed harmlessly in the air.

Raven had already computed a course back to Mao Man. Interestingly enough, the hostile action had no effect on its evaluation of the target. It remained locked at 98.2.

Melissa turned to the Predator screen to watch the aircraft come around. There was a second SAM warning, this one from the Predator.

Then a proximity warning blared.

"Watch out!" Melissa yelled. "You're too close!"

But it was too late. A black tail filled the Predator screen. Then the video went blank.

Melissa looked back to the Raven panel. It was off-line.

5

Southeastern Sudan

LI HAN THREW HIMSELF TO THE GROUND, KNOWING HE was dead.

There was a loud explosion high above him—the missile fired from the cave.

Then a second sound, closer, though this one softer and longer, more a smack and a tear than a bang.

Another explosion, farther away from the others. A loud crack similar to the first sound.

Li Han lay on the ground for several seconds. He knew he wasn't dead, yet he didn't entirely believe it. The aircraft had been so very close to him this time. Finally he pushed up to his knees and turned around. The sky was empty; the aircraft that had been following him were gone.

Once more, Li Han had cheated the Americans. Or God. Or both.

He took a few steps toward the car, then stopped. The aircraft must have been hit by the missiles. If so, their parts would be nearby. There would certainly be something worth scrounging or selling.

One of the Brothers ran from the cave, yelling at him in Arabic. The Brothers—they were all members of a radical group that called itself the Sudan Brotherhood—used Arabic as their official language of choice. It was a difficult language for Li Han; he would have much preferred English.

But the gist of what the man was saying was easily deciphered: *Praise Allah that you are alive.*

You fool, thought Li Han. It was God who was trying to kill me.

"Where are the planes?" he said to the man in Arabic.

The brother shook his head. Li Han couldn't be sure if he didn't know or couldn't understand his Chinese-accented Arabic.

"The airplane," he said, using English, and held his hands out as if they were wings. The brother pointed toward the hills.

"Let us take a look," said Li Han.

The brother began to protest.

"Don't worry. The Americans never send three planes," said Li Han, starting away. "We are safe for a while."

6

CIA Headquarters Campus (Langley)
McLean, Virginia

JONATHON REID FROWNED AS SOON AS HE ENTERED THE director's dining room. Reginald Harker was sitting at the far end of the table, holding his coffee cup out for the attendant.

Worse news: there was only one other place set. When Reid had received the "invitation" to breakfast with CIA Director Herman Edmund, he assumed Edmund would actually be there.

As an old Agency hand, he should have known better. Reid's official title was Special Assistant to the Deputy Director Operations, CIA; in fact, he ran his own portfolio of projects at Edmund's behest. Officially "retired" and back on a contract basis, Reid was the grayest of grayhairs in the Agency.

"Jonathon." Harker nodded, but didn't rise.

Reid pulled out the chair opposite him and sat down. Harker had been with the CIA for a little over twenty years. In the old days, he'd been a Middle East expert, and had done his share of time in the region. Reid wasn't sure what he'd done in the interim, but at the moment he was a deputy in the action directorate, a covert ops supervisor in charge of restricted projects. Reid didn't know what they were; in fact, he didn't even know Harker's formal title. Titles often meant very little in their line of work.

"Just coffee," Reid told the attendant. "Black."

"I was glad you could make it," said Harker after the woman left.

"I was under the impression Herman would be here," said Reid.

"Very busy morning," said Harker.

"We have business, then?"

Harker made a face, then looked to the door as the attendant knocked. The woman had worked for the Agency for nearly forty-five years, and un-doubtedly had forgotten more secrets than either man had ever been told. But neither Harker nor

Reid spoke until she finished laying out Harker's meal and left a fresh pot of coffee for Reid.

"I understand you're working with the Office of Special Technology," said Harker finally. "Heading our half of it."

"*Mmmm*," said Reid noncommittally.

"We need help on an assignment."

"Who's 'we'?"

Harker put his elbows on the table and leaned forward over his untouched egg. This was all just show and posture—exactly the thing Reid hated about the Agency bureaucracy. The man obviously needed a favor. He should just come out and say it.

"I've been working directly under D-CIA," said Harker, meaning Edmund. "It's a special project."

"So far you've told me nothing."

Harker frowned, then changed tact. "I thought you were retiring, Jonathon."

"I am retired. Back on contract. At my pleasure."

Harker picked up his fork and took a mouthful of egg. Reid could now guess what was up: something Harker was in charge of had gone to crap, and he needed help from Whiplash.

"How is it?" asked Reid.

"Cold," said Harker, putting down his fork.

"So what went wrong?" said Reid finally.

"Why do you think something went wrong?"

"Reg, I have a lot of things to do today."

"We have a project called Raven," said Harker. "Have you heard of it?"

"No," said Reid.

"Well that's good, at least." Harker rubbed his face. His fingers pushed so hard that they left white streaks on the skin. "It's a follow-on to the Predator program. In a sense. We lost one of the planes last night in Africa. We need to recover the wreckage. One of our agents is headed there now. We wondered—the director wondered—if it would be possible for Whiplash to back her up."

7

Brown Lake Test Area, Dreamland

CAPTAIN TURK MAKO STRETCHED HIS ARMS BACK AND rocked his shoulders, loosening his muscles before putting on the flight helmet for the Tigershark II. For all of its advanced electronics and carefully thought-out interface, the helmet had one serious shortcoming:

It was heavy, at least twice the weight of a regular flight helmet. And the high-speed maneuvers the Tigershark II specialized in didn't make it feel any lighter.

Then again, the brain bucket did keep the gray matter where it belonged.

"Ready, Captain?" asked Martha Albris, flight crew chief for the test mission.

Though standing next to him, Albris was using the Whiplash com system, and her voice was so loud in the helmet that it hurt Turk's eardrums. Turk put his hand over the ear area of his helmet and rotated his palm, manually adjusting the volume on the external microphone system. The helmet had several interfaces; besides voice, a number of controls were activated by external touch, including the audio volume. It was part of an intuitive control system aimed to make the Tigershark more an extension of the pilot's body rather than an aircraft.

Turk gave her a thumbs-up.

They walked together to the boarding ladder. The Tigershark II was a squat, sleek aircraft, small by conventional fighter standards. But then she wasn't a conventional fighter. She was designed to work with a fleet of unmanned aircraft, acting as both team leader and mother hen.

Turk went up the four steps of the ladder to a horizontal bridge, where he climbed off the gridwork and onto the seat of his airplane. He folded his legs down under the control panel and into the narrow tunnel beneath the nose of the plane, slipping into the airplane much like a foot into a loafer.

Albris bent over the platform to help him. As crew chiefs went, she was particularly pleasing to the eye, even in her one-piece coverall. Turk had actually never seen the civilian mechanics supervisor in anything but a coverall. Still, her freckled face and the slight scent of perfume sent his imagination soaring.

Maybe he'd look her up after the postflight debrief.

Turk's fantasies were interrupted by a black SUV that pulled across the front of the hangar, its blue emergency lights flashing. The passenger-side door opened and his boss, Breanna Stockard, emerged from the cab.

"Turk, I need to talk to you," she yelled. "There's been a change in plans."

Turk pulled himself back upright.

"Flight scrubbed, boss?" he asked. The helmet projected his voice across the hangar.

"The test flight is. But you're still going to fly."

"Really? Where to?"

"We'll discuss it inside," said Breanna.

BREANNA WATCHED TURK CLIMB OUT OF THE PLANE AND run over to the truck. That was the great thing about Turk—he was enthusiastic no matter what.

"Another demo flight for visiting congressmen?" he asked.

"Not really," she said, turning toward the hangar. "We have to go downstairs to discuss it."

The Office of Special Technology used a small area in the Dreamland complex to house Tigershark and some related projects. Besides a pair of hangars, it "owned" an underground bunker and a support area there.

The Office of Special Technology was an outgrowth of several earlier programs that brought cutting-edge technology to the front lines. Most notable of these was Dreamland itself, which a decade and a half before had been run by Breanna's father, Tecumseh "Dog" Bastian. But the walk down the concrete ramp to the secure areas below held no special romance for Breanna; she'd long ago learned to steel herself off from any emotion where Dreamland was concerned.

"You're flying to Sudan," Breanna told Turk when they reached the secure area below. Once a medical test lab, the room was now used to brief missions. It was functionally the equivalent of a SCIF, or secure communications area, sealed against possible electronic eavesdropping.

Breanna walked to one of the computer terminals.

"Less than twelve hours ago, a UAV called Raven went down in a mountainous area in the southeast corner of Sudan, not far from Ethiopia," she said. "I have a map here."

"That's pretty far to get some pictures," said Turk, looking at the screen. "Going to be a long flight, even supersonic."

"It's not just a reconnaissance mission, Turk. Whiplash has been deployed. Our network satellite in that area is down for maintenance. It'll be at least forty-eight hours before we get the replacement moved into position."

"Gotcha."

Whiplash was the code name of a joint CIA–Defense Department project run by the Office of Special Technology. It combined a number of cutting-edge technologies with a specially trained covert action unit headed by Air Force colonel Danny Freah. Freah had helped pioneer the concept at Dreamland as a captain some fifteen years before. Now he was back as the leader of a new incarnation, working with special operators from a number of different military branches as well as the CIA.

Unlike the Dreamland version, the new Whiplash worked directly with the Central Intelligence Agency and included a number of CIA officers. The head of the Agency contingent was Nuri Abaajmed Lupo, a young covert agent who, by coincidence, had spent considerable time undercover in roughly the same area where the Raven UAV had gone down.

Nuri had been the first field agent to train with a highly integrated computer network developed for Whiplash. Officially known as the Massively Parallel Integrated Decision Complex or MY-PID, the network of interconnected computers and data interfaces, the system allowed him to access a wide range of information, from planted bugs to Agency data mining, instantaneously while he was in the field.

The high volume data streams traveled through a dedicated network of satellites. The amount of data involved and the limitations of the ground broadcasting system required that the satellites be within certain ranges for MY-PID to work. The Tigershark II could substitute as a relay station in an emergency.

"You're to contact Danny Freah when you arrive on station," Breanna continued. "We'll have updates to you while you're en route."

"All right, I guess."

"Problem, Captain?"

"No ma'am. Just figuring it out."

Turk folded his arms and stared at the screen.

The target area in southeastern Sudan was some 13,750 kilometers away—roughly 7,500 nautical miles. Cruising in the vicinity of Mach 3, the Tigershark could cover that distance in the area of four hours. At that speed, though, it would run out of fuel somewhere over the Atlantic. He'd need to set up at least two refuels to be comfortable.

"The first tanker will meet you in the Caribbean," said Breanna. She tapped a password into the computer and a map appeared. "It's already being prepped. You fly south with it, then head across to the Med. A second tanker will come on station over Libya."

"How long do I stay on station?"

"As long as it takes. We'll find another tanker; you can just stay in transmission range if you have to refuel off the east coast of Africa. Obviously, you won't be able to provide any surveillance, but we'll have to make do until we get more gear there. Frankly, it doesn't seem like it'll even be necessary. The mission looks very straightforward."

Breanna double-tapped the screen, expanding the map area of southern Sudan. Next she opened a set of optical satellite images of the area, taken about an hour before the accident.

"This satellite will pass back over that area in three hours," she said. "It's possible that they'll find the wreckage before you arrive. If not, you're to use your sensors to assist in the search. All right?"

"Sure."

"Colonel Freah will have operational control."

Breanna looked up from the screen. The frown on Turk's face hadn't dissipated.

"What's wrong, Captain?"

"Nothing."

"Out with it."

"Tigershark's unarmed."

"And?"

"I could do a much better job with the gun."

The gun referred to was the experimental rail gun. The weapon was undergoing tests in a second aircraft, which was also housed at the leased Dreamland base.

"The weapon's not operational. And there shouldn't be any need for it." Breanna clicked on another folder. A set of images opened. "This is Raven. It's smaller than a Flighthawk or a Predator. It's armed with Hellfire missiles at the moment, but eventually it will be able to house a number of weapons."

"Looks more like a Tigershark than a Predator."

"It is. The contractor is the same for both systems." Breanna closed the file, returning to the map. "It was flying with a Predator, which also crashed. Danny will be working out of Ethiopia. You'll be able to land there in an emergency."

"I didn't think Ethiopia was an ally," said Turk.

"They're not."

8

Western Ethiopia

DANNY FREAH STARED OUT INTO THE BLACK NIGHT AS the MV-22 Osprey whipped over the hills.

"Hasn't changed," said his companion bitterly. Nuri Abaajmed Lupo was sitting in the sling seat nearby, slumped back, arm draped over the canvas back.

"Maybe it has. Too dark to see," said Danny.

"Never changes," said Nuri. "It's a shit hole."

Danny was silent for a moment. He'd been here a few months back, on his very first mission with Whiplash—the *new* Whiplash. They'd pulled Nuri out of a tense situation, and nearly died in the process.

A good christening.

Since that time, the lawless situation in south-eastern Sudan had gotten worse. Worried about violence spilling over the border, the Ethiopian government had declared its "neutrality" in the civil war, but was ineffective in keeping either side out.

At the same time it was engaged in an unrelated feud with the United States, Ethiopia had dismissed the U.S. ambassador a few weeks before. This made the existence of a secret American base in the northwest corner of the country even more problematic.

"Wish you were still in Alexandria?" Danny asked Nuri.

Nuri shrugged.

"We'll wrap this up and get back," said Danny. "She'll remember you."

Nuri frowned. "She" was a colonel in the state police administration, assigned as one of their liaisons. The sudden assignment had interrupted Nuri's plans to take her out.

The Osprey dipped into a valley, skimming close to the treetops. As the aircraft slowed, the engine nacelles on the wings swung up. Danny cinched his seat belt, the aircraft fluttering down onto the landing strip.

Outside, the air was cool and crisp, a welcome change from Egypt, where it had been oppressively hot. Danny zipped his jacket to his neck. He was dressed in civilian clothes, unsure exactly what to expect.

"They didn't even send anyone to meet us," said Nuri, surveying the field.

"We probably got here faster than they expected," said Danny. He pulled the strap to his rucksack over his shoulder and started walking toward the low-slung buildings beyond the small strip where they'd been deposited. Ras Dashen, the highest peak in the Semien Mountains, rose in the distance, its brown hulk clearly outlined by the glow of the full moon. The mountain was a popular destination for adventure tourists, but this sparsely populated valley was more than fifty miles from the nearest route taken by tourists. Accessible only by a scrub road or aircraft, the CIA had been using the field for Raven for nearly two months.

The Osprey rose behind them, spitting sand

and grit in every direction. The aircraft would fly back to southern Egypt, refuel, then go north to Cairo to wait for the rest of the Whiplash team.

Assuming they were needed. Danny wasn't exactly sure what the situation was; Reid hadn't given him many details, saying only to get there and find out what had to be done.

"Lonely place," said Danny as they walked.

Nuri grumbled an answer.

"This place operational when you were here?" Danny asked. "Before Whiplash?"

"Not that I knew."

A thick clump of clouds floated in front of the moon, casting the base in darkness. As they passed, a pickup truck emerged from the shadows near the building, riding toward them without its lights.

"Here comes our ride," said Nuri.

"You don't sound too enthusiastic."

"I wouldn't trust anything the Agency is doing out here." Nuri stopped. "Black projects have a way of becoming rodeos."

The pickup arrived before Danny could ask what he meant. The driver rolled down the window. He was white, and spoke with a British accent.

"You're Colonel Freah?"

"That's right."

"You can put your bags in the back." The man didn't introduce himself. He waited silently for Danny and Nuri to get in, then put the truck into reverse, made a slow-motion U-turn, and drove toward the buildings. There were five; two about the size of a small ranch house back home, and three slightly smaller.

"Which building?" Danny asked.

"You can wait in the one on the far right." The building was one of the larger structures.

"Wait?" snapped Nuri.

"What do you mean wait?" asked Danny. "We're here to meet Melissa Ilse."

"I don't know where she is." The driver seemed almost offended that they would imply he did know.

"How long you been on contract?" asked Nuri.

The man looked at him. "That's not your business."

"That's what I thought."

Danny and Nuri got out and went into the building. It consisted of a single room. A set of tables formed two long rows in the center, with chairs running down one side. Dim red lights shone from overhead fixtures; there wasn't enough light to read a watch by.

"Most of them bugged out already," said Nuri, surveying the room. "Shit."

"Why do you say that?"

"Too few people. If they were running UAVs from here, they would have needed dozens of people. Even if it was just a skeletal crew. Even if they were flying from somewhere else. And the security would have been tighter. I'll bet they had tents, and just took everything away. I don't like this."

Dubious, Danny looked around the room. It looked more like an empty Knights of Columbus hall than a command post.

"So where's this Melissa, you think?" he asked Nuri.

Nuri pulled out a chair and sat down. "Damned if I know. I never even heard of her."

He shook his head. Danny was used to dealing with Nuri—he tended to be a bit of a crank—but this was cantankerous even for him.

"There aren't that many people who can deal with East Africa," Nuri added. "I know them all. And she's not one of them."

"Maybe it's a pseudonym."

"Yeah."

"Well, this is a bullshit way to treat us," said Danny. As he turned to go back to the door, it opened. A short, thin man with several days' worth of stubble on his face entered.

"Colonel Freah?"

"That's right."

"I'm Damian Jordan." He reached out and shook Danny's hand. He had a grip that could crush rocks.

"We're supposed to meet Melissa Ilse," said Danny.

"She's not here," said Jordan. He offered his hand to Nuri. Nuri just stared at him.

"Where is she?" asked Danny.

"She got a lead on the aircraft and she went to check it out."

"By herself?" asked Nuri.

"Melissa is like that."

"You're in charge?" asked Danny.

"Melissa is."

"Where's the rest of your team?" asked Nuri.

"With the aircraft down, we were ordered to move to a more secure location. We're pretty wide-open over here. So it's just me, Ferny—who drove out to get you—and two Ethiopian nationals working as bodyguards."

"You trust them?" asked Nuri.

"Only until the shit hits the fan," said Jordan. "Then they'll take off for the hills. Come on into the other building and we'll get something to eat. I'll brief you on the way."

9

Southeastern Sudan

IT TOOK LI HAN SEVERAL HOURS TO REACH THE CRASH site, most of it on foot. A boy in a village allied with the Brothers had seen the aircraft fall from the sky. He showed Li Han the way himself, plunging down hillsides and scrambling over the rocks like it was a game. The Brothers who were with Li Han couldn't keep up, and in fact even Li Han, who prided himself on his excellent condition, had a hard time toward the end. The moon kept poking in and out of the clouds, and he stumbled several times, twisting his ankle and knee, though not so badly that he gave up.

And then they were there.

One of the wings had broken off in flight, but the rest of the aircraft was nearly whole. It looked like a black tent, sitting in the ravine where it had landed. Li Han approached it cautiously, afraid that the Americans had booby-trapped it. They were capable of anything.

Li Han knelt down next to the fuselage, examining the strange-looking aircraft. It had landed on its back. A missile was attached to the wing.

Li Han caught the boy as he started to scramble onto the wing near the missile.

"No," said Li Han. He used English. The child may not have understood the language, but the tone was enough to warn him away. Li Han pointed, telling the boy to move back.

Li Han rose and walked to the nose of the small plane. Its skin was covered with a black, radar-absorbing paint, obviously intended to lower the radar profile. He took an LED flashlight from his pocket and ran its beam over the wreckage. The antennas might be hidden under the wreckage; they would be on the top of the aircraft most likely, where they could receive signals from satellites. But where was the sensor pod with its cameras?

Integrated into the hull. The material seemed almost porous.

The two Brothers who'd accompanied him came over the hill, huffing for breath. They slid down the ravine on the sides of their feet.

"Careful," said Li Han, forgetting for a moment and speaking in his native Mandarin.

They looked at him sheepishly.

"We must get the wreckage out of here before the satellite comes," he said, switching to English. "Before it is dawn. We have only three hours. Do you understand?"

The taller one, Amara of Yujst—they all had odd, African names—said something in Arabic.

"Pick it up and carry it out," Li Han told him, still in English.

"It will be heavy," said Amara.

"Then get more help," said Li Han.

10

Western Ethiopia

"WE'VE BEEN TARGETING HIM," SAID DAMIAN JORDAN, pointing at the hazy black-and-white image of an Asian man on the screen. "Mao Man."

"Sounds archaeological," said Danny, looking at the face.

"Li Han," said Nuri coldly.

"You know who he is?" asked Jordan. He cracked his knuckles, right hand first, then left. The sound echoed in the room. Except for a pair of cots and a mobile workstation, the room was empty.

"I never heard him called Mao Man," said Nuri. "But I know who he is. He's a technical expert, and a weapons dealer. A real humanitarian. You've heard of A.Q. Khan, right?"

Khan was the Pakistani scientist who had helped Iran—and possibly others—develop their own nuclear weapons program.

"This guy is similar, except he's Chinese," said Nuri. "He had some sort of falling out with the government and military. Probably over money. Anyway, he's been in a number of places in the last few years, selling his services. He's pretty smart. And absolutely no morals." Nuri turned to Jordan. "He has a team here?"

"Not a team. He's working with the Sudan Brotherhood."

"Lovely." Nuri turned back to Danny. "Muslim fanatic group. Gets some money and help from al Qaeda."

"I don't know about the link—" started Jordan.

"I do," said Nuri flatly.

"Well you know more than me," said Jordan. "All I know is we're targeting this guy. It's a non-contact situation."

Nuri frowned. "How long?"

"We've been here almost five weeks," said Jordan. "Most of that time was getting the air-craft ready, though. We only just started tracking him."

Jordan began briefing them on Raven, an armed UAV they had used to track Mao Man. Its function was similar to Reaper—the armed Predator drones—but it was newer, more capable.

"How?" asked Danny.

Jordan shrugged. "Faster. A little smaller. More robust."

Nuri snorted.

"This was its first mission," said Jordan. "Really more of a shakedown cruise. They picked a quiet area for a maiden flight. Afghanistan was too hot."

"Yeah," sneered Nuri.

"Have to try it somewhere," said Jordan. "It wasn't my choice. There was some sort of mechanical problem about a third of the way through the mission. There were temperature spikes in the right engine. My guess is that there was impurity in the fuel and something blew in the chamber. The power profiles were off, and we got a lot of ambient sound, kind of like you'd get in a car if there was a hole in the muffler. It may have been loud—that's what may have tipped off Mao Man and the guerrillas he's working with. Or maybe they heard the Predator, or saw something somehow. Anyway, they came out of the mine and fired a couple of MPADs—shoulder-launched antiaircraft missiles. It was a Stinger Block 2."

"An American missile?" asked Danny.

"Oh yeah."

"How'd they get that?"

"Don't know. They get a lot of stuff out here."

"Sold by a friendly government," said Nuri. "Allegedly friendly."

Danny shook his head. "So they shot it down."

"No, that's the damn shame of it. Raven was flying with a Predator on overwatch. The two aircraft collided."

"You know where it went down?" asked Danny.

"Roughly. That's where Melissa went. We have transponders, but the accident knocked one of them out, and separated the other two. So it's in one of two spots. At first there was no signal because of a sandstorm."

"A sandstorm?" asked Danny.

"Happens all the time here," said Nuri.

"The particles screw up the low-power transmissions," explained Jordan. "It's a trade-off—if you have a transmission that's too strong, anyone can find you. At any rate, we can see them now. It's over the border about fifty miles."

Nuri whistled. "That's not the best place for a woman."

"It's not *that* bad," said Jordan. "She's been out there before."

"How is one person going to bring back an aircraft?" asked Danny.

"She said she just wants to locate it." Jordan shrugged. "When they told us you were coming, she said she'd get there and you could follow."

"Is she nuts?" asked Danny.

"Well yeah, actually, she is," said Jordan.

"WE'RE GETTING ABOUT A TENTH OF THE STORY HERE," Nuri told Danny when they went outside. "No-contact mission. You know what that means?"

"No," said Danny.

"That means they don't have to ask permission to kill this guy," said Nuri.

"Okay."

"They're out here testing a new UAV on a high-value target? CIA officer goes out by herself to locate it? Granted it's not as bad as it was a year ago, but it's still not Disney World. There's a lot more to the story, Danny. A hell of a lot more."

Nuri folded his arms. He didn't know exactly what else was going on here, but it smelled bad. Predators had never been used against the rebels here, not even the Sudan Brotherhood, because they'd never taken action against the U.S. In fact, except for their religious beliefs, one could have argued that they were much friendlier toward America philosophically than their government was.

As for Li Han, targeting him made a hell of a lot of sense. But bugging out didn't. The bureaucratic bs needed to authorize a strike was so immense that an operation like this would continue for years.

Unless they hadn't gone through with the bureaucratic bs.

Which meant the operation wasn't just black; it was unauthorized; aka illegal.

Nuri felt his lower lip starting to shudder. The cool air was getting to him.

"How long before we can hook into the Voice?" asked Nuri, using one of his pet names for the MY-PID system.

"Tigershark won't be on station for a few hours," said Danny, checking his watch. "I'll find out—I have to tell Bree we're here. Hang around, all right?"

"I'm not going anywhere."

Danny took out his encrypted satellite phone—

it used standard military satellites, not the data-heavy Whiplash network—and called in as they walked toward the airstrip, as much to keep warm as to avoid being overheard. Nuri put his hands in his pockets, rocking back and forth as he listened to Danny's side of the conversation.

"Hey Bree, this is Danny. We're here. What's the ETA on Tigershark? . . . Uh-huh."

Nuri felt a twinge of jealousy at how close the colonel and Breanna Stockard were. There was a level of trust there that he'd never had with any of his supervisors, and certainly not with Jonathon Reid. It wasn't that he thought Reid or any of the men he'd worked for were less than dedicated, or would leave him purposely in the lurch. It was more a question of how far beyond their duty they would go. He'd already seen Stockard risk her career and her life for Danny.

For *them*. For the entire team. But it was personal for Danny in a way it would never be for Nuri.

"Nuri thinks there's a lot more going on here than we're being told, Bree," said Danny. "Uh-huh."

Nuri watched Danny listen to something she said, but in the darkness he couldn't see his face well enough to interpret his reaction.

"She wants to talk to you," said Danny, handing him the sat phone.

"Ms. Stockard, hello."

"Nuri, what do you think is going on?" asked Breanna.

"I can't say exactly."

He explained that the Agency didn't seem to be following its usual protocols when targeting a high-value terrorist like Li Han. On the other hand, he had to admit that because he had no direct information about either Raven or the particular mission, he simply didn't know how suspicious to be.

The more questions Breanna asked, the less confident Nuri felt. And yet, things still seemed a little off, a little unusual in ways that made him believe the CIA wasn't telling them everything.

Well, duh, he thought, handing the phone back to Danny. When did the Agency *ever* tell anyone everything?

"SHE'S GOING TO TALK TO REID," DANNY TOLD NURI after he signed off. "I don't think Reid would lie to her."

"Probably not," said Nuri.

"You think Reid would lie?"

Nuri shrugged.

There were all sorts of reasons Danny didn't particularly like the fact that Whiplash was a joint project between the military and the CIA, but they all came down to Nuri's two words: *probably not*.

You never knew exactly what the CIA was up to. The Air Force and the rest of the military might have its problems and its politics, but these paled compared to Central Intelligence.

"Tigershark will be here in another three hours," said Danny. Once the aircraft was overhead, they would have real-time surveillance as well as a connection with their computer system, MY-PID. The rest of the team was scheduled to arrive roughly two hours later. Assuming that Melissa Ilse had located the wreckage by then, they would fly in, retrieve it, and come home.

Danny noticed Nuri staring into the distance.

"What are you thinking?" he asked.

"Just how lovely it is to be back in this stink hole," said the CIA officer.

11

Southeastern Sudan

MELISSA ILSE CUT THE MOTORCYCLE'S ENGINE, COASTing in the dark as the indicator beeper became a steady hum. She was a mile from the UAV.

Hand-built by Ducati to CIA specifications, the lightweight motorcycle had a pair of over-sized mufflers that kept engine noise to a low rumble. But sound traveled far in the desert foot-hills, and she couldn't afford to take a chance of alerting anyone that she was near. She needed to locate the UAV and recover its brain, or her career was shot.

Harker had told her that in so many words.

Melissa glided off the dirt trail she'd been riding for the past half hour or so, letting the bike's momentum carry her to a trio of rocks a few yards up the hillside. She put on her brakes as she reached them. Hopping off the bike, she set it down gently against the largest of the rocks. She pulled the MP-5 submachine gun from its holster on the side of the bike and trotted down to the trail, turning back to make sure the bike couldn't be seen.

Her night vision goggles were heavy against her face. She pulled them off and rubbed her cheekbones and eyes. She was surprised there was enough light to see fairly well, and it was such a relief not to have the apparatus pressing against her face that she decided she would do without it for a while. She stuffed it into her rucksack, then examined her GPS.

The handheld device wasn't coordinated with the UAV's homing signals, but it wasn't hard to get her bearings. The aircraft had gone down on the other side of the ridge. She could either climb directly over it or circle around parallel to the trail she'd been riding.

Direct was always better.

Melissa paused every few steps to look around and make sure she wasn't being followed. She'd been through this general area several times in the past two months, before Raven was brought in. She might even have been on this very hillside, though she didn't remember it.

The chapped land and rugged hills reminded her of southwest Nevada, where her dad used to take her camping and hiking when she was a girl. He and her mother had divorced when she was only three; he had custody only a few weeks each year, and they always spent at least one week of that camping. She cherished those trips now, and looked forward to the next, not due for several months.

Melissa scolded herself. It was dangerous letting her mind drift. Crouching at the top of the ridge, she put one hand on the rocky crust, then folded herself against the hillside, peering over the top.

Shadow covered everything before her. She slid down a few feet, pulled off her pack and removed her night vision goggles.

A small settlement sat in the valley on the left, not quite two miles away. There was no sign anyone was awake.

So where was the plane?

From the signal, it should be to her right, maybe a thousand yards away.

Melissa surveyed the area again. The submachine gun felt heavy in her hands. She'd never fired it at an enemy. She'd never used a gun against a real person at all.

She took a slow breath, controlling her nerves, and started down the hill in the direction of the signal.

She came to the wreckage sooner than she thought. The aircraft's left wing jutted from the rocks. It had sheered at the wing root, pulled off by the force of the midair collision.

Melissa took over, scanning the area. This was bad luck—she'd gone after the wrong part of the plane. The flight computer was in the forward section of the fuselage—the other signal nearly five miles to the northeast.

She cursed silently, then took the camera from her pocket. They'd want to know what the wrecked wing looked like.

12

Washington, D.C.

SENATOR JEFFREY "ZEN" STOCKARD LOOKED UP AT THE receptionist as he rolled into the rehabilitation ward in Building 5123 at the Walter Reed Hospital complex. They were old friends by now, so well-acquainted that Zen knew she took her coffee black with two sugars.

It was important, after all, to get those little things right.

"Luciana, you are looking very chipper this morning," he said, rolling toward her. "How is my favorite receptionist and nurse in training?"

"Big test tonight," she told him.

"Better hit the books."

"I am." She raised the textbook from behind the counter. Building 5123 was a special facility at the hospital complex, with the highest level of security possible—so high, in fact, that even Zen had to submit to a rudimentary pat down. His aide—Jason Black—couldn't even go downstairs with him.

Which, in some ways, was just as well.

While the staff members were all medical professionals, they worked for the Walter Reed Army Institute of Research, a special branch charged with investigating biology and medicine and their implications on the battlefield as well as society.

"Jay brought you coffee," said Zen, glancing back at his aide. Black handed over the cup of Starbucks.

"You look like you're still asleep, Jason," said Luciana.

Jason blushed. "Naw."

"I ride him hard, Lucy," said Zen. "Twenty-four/seven, around the clock. How's my patient?"

"They don't tell me anything, Senator. But I haven't heard anything bad."

"That's good to know."

Zen rolled himself toward the security checkpoint a short distance away. Contrary to what she'd told Zen, the staff downstairs would have passed the word if there was a problem. Not that it would have kept Zen from going down to see their patient, Mark Stoner.

Stoner had been a close friend years before. They'd worked together at Dreamland; at one point, Stoner had saved Zen's wife Breanna's life.

Stoner had been lost on a mission in Eastern Europe some fifteen years before. Everyone, Zen included, had given him up for dead.

A recent Whiplash mission had discovered him still alive, though so physically and mentally altered, he was barely recognizable. Zen had helped rescue him. Now he felt obligated to help him back to health.

Mental health. Physically, he'd never be what he was. He'd always be much, much better.

Rescued from a helicopter crash by a scientist working with Olympic athletes, Stoner had been the recipient of numerous biomechanical improvements and a host of steroidlike drugs that had turned him into something approaching a Superman. While he had been weaned from most of the drugs the scientists had put him on, he still retained much of his strength.

A single nurse was on duty in the basement ward. Two guards with loaded shotguns stood behind her.

"Good morning, Senator."

"Katherine."

"Dr. Esrang is with him."

"OK."

Zen wheeled himself next to a chair, then waited as one of the guards ran a wand around him and looked over his wheelchair to make sure there were no weapons or other contraband. Cleared, he got back on and wheeled himself to the steel door. A loud buzzer sounded; the door slid to the side. Zen entered a narrow corridor and began wheeling toward a second steel door. The doors acted like an airlock; only one could be opened at a time, even in an emergency.

Two more guards waited on the other side of the door. Zen was searched once more. If anything, the second search was more thorough. Cleared, Zen went down the hallway to a set of iron bars. The burly man on the other side, dressed in riot gear but without a weapon, eyed him, then turned and nodded. The bars went up; Zen wheeled through. He said hello, not expecting an answer. He had never gotten one in the weeks since he'd been coming to visit Stoner, and he didn't get one now.

Past the last set of iron bars, the place looked pretty much like a normal hospital suite again. It was only when one looked very closely at things, like the double locks on the cabinet drawers and the ubiquitous video monitors, that one might realize this was an ultra-high-security facility.

The hall turned to the right, opening into a large, glass-enclosed area. The glass looked into four different rooms. Zen pivoted to his left, facing a large physical therapy space on the other side of the glass. Stoner, dressed in sweats, was lying on a bench doing flying presses with a set of dumbbells. If the numbers on the sides of the plates were to be believed, he was swinging two hundred pounds overhead with each arm as easily as Zen might have lifted fifty.

Zen caught a reflection in the glass. Dr. Esrang was leaning, arms folded, against the glass almost directly behind him.

"You're trusting him with free weights," said Zen.

"He's making good progress," said Esrang, coming over. "He's earning our trust."

"Are the new drugs working?"

"Hard to say, as usual. We look at brain waves, we look at scans. We are only guessing."

Zen nodded. They'd had variations of this conversation several times.

"You may go in if you wish," said the doctor.

Zen watched his old friend awhile longer. Stoner's face was expressionless. He might be concentrating entirely on his body's movements, feeling every strain and pull of his muscles. Or he might be a million miles away.

Zen wheeled over to the far side of the space. There was a bar on the frame. He slid it up, then pushed the door-sized pane of glass next to it open. He made sure to close the door behind him, then wheeled around to the room where Stoner was working out.

Stoner said nothing when he entered. Zen wheeled about halfway into the room, waiting until his friend finished a set. Stoner, six feet tall and broad-shouldered, weighed about 240 pounds, nearly all of it muscle.

"Working with the dumbbells today?" said Zen.

Stoner got up from the bench and went to a weight rack on the far side of the room. He took out another set of dumbbells and began doing a military press.

"Enough weight for you?" asked Zen.

He hated that he was reduced to ridiculous comments, but he couldn't think of much else to say. Stoner worked in silence, pushing the weights up with steady, flawless efficiency. These were the heaviest set of weights in the room, and he knocked off thirty reps without a problem. He was sweating, but that might have been due to the heat—the place felt like a sauna.

"I can stay for breakfast if you want," said Zen. "Give me an excuse to blow off a committee meeting."

No answer. Stoner put down the weights, then went back to the bench and started on a set of sitting curls. His face remained the same: no sign of stress.

"Nationals are doing well. They won last night," said Zen. "They'll be back home soon. Maybe we can take in a game."

"Baseball?" asked Stoner.

"Yeah. You want to go to a game?"

Instead of responding, Stoner went back to his workout. During his treatment in Eastern Europe, he had been essentially brainwashed, his personality and memory replaced with an almost robotic consciousness. His old self or at least some semblance of it remained, but exactly how much, no one could say.

Zen had managed only a handful of conversations with him since he'd been here. Stoner hadn't said more than a dozen words in each. But that was more than he'd said to anyone else.

Stoner did two more circuits, pumping the iron without visible fatigue. As he finished a set of standing presses, he glanced over at Zen.

The look in his eye frightened Zen. For a split second he thought Stoner was going to toss one of the dumbbells at his head.

He didn't. He just glared at him, then pumped through another twenty reps.

"Man, you're in good shape," said Zen as Stoner racked the weights.

Stoner turned to him. "Need heavier weights. Too easy."

"Did you ask the doctors?"

Stoner pulled his hood over his head.

"I can try and get more for you," said Zen. "What weight?"

"Big disks," said Stoner. "I need more."

He started walking toward the door next to the rack.

"Feel like having breakfast?" Zen asked.

"No," said Stoner. "Gonna shower."

"OK," said Zen. "I'll see you tomorrow, then, maybe."

Stoner said nothing. Zen watched him walk down the hall, turning right into his room.

"I've already ordered more weights," said Esrang when Zen met him outside. "We didn't want to give him too much at first, in case he decided to use them as weapons."

"You still think he's dangerous?"

Esrang pitched his head to one side, gesturing with his shoulders. He was one of the world's experts on the effects of steroids and other drugs on the human brain, but he often pointed out that this meant he knew that he didn't know enough.

Zen glanced at his watch. "I'm afraid I have to go. I'll be back tomorrow."

"I'm sure he'll appreciate it."

Zen smiled. It was a nice thing for the doctor to say, but they both knew it wasn't necessarily true.

13

Southeastern Sudan

LI HAN WATCHED AS THE AIRCRAFT WAS LIFTED INTO THE back of the pickup truck. It was a lot lighter than he'd expected; three men could easily handle it.

It would fetch a decent amount of money. The design was unique, the materials, even the on-board flight control computer, which had considerably more processing and memory chips than Li Han expected—the right buyer would pay a good price.

The question was finding the right buyer. The best price would come from his former countrymen, though there was no way he could deal with them.

The Russians were one possibility. The French were another. The Iranians, but his last dealings with them had turned sour.

The biggest payday might actually come from the Americans, who would want their equipment back.

Maybe they could make a deal.

He needed to find a place to examine it more carefully, and think. That meant going north, away from the area controlled by the Brotherhood. They would only complicate things.

The Brother holding the forward end of the aircraft slipped as they were placing it into the bed of the pickup. The fuselage fell hard against the truck.

"Careful, you idiots!" yelled Li Han in Chinese.

He ran over to the plane. It didn't appear to be damaged, at least not any worse than it had been.

"Come," he said, switching to English. "We need to be away from here before the satellite appears."

MELISSA WAS A MILE AND A HALF FROM THE TRANsponder when the signal went from a steady beep to a more urgent bleat.

The aircraft was being moved.

She squeezed the throttle on the motorcycle, hunkering down against the handlebars as its speed jumped. A second later she realized that was a mistake. Backing off the gas, she pulled her GPS out from her jacket pocket and got her bearings.

The transponder was in a valley roughly parallel to the one she was riding through. Both ran east to west. According to the map, a road that intersected both valleys lay two miles ahead. She could go to that intersection and wait.

Unless whoever had the UAV turned north rather than staying on the road. There were at least two trails running off the valley in that direction before the intersection. And sure enough, the signal soon indicated that the UAV was moving farther away.

It was starting to get light. Melissa went up the connecting road and stayed on it, speeding roughly parallel to whoever was taking the UAV away. They were about a mile and a half away, but the trail and road ran away from each other, her path going due north while the other gradually tailing eastward.

Finally she stopped and examined the map on the GPS to try and guess where they were going. The trail wound through a series of settlements, intersected with several unpaved roads, and finally ended at what passed for a super highway here, a double-lane asphalt paved road that ran to Duka, a small town that sat on a flat plain at the eastern foot of the mountains. She slipped the GPS back into her pocket. Who had the UAV? Mao Man?

She hoped not. The fact that it was being taken north argued against it: the Brothers' stronghold was well to the south, where she assumed he'd been heading when attacked. He had only come this far north to arrange for a meeting with weapons suppliers.

Most likely either a government patrol spotted the wreckage and decided to take it, or some local farmer found it and decided to take it to the authorities and claim a reward.

Either could be easily bought off. A hundred dollars here would bring a family luxury for a year.

Melissa slipped the bike out of neutral and began following the signal once more.

LI HAN FELT HIS EYES STARTING TO CLOSE AS THEY ZIG-zagged through the hills. He'd been up now for nearly thirty-six hours straight, long even for him.

Shaking himself, he sat upright in the cab of the truck, then rolled down the window, sticking his head out into the wind. He could sleep in Duka. He'd used a building there to house some explosives about a year and a half before; it was sure to be still unoccupied. And though the town was controlled by two different rebel groups, neither would bear him any malice, especially if he promised fresh weapons and ammunition as he had the last time.

But he had to stay alert until he reached the small city. The army occasionally sent patrols through the area. It was unlikely that they would meet any at night, but if they did, the soldiers would assume they were rebels and immediately open fire.

One of the men in the back of the pickup began banging on the roof of the cab. The driver slowed, then spoke to him through his window.

"What?" asked Li Han in English.

"Following. A motorbike follows," said the driver.

A motorcycle?

Li Han twisted around, trying to see. It was too dark, and the hulk of the UAV blocked most of his view.

It wouldn't be the army. More like one of the many rebel groups that contested the area.

"Shoot them!" yelled Li Han. He turned back to the driver. "Tell them in the back to shoot them. Don't stop! Drive faster. Faster!"

MELISSA KNEW SHE WAS PRESSING IT, PULLING CLOSER and closer to the truck. But it was alone, and while there were definitely men in the back, none seemed armed or particularly hostile. If she caught up, she could work out a deal.

A poke of white light from the back of the truck told her she'd miscalculated. They did have weapons, and they weren't in the mood to bargain.

Melissa raised her submachine gun and fired back. The barrel of the MP-5 pushed up from the recoil harder than she'd anticipated, and the shots flew wild over the truck. She tucked the weapon tighter against her side. The road rose, then veered to the right; she shifted her weight, trying not to slow down around the curve. Tilting back, she saw the truck square ahead of her, fat between her handlebars and no more than thirty yards away.

She pressed her finger against the trigger. As she fired, the front of the bike began to turn to her right.

Starting to lose her balance, Melissa let go of the gun and grabbed the handlebar. But it was too late—she went over in a tumble, rolling around in the dust as a hail of bullets from the truck passed overhead.

14

Room 4, CIA Headquarters Campus

JONATHON REID SAT AT THE LARGE CONFERENCE TABLE, staring at the gray wall in front of him. He was alone in the high-tech headquarters and command center.

The top of the wall began to glow blue.

"Open com channel to Ms. Stockard," he said softly.

The rectangular window appeared in the middle of the wall. It expanded, widening until it covered about a third of the space. The outer portion of the wall darkened from gray to black. The interior window, meanwhile, turned deep blue, then morphed into an image of Breanna Stockard in a secure conference room in Dreamland.

She was alone, and she was frowning.

"Breanna," said Reid. "Good morning again."

"Jonathon, what's really going out there in Africa?"

"I told you everything the director told me."

"Nuri says there's a lot more to the project than we're being told."

"I don't doubt he's right."

"And?"

Reid said nothing. The Raven program was clearly an assassination mission, and clearly it involved top secret technology that the Agency had developed outside of its normal channels. But Harker hadn't spelled any of this out; he had merely said the UAV must be recovered. All Reid had were guesses and suppositions, not facts.

"Jonathon, you're not saying anything."

"I know, Breanna. I don't have more facts than I've shared."

"Listen, the only way this is going to work is if we're completely honest with each other."

Reid nodded.

"Well?" prompted Breanna.

"Clearly, this is a CIA project that's highly secret, and they don't want to tell us any of the details," he said. "And they haven't."

"I got that."

Breanna and Reid had gotten along fairly well since the program began, despite the vast differences in the institutions they reported to, their backgrounds, and their ages. Cooperation between the military and the CIA was not always ideal in any event, and on a program such as Whiplash and the related MY-PID initiative, there was bound to be even greater conflict. But so far they had largely steered clear of the usual suspicions, let alone the attempts at empire building and turf wars that typically marred joint projects. Partly this was because they had so far kept the operation—and its staffing—to an absolute minimum. But it also had to do with their personal relationships. Reid, much older than Breanna, liked and admired her in an almost fatherly way, and she clearly respected him, often treating him with professional deference.

Not now, though. Right now she was angry with him, believing he was holding back.

"I can only guess at what they're doing," Reid told her. "I have no facts. I know exactly what you're thinking, but they've put up barriers, and I can't just simply whisk them away with a wave of my hand."

"We need to know exactly what's going on," Breanna told him.

"Beyond what we already know? Why? We have to recover the UAV. It's already been located."

"What we don't know may bite us."

"Granted."

"God, Jonathon, you've got to press them for more information."

"I have."

"Then I will."

"I don't know that that will work," said Reid. "I have a call in to the director. I am trying."

Reid could already guess what Herm Edmund was going to say—this is on a need to know basis, and you don't need to know.

"Jonathon, I've always been up front with you," said Breanna.

"And I'm being up front with you. It's a UAV, it's obviously an assassination program, though they're not even saying that. Not to me, anyway."

"If one of our people gets hurt because of something we should have known—"

"I feel exactly the same way."

The window folded in on itself abruptly. Breanna had killed the transmission.

Reid sat back in his chair. One of the rock bed requirements of being a good CIA officer was that you stopped asking questions at a certain point. You stopped probing for information when it became clear you were not entitled to that information. Because knowing it might in fact endanger an operation, and the Agency.

On the other hand . . .

"Computer, show me the personnel file for Reginald Harker," said Reid. "Same with Melissa Ilse. Unrestricted authorization Jonathon Reid. Access all databases and perform a cross-Agency search for those individuals, and all references to Raven. Discover related operations and references, with a confidence value of ten percent or above."

"Working," replied the computer.

15

Southeastern Sudan

MELISSA ROLLED IN THE DIRT AS THE MOTORBIKE FLEW out from under her. She threw her arms up, trying to protect her face as the rear wheel spun toward her. A storm of pebbles splattered against her hands as the wheel caught in a rut; the bike tumbled back in the other direction.

Her shoulder hit a boulder at the side of the ditch. Her arm jolted from its socket and an intense wave of pain enveloped her body. Her head seemed to swim away from her.

My shoulder, she thought. Dislocated. Something torn.

I need the gun.

Get the gun.

Melissa pushed herself to her belly. Her eyes closed tight with the pain.

For a moment she thought she was still wearing the night goggles, and feared that the glass had embedded in her eyes, that she was blind. She reached with her left hand to pull them off, then realized she hadn't had them on.

There was dirt in her eyes, but she could see.

Get the gun!

Her right arm hung off her body as she pushed herself to her knees. The bike was a few yards away, on the other side of the road. But where was her gun?

Melissa crawled onto the hard-packed dirt road, looking for the MP-5, then shifted her weight to rise to her knees. The pain seemed to weigh a hundred pounds, throwing off her balance.

Another wave of dizziness hit her as she got to her feet.

The gun! The gun!

Melissa turned back in the direction she'd taken. She started to trot, then saw a black object just off the shoulder on her left. After a few steps she realized it was just a shadow in the rocks. She stopped, turned to the right, and saw the gun lying in the middle of the road.

"THE MOTORCYCLE HAS STOPPED FOLLOWING US," THE driver told Li Han.

Li Han twisted in the seat, looking behind them. The men in the back were clutching onto the wrecked aircraft, holding on for dear life as the truck flew over the washboard road.

One of the men leaned over the cab and yelled at the driver through his window.

"They fired at us," said the driver. "One of our men is hurt."

"How many were there?" asked Li Han.

"Two, maybe three. But they're gone now. Amara says that we kill both. In the dark, hard to tell."

Li Han considered going back to check the bodies. It might be useful to know which band they were with. The fact that they had motorcycles was unusual—perhaps they were future customers.

"The Brother needs a doctor," said the driver. "He was hit in the chest."

"Tell them to put a compress on," said Li Han.

The driver didn't understand. Li Han decided not to explain; they'd figure it out on their own eventually.

"Turn around," he told the driver. "Let's go find out who they were."

"Turn around?"

"Yes, a U-turn."

"There may be more."

"I doubt it," said Li Han. "Let's go see."

16

Western Ethiopia

"Colonel Freah?"

Danny looked over at the door to the building as Damian Jordan came outside. The sun was not quite at the horizon; gray twilight filtered over the base, making it look like a pixilated photograph pulled from a newspaper.

"What's up?"

"Melissa is on the radio. She's located the UAV. I figured you wanted to talk to her."

"Exactly," said Danny.

"Uh, she says she's been hurt."

"Bad?"

"Dunno. She's crabbier than usual, so probably fairly bad."

Jordan led Danny inside to the table where he'd set up an older satellite radio, a bulky unit with a corded handset. The console, about the size of a small briefcase, was at least ten years old. While it was powerful and had encryption gear, it was hardly state of the art. Nuri had pointed out that the operation surely had access to much better equipment; this was some sort of wrongheaded attempt to keep an extremely low profile.

"Here you go," said Jordan, giving Danny the handset.

"Ms. Ilse, this is Colonel Freah. Where are you?"

"Who are you?"

"Danny Freah. I'm the person who's going to get you and your UAV back here. Now where the hell are you?"

She grunted, as if in pain.

"Are you OK?" Danny asked.

"I dislocated my shoulder. I'm all right. Some of the natives grabbed the UAV. They're taking it in the direction of Duka. I have to get it. If you're going to help—"

"My team is going to be here in about twenty minutes," Danny told her. "You're roughly seventy miles away—we can get there inside an hour."

"All right," she said weakly.

"Are you OK?" he asked again.

"I'm fine." She snapped off the radio.

Danny handed back the handset.

"She goes her own way," said Jordan. He smiled, as if that was a good thing.

17

Over the Sudan

THE PROBLEM WITH FLYING THE TIGERSHARK, ESPECIALLY at very high speeds over long distances, was that it was boring.

Exceedingly, even excruciatingly, boring.

The plane flew itself, even during the refueling hookups. In fact, the Tigershark II had been designed to operate completely without a pilot, and very possibly could have handled this mission entirely on its own.

Not that Turk would have admitted it. He wouldn't even say it out loud, especially not in the plane: he'd come to think of the Tigershark almost as a person. The flight computer was *almost* sentient, in the words of its developer, Dr. Ray Rubeo.

Almost sentient. An important word, "almost."

Turk checked his instruments—everything in the green, perfect as always—then his location and that of the area where the UAV had gone down. The robot aircraft had a set of transponders that were sending signals to a satellite.

"Tigershark, this is Whiplash Ground. You hearing us?"

"Colonel Freah." Turk reached his right hand up to his helmet, enabling the video feed on the Whiplash communications system. Danny Freah's face appeared in a small box on the virtual screen projected by the Whiplash combat helmet. "Got good coms up here, Colonel."

"One of the operators has been tracking our item in country. She's hurt. We're going to be en route in a few minutes to her location. We're wondering if you can take a pass and check on her."

"Uh, roger that if you give me a location," said Turk. "I'm just about ten minutes from the target area," he added, pointing at part of the virtual instrument panel where the course way markers were displayed. "Eight and a half, to be exact."

"I have GPS coordinates," said Danny. "Stand by."

Turk waited while Danny uploaded the GPS tracking channel used by the CIA officer in western Sudan. He then increased the detail on the sitrep panel.

"Colonel, do you know that one of the transponders is moving?" said Turk. "It looks like it's approaching her location."

"Are you sure about that, Tiger?"

Turk double-tapped on the GPS locator and

told the Tigershark to fly to that spot. Then he went back to the radio.

"Yeah, roger that. Affirmative," he added. "Be advised I'm unarmed at this time."

"We copy."

"Operative got a name?"

"Melissa Ilse."

"It's a girl?"

"I already told you it's a she, Tigershark. And that would be a woman, not a girl. Copy?"

"Roger that. I'll do what I can."

18

Southeastern Sudan

MELISSA HEARD THE TRUCK RATTLING TOWARD HER. She glanced around for cover, but nothing was handy. She decided her only option was to move up the nearby embankment, to get out of easy view.

If they found her, she'd have to make her stand.

Her right arm and shoulder screamed with every step and jostle. She tried to keep it from moving too much by gripping the bottom of her jacket with her hand. The pain was so intense that she couldn't fold her fingers into a good grip, and had to simply hook her thumb around the cloth.

It was almost ironic. As part of her training for the mission, she'd been put into a rush course as a nurse so she could learn enough to use that as a cover. She had then treated two colleagues for dislocated shoulders during a particularly difficult survival refresher course she'd taken right afterward. Putting their arms back in place didn't seem like such a big deal.

Being on the other side of the pain gave her an entirely different perspective.

The sound of the truck grew louder. She dropped to one knee, then eased down to spread herself flat against the side of the hill. She was no more than twenty yards from the roadway, if that.

Her headset buzzed with an incoming call on her sat line, but she didn't answer it—the truck's headlights swept across the road ahead.

Maybe she could shoot them now. But she'd have to fire with her left hand.

She wasn't even that good with her right.

God, what a mistake she'd made getting close to the truck. What the hell was she thinking?

The truck jerked to a stop near the bike.

Melissa tried to will away the pain, extending her breathing, pushing the air all the way into her lungs before slowly exhaling.

The men got out of the truck.

Her headset buzzed again. She still didn't dare answer it.

TWENTY THOUSAND FEET ABOVE, TURK SWITCHED TO the Tigershark's enhanced view, trying to get a good read on what was below. The UAV and its CIA operator were roughly twenty yards from each other.

The Tigershark had been designed to carry a rail gun, which could fire metal slugs accurately to twenty miles. It still had some kinks, but would have come in very handy now.

"Whiplash Ground—Colonel Freah, I'm looking at a truck with people getting out of it. Our contact should be nearby. Are these hostiles?"

"We believe so, Tigershark. But stand by. We're trying to contact her now."

There was no time to stand by—the men in the truck were spreading out, moving in the direction of the CIA officer. They were carrying weapons. That made them hostile in Turk's book.

The only weapon he had was the Tigershark itself. He pushed down the nose, determined to use it.

MELISSA WATCHED AS THE MEN MOVED UP THE ROAD. They moved quickly—too quickly. They're scared, she thought.

A good sign, in a way: their fire would be less accurate.

She'd take the man closest to her, the one going to the bike. Then sweep across left, then back to the truck.

She'd have to reload before she took out the truck.

Her finger started to twitch.

I can do it.

I have to do it.

Melissa took as slow a breath as she could manage, then pulled the gun up. It was awkward in her left hand. She forced her right arm toward the front of the weapon, hoping to steady it. The pain was excruciating. She twisted her trunk, putting her hand, still gripping her shirt, closer to the weapon.

Steadying herself as best she could, Melissa raised the barrel with her left arm, ready to fire.

Suddenly there was a rush of air from above, the sky cracking with what seemed a hurricane. Dirt flew everywhere, and the night flashed red and white. A howl filled her ears. Melissa threw herself down, cowering against the force of whatever bomb was exploding.

Li Han had just started to get out of the truck when there was a vortex of wind and a hard, loud snap directly above him. It didn't sound quite like an explosion, but the wash threw him back against the vehicle. Dirt and dust flew all around; he was pelted by small rocks.

"*Dso Ba!*" he yelled in Chinese, even before he got back to his feet. "Go! Leave! They're firing missiles! Go! Go!"

He pulled at the door. There had been no explosion: whatever the Americans had fired at them had missed or malfunctioned.

"*Wo-men! Dso Ba!*"

The driver looked at him, paralyzed. Li Han realized he was speaking Chinese.

"Go!" he shouted in English. "Leave! Leave! Get the truck out of here."

One of the men in the back pounded on the roof of the cab. It was Amara, yelling something in Arabic.

"Go!" he added, switching to English, though it was hard to tell in his accent and excitement. "Mr. Li—tell him go!"

"Go!" repeated Li Han. "Let's go!"

The driver began moving in slow motion. The truck lurched forward.

"Faster!" yelled Li Han. "Before they fire again."

BY THE TIME MELISSA RAISED HER HEAD, THE TRUCK had started moving away. The men on the road picked themselves up and began scrambling after it.

What the hell had just happened?

Had someone fired a missile? Or several of them?

But there didn't seem to have been an explosion, just a massive rush of air.

When the men were gone, she rose slowly. She'd forgotten the pain, but it came back now with a vengeance, nearly knocking her unconscious. She fell back on her rump, head folded down against her chest. The submachine gun fell from her hand.

In a mental fog, Melissa began to gently rock back and forth, trying to soothe her injured arm as if it were a baby. Gradually her senses returned, though the pain remained, throbbing against her neck and torso.

She swung her knees around and rose, trying to

jostle her arm as little as possible. Finally upright, she walked down to the road. There was no bomb crater, no debris.

Melissa retrieved her gun. Her ruck was a few yards farther up the hill. She had no memory of taking it off.

The sat phone was on the ground as well, near where she'd been crouched. She picked it up and called Jordan back at the base camp. Instead of Jordan, however, a man with a deeper, somewhat older voice answered.

"This is Danny Freah. Melissa, are you OK?"

"Who are you?"

"It's Colonel Freah again. Are you all right?"

"Yeah."

"Stay where you are. We'll be at your location in twenty minutes. My Osprey is just taking off now."

"What Osprey?"

"Listen, Ms. Ilse, you don't know how lucky you are to be alive. Just stay where you are."

"I'm not moving," she said. She tried to make her words sharp, but the pain in her shoulder made it difficult to talk; she could hear the wince in her voice.

"We'll be there as soon as we can," said Danny, his voice softer. "Just stay on the hill, behind those rocks. You'll be OK. The truck has moved on. I have to go—the aircraft is here. We'll contact you when we're zero-five from your location."

The connection died. Melissa lowered herself to the ground, sitting as gently as she could.

Over the Midwest

BREANNA STOCKARD WAS NEVER COMFORTABLE AS A
passenger on an airplane.

It wasn't that she didn't like to fly; on the contrary, she loved flying. Or rather, she loved *piloting*. She loved it so much that being a passenger
made her feel extremely out of sorts. Even sitting
in the back of a C-20 Gulfstream, she felt as if she
ought to be doing something other than studying
the thick folders of reports on her iPad, or tracking through the myriad classified e-mails related
to her duties at the Office of Special Technology.

The Gulfstream was assigned to the Pentagon
for VIP travel, and carried a full suite of secure
communications. So she was surprised when her
own secure sat phone rang.

Until she saw the call was from Jonathon Reid.

"This is Breanna."

"Breanna, can you talk?"

Breanna was the sole passenger on the plane.
The cabin crew consisted of a tech sergeant who
was sitting in the back, discreetly reading a magazine.

"Yes," she said.

"I've pieced together information," said Reid. "I
don't have everything. But I think what I have is
accurate."

"OK."

"The UAV was contracted for about three years
ago, an outgrowth of the same program that pro-

duced Tigershark, as we already know. The development was entirely covert; obviously I don't have all the details."

The CIA had a long history of developing its own aircraft, going all the way back to the U-2. At times it had worked with the Air Force, and in fact it might very well have done so in this case.

"But it's not the aircraft that's important," continued Reid. "I think there's a lot more to it."

"Like what?"

"I don't feel comfortable talking about it, even over this line," he said. "We'll have to talk when you come back. I know you're supposed to go directly to SOCCOM for that conference in Florida, but I'd like to speak to you in person as soon as possible. Tonight, in fact."

"Can you meet me there?"

"I'd rather spend the time looking into this further, if possible," said Reid. "How important is the conference?"

The "conference" was actually a two-day meeting with members of the Special Operations Command to listen to requirements they had for new weapons. It was starting the next morning at eight, but Breanna was due to have breakfast with the commanding general and his staff at 0600—6:00 A.M. sharp, as the general's aide had put it to her secretary, noting that his boss was a notorious early riser with a packed schedule and an almost hyperbolic sense of punctuality.

Breanna didn't want to cancel—informal sessions like that were almost always more valuable than the actual meetings themselves. But if she detoured up to Washington, she'd get almost no sleep.

So what else was new?

"All right," Breanna told him. "I'll meet you at Andrews."

"Yes. Good."

"Jonathon—do we have a problem here?"

Reid didn't answer for a moment. "I don't know that it's a problem specifically for us," he said finally.

"All right. I'll talk to the pilot, and text you a time."

REID STARED AT THE BLANK VIRTUAL WALL FOR SEVERAL minutes after Breanna had hung up.

No, the UAV wasn't the whole story, not by a long shot. The code word "Raven" didn't even refer to the aircraft.

If he was right, Whiplash had just been inserted into the middle of a perfect storm: an illegal assassination program, an off-the-books CIA tech development operation, and an Agency screwup that had just made an unstoppable weapon available to anyone who happened to spot the UAV wreckage in the middle of the desert.

MORAL DILEMMAS

___

1

Southeastern Sudan, Africa

DANNY FREAH JUMPED FROM THE OSPREY JUST BEHIND Ben "Boston" Rockland, the team sergeant, and John "Flash" Gordon, the second-ranking NCO. Melissa Ilse was huddled near the rocks.

"Flash, grab the bike!" yelled Boston. "Let's go, people, we need to get moving!"

Danny trotted over to Melissa. She was crouched down, in obvious pain, holding her shoulder. Sugar—CIA covert officer Clare Keeb—was standing over her, her SCAR-H/MK-17 rifle poised, even though a scan of the area had shown no one nearby.

"Probably dislocated," said Sugar, keeping her eyes on the terrain.

"It's definitely dislocated," said Melissa.

Danny knelt down. Melissa wasn't what he expected. She was young—twenty-four, maybe, slim and tall, nearly five-ten, he thought, helping her up gently. Even in pain she had a beautiful, flawless face. Her skin was a half shade lighter than his; he hadn't realized she was African-American.

"I'm all right," she insisted. "We have to get the aircraft back. Do you know where they went?"

"We'll take care of that," said Danny. "Right now we have to get of here. The sun's coming up. We don't want anyone to see us."

"That's not important."

"The hell it's not," said Boston gruffly.

"Come on, into the aircraft," Danny told her. "Or do we put you on a stretcher?"

"Ow, my arm!" Melissa shrieked as Boston tried to help her on the other side. "Do you know how to pull it back into place?"

"Sure, but I ain't doing that here."

"We'll treat it," said Danny. "Get into the aircraft."

Boston put his hand on her back. "Come on, sister."

"I'm not your sister, asshole."

Boston gave Danny a grin behind her back.

Just like Boston to start pushing buttons, thought Danny.

A HALF HOUR LATER THEY WERE BACK AT THE BASE IN Ethiopia. The team had taken over one of the smaller buildings to use as a combination common area and command post. Sugar and Danny brought Melissa there and examined her shoulder. It was swollen, and seemed to have some ligament damage as well as a dislocation.

"Best place for you is up in Alexandria," Danny told her. "They'll put you out, get the shoulder right, and send you home."

"What?"

"There's a good hospital there. And—"

"I'm not going to a hospital," she insisted. "There's no need. It's just dislocated. Just push it back in place."

"This ain't like the movies," said Sugar. "You don't know what else might be screwed up or broken. You need X rays, and really they oughta do an MRI on you. I'd guess you have rotator cuff tears—"

"Just can the talk and put it back in place."

"Don't go ghetto with me, girl," snapped Sugar. She had earned her nickname because of her extremely sweet nature, but she could be a demon when someone rubbed her wrong.

"I know what I'm talking about," insisted Melissa. "I'm a nurse."

"Yeah, and I'm the President of the United States."

"I'll handle this," said Danny. "Shug, go see what Nuri's up to. All right?"

"Anything you say, Colonel." Sugar rolled her eyes and left.

A half-dozen small canvas camp chairs had been left in the building. They were the only furniture, if you didn't count the boxes and gear the Whiplash team had brought. Danny pulled over one of the chairs and sat down in front of Melissa. She had her shirt pulled down, exposing the top half of her breast as well as her shoulder.

Danny concentrated on her shoulder, gently touching the large bruise.

"I don't think popping it back into place is a good idea," he said.

"Have you ever done it before?"

"Have you?"

"Twice."

"On yourself?"

"No."

"If the muscle and ligaments are torn—"

"I need to get Raven back. It's in Duka. I'm the only one here who can get in there and find it."

"That's not even close to being true," said Nuri, standing near the door. Sugar was next to him. "Who are you working for?"

"Who are you?"

"Nuri Lupo. I spent six months out here, living with the rebels. I'll tell you one thing, you're damn lucky you're alive. Riding out through those hills? American? Woman? Anyone who found you could have hit you over the head and hauled you back to their village. Ransom on your dead body would have set them up for life. And that's if they dealt with us—give you to al Qaeda or one of the groups they support, you'd be worth a lot more."

"I can take care of myself."

"I'll bet. Who do you work for?" Nuri asked. "Are you even authorized to be here?"

"If my shoulder didn't hurt so badly, I'd slap your face."

"All right, kindergarten time is over," said Danny. "Sugar, get her some morphine."

"I'm not taking any morphine," insisted Melissa.

"If you want us to fix it, you're getting a shot," said Danny.

"I have a job to do here, Colonel. I'm not doing anything that will endanger it. And I'm sure as hell not going to Alexandria or anywhere else for a hospital. I'm not leaving until we have Raven."

"That may be a while," said Nuri.

Danny looked over at Nuri. "Let's talk outside," he told him.

Melissa grabbed him as he started to get up.

"I need to do my job," she told him. "I don't want morphine. I don't want to be knocked out. Give me aspirin. That's all I need."

"I doubt that," said Sugar. "Your muscles are in splint mode. Super hard. You need something to relax them."

"Just get aspirin."

Sugar glanced at Danny.

"Try aspirin," he said. "Can you get her shoulder back into place?"

"I can try," said Sugar. She sounded doubtful. "If her muscles relax enough."

"How about a half dose of the morphine?" asked Danny. "Just enough to loosen up."

"All right," said Melissa. "Half a dose."

"THEY TOOK THE AIRCRAFT TO AN OLD WAREHOUSE building near a train line," Nuri told Danny outside. MY-PID superimposed the locator signal on a satellite image of Duka and the surrounding area, projecting it onto a large slate computer Nuri had tied into the system. "The train line was built about a decade ago for some mining operation, but it hasn't run in years. Most of the locals live in huts on the south and western ends of town, but people will squat in empty buildings all the time. We can't really be sure what the hell's going on there without having a look from the ground."

He moved his finger over the screen, increasing the magnification.

"There were at least two different rebel groups in Duka when I was here," Nuri went on. "They sometimes work together, at least to the extent that they don't kill each other. Which is saying something out here."

"MY-PID have anything new?"

"Nothing more than I've said. They're really small bands."

"What about this Raven project? Is it related to the place, Duka?"

"I don't think so. There's no connection with Li Han and the town. He may have been in the area, but he's been working with the Sudan Brotherhood. They're much farther south."

"So he's out of the picture?"

"Probably ran off," said Nuri.

"Anything new on Raven?"

"Totally black," said Nuri, with more than a hint of I-told-you-so. "Not available in any system MY-PID has access to either. I thought of telling it to go over the wall."

"Don't," said Danny sharply.

"I didn't."

Going over the wall meant telling the system to break into Agency computers and other systems that were supposed to be off-limits to it. Theoretically, the safety precautions built into the computer system—meant to prevent it from ever being used against the U.S.—would prevent this.

But MY-PID had enormous resources, and Nuri was sure the system could get in if asked.

Which he still might do. He just wouldn't tell Danny about it.

"What's Duka like?" asked Danny.

"Typical shit hole. Little city. Used to be about ten times the size but shrunk with the fighting over the past two years. Relatively peaceful now. Two rebel factions share control. One's religious. The other's just crazy."

Nuri had been in Duka twice. He'd had dealings with a man named Gerard, who was the unofficial head of a band of rebels from a tribe whose name—phonetically, "Meur-tse Meur-tskk"—was bastardized by Western intelligence services into Meurtre Musique—"murder music" in French.

The group was actually a subgroup of the Kababish tribe, with a historical connection to French colonists or explorers who had apparently intermarried with some of the tribe during the eighteenth or nineteenth century. It was now more a loose association of outcasts and their families than an extended family, too small to have any influence outside the area where they lived.

The other group—Sudan the Almighty First Liberation in the Name of Allah, to use the English name—was larger, with informal and family ties connecting them loosely to other groups around the region. Like Meurtre Musique, the members were Islamic, but somewhat more observant. Despite their name, they were not affiliated with the powerful radical Islamic Sudan Brotherhood, which was a dominant rebel force in the south.

Meurtre Musique and First Liberation ran the city; the only government presence was a police station "staffed" by a sixty-year-old man who spent most of his time in Khartoum, the capital well to the west.

"You think we can get into the city with the Osprey?" Danny asked.

"Attract a hell of a lot of attention," said Nuri. "We'd be better off going in low-key, or maybe waiting until night and scouting around."

There was a short, loud scream from inside the hut. A string of curses followed.

"Sounds like Sugar fixed the princess's shoulder," said Nuri.

"What's her story, you figure?" Danny asked.

"Besides the obvious fact that she's a bitch?" Nuri shook his head. "Women officers are all one of two kinds—either they use sex to get what they want, or they play hard-ass bitch. She's the second. We should get rid of her. Shoot her up with morphine and pack her off. The shoulder's the perfect excuse."

"This is her operation."

"No, it's our operation," said Nuri. "Her operation ended when the aircraft crashed and we were called in to clean up. I don't like the fact that it's walled off, Danny. There is a huge amount here that they're not telling us."

"I know."

Sugar came out of the building. She was smiling.

"Done," she told Danny. "She didn't want to wait for the aspirin to take."

"She gonna be all right?"

"*Phhhh*. That attitude tells me she wasn't all right to begin with. I'm gonna get some chow and get some rest, Colonel, all right?"

"Sure. You setting up your own tent?"

"You got that right. I'm not sleeping with those pervs. No way, Colonel." She thrust her finger at Nuri in mock warning. "And you watch yourself, too, Mr. Lupo."

Sugar exploded with laughter and sauntered away.

Danny picked up the small touch screen and looked at the satellite image. The warehouse where the UAV was located could be attacked easily enough, but he'd prefer to make the assault at night for a host of reasons, starting with operational security. The question was whether they could wait that long.

"How likely are they to move the UAV, you think?" he asked Nuri.

"I have no idea. We don't even know who has it. If it's one of these groups, they won't bother. They have no place to go with it. If it's just someone moving through—which I doubt—they'll probably wait until nightfall and start out again. In that case, they'll be easy to take on the road. Shoot out the driver, grab the bird, and go home."

"What about Li Han?"

"It could be him," said Nuri. "This isn't a Brother village, though. He'd be a fish out of water."

"Isn't he already? Being Chinese?"

"True. Maybe we should go in and nose around a bit."

"Just walk in?"

"Drive in," said Nuri. "I've been here before. I'll use my old cover. We can plant some bugs for MY-PID to use. Augment the feeds from the Tigershark."

"OK."

"Hell, I may be able to buy the damn thing," added Nuri. "Save us a lot of trouble."

"Buy it?"

"We're in Africa, remember? Everything's for sale."

"Not to us."

Nuri laughed. "I'm a gun dealer. I had some dealings with a man named Gerard, trying to sell him some guns. If he's involved, it'll be for sale. And if he's not, he'll tell us who is."

"That's safe?"

Nuri laughed again, this time much harder.

"Of course it's not safe," he said when he regained control.

2

Over Sudan

WITH THE UAV LOCATED AND THE CIA OFFICER RECOV-
ered, Turk's job settled into a sustained fugue of
monotony. He had to orbit above Duka, watching to make sure that the rebels or whoever had
grabbed the UAV remained in the warehouse
building with it. He had two problems: conserv-
ing fuel and staying awake.

The second was by far the hardest. Turk had a
small vial of what were euphemistically known as
"go pills" in the pocket of his flight suit, but he
preferred not to take them. So he ran through his
other, nonprescription bag of tricks—listening to
rap music tracks and playing mental games. He
tried to trace perfect ellipses in the air without
the aid of the flight computer, mentally timing his
circuits against the actual clock.

His eyes still felt the heavy effect of gravity.

He was at 30,000 feet, well above the altitude
where anyone on the ground could hear him, let
alone do anything about him. As far as he knew,
his only job now would be to circle around until
the Raven was recovered. At that point he could
land, refuel, and head home.

Maybe with some sleep in there somewhere.

Turk amused himself by thinking of places he
might stop over. The Tigershark had been at a
number of air shows—the aircraft had been built
as a demonstration project and toured before being
bought by the Office of Special Technology—so

as long as he could get Breanna to agree, he could take it just about anywhere.

Maybe Paris. They said the women were pretty hot there.

Italian women. Better bet. He could land at Aviano, find some fellow pilot to show him the city . . .

"Tigershark, this is Whiplash Ground. How are you reading me?"

"I read you good, Colonel. What's our game plan?"

"We're thinking of sending someone into the city to scout around. If we have an operation, we're not going in until tonight."

"What's the status on that tanker?"

"We're still waiting to hear."

A tanker had been routed from the Air Mobility Command, but it wasn't clear how long it might be before it would arrive. Not only had the mission been thrown together at the last moment, but Whiplash's status outside the normal chain of command hurt when it came to arranging for outside support. Tankers were in especially short supply, and finding one that didn't have a specific mission was always difficult.

"I can stay up where I am for another two hours, give or take," said Turk. He glanced at the fuel panel and mentally calculated that he actually had a little more than three. But it was always good to err on the low side. "If the tanker isn't going to be here by then, it might be a good idea for me to land and refuel at your base. Assuming you have fuel."

"Stand by."

Turk gave the controls over to the computer and stretched, raising his legs and pointing his toes awkwardly. This was the only situation where he envied Flighthawk pilots—they could get up from their stations and take a walk around the aircraft.

Not in the B-2s that were controlling the UAV fighters now, of course, but in the older Megafortresses and the new B-5Cs. Then again, most remote aircraft pilots didn't even fly in mother ships anymore; they operated at remote bases or centers back home, just like the Predator and Global Hawk pilots.

Scratch that envy, Turk thought.

"Tigershark, we have a tanker en route. It'll be about an hour," said Colonel Freah, coming back on the line.

"I'll wait," he told Danny. "Give me the tanker frequency and his flight vector, if you can."

"Stand by."

3

Western Ethiopia

NURI NEEDED TO GEAR UP TO GO INTO DUKA. THE FIRST thing he needed was better bling. An arms dealer could get away with shabby clothes, but lacking gold was beyond suspicious. At a minimum, he needed at least a fancy wristwatch. Transportation was critical as well.

Most of all, he needed American dollars.

Which was a problem. The CIA had temporarily closed its station in Addis Ababa, the Ethiopian capital. The nearest officer was in Eritrea somewhere.

"Use the cash the existing operation has," said Reid. "I'm sure they have plenty."

Reid seemed grouchy, probably because of the hour. D.C. was eight hours behind eastern Africa, which made it close to two in the morning there.

"I'm not getting a lot of cooperation," said Nuri.

"Shoot them if they don't cooperate."

It didn't sound like a joke.

"Get back to me if there's still a problem," said Reid before hanging up.

Melissa had gone to rest in her quarters, one of the smaller huts farthest up on the hillside—not a coincidence, Nuri thought, as she had undoubtedly chosen it for the pseudo status its location would provide.

From a distance, all of the buildings looked as if they had been there for ages. But up close it was obvious they were recent additions—the painted exterior walls were made from pressboard, relatively rare in this part of Africa.

Even rarer was the door on Melissa's hut, all metal. Nuri knocked on it.

"What?" she snapped from inside.

"You awake?"

"I'm awake," she said, pulling open the door. Her right arm was in a sling.

"Can we talk?"

Melissa pushed the door open and let him in. There was a sleeping bag on the floor. A computer and some communications gear sat opposite it, pushed up against the wall. The only other furniture was a small metal footlocker. A pair of AK-47s sat on top, with loaded magazines piled at the side. A small, battery-powered lantern near the head of the sleeping bag lit the room.

"I need some cash," Nuri said.

"And?"

"I need money."

"Why do you think I have money?" snapped Melissa, sitting down on the sleeping bag. She pushed back to the wall, spreading her legs in front of her. She was wearing black fatigues.

"Look, I just got off the line with my boss," said Nuri. "He told me I should shoot you if you didn't cooperate. And he was serious."

"Give me a break."

"I know you got a stash of money," he said. "Nobody works in Africa, especially out here, without bribe money. Piles of it."

"Why do you need money?"

"I'm going into Duka and nose around. I have a cover as an arms dealer."

"I have a few thousand, that's all."

"It's a start."

"I go with the money."

Nuri shook his head. "Ain't gonna work."

"It has to."

"Nope. Come on. I have a cover here I've established. I go in with an American girl—I'd be dead."

"You don't exactly look like you belong," said Melissa. "You're the wrong color."

"I'm from Eritrea," said Nuri. His cover story wasn't that far from the truth, if you went back two generations. "I'm an Italian. Don't make a face—it worked for months. I can speak most of the tribal languages, including Nubian, as well as Arabic."

"I'll bet."

"You want Lango or Madi?"

"Nobody speaks Lango up here," said Melissa.

"No shit. That wasn't my point."

"Look, we can work together," she told him. "We don't have to be enemies."

"Just give me the cash."

"You're stuck if I don't. There are no cash machines outside of the capital, which is too far for you to go, right? And Eritrea isn't going to help. Because there's one person in Eritrea, and you can never get ahold of him. And the embassy is useless."

"I can call Washington," he told her. "And have you ordered back home."

"Look, there's no need for us to spit at each other," she told him. "Let's work together."

Nuri frowned.

"You can't cut me out," she told him. "Tell your boss I want to be involved."

"My boss?"

"Colonel Freah."

"Danny's not my boss. He commands the military people."

"And what are you?"

"I'm Agency, just like you. We work as a team."

"Who's in charge of the operation?"

"We both are."

"There has to be *one* person in charge. One."

"You going to tell me how to run my operation now?"

"I'm not trying to argue with you. I'm sorry." She shifted against the wall. "Let me go into town with you."

"So the guys in the truck can recognize you?"

"They never got close enough to see me. It was dark."

"What part of the company do you work for?"

Melissa didn't answer.

"How long have you been covert? Or are you a tech geek who found her way over to the action side?"

"I'm not going to play games," Melissa said. "I work for Harker—talk to him."

"Look, give me the money," he told her. "I need to go in right away. You're in no shape right now. You should have taken more morphine. At least you'd get some rest."

"You're a doctor now?"

"Are you?"

"I trained as a nurse."

Nuri put up his hands. She had an answer for everything.

Finally, Melissa went over to the footlocker and opened it. She hunched over it, counting money out.

"This ought to be enough," she told him, handing over a wad of hundred-dollar bills.

Nuri started to count it.

"There are fifty," she told him. "Five thousand."

"That may not do it."

"It'll have to." She slammed the top down with her right hand, pulling it halfway out of the sling.

"You should get your arm fixed."

"It'll be fine. You go and scout. OK. But I want to go on the mission."

"If there is a mission, that'll be up to Danny."

"I thought he wasn't your boss."

"He's not. But he's more objective than I am."

BOSTON MANAGED TO PATCH UP MELISSA'S MOTORCY-cle well enough for Nuri to ride it across the border into Elada, a medium-sized town in Eritrea, about an hour and a half away. He bought a counterfeit Rolex, some AK-47s, an old Colt service automatic, ammo, and two pair of khaki uniforms for a hundred American dollars; he could have shaved at least another ten off the deal if he'd had exact change.

Finding a decent vehicle was a different story. Pickup trucks, even those in poor condition, were valuable and rare. Nuri wanted either two trucks, or a truck and Land Rover; he'd stick a few of the Whiplash people in the back of the pickup as bodyguards. But he couldn't find anyone willing to sell. The best he could do was work a trade for a battered Mercedes sedan—his motorcycle, a thousand American in cash, and three stolen credit cards.

The credit cards were Agency cards, disabled

by MY-PID two minutes after the transaction. It would undoubtedly be at least a full day before the buyer found out: Elada didn't have any ATMs, nor were there any in the rest of the country.

The car ran decently, and came with three-quarters of a tank worth of diesel. Which was enough—Nuri drove it about five miles south to a field where the Osprey was waiting. Danny had decided to speed things up by flying it across to Sudan.

"I have uniforms for two bodyguards," Nuri told Danny as the Osprey took off with the car chained beneath its belly. "How about Flash and Boston?"

"Boston can go, but Flash is going to stay with the aircraft in case we need backup," said Danny. "I want to come."

Boston was imposing physically, but his real asset was an angry, craggy face that would scare even a close friend into thinking he was just waiting for an excuse to kill. Flash, though white, had the lean, undernourished look of a down-on-his-luck white mercenary who very likely was nursing sociopathic tendencies.

Danny was big physically, and Nuri knew from experience that he was in excellent shape and was a great shot. But he had a quieter, almost benign face—too relaxed, too in control. The ideal bodyguard out here was just this side of criminally insane.

"You think you can do it?" Nuri asked.

"I've gone undercover here before."

"This is different. You'll have to be completely silent. If they hear your accent up here, we're dead."

"I'm not worried," said Danny.

Nuri picked up one of the uniforms. "Here you go, then. I hope it fits."

4

Andrews Air Force Base, Maryland

BREANNA SPOTTED JONATHON REID'S GRAY TAURUS parked with its running lights and engine on near the edge of the tarmac as the C-20 turned off the access ramp from the runway. She unbuckled her seat belt and went to the door, waiting while the aircraft taxied over.

"Pilots say the plane should be refueled inside an hour, ma'am," said the sergeant who was working as the crewman. "If you'd like, I can try and hunt up something to eat."

"A bagel?" she asked. "With butter?"

"I'll give it a shot, ma'am."

Breanna waited impatiently for the aircraft to halt. It seemed to take forever to travel the last twenty or thirty yards. Finally it eased to a stop. The crewman dropped the fold-down stairs, and Breanna trotted down them into a light rain. She walked over to the car and got in on the passenger side.

Reid handed her a cup of coffee.

"The news is that bad?" she asked.

Reid had an extremely droll sense of humor, but he didn't laugh now.

"I'm guessing what's going on here," he told her. "I'm guessing there's an unauthorized assassination program involved. There are no official records or minutes anywhere. No NSC notes. And I did check, through the back channel."

"OK." Breanna had suspected as much when he said he wanted to talk about it in person.

"But it's the weapon that worries me," said Reid. "Raven doesn't refer to the UAV. It was a program to develop software that could seek out and destroy whoever it was targeted against. It could control a variety of platforms. In fact, it could go, on its own, from one to the other. That was its goal."

"Is that possible?"

"I don't know." Reid took a sip from his coffee. "After seeing everything Dr. Rubeo has come up with, I'd say anything is possible."

"Hmmm."

"This weapon would be able to take over programs of other countries," continued Reid. "There was a white paper, very restricted access, that talks about guarding against these things."

"You should really talk to Ray about it."

"I'd like to. But I don't know how much to trust him."

"I trust Ray implicitly."

"Would he feel obliged, morally, to discuss it with anyone else?"

"What do you mean?"

"If the Agency has created a weapon that can't be controlled, and accidentally set it loose, who would he feel he had to tell?"

"What do you mean, it can't be controlled?"

Reid sipped his coffee, momentarily turning his gaze to the drops of rain landing on the windshield.

"The implication of the white paper was that this software would be like a virus, released into the wild," he said, still looking at the rain. "Once out there, it would just run relentless until its target was found."

"You think the Agency would test that without any safety protocols?" said Breanna. "That would be insane."

"I don't know what they're doing. I would assume they would have *some* sort of safeguard. And I don't know if any of this is even possible. But . . ."

"But?"

"But they're definitely going after someone in the Sudan, they're definitely using a UAV no one else has known about, and they're definitely being extremely secretive. And the person the Whiplash team rendezvoused with in Africa joined the Agency as a software scientist before transferring about a year ago to covert ops."

"We have to ask Edmund what's going on," said Breanna.

"I have. He won't say. I have a few favors to call in," added Reid. "And I'll talk to Dr. Rubeo."

"Then what?"

"I'm not sure." Reid put his coffee cup back in

the holder. "I have to ask you not to share this with the senator."

"Zen?"

"I don't— This could be a real political football in Congress. And . . ." He paused. "I'm not sure the President knows. In fact, I'd almost bet she doesn't. Just from Edmund's reactions."

"You think they'd run an assassination program without telling the President?"

"Without a doubt," said Reid.

BY THE TIME SHE REBOARDED THE C-20, BREANNA FELT drained. Recovering the UAV—they had located it and were planning to go in as soon as it was dark—was exactly the sort of mission Whiplash had been created for. The political implications of Raven, even if it were "just" an illegal assassination mission, were something else again.

She hadn't even been thinking of Zen until Reid mentioned that he couldn't be told.

They both had jobs where it was necessary to keep a certain amount of separation between work and home, and therefore to keep certain state and political secrets from one another as well. But if Breanna knew that the CIA was breaking the law, and being extremely irresponsible as well—could she in good conscience *not* tell Zen about it? What would he say to her when he found out?

Because something like this would eventually come out. Surely.

Hopefully, Reid was overthinking the situation. Losing a top secret UAV would certainly be enough to circle the wagons.

And just because he couldn't find any approval in the system for the assassination didn't necessarily mean there hadn't been one.

"Ma'am?"

Breanna looked up at the tech sergeant, standing in the aisle next to her seat.

"Got you your bagel," he said, smiling as he handed her a tray. "I have to ask you to buckle your seat belt."

5

Duka, Sudan

LI HAN CIRCLED THE WRECKED AIRCRAFT. IT WAS WORTH even more than he'd thought at first glance. It was unique, far more advanced than anything he was familiar with. Granted, he wasn't an expert in UAVs, but he knew a great deal about computers and processing technology, and what he saw here was truly impressive.

The building in Duka hadn't changed at all since he'd been there last. Nor had Duka itself—still a sleepy backwater occupied by tribesmen barely removed from the medieval ages. The people walked around in a mixture of modern and ancient dress, and were armed with AK-47s and the like, but they still thought the way people thought in the Stone Age. If he had been a sociologist, he'd have found it fascinating.

But he was not. He was a scientist, and not even that.

His escorts were all sleeping upstairs, even the two men who had been posted by the door as guards. Just as well.

While the locals posed no threat, Li Han knew the Americans would be looking for the aircraft. Embedded in its skin were two devices sending repeater-type radio beacons, obviously intended for tracking. One of them had been damaged in the crash, but the other was still working. Carefully removing them, he'd placed them into the back of the truck, covered them with a tarp, and had the Brothers drive them to another building a kilometer away. It was an elementary ruse, but at least he'd have some warning if the Americans came.

He put his knee down on the dirt floor as if genuflecting before the marvel in front of him. The airfoil was made of carbon-fiber and metallized glass, with a few titanium elements. The manufacturing process was so advanced he doubted it would be of interest to any Third World country, even the Iranians. The Russians might not even be able to duplicate it.

The Chinese, of course, would be highly interested, but they were the one country he could never deal with. Not even on this. The ministry considered him a traitor, and would pay any price for his head.

Selling the engine would be easier. It was a downsized turbine, nothing particularly fancy or difficult to copy. The Israelis were very much interested in lightweight engines for their own UAVs, and they paid extremely well. But being that this was American technology—markings indicated at least some of the parts had been manufactured by GE—it was possible, perhaps even likely, that they already had access to it. They might even have helped develop it.

As far as he could tell, the optical sensors were trashed beyond use and even recognition when the aircraft crashed. The same went for the infrared sensor, though in that case he thought some of the parts might be salvageable and potentially salable to Iran for their own research. The price wouldn't be high; it was more likely something he could throw in to make a larger deal.

The weapons system was a straight Hellfire missile setup. He could get about three thousand dollars for the salvageable mount and related electrical parts—not even pocket change. The missile itself would have fetched much more, but part of the propulsion system had shattered on impact and appeared irreparable.

And then there was the computer and guidance system, which looked to be the equivalent of a mainframe computer stuffed into a box no bigger than a woman's purse.

UAVs were essentially radio controlled aircraft. Their "brains" received radio signals, then translated those inputs into electrical impulses that guided the throttle and the various control surfaces. In truth, it wasn't all that complicated—children's toys had been doing something similar for decades. The circuitry for sending flight data and information from the other sensors was trivial.

But this UAV's brain was far different. It had six processor arrays, all clearly custom-built. This suggested a parallel computing architecture that would be overkill for even the most complicated aircraft. Not only could you fly a Boeing Dreamliner with this much power; you could fly an entire fleet of them.

And still have plenty of processing room left for a championship game of chess.

The obvious conclusion was that the computer flew the aircraft without the help of a ground pilot. But what else did it do?

Li Han was determined to find out. His only problem was to do that without destroying the programming.

And to do it here. It seemed safer to hide out in Duka than attempt to return to the Brothers. But that meant limited power. The electricity in the house worked only a few hours a day, and he didn't want to attract attention by getting a gas generator like some of the locals. He had battery lanterns, and his laptop was extremely powerful, but there was no mistaking the musty basement for a Shanghai computer lab. He was lucky to even be in a building with a basement, as crude as it was.

The overhead light flickered as Li Han leaned over the computer box. There were two network interface plugs, the standard 5E receptacles used by local area networks around the world. There was also a pair of much larger connectors that looked to Li Han like specialized optical cable receptors. These were irregularly sized, larger than the thumb-sized hook-ins one would find on advanced audiovisual equipment in professional studios or similar applications.

Clearly, the 5E connectors were his way in, but he didn't have any 5E wiring.

Could he find it here?

There was a sound outside, upstairs—an engine. Li Han froze. For a moment he expected the worst: a missile crashing through the roof. But the noise was just a truck passing on the road.

He took a deep breath and began thinking about where he might find a computer cable in this part of the Sudan.

6

Georgetown, Washington, D.C.

IT WAS WELL AFTER 2:00 A.M. BY THE TIME JONATHON Reid got home. The house was quiet, his wife sleeping. It was a modest house by Georgetown standards—three bedrooms, a bath and a half, no granite or marble on the property, and the only thing "faux" was the fake flower on the kitchen windowsill. Reid or his wife cut the small lawn themselves. But the house felt like an immense place tonight. He walked through the downstairs rooms quietly, absorbing the space and the quiet. Thinking.

Possibly, he was making too much of this. There was always that danger when you only saw parts, not the whole.

Reid slipped quietly into the master bedroom. He took off his clothes and reached to pull the blanket down. But as he started to slip into bed, he realized there was no way he would sleep. He looked at his wife, her face turned away from him. As good as it would feel to curl his body around hers, he didn't want to wake her.

He left the room and walked to the far end of the hall, to the guest room. It had been his oldest daughter's room years before. Repainted several times, it bore no visible trace of her, but to Reid it still felt as if she were there. He could remember setting up her bed the first night they moved in. He'd sat here countless times, reading her stories.

He could close his eyes and imagine himself on the floor next to her bed, telling her while she slept that he had to go away again, explaining that it was his job and that even if he didn't come back—something he would say only when he was positive she wasn't awake—he still loved her, and no matter what, would be her father and protector.

Reid eased himself down to that very spot on the floor next to the bed, then leaned back and stared at the ceiling. A dim brownish light filtered in from the window, casting the room in faded sepia.

If the CIA was running an illegal assassination program, from a country it had been ordered to leave, with a potentially uncontrollable weapon, what should Jonathon Reid do? Where was his loyalty? What was his moral obligation?

The CIA was his life. He had a deep personal relationship with the director, not to mention countless fellow officers, present and retired, who would surely be affected by any scandal.

He also had a deep personal relationship with the President. He was one of her husband's best friends, and hers as well.

And there was his obligation to his country, and to justice.

How did those obligations sort themselves out here? What exactly was he supposed to do?

Li Han was not on the preapproved target list. It was possible, though unlikely, that he had been added under a special mechanism allowed by national security law; those proceedings were compartmentalized, and there was always a chance that Reid's search—thorough, and itself skirting the bounds of his legal duties as a CIA officer— had missed this particular authorization.

Even so—even if there was no authorization— did that make the targeting wrong? Li Han was such a despicable slime, such a threat to the country, that his death could easily be justified. Truly it would save lives; he wasn't running an agricultural program in Sudan, after all.

The Agency's development of the UAV clearly

had begun under the previous administration. While the recent reorganization did not allow for such programs, there were always gray areas, especially when it came to development.

Given the CIA's long history of producing such weapons, not to mention the Agency's record of success, this was another area that at worst might be a minor transgression. And certainly in his case, given Reid's relationship with the Office of Special Technology and Whiplash, Reid could easily be criticized for trying to guard his turf. And in fact he might even be doing that, unconsciously at least.

Utilizing a software program that could hunt down and kill on its own? Without authorization?

Raven sounded like science fiction. But then, nearly everything that they did at the Office of Special Technology sounded like science fiction as well. So did half the gadgets covert officers carried in their pockets these days, at least to an old-timer like Reid.

What should he do?

He'd need more information—talk to Rubeo, look at the authorizations he hadn't had a chance to access. Confront Edmund. Ask what exactly was going on.

Then?

Well, he had to go tell the President, didn't he?

She *might* actually know about the program. She might have authorized every single element. It was possible.

Maybe he just didn't know the whole story. Maybe the original Raven was just a pipedream, and had become a sexy name for a cool looking aircraft. Maybe there was nothing special about the aircraft at all.

"Jonathon, what are you doing on the floor?"

Reid looked over at the doorway. The dim light framed his wife's silhouette. In that instant she was twenty-five again; they had just met, and she was the most beautiful woman he could ever imagine, in every sense of the word.

She still was, to his eye.

"Jon?"

She came over and knelt by him. "Are you OK, honey? Is your back bothering you?"

"I was feeling a little . . . stiff," he said. It wasn't a lie, exactly, just far from the truth. "I didn't want to wake you."

"Sitting on the floor isn't going to make your back better," she said. "Come on and get a heating pad."

"I'd rather a nice backrub," he said.

He reached his hand up to hers. She took it. Forty some years flew by in her grip.

"Come to bed," she told him softly.

Reid got up and followed her to their room.

7

Approaching Duka, eastern Sudan

DANNY FREAH HATED TO LIE, EVEN IN THE LINE OF DUTY. It was the one aspect of Whiplash and working with the CIA that he didn't particularly like.

In his role as a covert officer, Nuri often pretended to be someone else. He was a smooth liar, a born bullshit artist and a good actor: as soon as he put on the watch and jacket he'd bought in Asmara, he became a slime-bag arms dealer. The performance was utterly believable.

By contrast, Danny felt awkward in the uniform, and not just because it was a little tight around the chest. Fortunately, his job was simple—follow Nuri and keep his mouth shut.

Duka had grown around a small oasis on a trading route that led ultimately to the sea. It had never been a particularly large city, though during the short period when the railroad was active it quadrupled in size. Most of the people who arrived during that tiny boomlet had left, leaving behind a motley collection of buildings that ranged from traditional African circular huts to ramshackle masonry warehouses. The place was far from prosperous, but what wealth was here was expressed in odd pieces of modern technology. Power generators hummed behind a number of grass-roofed huts, and Danny saw a few satellite dishes as well.

The huts were the most interesting to him. These were in the oldest part of town, clustered along the western edges. Most sat in the center of small yards and garden patches. A few of the yards had goats and even oxen. There were also chickens, which wandered near the road as the Mercedes approached.

Danny hit the brakes several times before Nuri told him it was senseless—the birds would only get out of the way at the last moment, no matter how fast or slow he was going.

"You're sure about that," said Danny.

"They always do."

"Why do they let the birds roam around? Aren't they afraid of wild animals?"

"Lions?"

"Well—"

"I doubt there have been lions or even hyenas around here for centuries," said Nuri. "Lions would be worth a fortune. The hyenas they'd kill for meat."

Though Danny's ancestors had come from Africa, he wasn't sure where. He felt no connection to either the land or the people.

"This place was pretty poor, right after the railroad stopped," continued Nuri. "A bunch of aid organizations got together and tried to help. Most of the money was siphoned off by the central government."

"That why there are so many rebel groups down here?"

"Not really. People expect corruption. The resentments with the government have more to do with tribal rivalries and jealousies, and outside agitators," added Nuri. "The outside people come in, find a malcontent or some crazoid, give him a little money and weapons. Things escalate from there."

"Are the Iranians here?"

"Not so much. Hezbollah tried getting some traction a little farther north, but it didn't work out. The Brotherhood, which is made up of Sudanese, isn't even that strong. You can be from the next town or a related tribe and still be considered an outsider."

"Like us."

"Oh, we're definitely outsiders. But we have money," said Nuri. "And we're not going to stay. So we're in a special category. They like us. Until they don't."

Danny swerved around a goat that had wandered near the highway. The Mercedes fishtailed and the rear wheels went off the road. He fought the car straight, half on and half off the pavement, then gently brought it back.

"About a half mile more," said Nuri calmly. "There should be a road heading to the east."

WORRIED THAT EVEN GOING NEAR THE ABANDONED warehouse buildings would seem suspicious, Nuri had Danny drive through the city to a rise about three-quarters of a mile north of the warehouse area. He got out there, making a show of stretching his legs and then pretending to go off to the side to relieve himself in case anyone was watching.

Reaching into his pocket, Nuri took out a small case about the size of a quarter. He opened it, then gingerly removed what looked like an over-sized mosquito from the interior. It was literally and metaphorically a bug—a tiny video camera was embedded in the eyes; the legs were used as antennas. The rest of the body was a battery, with about a twelve-hour life span.

He walked into the weeds and positioned the mosquito. Its circuitry had woken up as soon as he took it from the box.

"MY-PID, are we connected?" Nuri asked, tapping his ear set. The control unit he was using looked exactly like a higher-end civilian cell phone system such as a Jawbone Icon; rather than using Bluetooth to connect to a cell phone, it had a proprietary burst radio connection to talk to the control unit in his pocket. The control unit in turn connected to the MY-PID system via a link with the Tigershark, orbiting overhead.

"Connection established," replied the Voice.

"Do you have a visual on the target warehouse?"

"Affirmative. Visual on target."

"Gotcha."

"Rephrase."

INSIDE THE CAR, DANNY USED A PAIR OF BINOCULARS TO examine the building where the UAV transponder was located. It was a simple metal structure, roughly two stories high and about 200 by 200 square feet. There were a dozen other buildings, most very similar, scattered around the area, all butting close to the railroad tracks and now disused sidings. There were clusters of houses near them, run-down shacks and battered brick buildings. Most were not occupied, according to MY-PID, which based the claim on the infrared readings from Tigershark's sensors.

There were two openings in the target building: a large garagelike door facing the road, and a standard-sized door nearby. There were no windows.

MY-PID said there were two people inside the building. They appeared to be sleeping.

"No guards outside," said Danny as Nuri got back in the car. "Just the two inside."

"Not that we can see," answered Nuri. He pulled out the MY-PID control unit, which was dummied up to look like an iPod Nano. He could have the computer tell him what it saw, but preferred to see it himself, even if it was on a ridiculously small screen. "There are kids playing on the other side of the railroad track. They probably get a few dinars for spotting strangers. Or anybody else."

"Those kids are only seven or eight years old," said Danny.

"Another year and they'll all have guns," said Nuri, sliding into the car. "Center of town is back the way we came."

Danny toyed with the idea of simply driving up to the building and having a look. The Osprey and two of his men were a few minutes away, hunkered down in the desert. If things looked easy, he could call it in quickly and they could haul the UAV away.

But things rarely went as easily as they looked. Most of Whiplash's advanced gear was still back in the States and wouldn't be available for at least another twenty-four to forty-eight hours. While he wasn't about to wait that long, it was better to wait for dark and come in with the whole team.

"Take a left ahead. There," said Nuri, pointing. "The roads are all dirt from here on. I'll warn when the next turn is coming up."

They worked their way around a patch of houses to an open area that served as Duka's business section. Small buildings were arranged haphazardly around the large dirt lot. There was a garage with several cars out in front; next to it were a pair of buildings with tin roofs that held small storefronts. A larger building, this one of brick, stood opposite the shops. About the size of a small ranch house in the States, the structure was shared by a medical clinic, a post office, and a store that sold farming gear.

Their destination was next to the clinic building: a squat, thatch-roofed pavilion that looked like an open-sided tent. About the size of a train car, it ran back from the open square at a slight angle, and was filled with a variety of benches, picnic tables, and cast-off plastic chairs. It was filled with people, more than two dozen, scattered in various groups. A pair of white-headed gentlemen played chess near the front; farther back, two men with machetes stood behind a squat, pale-skinned man whose face was covered with pimples.

The man was Gerard, the de facto leader of Meurtre Musique. He sat in a red plastic chair, gazing straight ahead.

"Someone should stay with the car," said Nuri.

"Boston, you stay," said Danny. "I want to get a look at him."

"You got it, boss."

Danny got out and followed Nuri into the pavilion.

"*Bonjour, Gerard,*" said Nuri, rattling off a greeting in French.

Gerard stared straight ahead. Danny thought he looked like a strung-out heroin addict.

"I hope you have been well." Nuri pulled over a chair and sat down, just off to the side of Gerard.

Danny walked over and stood behind him. He had arranged the strap on his rifle so it hung down near his hand; he kept his fingers on the butt grip, ready just in case.

The two men with the machetes eyed him fiercely, but soon turned their attention back to the general area. Danny wondered why: most of the people beneath the shed roof were old, and couldn't have hurt themselves, let alone Gerard. His gun was the only one visible.

"*Je voudrais de l'eau,*" said Nuri. "I'd like some water. What about you?"

Gerard's head moved ever so slightly downward. Nuri straightened in his chair and turned toward a woman standing nearby. Gerard said something; the woman replied, then left, crossing the street.

NURI CONTINUED HIS SLOW ASSAULT ON GERARD'S SI-lence, telling him that he had been doing much traveling in the past several months, seeing many people and learning many new things. He used French, even though it wasn't his best language. He'd taken off the MY-PID ear set—Gerard might have wanted it if he'd seen it—but could speak the language reasonably well without the computer translator's help.

He could have been speaking Portuguese for all the results he was getting. Gerard remained silent.

The man was a cipher. The first time they had met, Nuri thought he was stoned on some local alcoholic concoction; there were an almost infinite variety. But he'd spent considerable time with Gerard at their second meeting, and saw that he only drank pure water. And when the barrier actually came down—when Gerard broke his silence and spoke about the guns he was interested in buying—he was quite articulate and even a good negotiator. Nuri had decided that the stony glare was part of some sort of religious commitment, Gerard's version of meditation or prayer.

His girl brought back two bottles of water. Nuri checked the seal to make sure his hadn't been refilled from a local tap—always a possibility, and sure to induce diarrhea—then opened his. Gerard stared at the bottle, then took it. He had a small sip. Nuri sensed he was ready to talk.

"Are you happy with your current supplier?" Nuri asked in French.

"*Hmmmph*," answered Gerard.

"I don't want to make trouble," said Nuri. "If there comes an opportunity, I am always ready."

Gerard handed the water bottle back to the girl.

She was thirteen or fourteen, probably a relative as well as a mistress. Nuri tried not to be judgmental. Things were different here, and he had a job to do.

"We are satisfied with the Russians," said Gerard in English.

"Russians?" Nuri switched to English as well. "They're supplying you now?"

Gerard said nothing.

"They do give good prices," admitted Nuri. The dealer might or might not be Russian; anyone from Eastern Europe was likely to be considered a Russian—Poles, Ukrainians, Georgians. All were more likely candidates, and most likely operating on their own. When he was last here, the *real* Russians were notably absent. "If you are satisfied, then there is no need to change. A good relationship is worth more than a few bullets, one way or the other."

Gerard remained silent.

"And the government—have they been giving you much trouble?" Nuri asked.

"They are monkeys," said Gerard. "Imbecilic monkeys."

"Yes."

"What would be of use to us would be medicines," he said. "Aspirin would be a very good thing."

"Aspirin? Of course. Yes. I believe I could arrange to find some of that. For the clinic?"

"The clinic is run by thieves," said Gerard. "We have established a new one."

"What other medicines?" asked Nuri.

Gerard rose. He moved stiffly, but compared to how Nuri had found him, he was a dynamo.

"I will take you to talk to the doctor. We will go in your car."

DANNY FOLLOWED NURI TO THE MERCEDES. GERARD, the girl, and the two guards came as well. They got into the back with Boston, while Nuri took his place up front. Danny didn't like that—it was far too dangerous, he thought—but there was no way to tell Nuri that.

Gerard gave directions from the back in French. Nuri translated them into African, and MY-PID—connected via the team radio—retranslated to English.

The directions took them to a single story building that looked very much like an American double-wide trailer.

"Wait in the car," Nuri said as the others got out.

"No way," said Danny.

They exchanged a glance. Nuri frowned, but didn't protest when Danny followed him inside the building.

THEY WERE MET NEAR THE DOOR BY A BLACK WOMAN IN her early twenties. She was enthusiastic and friendly, and clearly didn't speak the local language—she fumbled worse than Nuri did over the greeting.

"Do you speak English?" she asked. She had a British accent; Nuri pegged her as a volunteer, here to do her part for world peace.

"Certainly, Doctor," Nuri answered.

"I am not a doctor," she said, leading them through the crowded reception room. "I am just a nurse. Marie Bloom."

"I'm sorry. Gerard introduced you as a doctor."

"I think they use the word for anyone with a medical interest." She smiled at Gerard, nodding. "He has been very good to us. You are here to see our clinic?"

"We may be able to supply some medicines for you," said Nuri. "Through Gerard's generosity. If I knew what it was you needed."

"Oh that would be wonderful. Let me show you around."

The two examining rooms were austere, furnished with basic tables and some cabinets. There were two rooms with beds where patients could rest, a pair of small offices, and a storeroom. A dozen people, all women or children, were being seen by two aides, both locals whom Marie had trained. They had been open only a few weeks, said Marie, but already had seen a number of difficult cases, including many patients with AIDS.

"We are going to be involved in a program," she said. "But for now, we send those with AIDS to the capital. We can't really help."

"What about the other clinic in town?" Nuri asked.

Marie glanced at Gerard before answering.

"Many people won't go there."

That had to be because the other clinic was associated with Sudan First. The friction between the two groups was new.

Most likely it wasn't serious, or Gerard would

not have been in the city center. But you could never tell.

"Give me a list of what you can use," said Nuri as the tour ended. "And I will see what I can do."

NURI LED DANNY BACK TO THE CAR WITHOUT GERARD and his small entourage. Boston was in the driver's seat; Danny got in the back.

"Why didn't you ask about the UAV?" asked Danny as Boston backed out onto the road.

"The time wasn't right," said Nuri.

"Why not?"

"Let me handle this, all right? We have to get this medicine."

"That'll take weeks."

"No. They just want over-the-counter drugs mostly. I'll fly to Egypt and buy it. It's all simple stuff. The clinic's a gold mine of information. If we could find a way to talk to some of the women who are waiting to see someone, we can figure out what's going on."

"It's not worth waiting," said Danny. "The longer we wait, the better the odds someone else will come and get in the way. We can take two men out pretty easily."

The sun had set; Boston turned on the headlights and found that only one worked, and only on high.

"I know we have different approaches to things," Nuri told him after a few minutes of driving in silence. "But I don't think there's any harm in waiting."

"I agree giving medicine to these people is a

good thing," said Danny. "But we can give it to them after the operation. My orders are to recover the UAV as quickly as I can. We're going in tonight."

"The only reason I'm giving it to them is so we can recover the UAV with a minimum of fuss," said Nuri. "I don't really care about helping them."

"That hardly cements your argument."

"Well it's true. Listen, if we can do it with a minimum of fuss—"

"We can," said Danny. "We go tonight."

8

Duka

IN THE END LI HAN SOLVED THE PROBLEM LIKE HE solved many problems: shortly after sunset, he had Amara bring him three teenage boys, gave them each five American dollars, and told them he would give the first to return with the proper cord another twenty dollars.

Amara predicted they would have a cord by morning. Instead, all three of the boys returned within the hour. One had a cord with RCA plugs; the other two, however, had found network cables. Which building in town they'd stolen them from was irrelevant to Li Han; he paid both young men as promised.

"You should give that one something as well," suggested Amara as the other two were paid. "Having an angry thief in the city is not a good thing."

"Yes," said Li Han, nodding. It was a wise suggestion; Amara had more intelligence than he'd thought. He gave the boy three dollars in consolation, then watched as Amara explained.

Amara spoke English as well as Arabic and the local lingo, but there was something else about him. He had a curiosity about him that the others lacked, and he seemed to put it to good use. Perhaps he could be useful.

"Are you good with computers?" Li Han asked him when the boy was gone.

"I use them for e-mail. The Web, that is all," answered Amara.

"You can't program?" Li Han booted his laptop up.

"No, I cannot."

Amara's accent was thick, and at times his vocabulary strained, but his grammar seemed perfect. Li Han suspected that he had been to the States or at least Europe, something rare for a Brother.

He let Amara watch as he hooked up his laptop to the aircraft's brain. There was no response, and he couldn't get his system to recognize it as part of a network. He tried the other plug with similar results.

The problem, he thought, might be that the UAV's brain wasn't powered; he made sure he had voltage flowing from a battery to the motherboard, but had not bothered to examine the network hook-ins.

"Here, watch me," said Li Han, starting to examine the circuitry.

"What are we doing?" asked Amara.

"We are looking for a break. A cut wire, a bad solder connection. It's a guess," Li Han added.

He quickly found a small unattached wire. Unsure where it had been attached, he narrowed down the possibilities until he found what looked like a match to the broken solder on a small post near the transformer section. This was some sort of last minute patch, something added possibly to allow the network connector, though it was impossible to tell without a schematic.

Solving the connection mystery gave him another problem: he had no soldering gun. And he suspected that would be a hell of a lot harder to find than a network cable.

Li Han went upstairs to the common room and looked over their supplies. There was a large medical kit with syringes. Filled with morphine, they had been stolen some weeks before from an aid group.

He squirted the drug out. Amara eyed him curiously.

"Do you have a lighter?" Li Han asked him.

"No."

"Does anyone?"

"Swal smokes, though it is forbidden."

"Get the lighter from him."

Amara went over to one of the youths sleeping on the side. He woke him, then had him walk to the opposite side of the room. They argued a bit—Li Han could tell the boy was lying about not smoking. Amara insisted. Swal, who was bigger, pushed him and started back to the nest of blankets where he'd been sleeping. Amara grabbed him; Swal shoved him violently across the floor.

Li Han put down the needle. With two quick strides he was halfway to Swal. He took his Glock from his belt and raised it just as Swal pulled his arm back to swing at Amara.

Swal froze. He held out his hands. Amara said something to him. Swal reached into his pocket slowly, then took out the lighter.

By now the others were awake, and staring at them.

"Translate, Amara," said Li Han. "When I ask for something, I want it immediately."

"But—" started Amara.

"Translate!"

Amara did so.

Swal nodded that he understood. When his head stopped bobbing, Li Han put a bullet through his temple.

"We will have no traitors in our group," said Li Han. He held out his hand. "Now give me the lighter."

9

SOCCOM Headquarters, Florida

BREANNA THANKED THE MAJOR WHO HAD SHOWN HER to the secure communications area. The sergeant waiting at the console handed her a handset, then walked to the other side of the room to give her a little privacy, pretending to fuss over something there.

"What's the situation, Danny?" she asked, holding the phone to her ear.

"We're going to go in tonight to the building where the UAV is," he told her.

"Good. You spoke to Jonathon?"

"Yes. He made quite a deal about our being discreet. Don't worry," said Danny. "I should mention that Nuri wants to hold off until the morning. He thinks he may be able to make a deal for us to get it back without any bloodshed. But that may take at least another day, probably two or three."

Under other circumstances, Breanna might have been inclined to wait. But given what Reid had told her the night before, the decision was easy.

"Get it back now. Go in ASAP."

"I intend on it."

Breanna hesitated. How much should she tell him?

Her inclination was everything. But if something went wrong—if he was captured and started to talk, that would make things worse.

"Call me as soon as the operation is complete," she said. "Danny—this one's important."

"They always are."

10

Duka

DANNY FREAH CHECKED HIS WEAPON AND HIS WATCH, waiting for the signal from Boston. Boston and Sugar were approaching the front of the target building from opposite directions, aiming to cut off any reinforcements from the nearby warehouse. Both had grenade launchers on their SCAR assault guns; their job was simply to delay any response from that direction until the Osprey could swing overhead and back them up. The aircraft's Hellfire missiles and chain guns would make short work of the building and anyone trying to take them on.

The rest of the Whiplash team, six men, were all with Danny. Once Boston and Sugar were in place, the two teams would move up to the north side of the warehouse. They'd plant charges on the sides, and at a signal, blow themselves a doorway.

Whiplash used a patterned explosive string that was designed to act like a can opener on a metal wall. The explosive in the device was metered and focused in a lenslike pattern that peeled down the top of the panel as it blew in.

The Whiplash team members were armed with SCARs configured either as submachine guns or as submachine guns with grenade launchers. Each wore special lightweight body armor that could resist anything up to a .50 caliber machine gun bullet at fifty yards. Their smart helmets had full face shields whose screens could provide either infrared or optical feeds from the cameras embedded at the top; the circuitry also provided some protection against sudden bright flashes—handy when using flash-bang grenades during an assault. The helmet com systems connected them with the others in the team, MY-PID, and a dedicated Whiplash com channel that connected with Room 4.

There were still only two men inside, both at the south end of the building. If they resisted, they'd be killed. If they surrendered, they'd be bound and then left after the operation—they were of no value once Whiplash had the UAV.

Danny flexed his fingers, waiting for Boston to check in. The air felt cold, even though it was well into the fifties. His stomach started to churn—that always seemed to happen lately, the acid building right before the action.

"I have someone moving inside the building," said Turk, watching from above in the Tiger-shark. "Uh, going to the north, maybe that front door."

"What's up with Building Two?" asked Danny quickly, asking about the nearest building, which was roughly seventy yards away, diagonally across the road.

"No movement. Guy is definitely heading for the door in Target Building."

"Copy," said Danny. "Boston? Sugar?"

"Yeah, I copy," said Sugar. She was huffing, obviously running to get in position. "Hang on."

"Subject at the door," said Turk.

Danny switched his view to an overhead feed from the Tigershark. He could see Sugar moving up to take the man when he came out, Boston covering her nearby.

"Team, get ready," he told the others. "You hear a gunshot, move in. Blow the panels and go."

"Subject is outside," said Turk.

The circuit was silent. Danny waited, acid eating at his stomach. The Tigershark, orbiting to the north, lost sight of the front of the building.

"Down," huffed Sugar finally. "He's down. I bashed him on the back of his head. Went down like a bowling pin."

"Truss him and drag him away from the building," said Danny. "Tell me when you're ready."

More waiting. The acid started creeping up toward his windpipe.

"I'm good," she said finally.

"We're good, boss," added Boston. "Go for it. We got your back."

"Teams up," said Danny. "MY-PID—what's the other tango inside the target building doing?"

"Subject is immobile. Appears to be sleeping."

The explosives were set. The team backed away, just far enough to stay clear of the blast.

"On three," said Danny, reflux biting at the back of his mouth. "One, two . . ."

11

Room 4, CIA Campus

JONATHON REID PUSHED THE SHEAF OF PAPERS ACROSS the conference table toward Ray Rubeo.

"This is the white paper," Reid said. "Is the program discussed here feasible?"

Rubeo frowned.

Perhaps it was because of the hour, Reid thought. It was not yet 5:00 A.M. But Rubeo himself had suggested the time.

The scientist always frowned. In fact, he seemed to be in a perpetual bad mood. He was a genius—his track record at Dreamland alone was proof—but he was a sourpuss even so. He gave the impression that he walked around in a different universe than mortal men. When he spoke to someone, it was as if he was coming down from Mount Olympus. How he had ever managed to get along with the Air Force command, let alone the bureaucracy of the Defense Department, was unfathomable.

Rubeo's company was one of the Office of Special Technology's main contractors, and among other things was responsible for building the highly secure facility they were sitting in. Rubeo had enormous influence at the Pentagon, but how he managed to deal with the generals there without being knifed—literally—Reid would never know.

The scientist turned the paper around and looked at the title. He frowned again. He turned over a page, looking at the names of the authors.

The frown deepened.

He turned over another page, reading a sentence or two of the executive summary, then flipped into the body of the paper, seemingly at random.

The frown seemed to reach to his chin.

Rubeo turned to the references at the back.

"It would have been nice if they had at least got the citations right." He pushed the paper back toward Reid.

"So your opinion?" asked Reid.

"About the paper? Or the possibility of the program you're referring to?"

"The latter, Doctor."

"Of course it's feasible," said Rubeo. "The individual elements are trivial. The main difficulty is designing a tool that can interface with unknown control systems."

"Layman's terms?"

"*Hmmmph.*" Rubeo took hold of his earlobe, as if pulling it might turn a lever inside his brain that allowed him to speak in plain English. "The difficulty is re-creating in software the flexibility of the human mind, and at the same time enabling that software to use the benefits of its computing power."

Rubeo paused. Translating his thoughts seemed several times more difficult than working out a complex mathematic problem for him.

"A man can drive a car," he continued. "He can fly an aircraft. He can shoot a gun. He can fire a missile. The same man can do all this. If you have the right man. If he has the proper training. His software, if you will, is designed precisely for this function. To duplicate that is not a trivial matter."

"Can we duplicate it?"

"Of course. The question is whether it's worth the effort. And, as these authors point out—somewhat sloppily, I might say—whether it's worth the risk."

"Is it?"

Rubeo reached for his coffee cup. It was filled with hot water—probably some sort of health fad, though Reid didn't ask.

"Why is this important?" Rubeo asked after a small, birdlike sip.

"I'm not sure I can tell you. I don't know all the facts yet either."

The frown became a smirk.

"Doctor, have you worked on a program similar to this?" Reid asked.

"I'm not sure you understand, Mr. Reid. The ultimate goal of any advanced artificial intelligence regime implies this ability. Creating an autonomous intelligence in and of itself implies that you have mastered the prerequisites for this. A program that can learn to fly an airplane can learn to do other things."

"So the program used to guide the Flighthawks could do this?"

Rubeo raised his right hand to his face, running his index finger along his eyebrows. It almost seemed to Reid that he was underlining some thought behind his cranium.

"Of course not," said Rubeo finally. "Those codes are strictly limited. There are difficulties with propagating the intelligence in an autonomous manner such as what's laid out here. I don't want to get too technical for you, and you'll excuse me, as I don't intend to insult you, but there has to be a certain amount of space for the program to function. Constraining it—well, it might work, but not as intended."

"Have you worked with something like this?"

"Mr. Reid, you will recall that my curriculum vitae includes heading the scientific team at Dreamland. We had many, many projects under development there. More specific, I cannot be. Even with you," added Rubeo. He took another sip of his water.

"Can I speak to you in confidence?" Reid asked.

"You have my confidence."

"What I mean, Doctor, is can I ask you some questions without them leaving the room?"

"It would depend on the questions."

That wasn't good enough, Reid thought. Yet he needed a candid opinion. And he wanted to discuss the issue with someone like Rubeo—with anyone, really.

But what if Rubeo felt obliged to talk to someone at the Pentagon or in the administration about it? What if he saw it as a moral issue that had to be aired?

Reid wanted to be the one to make that decision. Assuming it had to be made.

But he needed to know. Perhaps he could back into the answer without arousing Rubeo's suspicion.

"If another government had this weapon—" Reid started.

"I doubt anyone has this ability," said Rubeo flatly. "We would see it in other weapons."

"So no one is this advanced?"

"The Israeli drones can't do a third of what the early versions of the Flighthawk could handle," said Rubeo. "And I would use that as a measuring stick."

"What about us?" said Reid. "Could we do it?"

Rubeo took another sip of his water, then set it down and leaned forward on the table.

"Have we done it?" asked the scientist.

"I don't know," admitted Reid. "That's why I wanted to talk to you."

"I see."

"I'm concerned about the implications," explained Reid.

"As well you should be."

"Can safety precautions be built into it? The paper says that they would be ineffectual."

"*Potentially* ineffectual," said Rubeo. "I can't make a judgment without knowing much more about the specifics of what we're talking about."

Fair enough, thought Reid.

"There would be physical limitations, depending on the hardware. And different contingencies.

I'm sorry to be vague—the portability issue is not trivial, but it can be overcome. Conceivably."

"If it were up to you, would you allow such a weapon to be used?" asked Reid.

Now Rubeo's lips curled up in the faintest suggestion of a smile—a rare occurrence.

"I don't make those sorts of decisions," he answered. "In my experience, it is a very rare weapon that, once created, is *not* used."

12

Duka

DANNY JUMPED UP AN INSTANT AFTER THE EXPLOSIVES blew out the panel. It was a neat penetration, a literal door for the Whiplash team to run through. The first trooper inside tossed a flash-bang grenade in the direction of the lone occupant. The man fell from the chair where he'd been sleeping; two Whiplashers reached him before the room stopped reverberating. One put his boot against the man's back and his gun against his head, just in case he had any notion of moving. The other trussed his arms and legs with thick zip ties.

"Where the hell is the plane?" yelled Thomas "Red" Roberts, who'd been tasked to secure the UAV. "All I see is the pickup truck."

Danny nudged Red out of the way. He was right. The only thing inside the building was the truck.

Danny flipped the shield on his helmet up. A single lightbulb near the front threw dim rays around the large room. As his eyes adjusted to the light, he pulled the signal receiving unit from his pocket and turned it on. The device was relatively simple—it beeped as it tracked the transmitter, the signals getting closer and closer together.

It was a solid tone.

He went over and peered over the back of the truck. There was a small jumble of what looked like debris near the cab. He picked it up—it was a hunk of plastic with some circuitry attached. Undoubtedly the tracking transmitter.

Damn.

"Movement in Building Two," said MY-PID.

"Two, three people moving to the front," added Turk, who was watching the feed.

"Osprey up," said Danny. "Red, Marcus— search this damn place."

"Already on it, Cap," said Marcus. He was another of the new recruits, a former Ranger, also trained as a helicopter pilot. Danny hoped to use that specialty in the future.

There was a burst of gunfire from the front of the building.

"Boston?"

"They ducked back inside," said Boston. "Didn't look like they had weapons."

The Osprey's heavy rotors pounded the ground

as it approached. Red went to the passenger side door of the pickup truck.

"Wait!" yelled Danny. "Check—"

His warning was too late—the truck exploded as Red pulled open the door.

13

Walter Reed Army Hospital
Washington, D.C.

THE PAST WAS GONE, ERASED AND BURIED FROM HIS memory, shocked out of him, drugged away. The past was gone and the future was blank; only the present remained, only the present was real.

Mark Stoner shifted in his bed, staring at the ceiling.

What was the present, though? Working out? Getting better?

Better from what?

It was all a jumble, a knot of torn thoughts.

Zen. Who was Zen?

A friend. Someone he knew.

But why was he in a wheelchair? And what was a friend, exactly?

Someone he saw a lot.

What was he supposed to say to him? What was he supposed to do?

Stoner leaned to the side. Dr. Esrang had given him a radio. He turned it on and began flipping through the stations.

". . . Two out, and here comes Granderson. He flied out his last at bat. The former Yankee is batting just .230 this year . . ."

The words were strangely familiar. Stoner tried to puzzle out what they meant.

Baseball.

He knew that. The game.

He knew everything about it, didn't he? He could picture what was happening in his head. He saw the batter swing and miss.

A memory floated up from deep within his consciousness. He was at a game with his grandfather.

His grandfather!

There was a past.

Baseball.

Stoner folded his arms across his chest and listened as the game progressed.

14

Duka

THE EXPLOSION BLEW RED BACK INTO DANNY. BOTH men fell against the floor. The explosive charge was relatively small, and their body armor absorbed most of the blow. Still, there was enough of a shock to knock both of them out for a second. Danny came to with Flash leaning over him.

"Cap, you OK?"

"Yeah," managed Danny. He got to his feet with Flash's help. Red was shaken, but uninjured except for some cuts and bruises—the biggest one to his pride.

"Nothing in here," said Flash. "You want to evac?"

"Right. Let's get out of here. Take the prisoner with us. Both of them—get the guy Sugar knocked out."

"On it."

They left through the hole at the side. Boston and Sugar joined them as they crossed over the railroad tracks, running into a small clearing where the Osprey could land and pick them up. Danny could smell the exhaust in the wash from the Osprey's rotors as the aircraft swooped toward them, its engine nacelles angled upward in helicopter mode.

His head was pounding. He paused as the aircraft settled down, counting his men to make sure they were all there. Flash had cut their prisoner's leg restraints away, but he held his man by the arms as they moved double-time toward the rear of the Osprey. The prisoner was small and skinny, a young teenager.

Sugar had the other POW on her back. This one was tall—close to six feet—but just as skinny as the other.

Both were probably useless, Danny realized.

Whoever had booby-trapped the truck probably figured they were disposable.

"We're all here, Cap," said Boston, taking up the rear.

"All right, let's get the hell out of here."

"What happened?" asked Boston as they ran up the MV-22's ramp.

"They booby-trapped the door of the truck and we missed it," said Danny. "We were lucky. And sloppy."

15

Duka

LI HAN CROUCHED AT THE EDGE OF THE CULVERT, watching as the Osprey rose. Its wings began to tip forward; it seemed to stutter to the right, and for a moment he thought it would crash. But the stutter was an optical illusion—the aircraft pivoted, turning away smoothly as it accelerated into the distance.

He had a clear shot for a Stinger missile.

But even if he'd had an antiaircraft weapon ready, it would have been foolish to attack. The aircraft was undoubtedly equipped with a detector and countermeasures, and even if he did succeed in taking it down, he'd be telling them he was still nearby. Better to remain a mystery.

Afraid he might be given away by the locals, Li Han had slipped out of the warehouse with Amara and most of the others, taking over a house about a quarter of a mile away and working on the UAV there. But even that had seemed too close, too small a precaution—as soon as he'd heard the explosion, Li Han had taken Amara with him and run from the building, using a door in the basement.

Now he felt just a bit like a coward.

But caution was always in order, especially when dealing with the Americans.

"What now?" asked Amara behind him.

"We'll go back inside the house," said Li Han, thinking. "They won't attack again tonight."

They would be watching. He'd have to lay low for a while.

What if he sold the UAV back to the Americans? They'd certainly be motivated buyers.

Amara might be able to broker the deal. He was a little puny physically, but he was smart. And the sight of Swal being shot hadn't unnerved him; he'd disposed of the body quietly. He seemed to realize that Li Han had done it for him, to reinforce his authority with the others.

"Are we going?" asked Amara. "How long can we stay in this city?"

"Your English is getting better all the time," said Li Han.

"You didn't answer the question."

Li Han smiled to him, then turned and led the way back to the house.

16

Room 4, CIA Campus

REID FLICKED OFF THE VIEWER AS THE OSPREY TOOK off. He didn't like monitoring the missions; there was too much temptation to micromanage. When he was in the field, he would never have allowed it.

But times were different now. The best he could do was not interfere.

He was about to call Breanna when the computer announced that she was holding on the line.

"You're psychic," he told her, picking up the phone. "I was just about to contact you."

"Do we have it?"

"Regrettably, no. The tracking transmitter was removed from the body of the UAV. It was booby-trapped, but we had no injuries."

"Well that's something, at least."

"We're reasonably sure that the UAV itself remains in Duka. But at the moment I think even that's a guess. Nuri is planning to go in tomorrow and check around. I don't know that there's much alternative."

"The replacement satellite should be on station in a few hours," said Breanna. "In the meantime, I've found a Global Hawk to augment the Tigershark so Turk can get some rest. We'll have surveillance, but no connection to MY-PID."

"That shouldn't be an immediate problem."

"We may need more force there," added Breanna. "And I'm going to get more of their equipment over there. This is more serious than we thought at first."

"The military side is your prerogative," said Reid. "But I can't emphasize enough that we have to be very quiet about it. If the Iranians or the Chinese or anyone else sees we're making a big fuss, they may get nosy. Even if we recover Raven at that point, we may have jeopardized the weapon."

"I understand, and Danny does, too. Did you talk to Ray Rubeo?"

"I did." Reid stopped pacing. "I'm going to talk to Edmund again. Based on that conversation . . . Based on that conversation, I may have to talk to the President. A number of things trouble me."

"Do you want me to come?"

"I think under the circumstances it would be best if I handled that myself," said Reid. "I still don't have the whole picture. Whether Edmund will give it to me or not remains to be seen."

17

Duka

MILOS KIMKO STOOD IN THE SHADOW OF THE SMALL hut, watching the aircraft fade into the distance. He was nearly three miles from where it had landed, but even without his binoculars he could tell it was an Osprey: only the American aircraft could move so quickly from a hover.

And what were the Americans doing in this forsaken corner of Africa? Taking sides with one of the two rebel groups who shared control of the town? Simply meeting with them?

Possibly. But what to make, then, of the explosion that had woken him?

The Russian rubbed his eyes. He was tired, physically worn by his job to assess the rebel movements in eastern Sudan. The SVR— Sluzhba Vneshney Razvedki, or Foreign Intelligence Service—had sent him to Khartoum a few weeks before, and he'd been traveling in the brush ever since.

He had a cover, and a side job, as an arms dealer. It was an excellent entrée to the locals, given the prices he was able to offer. The SVR subsidized the price; in fact, Kimko suspected his supervisors were keeping a portion of the money he sent back for themselves.

The sound of the Osprey's engines faded. Kimko debated with himself. Should he go and see what they'd been up to now, or should he wait for the morning?

He'd been planning on continuing north at dawn, but that could be changed; it wasn't like anyone there was setting their watches by him.

But why not take a look around now? He had nothing better to do, truly. The fresh air felt good.

It would also take his mind off the fact that he desperately wanted a drink.

Kimko went back inside. The round hut was tiny, a one room refuge that combined a bedroom, sitting area, and primitive kitchen in the space of four or five square meters. He went to his knapsack on the far side of the bed and took out his gun and holster; he picked up his thick sweater from the floor where it had fallen. He was still losing weight—even with the sweater and the shoulder holster, the jacket hung from his shoulders like an oversized bathrobe, two or three sizes too large. Not long ago it had been tight.

But that's what Africa did to you. It shriveled you to nothing. It was terrible to foreigners, but just as hard on the natives; everyone he met had an empty look in their eyes, as if their souls had drilled through their skulls and fled.

A pile of clothes lay at the foot of the bed. Kimko took a five euro bill from his wallet and dropped it on the clothes. Hopefully, the woman who owned the clothes would be gone before he returned.

18

Western Ethiopia

THE WHIPLASH TEAM WAS QUIET THE ENTIRE WAY BACK to Ethiopia. Even Sugar, who normally could have been counted on for a dozen wise cracks and half as many put-downs, said nothing.

Red, who'd been closest to the IED when it went off, had been cut in several places and badly bruised, but was spared more serious injury by his helmet and armored vest. A large piece of shrapnel had sliced past the outer fabric into the carbon-boron layer, exposing the intricate web of the protective material. He stared at the slice the whole trip back.

"I'm sorry, Cap—I checked for wires and didn't see anything," he told Danny after they hopped out of the Osprey. "I looked underneath, in the back—I didn't see explosives in the seat or anything—I just—I don't know."

"Forget it," Danny told him. "Focus on the mission."

"Lettin' him off easy," said Boston, watching Red head toward the hut the team had taken over for quarters.

"The bomb kicked him harder in the butt than I could," answered Danny.

"I doubt he checked it right," said Boston. "His helmet should've picked something up, even if it was a grenade."

"I'm sure he forgot to reset it inside," said Danny. "He won't forget next time. That's what counts."

The Whiplash helmets had embedded chemical sniffers designed to warn of IEDs, or improvised explosive devices. But these could easily be confused in a combat situation, where the detection threshold was fairly high—you didn't want your own grenade or explosive pack setting off the alarm. So the settings could be dialed back, or what the designers called "normalized," with a reading taken before the actual operation. That reading was supposed to pick up the presence of the chemicals already in the group making the assault. That reading set the threshold for subsequent readings. Roughly speaking, the gear would see that the team had twelve ounces of PETN before the action, and the chemical sniffers would sound the alert only when a thirteenth was detected.

In the situation inside the warehouse, the helmet should have been reset before the truck was examined. This took up to ninety seconds, and in the heat of battle was often forgotten. But there were other reasons the explosive could have missed, and Danny saw no point in calling one of his team members a liar.

"Whoever set the bomb was pretty smart," he told Boston. "He's a couple of steps ahead of us."

"I guess."

"Has to be their Mao Man, Li Han."

"I agree."

"Put the prisoners in separate tents," Danny told him. "I'll get Nuri and we'll talk to them."

"You got it, Cap. Hey, heads up—storm headed our way."

Boston pointed toward the small huts. Melissa Ilse, right arm in a sling, was striding in their direction, moving at a speed that clearly indicated she wasn't pleased.

Danny kept up his own deliberate pace toward the main building. "Ms. Ilse, what can I do for you?"

"Why didn't you wake me up?"

"I didn't know I was your alarm clock."

"Listen, Colonel . . ."

She took hold of his right arm. As Danny turned toward her, Melissa's glare reminded him of a look his wife had given him when he told her he wasn't running for Congress. Ever.

Not a good memory, that.

"I'm in charge of this operation here, Colonel," said Melissa. "This is my op."

"No, Ms. Ilse, I'm afraid—"

"Melissa."

"Right. This is a Whiplash operation. I'm in charge."

"You're supposed to help me. *Help.*"

"I really don't care to argue."

Danny started walking again. She fell in next to him.

"Obviously, you didn't recover the UAV."

"That's right," he said.

"I insist that you involve me in any other operation. Do you understand?"

"Your arm better?" asked Danny.

"Colonel, I insist."

She followed in a huff as Danny entered the main building. Nuri was inside, talking with someone on a satellite phone. Jordan was fussing with the coffeepot.

"Your guys are all right?" asked Jordan, glancing over as he came in.

"Yeah. Just barely," said Danny.

"Coffee?"

"Sure."

"Melissa?"

"No thank you," she said frostily.

"A little strong," said Jordan, handing the coffee over.

"I'll say," said Danny.

"Keeps me awake."

Nuri finished his call and came over.

"I'm sorry," he told Danny.

Danny nodded. Nuri was sincere; he wasn't an *I told you so* kind of guy.

"My drugs are on the way," said Nuri. "They should be here by first light. I'll go back and nose around."

"They're not going to connect you with to-night?"

"Nah. They may think you were coming to get me. I'm a criminal, remember? That'll only help my reputation."

"I think Li Han was behind this," said Danny.

"Could be."

"I think that's a very good guess," said Melissa. "I'm sure he's still in Duka."

"I think it's kind of hard to be that definite," said Nuri. "We thought he was in the warehouse."

"He's still in Duka."

"What do you think?" Danny asked Jordan.

"I don't know. Booby-trapping the truck would be very much like him. Finding the transponder? Definitely. But anything's possible. These people aren't stupid; they've lived by their wits out here for a long time."

"We brought two guys back," Danny told Nuri. "Maybe you can get something out of them."

"Sure," said Nuri.

Melissa followed them out of the building.

"Unless your Arabic's a lot better than mine," Nuri told her as they neared the tent, "I think you ought to stay outside. The less people who see you, the better."

She gave him a scowl but didn't argue.

NURI ADJUSTED THE MY-PID EAR SET AND FOLLOWED Danny inside the tent. A teenager lay on the floor, arms and legs bound by zip ties. The tent was illuminated by a 150-watt bulb in a work lamp hanging from the peak.

Nuri knelt next to the prisoner. The kid was so still that even though his eyes were open, Nuri thought he was sleeping.

"*As-Salamu Alaikum wa Rahmatullahi wa Barakatuhu*," Nuri said in Arabic. May the One True God's Peace and Blessing Be Upon You.

The young man's eyes opened a little wider, but he said nothing.

"Why did you try to kill my friends?" asked Nuri. When he didn't get a response, he switched to Nubian, the dominant tribal language of the North, and repeated the question.

Nuri's Nubian wasn't nearly as fluent as his Arabic, and the differences in the dialects added considerable difficulty. He would at least have no trouble translating: MY-PID could handle it instantaneously. Indeed, as soon as the Voice heard him use the language, it would make suggestions, allowing him to refine his speech as he went along.

The computer's help proved unnecessary.

"You think I don't know English?" said the prisoner.

"I didn't want to insult you by using it," said Nuri.

The kid made a face.

"How old are you?" asked Danny.

"What kind of question is that for a warrior of God?" snapped the boy.

"You're not fighting for God. You're trying to get Dr. Thorika into power," answered Nuri, referring to the opposition figure supported by the Brotherhood.

"*Phhhh*, Thorika." The prisoner tried to spit, but his mouth was so dry he couldn't even force spittle to his lips. "We fight for the rule of Islam."

"You're with the Brothers?" said Nuri, who of course had suspected as much, based on what he knew of Li Han. "Have they stopped backing Thorika?"

The prisoner frowned again, perhaps realizing he had given Nuri more information than he should have.

"I didn't know the Brotherhood had people this far north," said Nuri in a reasonable tone. "Why have you come into the territory of your enemies?"

"All Sudan is our territory. We have friends everywhere."

The kid switched to Arabic as he repeated several slogans popular with the Brothers. Nuri let him talk for a while before finally cutting him off.

"What about the Chinese scientist? Why is he in charge of you?"

"He is not in charge of us."

The interview continued in that vein for several more minutes. Nuri concluded that the prisoner was older than he looked, but even so probably didn't have much information that would be immediately useful.

The second prisoner stuck to Arabic, but was more talkative, volunteering that "the Asian" was in the city, though he didn't know where. He said he was fifteen, and Nuri believed it; he had clearly not been trusted with much information, and didn't seem to know that much about the UAV.

"They're the usual teenage riffraff the Brotherhood recruits," said Melissa derisively outside the tent. "They're ignorant. They don't know anything."

"The first one spoke English pretty well," said Nuri.

"So? It's the official language. One of them."

"The usual slugs don't speak it as well as he does," said Nuri.

"Li Han doesn't speak Arabic, or any of the local languages," said Melissa. "They needed someone who could communicate with him."

"If Li Han is so good, why is he working for them?" asked Danny. "Why isn't he working for Iran or Syria?"

"He *has* worked for them," said Melissa. "He's here because al Qaeda gave the Brotherhood money to hire him. He's being paid ridiculously well to help them set up communications networks, arrange their computers. Forge networks."

"Does he work for them, or the Brotherhood?"

"What difference does it make?"

"It makes a difference," said Nuri.

"The Brotherhood. They contacted him through an intermediary. I'd guess he knows where the money comes from."

"And where do they get it?" said Nuri. His tone made it clear he was speaking rhetorically. "The big oil states, Saudi Arabia, Bahrain, the rest. It's blood money—we'll pay you off if you don't try and overthrow us, or preach too hard in our mosques, or do something else that will upset our business arrangements. Whatever it is Li Han is doing out here, he's getting a ton of money for it. More than you and I will ever make in a hundred lifetimes."

"That's true," said Melissa. "He's helping them organize. That's why it's important to take him out now."

"Getting the UAV back is our priority," said Danny.

"Absolutely," she said.

"I want access to the file," said Nuri.

"What's our next move?" Melissa asked Danny.

"It's not 'our' next move," said Nuri. "I'm going back to see what's going on. We'll take it from there."

"I'm going in with you."

"No again," said Nuri.

"Colonel, this is my mission," said Melissa. "Raven is in Duka somewhere. I have to find it."

"This is *our* mission," said Danny. "All of ours."

Nuri tried to suppress his anger. He could tell what Danny was thinking: he saw this as a squabble between two Agency officers, a turf battle. But Nuri knew there was a lot more going on here than they'd been told—he doubted the assassination operation had been authorized, and there was no telling what else was up. Melissa was exactly the sort of gung-ho idiot higher-ups threw into a situation where the Agency didn't belong.

"I'm going to the clinic with the drugs," he said. "After that I'll check with the other group. I'm not convinced that Li Han is still in town, but if he is, I'll hear about it."

"I could go to the clinic," said Melissa. "I'm trained as a nurse. I'll gather information in the city."

"I don't think that's necessary," said Danny. "Your arm's in a sling."

"I don't need it." She pulled it out. Pain showed on her face, but she let it dangle. "Raven is mine. It's my job to find it."

"We can get the information ourselves."

"You haven't done very well at it to this point."

Danny scowled.

"I'm going," said Melissa. "I'd be there now if I hadn't taken a spill."

Why not let her? thought Nuri. If she was going to be a jackass, why not let her park herself inside the clinic? She'd be out of the way there.

Sure. And then they'd capture her, torture her, and she'd tell them everything she knew about Raven and whatever else she was involved in.

But on the bright side, maybe they'd kill her.

"You can't stop me," Melissa insisted to Danny. "This is *my* mission. My job."

That was another thing that bothered Nuri—she kept addressing Danny, not him, or at worst both of them.

"They'll think you're a spy in the clinic," said Nuri. "They'll know you're American."

"Of course they'll know I'm an American. I don't lie about that. There are a lot of Americans in Sudan."

"Not a lot," said Nuri. "And they're all aid workers."

"So?" She kept staring at Danny.

"Fine," said Nuri. "It's your funeral."

19

CIA Headquarters

HERMAN EDMUND'S SCHEDULE WAS ORDINARILY TOO tight for Jonathon Reid to expect an immediate meeting, even on an important matter, and given their conversation the other day, Reid doubted that Edmund would be motivated to make time. So he was surprised when Edmund's secretary kept him on the telephone when he made the request, and even more surprised to hear the CIA director's voice rather than hers a few seconds later.

"I was going to call you myself," Edmund said. "We need to talk."

"Have you had breakfast?"

"Much earlier."

"We'll call it an early lunch, then."

"We should talk in a very secure place," said Reid.

Edmund hesitated for the slightest of moments before telling Reid that he had exactly the same idea.

They ate in the director's dining room, only the two of them.

Reid ordered a cup of yogurt.

"You want to talk about Raven," said Edmund as soon as the attendant left.

"I do."

"Jon, it's an unfortunate situation."

"I think we both know it's more than that," said Reid.

Edmund raised an eyebrow. He pushed back in his chair, nearly reaching the wall. Photographs of all the Agency's past directors hung in a line above their heads; William Casey glared down above Edmund's.

"I understand that you've been making inquiries," he said.

"I've been discreet."

"As always," said Edmund.

"You can't expect me to put the lives of my people on the line without knowing what they're being risked for."

"Come on, Jonathon. That's bullshit and you know it. People do that every day here. You do it, I do it—it's the nature of the business."

"The program is illegal, isn't it?" said Reid.

"There's no executive order authorizing that Li Han be killed. And that's the mandated procedure."

"I never discuss specific orders like that."

Reid was tempted to repeat Edmund's line about bullshit back at him, but he didn't.

"The UAV project is probably borderline as well," Reid said. "But what I'm truly concerned about is Raven itself."

"You told me you had located the UAV."

"Raven is not the aircraft," said Reid. "I need to know about the software, Herman. I need to know how much of a danger it is."

"Software is software. It flies the plane."

"That's not all it does."

"In this case, it is."

"What are the safeguards?"

"I don't know the technical data. Obviously, I'd be out of my element discussing them. As would you."

"I want to speak to the people who developed the software and the computer that it runs in," insisted Reid. "I want them to talk to my experts."

"Can't happen."

"Why not?"

Edmund shook his head. "Can't."

A buzzer sounded.

"Come," said Edmund loudly.

In response, the attendant opened the door and wheeled in a tray with their food. The director had ordered a cheese omelet with home fries.

"I had the chef hold the onions," said Edmund. "I have meeting with the Secretary of State later.

Though on second thought, maybe that would have been a good idea."

He laughed at his own joke. Reid said nothing until the attendant left. "My fear," he said then, "is that the program, if it were to get into the wild, would be unstoppable."

"What do you mean, in the wild?"

"Like a virus. It has that sort of capability."

"It doesn't work that way, Jonathon. Your tech people should be able to tell you that."

Reid rose as Edmund took a bite from his omelet.

"Where are you going?" asked the director.

"I've lost my appetite."

"Sit down, Jonathon."

This was exactly the sort of situation Reid had dreaded when he decided to return to the Agency after his retirement. But it was also exactly the reason he had not taken the post of DDO.

"I don't think we have anything else to talk about," he said coldly. "If you're not going to give me full access to the Raven program, anything else either one of us says would be pointless."

"Jonathon—"

Reid hesitated, half expecting Edmund to change his mind, or perhaps appeal to their long friendship. But the director said nothing else.

"Maybe I'll be hungry later," said Reid, pocketing the yogurt before leaving.

20

Western Ethiopia

TURK HAD NOW BEEN UP FOR AN UNGODLY NUMBER OF hours, and while his own personal record was in no danger of falling, he was nonetheless feeling the strains of fatigue. With the Whiplash team back in Ethiopia and a Global Hawk now overhead for surveillance, he was no longer needed. Assuming the satellite arrived in a few hours, he could even go home.

Until then he had to stay nearby. So he called Danny and cleared himself to land at the Ethiopian base.

The runway was a long hash mark just off the peak of a ridge in the mountains, a little on the short side, though not a problem for the diminutive Tigershark. But the field wasn't exactly the smoothest, with an almost wavy pattern running across the tarmac about halfway down, and several dozen poorly patched craters scattered over its length. The Tigershark took a couple of hard bumps as she landed, knocking Turk against his restraints. A funnel of dust followed him down the runway.

One of the Whiplash team members took a truck out to meet him, and guided him to the maintenance area—a lone fuel truck standing in the middle of an open space.

The Tigershark had been designed to operate from forward bases, and the aircraft's engine intakes had special screens designed to lessen the possibility that they would ingest engine debris. This base was rough even by Whiplash standards, however; he'd need some help checking the runway before takeoff.

Turk popped the canopy, secured the aircraft, then clambered down to the ground. His muscles felt as if they'd atrophied after his long stint in the air.

"Captain Mako, welcome to Shangri-La," said Boston, hopping from the truck that had escorted him in.

"Hey, Boston." Turk stuck out his hand. "Long time no see. Call me Turk."

"Yes, sir, Turk."

"Where can I get some food and a bunk?" he asked.

"Empty beds in either that little building over there, next to the two big ones," said Boston, pointing. "Or else one of the tents. We have prisoners in the ones with guards outside them."

"I'll stay out of those."

"Not a bad idea."

"Where's Colonel Freah?"

"That would be the big building on the left."

"Wash the windows and check the oil," said Turk as he started for the building.

"Jeez, very funny, sir. I never heard that one. Har-har."

Turk cracked up. Corny jokes always put him into a good mood.

He walked up the slight rise toward the buildings, warmed by the sun as it poked between the nearby peaks. He was just pulling open the door to the large building when someone on the other side yanked it from his hand. A furious cloud flew out of the door, knocking him back.

It was the most beautiful cloud he'd ever seen.

"Wow, aren't you pretty," said Turk.

"And aren't you an asshole," said Melissa, practically spitting at him.

"Come on," laughed Turk. "You must have seen bigger ones."

"Asshole."

Turk watched her walk away. He had never seen a pair of fatigues move with such sexual energy before.

"Enjoy the show?" asked Danny Freah when he turned back around.

"I would have landed hours ago if I knew the sights were so pretty," said Turk.

"Watch yourself, Captain."

"I will, Colonel. Definitely. Say, you got a minute? I may need a little help inspecting the runway to make sure we don't have debris before takeoff. Plus, I have a couple of ideas about where the bad guys may be."

Danny frowned at him. "I have to go into town. Talk to me while I walk."

Nuri waited impatiently by the Mercedes for Danny to finish talking to the pilot. They should have been in Duka already. It was important to show that he had no connection with the raid; so important that he was willing to go in even without a connection to MY-PID.

Of course, this might be a wild-goose chase.

The rest of the aircraft could be hundreds of miles away by now.

"Sorry that took so long," said Danny, finally coming over. "I wanted to make sure we have some more people and gear in case you can't work out a deal."

"How long before it gets here?" asked Nuri.

"It's en route. It may be a while."

Nuri walked to the driver's side door. "I'll drive."

"Hold up," said Danny.

"What?"

"I thought we were taking Melissa."

"She's not here, that's her problem."

"What is it with you and her, Nuri?" said Danny. "What do you have against her?"

"She's not telling us the whole story," said Nuri. "And I don't trust her."

"You have to keep the Whiplash people cut out of the picture."

Harker was practically shouting. Melissa started to raise her right arm to rub her forehead, but a shock of pain stopped her. Sugar probably had been right—she almost certainly had torn a ligament.

"Look, the only way to get the UAV back is with their help," Melissa told her boss.

"That's not a question—get it back."

"Then I have to work with them. You sent them."

"I didn't send them. The director sent them. Not the same thing."

She glanced at her watch. She was ten minutes late. Nuri would have a fit.

Hell, he'd probably left without her. It would be just like him.

"I have to go," she told Harker.

"Melissa. Get this done. Take out Mao Man. If you—"

She killed the line, turned off the phone, and shoved the sat phone back into the safe box in her footlocker. Her other phone was already in her pocket.

Melissa locked up everything, then paused at the door. She didn't have a mirror; all she could do was glance down at her clothes.

Frumpy. But that was the best she was going to manage. She pulled open the door, locked it behind her, and started down toward the Mercedes. No one was standing near it, and her first thought was that she wasn't late at all. Then she realized that both Danny and Nuri were inside.

She started to run.

"ABOUT TIME YOU GOT HERE," SAID NURI AS SHE PULLED open the door. He started the car and put it in gear, not waiting for her to buckle her seat belt.

"Gonna be a long drive folks," said Danny. "Let's all relax. Where you from?"

"San Francisco," Melissa said.

Nuri felt his cheeks burning as the two began a trivial conversation about their backgrounds.

The problem was that she was good-looking. If she'd been ugly—or better, if she'd been a guy—Danny would have played it entirely straight.

He'd have kept her at arm's length, trusted everything Nuri said. She'd be back at the base, or even in Alexandria, where she couldn't screw anything up.

Granted, she might be useful at the clinic. Maybe.

Nuri's foul mood settled over him as he drove. About two miles from the border, he went off the main road to bypass the guards at the main crossing, using a trail he'd spotted from the satellite photos. It was clearly well traveled—though dirt, it was hard packed, and even doing fifty, the Mercedes raised little dust. Within an hour, they were approaching Duka.

"We're going to switch, right?" asked Danny. "I'm your driver."

"Right," said Nuri, feeling a little foolish. He took his foot off the gas and coasted to a stop. "Thanks. I forgot."

21

Washington, D.C.

IF THE AGENCY WAS RUNNING A DEEPLY DANGEROUS and illegal operation, how far would it go to keep the secret to itself?

The ends of the earth, and beyond.

The first step from the director's dining room

felt like liberation to Reid; he knew what he had to do, and there was power in that certainty.

But with every step that followed, doubt crept in, then paranoia.

Would Edmund order he be detained? Or even killed?

It was a ridiculous idea, Reid told himself. Even if they hadn't been friends, Edmund would never do such a thing. Nor would any director. He was sure of it.

And yet, he couldn't seem to shake the paranoia. It intensified as the day went on, until it began to feel like a hood over his head, furrowing his vision and pushing him physically closer to the ground. Reid spent the afternoon in Room 4, studying more of the data, reviewing everything that might be even tangentially related to Raven.

That alone would have stoked his fears—the more he learned about the class of programs, the more he realized Raven was potentially unstoppable. "Killer viruses," declared a paper written by an Australian researcher. The man foresaw a cyber war that would paralyze the world inside of five minutes.

A little past 4:00 P.M. the phone system alerted Reid to a call from the Senate Office Building. Thinking it was Breanna's husband or his staff looking for her, he took the call, and found himself talking to a member of Senator Claus Gunter's staff.

"Mr. Reid, can you hold for the senator?" asked the secretary.

Reid hesitated for a moment. Gunter was a member of the Senate Defense Appropriations Committee, but Reid barely knew him.

But of course he had to be polite. "Surely."

"Jonathon, how are you?" said Gunter, coming on the line.

"I'm fine, Senator. Yourself?"

"Very good, very good. I wanted to speak to you in confidence. Is that possible?"

"I'm at your disposal, Senator," said Reid.

"You know, between you and I, George Napoli is retiring from the DIA in a few months," said Gunter.

"I hadn't heard that." Napoli was the head of the Defense Intelligence Agency.

"In some quarters, your name has been raised," said Gunter.

Reid realized immediately what was going on—he was being bought off. He wondered—did Gunter know about the operation, or was Edmund using him?

Surely the latter.

"Interesting," said Reid.

"Is that the sort of post . . . you'd be interested in?"

"I hadn't really given the matter any thought," said Reid. It was best to be noncommittal—it might draw more information from Gunter. "I hadn't known it was even coming open."

"Well it is. And a lot of people think highly of you. On both sides of the aisle. I believe the President could be persuaded," said Gunter.

"It is an interesting opportunity," said Reid. "Who— Are there people putting my name forward?"

"I've heard in several places," said Gunter, so breezily it was clearly a lie.

"I don't know if I would have support," said Reid. "I don't know the members of the Intelligence Committee very well."

"This will go through my committee, Defense," said Gunter.

"I see. But even inside the CIA there might be people opposed."

"I wouldn't worry about a problem from that quarter. Perhaps we should have lunch."

"I'd love to," said Reid. It was a lie, of course; he'd sooner lay down across traffic on the Beltway. "When were you thinking?"

"I'll have my secretary check the schedule and give you some dates."

Reid's first reaction as he put the phone down was relief: Edmund clearly had decided to try to buy him off. This meant his paranoia was completely unjustified—you didn't try to kill someone you were bribing.

But once contracted, paranoia is a difficult disease to shake. He began thinking that it could every easily be a ploy to make him drop his guard. And the more he told himself that he was being ridiculous, even silly, the more the idea stuck.

He finally decided that he had to talk to the President as soon as possible, if only to retain his own sanity.

EVEN A LONGTIME FRIEND LIKE JONATHON REID COULDN'T just show up at the White House and expect the President to see him. Christine Mary Todd was far too busy for that. Most evenings she spent away from the White House, at receptions or in meetings. And getting a formal appointment without giving the reason to the chief of staff could take days, if not weeks.

Getting in to see her husband, on the other hand, was far less onerous.

At precisely five after five Reid left his office to go to his car. He took a deep breath before stepping out of the elevator, assuring himself there was no reason to be so paranoid, and that if there *was* a reason, he would face his fate with equanimity and honor.

There was an unexpected thrill in that—a sense of the old excitement he had felt as a field officer so many years before.

But he had an old man's heart now. Just walking to the car nearly exhausted him.

As Reid put his key into the ignition, he thought how easy it would be to attach a bomb to the wires, how quickly he would go.

There was no bomb; there was no plot; there was nothing but his paranoia. As far as he could tell, he wasn't followed from the lot, nor on the local roads as he wended his way across town.

But his caution didn't fade. Reid drove to the Metro and crisscrossed his way around the capital, changing trains willy-nilly amid the rush-hour throng.

He came up at the Mall and walked to the Smithsonian. Inside, he found one of the few pay phones left in the city, and called Daniel Todd's private cell phone.

"Danny, this is Jon, how are you?"

"Jon—I almost didn't answer. Where are you?"

"Knocking around in the city—it's a long story. What are you doing?"

"At the moment I was heading for dinner," said Todd.

"After dinner?"

"Probably watch the Nationals on the tube. They're playing the Mets. I'd love to see them win."

"You're going to the game?"

"Too late for that. I'm staying in to watch."

"Want some company?"

"You're stooping to baseball?"

"Yes."

"Game's on at seven. I'll leave word."

22

Duka

IT HAD BEEN TWO WEEKS SINCE MILOS KIMKO HAD drunk his last vodka, but the taste lingered in his mouth, teasing his cracked lips and stuffed nose. He longed for a drink, but there were none to be had, which was a fortunate thing for a man struggling to break the habit.

The locals all chewed khat, an ugly tasting weed that supposedly mimicked amphetamines. Kimko thought it made them crazy and wouldn't go near it. The homemade alchoholic concoctions, brewed in repugnant stills, were even worse. He therefore had a reasonable shot at staying sober long enough for it to take.

Africa was not exactly a punishment for the career SVR officer, much less a rehabilitation clinic. It was more a symbol of his diminishment. Milos Kimko had once been a bright star in the Russian secret service, a master of over a dozen languages, an accomplished thief and a persuader of men, a large number of whom were still in the SVR's employ as spies. For several years he'd headed the service's Egyptian operation, and at the time had contacts throughout the Middle East. He had even helped, behind the scenes, negotiate several of the secret pacts with Iran that Russian prime minister Vladimir Putin had used to outmaneuver the U.S. and its allies during the Clinton administration.

But that had been his high point. Instead of the assignment in Moscow he coveted, he was rotated into Western Europe, and from there, inexplicably, to South America. He could blame drinking for his downfall, but that was a lie; the drinking was a consolation, not a reason. He never knew whether he had inadvertently crossed someone or if one of his bosses had coveted his wife. Both, probably.

Petra had been gone five years now, a distant memory.

Kimko smiled at the server as she brought his

tea. He sniffed it first—you couldn't be too careful here—then took a sip. As he set down the cup, a short African with a scruffy beard entered the café.

Girma, the man he had come to see.

Kimko rose to get his attention, then sat back down. Girma sauntered over.

"Well, my friend, you are looking well this morning," said Girma in Arabic.

"And you."

Girma sat. He headed the local faction of rebels known in English as Sudan First, and had a reputation as slightly unbalanced. The waitress rushed over with a pot of fresh tea brewed especially for him. It was a local concoction, sprinkled heavily with khat.

"The weather is pleasant this morning," said Kimko.

The two men chatted about the weather for a few minutes, wary lions sizing each other up. The full name of Girma's group translated as "Sudan the Almighty First Liberation." Its beliefs varied according to the person and, as near as Kimko could tell from his two days here, the hour. But it was larger and somewhat richer than the other group, Meur-tse Meur-tskk. The leader of Meur-tse Meur-tskk, an improbable French-loving African named Gerard, was even crazier than Girma, spending most of his time staring into the distance. So Kimko knew that if he wanted information, Girma and Sudan First were the ones to deal with.

He had heard rumors in the south that the

Brothers were trying to forge an alliance with Girma, but had so far not put enough money on the table to cement it. That was the problem with true believers—they failed to see that corruption was the easiest way to a man's soul.

"Did the commotion last night wake you?" asked Kimko after Girma had his second cup of tea.

"The commotion?"

"The Americans attacked one of the buildings outside town." Kimko wasn't sure if Girma was faking ignorance or if it was genuine. "Near the train yard. I assume it was an attack on your rivals, Meurtre Musique."

"Meurtre Musique are our friends," said Girma carefully. He studied his tea before placing it down. "Why do you say they were attacked?"

"There was an Osprey in the air last night. I happened to be awake and went there for a look. There had been an explosion, but otherwise I saw nothing important. The children told me this morning it had once been a warehouse for rice."

"The rice warehouse." Girma shook his head. "That isn't Meurtre Musique's. Why would they take our building?"

"It's your building?"

"All of Duka is ours."

"Who were the Americans attacking?" asked Kimko.

"The Americans are not here. You are obsessed with Americans."

Kimko let the comment pass.

"There was a robbery last night, that is one

bad thing that happened," said Girma. "I know of that—and when I catch the thief, his hand will be cut off."

"Where was the robbery?" asked Kimko.

"The clinic."

Kimko nodded.

"Meurtre Musique is jealous. They cannot be trusted," said Girma darkly.

"Jealous?"

"They have opened their own clinic."

"I see."

"For a long time we have lived side by side, but now I see—they can't be trusted."

"What was stolen?"

"Wires for the computers."

"Wires?"

"To tie something up. They aren't even smart enough to take the computers. Imbeciles."

Kimko sipped his tea. The theft of computer wires was even more interesting, if perplexing, than an attack on a warehouse.

"If the Americans were to attack someone," said Girma finally, "it would be the Brothers."

"The Brothers? They're here?"

"Yes, the government chased them from the mines to the south. They haven't contacted us, but of course we know everything that goes on in the city."

Except for the most obvious things like Osprey attacks in the middle of the night, thought Kimko.

"I expect they will talk of an alliance again," said Girma. "They are always anxious for one."

"I wonder," said Kimko, "if there might not be a way to talk to them."

"Why would you talk to them? They have no power here."

"Of course not. You are the power," said Kimko. "Still, it might be useful."

"To sell them weapons?"

"Perhaps." Kimko saw the slight pout on Girma's face. "Of course, if I made a sale, I would pay a commission to whoever helped make that possible. A nice commission."

"*Hmmmm.*" Girma drained his tea and poured a fresh cup. "A meeting could be arranged."

"Good."

Girma rose. "Come with me."

"Now?"

"I believe I know where they are. There is no sense waiting, is there?"

"Certainly not."

23

Duka

DANNY LET NURI DO THE TALKING WHEN THEY ARRIVED at the clinic, hanging back and watching Marie Bloom. People who worked with NGAs— nongovernmental agencies—were always an odd mix, and for Danny at least, hard to read. Both

Nuri and Melissa had assured him that she was a volunteer, not a British agent. Naiveté and religious devotion had brought her here, Nuri assured him, in a way that made it sound several times more dangerous than warfare.

The two boxes of medicines were accepted almost greedily. Bloom didn't ask many questions of Melissa, whom Nuri claimed he had recruited while getting the supplies. Melissa said that she worked for WHO, the World Health Organization, and was due in Khartoum in three days. A colleague would pick her up in forty-eight hours and give her a ride.

As she was talking, one of the children who was waiting with his mother ran over and grabbed her leg, apparently playing a game of hide and seek with another kid. Melissa bent down and smiled at him, asking in Arabic what his name was.

Watching, Danny once more thought of Jemma, though this time in a much kinder way. She had always had a soft spot for kids, before and especially after they learned they couldn't have one.

He curled his arms in front of his chest and frowned the way he assumed a bodyguard would. The others took no notice.

"Next stop, Gerard," said Nuri when they were outside.

"You think Melissa is OK in there?" asked Danny.

"They won't hurt her," said Nuri. "I'm sure they think she's a spy, but they think that of everyone."

"I don't know."

"She wanted to be there. Relax, Danny. They don't generally kill women."

"Not generally?"

"We're in a lot more danger, I'll tell you that."

"That's not very reassuring."

"It wasn't meant to be."

24

Duka

THE LOOKOUT YELLED FROM ACROSS THE STREET AS soon as the Range Rover drove up.

"Who?" hissed Li Han.

"Girma. Sudan First," added Amara, naming the Islamic rebel group that shared control of the city. "He's coming to the house."

"How does he know we're here?" asked Li Han.

Amara didn't answer. It was probably a foolish question, Li Han realized—the town was so small any stranger would stand out.

"Let him come." Li Han moved his pistol in his belt, making it easier to retrieve, then pulled a sweatshirt over his head.

Amara opened the door as Girma and his small entourage approached. Besides the Muslim rebel there were two bodyguards and a blotchy-faced white man with greasy, dark hair. The white man was wearing a thick flannel shirt and a heavy suit jacket.

A Pole or a Russian, Li Han guessed. What did this mean?

Had the brothers betrayed him? They had seemed cowed since he shot the tall one, but that was the problem with Africans—they always snuck around behind your back.

"I have come to see the Brothers!" bellowed Girma, practically bouncing into the house. He was overflowing with energy—probably hopped up on khat, Li Han realized.

"We are here on other business," said Li Han in English. Amara translated.

"Who are you?" asked Girma, switching to English himself.

"A friend."

Girma gave him an exaggerated look of surprise, then turned and spoke to Amara in what Li Han gathered was Arabic, though it went by so quickly he couldn't decipher the words.

"They are wondering why we are here and have not greeted them," said Amara.

"Tell them we were afraid that we would bring them trouble."

"Why would you bring us trouble, brother?" said Girma. "Are you running from the Americans?"

"What Americans?" asked Li Han.

"The Americans attacked a building not far from here last night," said the white man in English. "Were they looking for you?"

"No," lied Li Han. "I didn't know there was an attack. Why would the Americans come here?"

"Then whose trouble are you afraid of?"

"Who are you?" asked Li Han.

"Milos Kimko. I work with friends in Russia. We are making arrangements to bring weapons and supplies to our friends here. Perhaps we could help you. You are part of a very impressive organization."

"I'm just a friend."

"I see. But these men are Brothers." He gestured at the others, whose white African clothes hinted at their alliance. "Pretty far north for the Brotherhood, aren't you?"

Li Han didn't answer. He didn't like the man, whose accent he had by now noticed gave him away as a Russian. Like many of his countrymen, he was clearly full of himself, a big talker who undoubtedly delivered less than half of what he promised.

This was, however, clearly an opportunity.

"I am always looking for a chance to do business," added the Russian. "I give many good prices."

"Do you buy as well as sell?" asked Li Han.

"Buy what?"

"You mentioned the Americans. I haven't seen them, but I have seen a weapon they have. It was an aircraft, a robot plane. I wonder if it would be worth money to you."

"We have Predators," said Kimko disparagingly. "Our own versions are better."

"This is not a Predator," said Li Han. "This is a much more capable aircraft."

"A Flighthawk?"

"Better even."

"How do you know?" Kimko asked skeptically.

"I've seen it fly."

"Show it to me."

"I don't have it," lied Li Han. "But I could arrange to show you parts, and give you a photo. Would your government be willing to pay?"

"I don't work for the government."

"Whoever you work for, then," said Li Han.

"Maybe."

"I will deliver a photo to you this evening in town," he said. "Where will you be?"

KIMKO EYED GIRMA CAREFULLY AS THEY GOT BACK INTO the Range Rover. Girma had started off the meeting with surplus energy. Now he was positively agitated, rocking as he sat in the backseat of the truck. He took his pistol out and began turning it over in his hand, examining it.

"This aircraft may be of great interest to me," Kimko said. "Have you heard anything about it?"

The African didn't answer. He reached into the pocket of his shirt and pulled out a small sack; he took out some dried, broken leaves and pushed them into his mouth.

More khat. Just what he needed, Kimko thought.

"Do the Americans fly UAVs here often?" he asked. "I wonder if there are other wreckages we could look at."

Girma shook his left fist in the air and pounded the seat in front of him.

"It is that Gerard's fault," he said loudly. "He stole our wires."

The back of the Rover was about the last place Kimko wanted to be. But there was no graceful way to escape. Or ungraceful, for that matter.

"I know my friends would be very, very interested in paying money for American weapons and technology," said Kimko, desperately trying to change the subject.

"I will kill him," said Girma. This time he slammed the seat with his right hand—and the pistol.

"Tell me what you need, my friend," said Kimko. "What wires? Let me make a present to you. It is fitting for our friendship. Show me the wires you need, and I will get you twice what you had. Because of our friendship."

Girma turned toward him, eyes wide.

"You are too good a friend," said Girma.

"Nothing is too good for you," said Kimko.

"I kill him!" yelled Girma. He pounded on the back of the driver's seat. "Take me to the square."

"Girma, it might be good if—"

"Take me now!" shouted Girma, raising the gun and firing a round through the roof of the truck.

25

Washington, D.C.

A DIEHARD BASEBALL FAN, ZEN STOCKARD HAD ADOPTED
the Nationals as his favorite team partly because
he loved underdogs, and partly by necessity—
they were the only team in town. He had a pair of
season tickets in a special handicapped box, and
often used them to conduct business—though
any baseball outing with Senator Stockard was
generally more pleasure than business, as long as
the home team won.

Tonight, with the Nationals down 5–1 to the
Mets after three innings, pleasure was hard to
come by.

"A little better pitching would go a long way,"
said Dr. Peter Esrang, Zen's companion for the
night. Esrang was a psychiatrist—and not coincidentally, a doctor Zen had personally asked to
take an interest in Mark Stoner's case.

"Jones always has trouble in the first inning,"
said Zen. "He gets a couple of guys on and the
pressure mounts."

"Psychological issue, obviously," said Esrang.

"But after the first, he's fine," said Zen as Jones
threw ball four to the Mets leadoff batter in the
top of the fourth.

"I don't know," said Esrang, watching the
runner take a large lead off first.

Jones threw a curve ball, which the Mets clean-
up hitter promptly bounced toward second. A

blink of an eye later the Nats had turned a double play.

"Now watch," said Zen. "He'll walk this guy on straight fastballs."

There was a slider in the middle of the sequence, but Zen was right—the player never took his bat off shoulder.

"How would you fix this guy?" he asked Esrang. He pushed his wheelchair back and angled slightly to see his guest's face.

"My specialty isn't sports," said Esrang. "But I wonder if it might be some sort of apprehension and overstimulation at first. Nervousness, in layman's terms. His pitches seem a lot sharper than they were in the first inning."

"Could be," said Zen.

"A variation of performance anxiety."

"So what do you do?"

"Have him pitch a lot of first innings," said Esrang. He laughed. "Of course, that's not going to work well for the team."

"Maybe if he pitched *no* first innings," said Zen.

"That would be another approach." Esrang sipped his beer. "Break through that barrier."

"Change the scoreboard so it looks like it's the second inning?" asked Zen. "Or hypnotize him."

"I don't trust hypnotism," said Esrang. "But if you could change his environment, even slightly, it might work."

A perfect segue, thought Zen. "I wonder if something like that would work with Mark."

Esrang was silent for a moment.

"Do you think it would?" asked Zen.

"I'm not sure what you mean."

"I was wondering if perhaps he might go out for short visits," said Zen. "Little trips."

"Senator, your friend is a potentially dangerous individual. Not a big league pitcher."

"Jones is pretty dangerous himself," laughed Zen as a ball headed toward the right field bleachers.

Zen let the subject rest for a while, ordering two beers and sticking to baseball. The doctor surely felt sandbagged, but in the end that wasn't going to matter one bit—eventually they were going to help Stoner. Somehow.

A pop fly to the catcher ended the Mets half of the inning. The Nationals manufactured a run in the bottom half with an error, a steal, and two long fly ball outs.

Jones struck out the side in the top of the second, his only ball missing the strike zone by perhaps a quarter of an inch.

A shadow swung over the sky near the edge of the stadium as the players ran to the dugout. Esrang's head jerked up. Zen followed his gaze.

"What's that airplane?" asked the doctor.

"That's security," said Zen. "The D.C. police are using UAVs to patrol some of the airspace over the past few weeks."

"It's a Predator?"

"No, civilian," said Zen. "The plane is smaller. But the idea is basically the same. They have infrared and optical cameras. They're just testing them for crowd control right now. A few weeks, though, and they'll be using them to give out tickets."

"Really?"

"That's what they claim."

"Hmmm."

"Personally, I think the money would be better spent on foot patrols." Zen was on the committee that oversaw D.C. funding, and had actually voted against the allocation, even though it was mostly funded by a private grant. "High tech has its limits. You need people on the ground, in the loop. Here you're spending the equivalent of six police officers—I'd rather have the people."

"I can't disagree," said the psychiatrist.

"Plus, I'll probably be the one getting the ticket," laughed Zen.

A roar rose from the crowd. Zen turned in time to see a ball head over the right field fence.

"Here we go," he told Esrang. "Brand new ballgame."

"I don't think it's necessarily a bad idea," said the psychiatrist. "But we have to be careful."

"The UAVs won't give out the tickets themselves."

"I mean with Mark."

"Oh, of course."

"The drugs they used, we don't have a good handle on the effects," said Esrang. "We don't know exactly if they've made him psychotic. He's very focused; he's very internal. I can't completely predict what he'll do."

"He hasn't harmed anyone since he's been in custody. Or done anything aggressive."

"I realize that. I know. But—"

The Nationals third baseman cracked a hard shot down the first baseline. Esrang jumped from his seat to watch as the player zipped past first, took a wide turn at second, and raced for third. He slid in under the tag.

"Not bad," Esrang told Zen, sitting back. "But I would never have given him a green light on three balls and no strikes."

"No." Zen held his gaze for a moment. "Sometimes you take a chance, and it works out."

"Hmmm," said Esrang.

26

Duka

NURI GAVE GERARD A BIG WAVE AS HE WALKED THROUGH the large pavilion. The African was more animated today than he'd been the day before; he actually nodded back.

"I just dropped off the medicines you asked for at your clinic," Nuri told him, setting down his rucksack and pulling over a camp chair. "They are very happy."

Gerard frowned. "You should have given them to me first."

"Those were just aspirins and bandages," said Nuri. "Little things that anyone could bring."

He pulled up his backpack and started to open it. One of the bodyguards lurched forward as if to stop him.

Gerard raised his hand and the man froze.

"This is ampicillin," said Nuri, taking out a bottle of pills. "*This* is important medicine that only an important person can deliver."

Pretending he wasn't flattered, Gerard feigned a frown and put out his hand. He took the bottle of antibiotics and opened it, pouring a few pills into his palm.

"Each of those is worth several dollars," said Nuri.

"*Hmph.*" Gerard held them up to his nose, sniffing them.

"They only work if you're sick," said Nuri, worried that Gerard was going to eat them. He didn't know how they would affect him.

Gerard poured them back into the bottle.

"Six bottles," Nuri told him. "And there are some other medicines as well. They're labeled. Your doctor will be very impressed."

Gerard handed the bottle back. "Let us have something to drink. Coke?"

DANNY SENSED TROUBLE AS SOON AS THE WHITE RANGE Rover turned the corner. Dirt and dust flew in every direction as the nose of the vehicle swung hard to the left and then back to the right. He took a step forward, closing the distance between himself and Nuri, who was sitting on one of the camp chairs in front of Gerard.

The Rover skidded to a stop. A man jumped out from the rear, raising his arm.

"Down!" yelled Danny. He threw himself forward, pushing Nuri to the ground as the man near the car began firing.

Gerard joined them as his bodyguards began returning fire.

"Go! Come on, let's go!" hissed Danny, grabbing Nuri and pulling him in the direction of the building next to the pavilion where they'd gone to meet Gerard. Someone got out of the Range Rover and began firing a machine gun; the bullets chewed through the tables at the front and the canvas overhead. There was more gunfire up the street, screams and curses.

"What is it? What is it?" demanded Nuri, as if Danny had an answer.

"The building—come on," Danny told him, pulling him to the back of the building where they had some hope of getting out of the cross fire. But a splatter of bullets from the machine gun cut them off. Danny spun back, ready to fire. But when he raised his head, the Range Rover was speeding down the street.

One of Gerard's bodyguards continued to shoot. The man's gun clicked empty; he dropped the magazine and reached for another, firing through that. He didn't stop until he had no more magazines.

A half-dozen people lay on the ground. Two or three moaned; the others were already dead. Blood and splinters were everywhere. One of the picnic tables had been shot in half, its two ends reaching up like a pair of hands praying to the heavens.

Gerard sputtered in rapid French.

"Stay down," Danny told Nuri, crouching next to him. "There were people firing from up the street."

"They were with Gerard."

"What's he saying?"

"He's asking who did this," said Nuri, who'd drawn his pistol. "Dumb question. Has to be Sudan First."

Nuri got to his knees, listening as Gerard continued to yell.

"He says it was Girma's truck. That's Sudan First."

"Time for us to get out of here," said Danny.

"We're going to have to help clean this up," said Nuri.

"What?"

"We have a car. We have to take the victims to the clinic."

This wasn't a particularly good time to be playing good Samaritan, thought Danny, but Nuri made sense. A half-dozen armed men had appeared from other parts of the square. They formed a perimeter around the battered pavilion. Gerard stood a few feet away, railing in French against whoever had done this. He'd taken a pistol out and was waving it around.

"Go get the car," Nuri told Danny. "I'll explain."

By the time Danny retrieved the Mercedes, two of Gerard's men were waiting with one of the wounded, a gray-haired old man whose face was covered with blood. Danny guessed that the man was already dead, but didn't argue; he helped three other people into the front seat, and took another into the rear.

"I'll stay," said Nuri, running up to him. "Gerard will help us now."

"Be careful," said Danny.

"I've been in much worse situations. Speak as little as possible," added Nuri. "Very little. They're going to be suspicious. The cover will be that you're a mercenary from Australia, probably a wanted criminal. They might accept that."

"I don't sound Australian."

"They won't know."

The two bodyguards climbed on the trunk; Danny rolled the windows down so they could hold on, then backed into a U-turn to get to the clinic.

MARIE BLOOM WAS NOT THE NAIVE DO-GOODER THAT Melissa had taken her for at first. On the contrary, Bloom was a steely and wily woman who started questioning her as soon as Nuri and Danny had left.

"What spy agency do you work for?" she asked, getting straight to the point.

"I'm not a spy," Melissa told her.

"Lupo didn't just find you on the street," she said. "You're an American. You're with the CIA."

"I am an American," Melissa said. She fidgeted in the office chair. It was a small room; if she held out her arms, she could almost touch both walls. "I was in Kruk last week. There were problems in one of the camps. I had . . . trouble."

"What sort of trouble?" asked Bloom. Her voice was borderline derisive. She leaned against the bare table she used as a desk; it doubled as an examining table for infants.

"There were problems with one of the supervisors," said Melissa. "He tried . . . let's say he pushed me around."

"And then what happened?"

"I took care of it."

Bloom frowned, and reached for Melissa's shoulder. She jerked back instinctively.

"I know it's hurt. Let me see it," said Bloom.

Melissa leaned forward reluctantly.

"Take off your shirt," directed Bloom.

Wincing, Melissa unbuttoned her blouse and slipped it back on her shoulders, exposing the massive bruise.

"You dislocated it," said Bloom, probing gently at the edges.

"I put it back in place."

"Yourself?"

"I had help."

"He pulled it from the socket?"

Melissa didn't answer.

"I would bet there's tearing," said Bloom. "The rotator cuff—"

"I'll be fine," said Melissa. "Someone is going to meet me. We'll go to the capital and I'll go home."

She pulled her shirt back into place. She didn't think Bloom fully believed her story, but the injury was certainly authentic, and it made everything else at least somewhat plausible. In general, that was all people needed—an excuse to find something believable.

"What are you taking for it?" asked Bloom.

"Aspirin." She shook her head. "I'm OK."

"We have hydrocodone."

"No. You'll need them for real patients."

"As if you're not hurt? You think you're more stoic than the next person?"

"I saw a hell of a lot worse at Kruk."

Bloom gathered a stethoscope, a thermometer, and gloves from a basket at the left side of the desk. "How do you know Gerard?"

"I have no idea who he is."

"Lupo?"

Melissa shook her head. "He was a convenient ride. I needed to go. It sounded like a good solution."

"You travel with people you don't know?" said Bloom, her voice once more harsh. "That's very dangerous."

"One of my supervisors said he could be trusted. He's a criminal, I know," added Melissa. "But he didn't try to hurt me."

"How much did you pay him?"

"When my friend comes, I'll give him a hundred dollars."

"You have it?"

"My friend will have it. I don't."

"I hope your friend has a gun," said Bloom. "Several."

Melissa rose and started to follow Bloom out of the office. As she opened the door, they heard gunfire in the distance. Bloom tensed.

"What's going on?" asked Melissa.

"I don't know." She turned around and went to the cabinet behind Melissa. Reaching inside, she took out a pistol—an older Walther automatic. She put it in her belt under her lab coat. "Get ready for anything."

DANNY DROVE THE CAR TO THE CLINIC'S FRONT DOOR, scattering a flock of birds pecking at the dirt. A thin man in a white T-shirt coming out of the building jumped back, fear in his eyes as Danny slammed on the brakes. The two men on the back leaped down and pulled open the doors, helping the wounded out of the car.

Except for the soft purr of the engine, it was eerily silent. Danny picked up a woman who had been shot in the arm and carried her inside. She was a limp rag, passed out from the loss of blood but at least breathing.

That was more than he could say for the man they'd lain across the backseat. Danny stopped the two guards as they picked him up and moved him out of the car. He put his finger on the man's pulse and shook his head.

They carried him in anyway.

The last person in the car was a young boy, unconscious but with a good pulse and steady breathing. Six or seven large splinters of wood were stuck in his face; small trickles of blood ran down across his chin and neck to his clothes. There was a stain on his pants where he'd wet himself, and another—this one caked blood, near his knee.

Danny picked him up, cradling him in his arms as he walked him inside the clinic. The reception room had become an emergency triage unit, with the patients spread out in the center of the floor. The people who'd been inside already stood at the far end, occasionally stealing glances at the wounded, but mostly trying to look anywhere else. Danny wanted to talk to Melissa, but she was tending one of the wounded, and he worried that going to her now would blow her cover, or his.

One of the men he'd come with tapped his shoulder, indicating that they should go back. Danny followed him silently. He glanced at the little boy as he left, hoping to give him some sign of encouragement. But the boy's eyes were still closed. Danny wondered if the kid would ever overcome the real wounds of the day.

"THE CHINESE MAN PUT HIM UP TO THIS," NURI TOLD Gerard as they surveyed the ruined pavilion. "Where is he?"

"I'll kill him," said Gerard. His glassy stare had been replaced by one even more frightening; his eyes were almost literally bulging from his sockets. Two veins pulsed in his neck.

"I'll pay good money for him," said Nuri calmly. "I know people who will pay us if we give him to them alive."

"I kill him."

"He's worth more to me. To us. More alive."

"Why would you save a murderer?"

The Mercedes rounded the corner, Gerard's

men hanging out the windows. Nuri went over to help the last of the wounded get in. Gerard stopped him as he bent to an old man.

"He's not hurt," said Gerard gruffly.

"He's holding his side." The man wasn't bleeding but seemed in obvious pain. "We have to get him in the car and take them to your clinic."

"No, they will find their own way," said Gerard. "You must take me to my house in the hills."

"I have other places to go."

"Take me," demanded Gerard.

The bodyguards bristled.

"What about the wounded?" asked Nuri.

"If you are my friend," said Gerard, "you will help me, not them."

"Get in the car," said Nuri, deciding it was the wisest thing to do.

27

Duka

IT HAD GONE TO HELL SO QUICKLY THAT KIMKO COULDN'T process all that had happened. But the basics were clear enough: Girma had shot up the center of town, killing or wounding at least a half-dozen people, all allied with Meur-tse Meur-tskk. There was certain to be a lot more fighting.

Kimko might have viewed the conflict as good for business if he hadn't been mixed up in the middle of it.

His best plan, he thought, was to get away as quickly as possible. But Girma didn't look ready to let him leave.

"You will see our great victory," Girma told him as the Range Rover sped across the desert to the foothills where Sudan the Almighty First Liberation had a fortress. "We will crush our enemies."

"You will need more ammunition. I can fetch it."

"We are fine. After the battle."

"Not before? Are you sure?"

"You will admire our mortars in action."

"What are you going to do with mortars?"

"We will fight. We will destroy our enemy."

"You can't attack them in the city."

"Don't tell me how to fight!" screamed Girma. He put his hand into his pocket and pulled out more khat leaves, thrusting them into his mouth.

LI HAN STUDIED THE LAPTOP SCREEN, LOOKING AT THE coding he had retrieved from the UAV's brain. With the proper connection—and power from the batteries—getting in was easy.

Relatively.

The control interface was written in a variation C++. If he'd been back in his lab in Shanghai, accessing the underlying code would be trivial; he'd have any number of tools and a large number of computers to help him. But here, all he had was a laptop with less memory than the UAV's brain.

The interface was designed to be easily accessed. Li Han managed to get a full dump of the program despite the fact that he couldn't get past the encrypted password, preventing access to the interface itself. He could see the logic of how it worked, though he couldn't yet access the commands. Until he managed that, he wouldn't be able to fully understand what he was looking at.

He might be able to replace the encrypted code section with his own revision, recompile and run the program. The problem was, he didn't have the tools. His Toshiba laptop, upgraded with the latest processor and a trunkload of memory, was state of the art and could easily run a suite of debuggers and other tools. But he didn't have them.

He could get the tools from any number of places online—Shanghai University would be his top choice, as he had a full set of broken passwords and knew the system intimately. But he assumed the Americans were tracking his satellite phone, so tethering the laptop to it would be as good as telling them where he was.

He noticed Amara staring at him.

"You're interested in what I'm doing?" asked Li Han, amused.

Amara shrugged.

"Do you know how to work these?" Li Han pointed at the laptop.

"I can work a computer."

At best, you can handle e-mail and Web surfing, thought Li Han. But the boy had potential. He could be trained.

At least to a degree.

"The UAV has a brain. I'm trying to tap into

it," said Li Han. "The program is written in a fairly common language. I think that's only the interface. They encrypted part of the underlying assembly language, but it uses this chip." He pointed at the encryption circuitry on the circuit board. "See, they were worried about someone breaking through the transmission, not physical security. So I can use what I know about the chip myself. I emulate it. Do you have any idea what I'm talking about?"

"Your program breaks the code."

"Something like that," said Li Han. Amara had missed a few steps, but that was the gist. "I need an Internet connection. I need to access some documents. Technical documents—I don't remember how some of these things work."

Lying slightly made the explanation simple.

"I don't know if there are Internets here," said Amara.

"If I had a sat phone, I could make my own connection," said Li Han. "But it would have to be one that the Americans couldn't trace to me. Or to you. You know how they are watching."

There was a commotion upstairs. One of the brothers called down to Amara and told him that a small boy had run up to the house and was knocking furiously on the door.

Li Han went upstairs. When they let the boy in, he collapsed just across the threshold, tears streaming from his face as he unleashed a long paragraph of words.

"There has been fighting," explained Amara. "The two groups."

"That's inconvenient."

"People have been killed," said Amara. "We should be ready to leave."

"Where do you suggest we go?"

Amara didn't answer.

"We stay here for now," answered Li Han. "Ask the boy if he knows what a satellite phone is. Tell him I'll pay for one—twice as much as I did for the wire."

28

Washington, D.C.

DAN TODD THRUST A GLASS INTO JONATHON REID'S hand as soon as Reid walked into his private den in the White House residence.

"Taste it," demanded Todd.

"What is it?"

"Bourbon. Taste it."

Reid sniffed dubiously at the glass. The color was a very dark amber, and the liquid had the consistency of gear oil.

"What do you smell?" Todd asked.

"Cigarette smoke."

"Ha!" Todd was a chain-smoker, and the room smelled of Marlboros. "Try it. It's supposed to be a hundred and three years old."

Reid took a very small sip from the glass.

"Well?" asked Todd.

"Hmmm," said Reid.

"One hundred and three year old bourbon," continued the President's husband. "Allegedly."

He laughed, then downed a shot.

"Smooth," said Todd. "This is what you get when the governor of Kentucky is trying to curry favor with the President. Of course, what he doesn't realize is that the President doesn't *like* bourbon."

"But her husband does."

"True. But if there's one person in the world who has no influence with the President, it's her husband." Todd took another sip. "Maybe it is a hundred years old. It's certainly dark enough. But how would I really know?"

"You don't," said Reid.

"Absolutely—but then we take much on face value. So what do you need to see her about?"

"I'm sorry to use you like this."

"Nonsense, Jonathon—you're not sorry to use me at all."

"It has to do with the Agency."

"Well, I figured that."

"Do you really want to know?"

"Absolutely not." Todd laughed. "She'll poke her head in around ten. Let's see how much money I can take from you in head-to-head poker before then."

THEY HAD A TWENTY-FIVE CENT PER HAND LIMIT, BUT Reid had still lost over five dollars by the time the President came by to see what her husband was up to.

Dan excused himself when the President came in, claiming he was going to raid the kitchen.

"I stumbled on something you probably don't know about," Reid told the President as soon as they were alone. "It's possible that you do. But one way or the other, I think you should."

Reid briefed her quickly, hitting the main points: illegal assassination, secretly developed UAV, potentially uncontrollable artificial intelligence program.

If she knew about any of it, it didn't show on her face.

"I'm not going to insult you, Jonathon, by asking if you're sure of all this," she said when he was done.

"I am sure of it, Chris."

She nodded. "Who else knows?"

Reid assumed that she was in fact asking whether Breanna Stockard's husband knew.

"Ms. Stockard is aware of most of what I've told you. She is in charge of the recovery. I don't believe she'll share any of the information with her husband."

A faint smile came to the President's lips.

"Zen and I are getting along fairly well these days, all things considered," said Ms. Todd. "It's not him I'm worried about."

"Of course. As far as I can tell, the information has been very tightly controlled in-house. But I simply don't know for sure. They're not exactly sharing."

"What's the status of your operation to recover the plane?"

"We've traced it to a village, and we're trying to get it back. We had one operation already, but unfortunately our information was incomplete and the UAV wasn't there."

"I see. Even when we get it back," added the President, "there's a much bigger problem here. Isn't there?"

"Exactly. That's why I wanted you to know."

29

Duka

THE LARCENY OF THE LOCAL YOUTH WAS ASTOUNDING. A half hour after Amara told the boy he needed a satellite phone, he had three. None of them had the proper circuitry to be tethered to his laptop, but that wasn't critical—Li Han simply removed their ID circuitry for use in his own. He was online within the hour.

He lost the connection with Shanghai some forty minutes later, but that was just as well— there was always the possibility of being detected if he remained on for too long. And the next set of operations could be done entirely with the laptop.

The battery was edging downward. The power was off and there was no indication when it would be on again. He'd need to get it recharged at one of the houses that used a generator.

Unless one of the children could steal one of those as well. No doubt they could.

Li Han moved his finger across the touch pad, then gave it a soft double tap.

And then, almost against his expectations if not his best hopes, the command screen for the UAV appeared.

Or at least what should have been the command screen appeared. It looked more like a database entry screen.

And half of it was filled with a photo of his face.

He leaned away, trying to make sense of the screen. What was this? The architecture of the program made it clear this *should* be the command module, and yet how could it be?

It was the command screen, if the logo at the top in thirty-six point Helvetica bold type was to be taken at face value.

How would this run a UAV? Li Han knew that the aircraft was flying itself when it came to simple flight commands, but he expected this section to contain an interface to a ground station.

The left side of the screen had location data at the top: a line with GPS coordinates that appeared to be in Africa, undoubtedly where he had been when the drone went down. Below that were the words SUBJECT CONFIRMED.

Then a blank space and the word: TERMINATE.

Below that: PROJECT ONGOING.

And at the bottom: STATUS: HOLDING.

All the words were in blue, except for STATUS: HOLDING, which was in red.

Li Han stared at the screen. He'd set up the

program to run with his debugger. He was about to go back to the shell so he could get a peek at a different part when the words on the screen began blinking: STATUS: SEEKING.

The program was active in the laptop, or at least thought it was.

What the hell was going on?

30

Duka

GERARD'S "FORTRESS" CONSISTED OF A ROW OF SLUM buildings behind a patchwork of round huts and small lots at the western end of the city. The buildings, most smaller than a one-car garage back in the States, were pushed together in a jumble behind an abandoned dump. It could be reached only on foot; Danny parked the Mercedes at the edge of the landfill and they hiked in through a maze of alleys.

Two men were sitting in the front room of the two-room shack, drinking some home-brewed concoction. Gerard shouted something at them and they leapt up, grabbed a pair of rifles from the floor and ran outside.

A piece of fabric separated the back room from the front. Gerard pushed it aside and led them into the room; there he introduced Nuri but not

Danny to the five men sitting on the floor, smoking hand-rolled cigarettes and talking. They were all members of the Meurtre Musique hierarchy. Gerard's overview filled the four youngest with energy, and they immediately left to rally different members of the group. The fifth, well into his sixties, sat stoically, nodding as Gerard repeated what had happened with more detail.

Danny wanted to get Melissa and get the hell out of there, the sooner the better, but Nuri sat down and started a conversation in French. They talked for nearly a half hour, Danny standing by the curtained door, sliding his hand up and down the barrel of his assault rifle, one eye on the front door. Finally, Nuri rose, and despite the others' protests, took his leave.

"What took so long?" asked Danny as they left the building.

"We're being watched," whispered Nuri. "Wait until we're back in the car."

They wended their way back out through the alleys. There were men with Kalashnikovs on the roofs. On the way in Danny had spotted a couple of kids playing and some women working in the yards; all were gone now.

"The older man had heard there were strangers in the village," Nuri explained when they got to the car. "One was Asian. I asked him where he thought he might be. He gave me a few different possibilities. They're on the other side of town."

"You're not suggesting we go there now, are you?" asked Danny.

"Why not? We're not part of their war."

"I'll remember to say that when the bullets start flying."

LI HAN WAS EXAMINING THE INTERFACE CODING WHEN Amara came trotting down the steps.

"Someone is coming," he said breathlessly.

"Who?" demanded Li Han.

"A white man," whispered Amara. "He's speaking Arabic."

"Ask what he wants. Then get rid of him."

Li Han went up with him, crouching in the front room while Amara went to the door. The African shouted something; the man outside answered in Arabic.

"He says he is looking for a man who found a UAV," said Amara. "He wants to make a deal."

"Tell him you don't know who it is."

"He named a man from Meur-tse Meur-tskk."

Li Han shook his head. "You don't know who it is. Say nothing else. If he talks, don't answer."

The man outside seemed reluctant to leave. Li Han watched from the corner of the window as he finally walked away with his bodyguard to a Mercedes and drove away.

"Who was he?" Li Han demanded, rising.

"A gun runner or spy, I guess," said Amara. "He had a foreign accent."

"Obviously. He's white."

"He said he would make a very good deal if he could find the man who had the aircraft."

"Did he speak English?"

"Not to me."

"You should have asked," said Li Han, though he hadn't thought of it himself.

31

Duka

A WOMAN'S VOICE ANSWERED FROM BEHIND THE DOOR of the second house. She knew nothing of an aircraft or a man from China.

"Can I come in and talk to you?" asked Nuri.

"You can talk to my husband when he comes home," said the woman.

"When will that be?"

"I don't know."

Nuri asked a few more questions, then told the woman he would try back later. He backed away, reaching Danny in a few steps.

"What do you think?" asked Danny.

"Could go either way. I stuck a bug near the door stop. MY-PID will activate it once the satellite comes overhead."

"I think it was the first house."

"Maybe," agreed Nuri. "But we still have two more to check. One thing that's very unusual—ordinarily, people are extremely friendly to strangers. The shooting has everybody on edge. Very on edge."

"So I see." Danny nodded in the direction of two men with AK-47s standing in the shadows at the side of the house across the way.

The muscles in Nuri's shoulders immediately tensed, and his throat tightened. But he'd been in situations like this dozens, even hundreds of times in Africa. He continued to walk toward the car, keeping an easy, almost lackadaisical pace.

"They're just watchin' us," said Danny.

"Yeah. Just move nice and easy."

Danny opened the driver's side door but didn't get in. Nuri went around and got in the car. He kept his eyes straight ahead, but took his pistol out from his waistband.

Danny eased into the seat, pulled the door closed and started the car.

"You have to make a U-turn," said Nuri.

The Mercedes stuttered as it started out of the turn, then stalled.

"Shit," muttered Danny.

He turned the car over—once, twice. It wasn't starting.

"Don't flood it," whispered Nuri.

"No shit."

"Maybe our friends will push us," said Nuri.

The car caught. Danny put it into gear gently and they edged forward.

"Maybe our friends will push us?" mocked Danny after they turned the corner.

"I was making a joke."

"It wasn't very funny."

"It was funny. A little."

"Not even a little. Which way to the next house?"

Nuri consulted the map on MY-PID.

"About a quarter mile down here. Take a left. There should be a bunch of huts."

There were. There were also three men with guns blocking the way.

"What do you think?" Danny asked, slowing to a stop in the middle of the intersection.

The men were standing about ten yards away. Each held a Belgian FN Minimi machine gun. They were relatively large guns, but the men were so big the weapons looked like scale models. The man in the middle had a bandolier of bullets around his neck and was dressed in generic fatigues similar to Danny's. The other two wore the dusty, cream-colored clothes more common there.

"I'll ask what's going on," said Nuri. "Stay in the car."

"I don't think that's a good idea," said Danny.

"Just wait."

Nuri pushed open the door and got out. His heart was pounding.

"Hello," he said, starting in English. "I am looking for a Chinese man named Li Han."

There was no reaction from any of the trio as he gave his spiel. He switched to Arabic but did no better.

"Are you with the Brothers?" Nuri asked finally.

"The Brothers are dirt," said one of the men, using English. He fired off a few rounds to emphasize his point.

"Right," said Nuri. "Can I get through?"

"You better leave, mister," said the man who'd fired. "Now."

Nuri thought it best to comply.

32

Duka

MELISSA FINISHED TAPING THE BANDAGES ON THE OLD man's arm and straightened. He turned his head toward her as she rose. The pupils in his eyes were large black disks, edged by the faintest gray. They met hers for a moment, drilling in with a wordless question.

Am I going to live?

"You're going to be OK," she said in Arabic.

The old man's eyes held hers as she put her hand on his back and eased him to his feet. Melissa helped him from her corner of the examining room, gently pushing him past the table where Marie Bloom was working on another patient.

Bloom's patient was a young boy who had caught shrapnel in his leg. He was much better off than the old man or any of the other patients they'd seen, but the pain on his face touched Melissa in a way none of the others had. She suddenly felt overwhelmed by sympathy for the people here, like a tree that had bent under the weight of heavy snow until finally it snapped.

"Who's next?" she asked in English.

The aide who'd been helping triage and organize the patients shook her head. They were done. For now.

Melissa went back to help Bloom get the boy down from the table. He winced, unable to put much weight on the leg.

"We'll have to get one of the men to carry him home," said Bloom.

"I'll take him," said Melissa. She dropped down to one knee, propping him up as he continued to test his leg. She guessed he was four or five. "Where's his mother?"

"She was one of the dead," said Bloom.

The boy's shirt was splattered with blood, and Bloom had cut off the bottom of his pants leg to work on him. He wore sandals rather than shoes.

"One of the women I treated earlier is his aunt," said Bloom. "I sent her home already. That's where he should go."

"It's terrible," said Melissa.

"Yes." Bloom frowned at her.

"What's wrong?" Melissa asked.

"Go ahead and take him home."

"Where?"

Bloom said something to the boy in Nubian. They spoke for a few moments, getting directions to his house.

"He'll show you where he lives," Bloom told

her finally. "He can't speak English, or very much Arabic."

"All right."

"Be careful. It should be quiet for a while, but there's sure to be a reprisal. They won't try to kill you since you're an outsider, but in the cross fire anything can happen."

"I'll be safe."

"Here." Bloom pulled a satellite phone from her pocket. "Call my number if you have a problem."

"I'll be OK."

Bloom gave her a stern look.

"What's your number?" she asked. "Let me try it and make sure it works."

THE BOY COULDN'T HAVE WEIGHED MORE THAN THIRTY pounds. Melissa took him in her arms, boosting him up against her shoulder as she started out. The clinic was at the top of a knoll; he lived in one of the round grass huts at the bottom. The boy jerked his arm forward, pointing with his whole hand, fingers spread wide to show her the way.

Small garden patches surrounded the huts; here and there a goat was tied to a post or wandered freely around the property. All the people, however, were hiding inside the structures. Melissa felt as if they were being watched but saw no one as she followed the boy's directions, turning right along a rutted path, then left and left again. Finally his hand swerved to the right, and she walked through an opening in a low fence of shrubs, entering a dirt-strewn yard just big enough to house the wreckage of an ancient flatbed truck.

The vehicle's tires had long ago rotted away. The metal body and frame were covered with red rust. There was a large hole in the center of the cab roof, and part of the front fender had disintegrated into flakes. Dirt was piled on the bed; a hodgepodge of weeds grew from it.

The hut was in better condition. Made of straw and mud, the thick fronds of straw on the roof stretched down gracefully in a circle over the body of the house, whose cementlike walls were smooth and seemingly impenetrable. A carpet hung in the doorway, shutting off the outside world.

"Hello!" shouted Melissa as she approached. "Hello!"

The carpet moved at the bottom. The head of a child about the age of the one she was carrying poked out from the side. The boy in her arms wiggled around, pushing to be freed. Melissa went down on one knee to release him, sure he wouldn't be able to stand. But after a few tentative steps he managed to hop to the door of the hut, shouting to the people inside.

The carpet was pushed away by a woman about her age. A worn, worried look on her face, she stared at Melissa a moment, then beckoned her inside.

"I have to get back," Melissa said. But the woman reached out and took her hand, nudging her forward with a forced smile. Even in extreme grief and danger, the local tradition of hospitality was still upheld.

The interior of the hut was practically bare.

Four children sat at one side on woven mats, a pile of grass dolls in front of them. The boy Melissa had taken home already sat among them, moving the doll as if it were a plane or perhaps an angel, leaving for heaven.

The interior walls were covered with shallow cracks where the mud had dried ages ago. A series of lines came down the sides, raised designs that to Melissa looked like random squiggles and rays, though they were obviously a conscious design. There were no windows, but the roof's circular rafters left an open space above the wall where air could circulate.

The woman who had invited her in scooped up a water bottle from the ground and offered it to her.

"Thank you, but I'm not thirsty," she said.

The woman didn't seem to understand. She said something unintelligible—Melissa only knew that the words were neither English nor Arabic— and pushed the water bottle toward her. Melissa took the tiniest sip possible from the water. When she handed it back, the woman refused—it was a present, gratitude for helping her nephew.

"Thank you," Melissa told her. "Thank you."

She nodded and backed out of the hut, trying to remember the turns she'd taken to get there.

"YOU WERE GOOD WITH THE PATIENTS," SAID BLOOM when she returned.

"Thank you."

"But you're not a nurse. Not with any experience here, at least."

Two hours before, Melissa would have argued and worked hard to keep her cover. But whatever change she'd undergone had affected every part of her.

"I am trained as a nurse," she told Bloom. "But that's not why I'm here."

"Why is it?"

"I'm looking for an Asian man. Chinese. His name is Li Han. He's a murderer."

"I don't know him."

"He came into the city a day ago."

"I don't know him."

"One of your aides may. He has something that doesn't belong to him, and I have to get it back."

"Are you going to arrest him?"

Melissa shook her head.

"You're going to kill him?" asked Bloom.

"If we can."

"Was he responsible for this?"

"I don't know," said Melissa.

"There's so much tragedy here. You're just going to add to it."

"No. Li Han has caused a lot of deaths. He helps people who want to murder others. We have to stop him. And we can."

"That won't end the violence here."

"It'll help."

Bloom raised her right hand to her mouth, biting her ring finger as she considered what to do. For the first time, Melissa noticed she wore a narrow wedding ring.

"You remind me of myself," said Bloom. "I was like you."

"How's that?"

"I worked for MI6."

IN FACT, BLOOM STILL DID, THOUGH NOW INFORMALLY. She'd quit the British Intelligence Service some years before, haunted by what she had seen in Africa, the suffering. She tried to join the Red Cross, then a group sponsored by the Anglican Church. For various reasons—very possibly her background as a spy—they wouldn't take her. Persistent, she finally settled on a little known agency called Nurse for the Poor. It received a considerable amount of money from the British government, undoubtedly at MI6's behest.

"The idea is to find terrorists before they become terrorists," said Bloom.

"Do you know who Li Han is?" asked Melissa.

Bloom shook her head. She seemed to have aged a decade, perhaps more, in the few minutes they'd been speaking.

"I give the service reports from time to time, but they don't tell me anything. I—I'm doing more by helping the people here."

"Even people like Gerard."

"Oh, he's a loon." Bloom smiled. Her British accent had suddenly become more pronounced. "But his group is better than the other, to be honest. They're all nuts here, the leaders. But the people are sincere. Loving."

Melissa nodded. She thought it odd that a spy, even a woman—especially a woman—would use the word "loving."

But maybe that's why Bloom was an ex-spy.

"I'll help you," Bloom told her. "But you must protect my people. These people."

"All right," Melissa said.

"Come." Bloom rose. "Let's talk to them."

33

Parsons, Maryland

WELL BEFORE SHE BECAME THE COUNTRY'S FIRST female president, Christine Mary Todd had carefully studied the power of the presidency. Among the many conclusions she had reached was that much of this power consisted of imagery. The pomp and circumstance of the office were not just props, but weapons that could be yielded by a prudent President.

So was the President's motorcade, especially when it pulled across a suburban lawn at five o'clock in the morning.

President Todd picked up the phone from the console as the limo came to a stop amid a swarm of black SUVs.

"Mr. Edmund, I hope you're up," she said when the head of the CIA answered his phone. "We're going to meet this morning."

"Uh—"

"Right now would be fine . . . Yes, thank you. Don't worry about the coffee; I've brought my own."

Todd put the phone down.

"David, are you ready?" she asked her chief of staff, David Greenwich, who was sitting in the front seat of the limo. Though generally an early riser, Greenwich gave a barely conscious "Yes, ma'am."

"Good. Let's go make Mr. Edmund's day."

Ms. Todd strode up the walk, heels clicking on the concrete. She wore pumps and a presidential skirt—knee length, a careful and distinguished drape. Her Secret Service detail buzzed around her; one or two of the agents may have had trouble keeping up.

Edmund's wife opened the door. She was in her bathrobe.

"Nancy, good morning," said the President.

"Herm is, uh—upstairs."

"Very good. I noticed a new bed of daffodils outside," added Ms. Todd as she walked into the hallway. "They're really lovely. Don't bother with me—I know the way."

It had been some time since Todd had been in the house, but it was easy to find the way to the master bedroom—up the steps in the main hall, a slight turn to get to the front of the house, then a short walk across a very plush red carpet.

Red is such an ugly color for a carpet, the President thought as she walked to the bedroom door.

"Mr. Edmund—are you decent?"

"Uh—uh, Madam President," stuttered Edmund from behind the door.

The President pointed to the door and nodded at one of her Secret Service escorts. He reached out and opened the door, filling the frame and entering quickly. Todd waited for a second agent to enter—out of discretion rather than fear that Edmund was waiting inside with a bomb.

Though he would surely wish he had been when she was through with him.

"I was just getting dressed," said Edmund, who had pulled on a pair of trousers but was still wearing his pajama top. "What's going on?"

"I want to know about the Raven project," she told him. She went to the upholstered chair at the side of the room, pushed it around so it angled toward him, and sat. "Everything. Assassination, drone, and most of all, software."

"I—"

"And when you are done, we'll discuss your letter of resignation," she added. "Coffee?"

34

Duka

THE AIDE OFFERED TO TAKE MELISSA TO THE HOUSE near the railroad tracks where she'd seen the armed strangers. Melissa glanced at Bloom. Bloom nodded.

"Let's go," said Melissa.

The aide's name was Glat. She spoke only a little English, but they didn't need many words to communicate. She led Melissa down the hill toward the main part of the town, then veered to the left, across the main road. They passed a small collection of cone-topped huts built so close to each other they looked like mushrooms, then hiked up a road lined by more prosperous houses, cement structures all recently built.

Yesterday, there had been a variety of sounds in the city, everything from the high-pitched whine of *boda-boda* motorcycle taxis to the shouts of children playing. Now it was dead silent.

Her guide slowed abruptly. Melissa put her arm on the woman's shoulder.

"It's all right," she said. "If you're scared, we can go back."

The woman kept going, though her pace was barely faster than a small child's. The road turned to the right and left the buildings behind. The railroad tracks were about fifty yards ahead.

Melissa had a pistol under her shirt, but she had no illusions of taking on more than one or two gunmen. Still, she kept walking, determined to at least figure out where the house was—to redeem herself, and her mission.

To impress Colonel Freah, too, though she didn't dwell on that as they neared the house.

Intending to keep his appointment with the Russian despite the fighting, Li Han hid the computer and the UAV's brain in the tunnel.

Upstairs, his young escorts seemed even edgier than normal. Shooting the tall one—whose body was buried somewhere outside—had made them fear him, but not to the degree that Li Han couldn't worry about getting shot in the back himself. He watched them warily, even as he stepped outside.

He spotted the insect then, a large mosquito perched in the crevice of the rocks just in front of the door. His instinct was to swat at it with his hand, but as he pulled back to swing, he realized there was something odd about it. Not only did it seem slightly too big, but it was abnormally placid.

Was it a listening device?

Li Han walked past it. He'd scanned the building for bugs when he arrived, but not since then.

He turned and walked back into the building as if he'd forgotten something. He went downstairs to his tools, got out the detection device, then held his breath as he turned it on, preparing himself for the worst.

Nothing.

But of course there was nothing here. He swept it around slowly, like a priest offering a blessing.

Still nothing.

He walked through the house slowly, moving around the walls. He paused at the front door, reaching up and down the frame, even though it wasn't strictly necessary to be that physically close. Still not getting anything, he moved outside and went to the mosquito.

Nothing. *Nothing.*

But it was clear to him now that the bug wasn't a real insect. Maybe it only turned on when it heard human voices.

Li Han knelt behind it. He held the detector next to it, then spoke softly in Chinese. There was no indication that the bug was transmitting. He spoke louder; still nothing.

It must be dead. Perhaps it would be worth something to the Russian. Li Han stuffed it into his pocket.

MELISSA GRABBED GLAT'S ARM AS SHE SAW THE shadow near the house thirty yards away.

It was a gun, swinging against the arm of the man as he walked toward a car.

Quickly, she pulled her guide to the side of the nearby building. The woman started to say something; paranoid, Melissa threw her hand over Glat's mouth and hushed her.

"*Ssssh*," she said, pointed to the ground, then nudged the young woman into a crouch. "Stay. Stay," she repeated. "Do you understand? Stay?"

Glat nodded that she understood.

Easing to the side of the building, Melissa dropped to her knees, then spread out along the ground, peering out around the bottom of the building. A truck had pulled to the front of a building. Two men were in the front seat. She couldn't see anything else. It was too dark to make out their faces.

The truck started and began moving in their direction. Melissa rose to get a better view. As the vehicle passed, she caught a glimpse of the man on the passenger side in the front.

Asian.

Mao Man.

Li Han.

35

Western Ethiopia

FRESH FROM HIS NAP, TURK WENT DOWN TO CHECK ON the Tigershark.

"Pimped it out for you, Captain," said Flash, who was pulling guard duty. "We were going to paint it pink, but we ran out of primer."

"Pity."

Turk reached up and put his palm on a panel just below the opening to the cockpit. The aircraft buzzed, then the forward area began to separate like a clamshell. The Tigershark did not have a canopy per se—all visuals were provided by a matrix of sensors embedded in the skin. This allowed for a much sleeker—and lower—cockpit area that was tucked into the body just in front of the wings.

"Looks a little like a sardine can," said Flash.

"An aerodynamic sardine can," said Turk, reaching into the cockpit and taking out the smart helmet. He put it on, made a link with the aircraft's flight systems, then had the computer begin a preflight instrument check.

Someone knocked on the back of his helmet. Turk pulled it off. It was Boston.

"Sorry to knock on your hat, Captain." Boston grinned. "Colonel Freah was wondering if you could talk to him for a minute."

"Sure. Where is he?"

"Back in the Sudan. Use this." Boston held up a sat phone. "I'll get him for you."

Turk put the helmet back on the seat of the Tigershark. The aircraft would perform its own self-check. Boston, meanwhile, made the connection.

"Colonel, you're looking for me?" asked Turk, taking the phone.

"Satellite is still a few hours away," said Danny. "We're wondering if you can get back on station. You can leave as soon as it's here."

"Yeah, roger that," said Turk. "Beats the hell out of hanging around here."

36

Duka

MILOS KIMKO EYED THE DRIVER NERVOUSLY AS THEY headed into the town. Two of Girma's men were sitting behind him, guns ready; another pair were in the back. Traveling with them was only a hair less dangerous than traveling without them, Kimko thought. Girma was clearly becoming crazed, and his band would surely follow his lead.

The driver stopped the truck abruptly. They had reached the gas station where Li Han suggested they meet. Fortunately, it was at the southeastern end of the city, a good distance from the areas favored by both sides.

The street was empty, the station closed. Kimko debated whether to get out. The vehicle offered a modicum of protection, but it was easier to see in the dusk, making it a logical target.

Nervous energy got the better of him. He opened the door. The others hopped out with him. Instead of fanning out like proper soldiers or trained bodyguards, they clustered together, clumped near the car as he prowled near the gas pumps, looking around the shadows of the building for ambushers or lookouts.

A flask would be welcome now. A drink.

No. He would play this through, get what Li Han had to offer, and turn it into a ticket out of here.

DANNY DROVE THE MERCEDES UP THE ROAD LEADING out of town and glanced at his watch. The Tigershark wouldn't be in range for another five minutes. At that point they could activate the bugs they had planted, and use the Whiplash system to communicate.

"Where the hell is Melissa?" grumbled Nuri. "She was supposed to meet us."

"We're a little early."

"I don't even trust that she saw Li Han."

"Where's the truck?"

"Still at the north end of the city."

Danny pulled the car off the road. They expected Li Han to get on the highway at some point, then try and go south in the direction of the Brotherhood's strongholds. The Whiplash team had loaded up in their Osprey and was en route. Once they were sure it was Li Han, Danny would order the team to prepare an ambush. They'd catch him on the road south.

If it was a false alarm, they'd go back to square one.

"Someone's walking up the road," said Nuri. "In our direction."

"Melissa?"

"Can't tell. Not enough resolution. They're holding something—could be a gun. Pistol."

"All right. Wait here," said Danny, opening the car door.

"Where you going?"

"I'm going to make sure it's not an ambush."

Danny slipped the door closed, then trotted down the road to a small cluster of bushes. He turned around, looking at the car, then took a few steps past the brush. Whoever was coming would see the bushes and expect someone to be waiting there.

He trotted another twenty yards down the road, then went off it into the open field and lay flat. The person would be focused on the brush if not the car, and miss him completely.

His right knee complained as he folded himself onto the ground. Middle age was creeping up on him; the sins and strains of his youth were coming back to haunt him.

"Nuri?" he asked over the team radio.

"A hundred yards," said Nuri. "I can't tell if it's her."

"Call her phone," said Danny.

LI HAN STOOD AT THE EDGE OF THE ROOF FINGERING HIS binoculars, watching the Russian at the gas station about a half mile away. Kimko had four bodyguards with him, but they were back by his truck, useless if he was attacked from anywhere but the road. From what Li Han had seen, he'd made only the most precursory check of the area before stopping.

He was disappointed. He'd always heard that Russian intelligence agents were the best in the world. But obviously they didn't send the best into Africa.

A vehicle drove past the gas station. Li Han watched as the bodyguards took cover behind their truck. They'd be dead meat if someone in the car fired a grenade.

No one did. The car sped past, continuing around to the eastern side of the city.

The Russian had stepped into the shadows as it approached. He moved out of them now, going toward the northern edge of the small property.

Li Han decided he would come from the south on foot.

"Go," he told Amara. "Drive as I told you. I will meet you there."

The Brother nodded.

MELISSA NEARLY JUMPED WHEN HER PHONE RANG. SHE took it from her pocket, telling herself to relax and move slowly. She crouched at the side of the road as she answered.

"Yes?" she whispered.

"Where are you?" asked Nuri.

"On the road where we were going to meet."

"Wait."

She could see shadows up the road ahead. She'd assumed it was Danny and Nuri's car, but now she wasn't sure.

"Danny is about ten yards on your left, on the east side of the road," Nuri told her. "Put one hand up. When you do, he's going to get up."

This is a bit much, she thought, but she did it anyway, turning in Danny's direction. A shadow emerged from the field.

"Hey," yelled Danny.

"Hey."

"The truck you spotted is parked near a building at the southern edge of town," said Danny, running to her. "Come on. We should have a pretty good view of the proceedings in a few minutes."

KIMKO SAW THE PICKUP APPROACHING AND HISSED AT the gunmen back by the car to get ready. Just as he ducked down, he realized someone was walking up from behind the service building. He turned around and saw the outline of a man with a pistol pointing at him.

His heart fell toward the ground; his lungs clutched.

"It's me," barked Li Han.

It took several seconds before Kimko could breathe again. Those seconds were filled with an incredible thirst.

God, for some vodka.

"Why are you playing games?" asked Kimko in English.

"Why did you bring so many people with you?"

"Bodyguards. There's fighting in the city. Two factions. Did you bring the photos?"

"I brought some things."

"Show me."

Kimko led him over to his truck. Meanwhile, the vehicle that had been approaching pulled into the gas station, stopping a few yards from the truck.

The guards are useless, thought Kimko. They were too used to intimidating people simply by flashing their weapons around. In a real fight, they'd be so much chum in the water.

Kimko got into the truck. Li Han got in on the other side, then took a cell phone from his pocket and turned it on.

"It has no SIM chip," said the Asian. "It can't be tracked. Don't worry."

"I'm not worried," said Kimko.

"Here," said Li Han, handing over the phone.

There was a small mélange of colors on the tiny screen. At first glance the image seemed to be nothing—indiscriminate shapes. Slowly, Kimko recognized a black triangle and a round sphere—the blurry outline of an aircraft.

He paged to the next image, and then the next. These were sharper. The object was definitely an aircraft, but it looked like no UAV he'd ever seen. Assuming it was a UAV, it would certainly be of interest back home.

Assuming.

"This looks like a model," said Kimko harshly. "A prop for a movie."

"It's not."

"How do I know?" Kimko started to hand the phone back.

"You can keep that," said Li Han. "Show it to your experts. Here. This is from the aircraft, the interior of the wing. Notice that it has writing."

He took a thin, long piece of metal from his pocket. Only a little larger than a fountain pen, it looked like a miniature shock absorber. It had a series of tiny numbers and letters stenciled on the bottom.

"It is an actuator," said Li Han. "It moved a piece of the wing that acted as a flap. The material is still attached. You can see it's a metallized glass. Very rare."

Kimko turned it over in his hand.

"How do I know this came from the aircraft?"

Li Han reached for the phone. He paged back through the images, stopping on a dark rectangular blur.

"It is the item on the right," said Li Han, handing the cell phone back. "Do you see?"

Kimko really didn't see, but others would. Even if the Chinaman was a fraud, this whole enterprise was certainly worth talking to Moscow about. It was definitely a ticket out of Africa.

But if he was a fraud, it could backfire.

"One million euros," said Li Han.

Kimko chuckled. "A million euros? For a broken piece of metal?"

Li Han didn't respond.

"I don't think this is worth a million euros," said Kimko. "A million euros would not be appropriate."

Kimko started to hand the phone back. Li Han wouldn't take it.

If it were a UAV, and if Moscow didn't know anything about it, then certainly it would be worth a million euros.

Maybe, maybe not. The best thing to do would be to let someone else make the call. In that case, if it were a fraud, then there would be no blame on him.

"I think one million euros is too much," said Kimko. He sighed, as if making a deep concession. "But if perhaps I could have one of my people inspect it, then we could negotiate seriously. People who know about these things," added Kimko. "I don't. I'm not an expert."

"No one sees it until I'm paid."

"Well that's impossible, then. This could all be a fraud." Kimko started to reach for the door handle, then remembered this was his truck—he shouldn't be the one to leave. They sat for a few moments in silence.

"Maybe an inspection could be arranged," said Li Han finally. "If you made a down payment."

Kimko snorted. "Impossible."

"I will give you something else. You'll pay for that."

Kimko made a face. Now he knew the man was a con artist. Whether it was his truck or not, he was getting out. He reached for the door.

"Here is a CIA bug," said Li Han, reaching into his pocket.

Once more Kimko's lungs seized. Li Han was worse than a con man—he was a plant, an agent.

"It's inactive," said Li Han, opening his palm. A small insect was inside. "Take it and I'll show you."

Unsure what else to do, Kimko reached for the insect. He picked it up gingerly. It felt real.

Men would be shooting at them any moment, he was sure. This was all a setup.

Li Han reached into his pocket again. He took out a small radiolike device and flipped it on.

"See?" said Li Han. "No radio signal. You see my needle. The bug doesn't work, but you can examine it and see how they do it."

"I'm sure we have millions of these," said Kimko.

"One thousand euros. Now."

"We have many of these," said Kimko. He didn't trust Li Han's detector, and in fact wasn't even sure the bug was a listening device. It looked more like a plastic model, a gag toy. He started to give it back.

"A thousand euros as a down payment." Li Han

pushed his hand away gently. "The device as a token of my sincerity."

"I will give you five hundred euros right now," said Kimko, deciding now it was the only way to get rid of him.

Li Han folded his arms and looked down at the floor of the truck. Kimko wondered if he should go higher. No, he decided—he shouldn't have made an offer at all.

"Five hundred will do for now," said Li Han. "There is a three-story building near the railroad tracks that once belonged to the stationmaster. You will meet me there at dusk tomorrow if you intend to purchase the aircraft. It won't be there," added Li Han, "so you needn't try any tricks. Come alone. I will take you to it, and you will transfer the money to an account. Once the transaction is complete, we can all be on our way. Come alone. Alone."

"Understood," said Kimko.

"THEY'RE LEAVING," SAID NURI, WATCHING THE VIDEO feed on the MY-PID slate. It was coming directly from the Global Hawk; the Tigershark was still a few minutes away, and MY-PID itself still wasn't online. "The car with Li Han seems to be going back to the house," said Nuri. "If it does, then we should follow the second truck, see where it goes."

"I want Mao Man," said Melissa, leaning forward in the backseat.

"We'll get him," said Nuri. "Relax."

Nuri zoomed the screen out as the vehicles

continued to drive. He couldn't watch both for very much longer.

"Li Han has to take priority," insisted Melissa.

"He's your problem," said Nuri. "We're here for the UAV. Danny, we have to choose. I say we go with the truck. We can relocate Li Han easily."

"You could say the same about the truck," answered Melissa.

"Nuri's calling the shots on the surveillance," said Danny. He put the Mercedes into gear. "Which way am I heading?"

As soon as Li Han was out of sight, Kimko told the driver to get on the road and go south. He pulled his ruck from the floor of the truck and reached inside, taking out a small fabric pencil case. He unfolded a metallic instrument from inside a small cocoon of bubble wrap, pushed its two halves together and turned. An LED at the end blinked red twice, then turned green. This was a bug detector, simpler in operation than Li Han's, though more sophisticated, or so Kimko thought. It detected all manner of radiation; if the mosquito was a listening device, it would find out.

The light stayed green, even when he put the other end of the stick against it. He began to speak.

"I wonder if this is really a listening device," he said in Russian. "I doubt it. He has taken my euros and I will never see him again."

The light remained green.

Probably it was phony. But then, so was the money he had handed over.

Kimko replaced the detector carefully back in its little nest. He took his satellite phone from the ruck and tapped the numbers; it was time to talk to Moscow.

TURK EASED OFF THE THROTTLE AS THE TIGERSHARK reached the ellipse marked out on his helmet display's sitrep map. The map gave the pilot a God's eye view of the world, with his target area in the center screen; he switched to the more traditional American view, showing the plane in the center, then keyed his mike to talk to Danny.

"Tigershark to Whiplash Ground—Colonel, I'm on station. You should have an affirmative hookup."

"Roger that, Tigershark. Ground acknowledges. Starting the handshake."

Turk smirked at the terminology. *Handshake.* All the damn radios did was squawk at each other.

HAVING FIVE HUNDRED EUROS IN HIS HAND MADE LI HAN feel almost insanely giddy. It was foolish and stupid—he had far larger sums than that in any number of his accounts, and several thousand in American dollars stuffed into his boots. Yet he couldn't help the intoxication. He'd been raised in a dirt-poor village in northwestern China; when he was growing up, the family pig ate better than he did. All the years since had done nothing to erase the memories of abject poverty and worthlessness, and only magnified the importance of money. Of cash. Of bills that passed smoothly between your fingers.

He folded them carefully, then put them in his pocket. Back to the problem at hand.

"Why did the program execute once it was in the laptop?" Li Han said aloud. He spoke in his native Chinese, trying to work out his problem with an invisible colleague. "And what does it think it's doing? Is it trying to go after me? I wonder what sort of intelligence it has. Because clearly it has intelligence."

"What are you saying?" asked Amara in English.

"Something you wouldn't understand," snapped Li Han in Chinese.

The young man didn't understand what he said, but the harsh tone came through, and his face turned to a frown. Li Han felt a twinge of guilt—Amara wasn't a bad kid. He should be kinder to him, especially since he thought he would be useful.

"I am exploring a problem," Li Han said in English, trying to make his voice kinder. "The aircraft's brain is a computer. When it interfaced with my computer, it acted as if it were alive. It started to operate. Do you know what that means?"

"The program began to work on its own."

"Exactly. Which is not something it should do."

He isn't completely ignorant, Li Han thought. He might be taught; he could be useful.

"I don't entirely understand it yet," continued Li Han. "I think it is some sort of control unit that is plugged into the brain and then programmed. But the programming is very involved. My face and a file of information about me was there."

"Why?"

"Good question. I'm not sure. It is clear I was its target. These weren't surveillance images. So was the aircraft programmed to watch me? I think so. How did they do it? How is this connected to the rest of the software, the part I haven't seen? I'm not sure. That is what I am pondering."

"Why is all this useful?"

Li Han couldn't help but smirk. Amara was not stupid, but there were clear limits.

"Let's say we want to watch someone," he explained. "Let's say we want to target the President of the United States for surveillance. If we gave the computer all of the information, could it do it? That is my question—because the information about me is in the command deck, the portion of the program that is supplying controls. Why would it be there otherwise? I don't know," added Li Han. "We must do more work."

"You are going to sell it to the Russian."

"Not that part," said Li Han. "Not the brain. The brain is self-contained."

Li Han explained how he had pulled it from the aircraft.

"I believe it could work in another aircraft," he added. "I'm not entirely sure. I need to experiment more."

They took a left turn off the main highway moving west, away from the city.

"Where are you going?" Li Han asked.

"You told me you wanted a new place."

"True," said Li Han.

Suddenly, a host of suspicions fell on him. Paranoia surged back. Where was Amara taking him?

Li Han put his hand down casually, letting it rest on his holster.

They drove about two miles, climbing up a low hill. Li Han's suspicions grew, then eased. If Amara had wanted to kill him, any place would do. They had already passed plenty of abandoned fields.

"It's just ahead," said Amara. "Twill will be there. If he waves, then we must go on by. You should duck then," he added. "It will be a signal that he is being watched."

"Why so far away?" asked Li Han.

"We expect fighting in the city. We don't need to be caught."

Li Han stared out the window. It was reasonable, but he wasn't sure—it still might be a trick.

Too elaborate for Amara. But he was being more assertive than before—far more assertive.

There was a small building near the road on the left. Twill, the thin man with the close-cropped hair, stepped out from the shadow.

He didn't wave.

"There he is," said Li Han.

Amara slowed, then pulled off the side of the road, stopping just in front of Twill. Li Han got out. There were two pickups parked near the building. Even in the dark it looked like a good burst of wind would knock it down.

"This isn't much of a building," he said, starting toward it.

"Too bad if you don't like it," said Amara, suddenly next to him.

Li Han, surprised by the sharp tone, started to turn.

Amara's first bullet caught him in the side of the head. By the time the second struck his forehead, he was already dead.

TARGETS UNKNOWN

———

1

Duka

DANNY FREAH TURNED ONTO THE HARD-PACKED ROAD, gingerly pressing his foot against the Mercedes accelerator. Their subject was only two hundred yards ahead.

"I have a full connection," said Nuri. "Everything's being routed back through MY-PID. All right. He's heading east . . . Whoa, slow down. He turned off onto a dirt road. I think there may be a lookout about fifty yards away. MY-PID, analyze and identify this position."

Danny concentrated on the road as Nuri pointed at the screen and talked to the computer.

"One of the bugs I set isn't in the proper location," Nuri told him. "It's in the truck we're following."

"What?"

"Yeah. I'm listening to a conversation in Russian."

"Russian?"

"*Shhh.*"

*   *   *

MY-PID PROVIDED THE TRANSLATION ON THE FLY, almost instantaneously. It heard not only the caller in the car, but was able to amplify the conversation on the other side.

> Voice 1 (in car): . . . I don't know exactly what it is. I have photos on a camera. I will upload them when I am at a safe location.
>
> Voice 2 (phone): How did he obtain it?
>
> Voice 1: It crashed somehow. I don't know. I can find out, if it's important.
>
> Voice 2: The price is ridiculous.
>
> Voice 1: I told him.
>
> Voice 2: These Africans think any scrap of metal is valuable.
>
> Voice 1: I need to meet him at dusk at the old stationmaster house. If you're not interested—
>
> Voice 2: We'll send someone. Who is he?
>
> Voice 1: He's Chinese. He's connected with the Brotherhood.
>
> Voice 2: Ah—I think I know who it is. Call at the usual time.

Voice 1 hung up. The man in the truck said nothing else.

"MY-PID, can you ID either of the voices?" asked Nuri.

"Call was made to a phone registered to the Stalingrad Export Company," reported the Voice. "Caller voice patterns are being compared to Russian SVG and GRU known agents."

"Good."

"Caller 1 is identified as Milos Kimko, known operative with Sluzhba Vneshney Razvedki," said the Voice a few seconds later. "He was posted to Africa 03-02-13. Dossier available."

"Hold it for me," said Nuri. "Where's the old stationmaster house?"

"Insufficient data."

"Is there a stationmaster house in Duka?"

"Two possible buildings identified," responded the computer. "Both are near the railroad tracks."

"Place them under constant surveillance."

"Are you talking to a person, or a machine?" asked Melissa.

"Nuri can fill in the details later," said Danny. "Right now we have to decide which way we're going. The turnoff the truck took is ahead."

"Don't turn," said Nuri. "Keep going. We'll have to head back to follow Li Han. This guy doesn't have the UAV. Not yet, anyway."

2

Duka

THEY DUMPED LI HAN'S BODY INSIDE THE BUILDING, raked over the dirt where he had fallen, then climbed into the trucks.

Amara started away. He drove quickly, exactly

as he had rehearsed, moving toward the main road south. It was dark but he didn't use his headlights. The fewer people who noticed him, the better.

He'd driven nearly halfway to the road when his hands began to sweat. Until now he'd been completely calm, unmoved by what he had done. Li Han was nothing to him, an infidel and worse. Ali Aba Muhammad had told him to kill Li Han and take the item back; obeying was as easy as breathing.

But his body began to rebel. The sweat was the first sign. It wouldn't stop. He wiped his right hand on his pants, put it back on the wheel, then wiped his left. The sweat kept coming.

"There is no God but the true God," he said to himself, beginning to pray.

The prayer calmed him, but only slightly.

By rights, he should hate Li Han and feel no remorse. His killing of Swal—a man whom Amara had, admittedly, despised—showed that he was a sinner and infidel of the worst sort. But for some reason Amara remained disturbed.

Li Han was not the first man he had killed. But the others had been during battles, and in truth Amara was not even sure that any of them had died—they had been far away, and he'd been either under cover or running. Nor had he known them. Here, Li Han had been right next to him. They had spent several weeks together. Even though Amara suspected from the beginning that he would kill him, even though he had quickly grown to despise the foreigner with his haughty manner, still, Amara had been close enough to him to actually see his face, his eyes, as he died bare inches away.

He had to die. It was God's will, as the Mentor had explained, and he was preparing to betray the Brotherhood to the Russians. But with all that, with all these good reasons, still Amara felt a tinge of regret and even fear. Twice as he drove he thought Li Han was in the truck beside him; once he even swore for a moment that he was there just before he glanced over.

The seat of course was empty, and he knew for a fact that Li Han was back in the building. But the feeling lingered.

When he reached the highway, Amara flipped the lights on and stepped on the gas, determined to put as many miles between himself and Duka as quickly possible.

He rolled down the windows. The wind rushed into the cab. It filled his lungs with energy and braced his cheeks. He would be in the south very soon. Li Han's ghost would be left far behind.

3

Duka

"VEHICLE LOCATED," MY-PID DECLARED.

"Display on a grid map," commanded Nuri.

The system popped the image onto the control

unit screen. Li Han's pickup was parked outside of a ramshackle house on the western outskirts of town.

"Can you locate the subject?" Nuri asked.

"Subject appears to be in building," answered the computer, interpreting the infrared heat signature inside. "Certainty is eighty-four percent."

"How many people are with him?"

"Subject appears alone. No activity."

"Looks like Li Han found a new place to stay," Nuri told Danny. "He's sleeping in a little shack outside the city."

"Why'd he change location?" Danny asked.

"Don't know." Nuri magnified the image, but it was impossible to see inside the building; the thick roof filtered and dulled the IR signal. "When's the rest of our gear getting here?"

"The MC-17 should check in any minute," said Danny. "I'll arrange a drop near here."

"Good."

Nuri told MY-PID to examine the house where Li Han had been earlier. Someone was there as well. The computer declared that there was too little data to positively rule out that Li Han wasn't in *that* building; only so much could be determined from studying heat signatures. They would have to watch both buildings.

Meanwhile, the bug tracked the Russian as he headed to a ramshackle compound southeast of the city, wedged into a trio of craggy hills. This was the Almighty First Liberation's "fortress." MY-PID counted twenty-eight man-sized heat signatures within the various buildings, accounting for the bulk of the rebel force. They were in defensive positions spread out in the rocks, guarding the approaches; clearly they expected retaliation for their leader's attack.

"Why are the Russians working with these guys?" Danny asked. "I thought Russia wasn't involved in Africa at all."

"It's something new," answered Melissa from the back.

Nuri tried to keep his teeth from grinding. She was right, but he still resented her, and something compelled him to answer everything she said. "They try to come in every so often."

"You know this guy?" Danny asked.

"Never even heard of him," said Nuri. "According to his dossier, he's been around awhile, was in Iran a while back. This may have been a demotion, or maybe he's interested in something special. Hard to tell."

"The computer keeps track of all this?" asked Melissa.

When Nuri didn't answer, Danny did, which only annoyed Nuri more.

"The system is like having a thousand assistants at your beck and call," said Danny. "It's a serious force multiplier."

"It's just a computer," said Nuri. His tone was so harsh that Danny glanced at him.

"Can I interface with it?" asked Melissa.

"You have to be trained," snapped Nuri.

"It responds to certain voices," said Danny, still staring at Nuri. "But we all benefit."

"I'm authorized to terminate Li Han," said

Melissa. "Once we're sure we have the UAV, we take him down. I don't think we should wait," she added, sliding forward and leaning near Danny. "I think we should get it now."

"We tried that already, and we missed," said Nuri quickly. "We're not positive where the UAV is. We can't afford another miss."

"Can't your device figure out where the plane is?"

Melissa said it innocently, but Nuri took it as a challenge.

"It's not omniscient," he said. "It needs data. The area wasn't under surveillance when it went down. We don't have our sensors in place."

"I'm for moving sooner rather than later," said Danny.

"You think we can take over the whole city?" asked Nuri.

"No, but we will have reinforcements soon," answered Danny. "Enough to deal with the people here. The problem is, if it's not here, we're losing a lot of time."

"If it's not here, where would it be?" said Nuri. "Anywhere in Africa."

"True," said Melissa.

God, thought Nuri, I must be wrong.

WITH THE CONNECTION TO MY-PID NOW PERMANENTLY supplied by the satellite, the Tigershark was no longer needed. Danny released Turk to fly home, which he reluctantly agreed to do.

Meanwhile, Danny located a spot for the Whiplash MC-17 to make an equipment drop. It was an open field about four miles northwest of the city. With the Osprey holding south in case the rest of the team was needed, Danny decided they would go up and meet the newcomers and their supplies, setting up a temporary base there. Driving or even flying back and forth to Ethiopia would take too much time. And ideally, he wanted to close the operation down quickly—as soon as he had a definitive word on where Raven was.

They got to the drop zone five minutes ahead of the aircraft. With Nuri monitoring what was going on in Duka through MY-PID, Danny got out and placed some chem markers in the field. The markers were small sticks that emitted a light visible only through infrared gear. Technically, the Whiplash MC-17 could make the drop without the lights, but Danny liked the extra measure of safety.

Melissa got out of the car with him, walking along as he set out the lights.

"I owe you an apology," she said after he had finished.

"What's that?" he asked, surprised.

"I was—I felt that you guys were barging in and trying to take over. I didn't realize how professional you were, and I acted . . . territorial. Bitchy."

"Forget it."

"I am sorry." She touched his hand and smiled. "I was afraid—this is my operation. You're trained to not let people in."

"Sure," said Danny.

Her hand lingered for just a moment.

"There were a lot of sick people in that clinic,"

added Melissa. "They're pretty desperate for help here."

"Yeah, I know. We were in a village to the west a few months ago, a couple of villages. It's a shame. They're so poor."

"Do you think—being black . . ."

"Like what? It could have been us?"

"Something like that."

"No. Not at all."

They were silent a moment. The wind picked up slightly, softly howling in the distance.

The MC-17.

"Plane's coming in," said Danny. "Come stand over here."

He led her back away from the target area. The Whiplash support aircraft was a specially modified Cargomaster II. Among other things, its engines had been muffled so they were barely audible even at a few thousand feet. Like the extremely capable stock aircraft, the Whiplash version could land on a small, rough airfield; in fact, it probably could have landed in this field, though taking off might have been problematic. There was no need to risk it.

The plane came in low and slow, dropping a trio of large containers on skids within a few meters of each other. The large crates bounced on air cushions attached to the bottom of the skids, giant air bags that inflated just before impact.

As the airplane cleared upward, three smaller figures appeared overhead—Hera Scokas and two Whiplash trainees, Chris "Shorty" Bradley and Toma "Babyboy" Parker. Hera hit her mark dead on, walking right up to the chem marker in the bull's-eye. The two men came in a bit to her left, blown slightly off course though still well within specs.

"Colonel, good to see you," said Hera. The short, curly-haired Greek-American gave Danny a wave, then immediately stowed her parachute and checked on the two newcomers who'd jumped with her.

A variety of Whiplash equipment had been packed onto the three crates, including tents, two motorbikes, surveillance gear, and almost a ton of ammunition. There was also a solar panel and battery array to provide the temporary camp with electricity, along with point defenses that included ballistic panels—high-tech versions of claymore antipersonnel mines—and a surveillance radar held aloft by a blimp. The body of the blimp was covered with an adaptive LED material that allowed it to blend in with the sky, making it virtually invisible to the naked eye.

As soon as they were unpacked, Danny launched two small UAVs to supplement the Global Hawk's coverage. Barely the size of a laptop computer, the robot aircraft looked like miniature versions of Cessna Skymasters, with twin booms to the tail and engines fore and aft of the cockpit. They flew neither fast nor high—sixty knots at 5,000 feet was roughly their top speed and ceiling, respectively. But their undersides were covered with LED arrays similar to those on the blimp, making them difficult to pick out even in daylight. And the top surfaces were covered with solar cells that supplemented and recharged the batteries powering their engines. As long as the day was sunny, MY-PID could manage the power consumption so the aircraft would fly 24/7.

Melissa pitched in, quietly working beside the others. She'd changed somehow, Danny realized, or maybe fatigue had just worn off the sharp edges.

Whatever the reason, she was actually pleasant to work with now. She volunteered to brief Hera and the others on the overall situation, and even helped set the posts for the command tent.

Maybe, thought Danny, they could work with her after all.

NURI DIDN'T UNDERSTAND THE SIGNIFICANCE OF WHAT was going on at first; he was too busy following MY-PID's brief on the Russian and his connections in Moscow. But the computer did.

"Large force gathering near the town center," the Voice told him as he paged through Kimko's file on the mobile laptop he'd hooked into the system. "Armed."

Nuri immediately brought up the image on the computer. Then he got out of the truck and went to find Danny.

The colonel was bent over a tent stake, hammering it in with a large mallet. Some technologies were impossible to improve on.

"Meurtre Musique is going to war," Nuri told him. "Two dozen of them, trucks, machine guns, grenade launchers. They're getting together near the town square."

"Do they have night vision gear?"

"Probably not."

"They're going to have a hard time hitting the hills where Sudan First is holed up," predicted Danny. "They'll spot them coming, even in the dark."

"That's not where they're going," said Nuri, watching the screen.

The trucks swung south down the main street, then formed two columns turning up different roads to the east. After they'd gone about three blocks, yellow and white flashes began appearing on the screen.

"Is something wrong with the image?" asked Melissa, peering at it over Danny's shoulder.

"They're shooting up houses," said Nuri flatly. "They're getting their revenge."

MELISSA FELT HER STOMACH SINK AS THE GUNFIRE continued on the screen. The trucks moved slowly through the streets, going no faster than four or five miles an hour, raking everything they passed with gunfire. In the western part of the city, a good portion of the bullets might be absorbed or deflected by the mud bricks of the buildings. But here the buildings were made mostly of discarded wood. There would be little to stop them.

Suddenly, something caught fire at the top of the screen. Danny poked his finger at it, increasing in magnification. A cottage had caught fire. The flames quickly formed a crown as they spread around the outer walls.

Something bolted out from the wall of fire. A finger of flame trailed it, even as it threw itself on the ground.

A person.

Two people, one big, one small.

A mother and child, Melissa imagined.

"This is terrible," she said. "We have to do something."

"Like what?" snapped Nuri.

"Colonel, we can't just let them shoot each other up," she told Danny. "They're killing innocent children."

"It's not our business," said Nuri. "Didn't you say something yesterday about not wanting these people to get in your way? You weren't worried about collateral damage."

"This is different."

"There's nothing really we can do," said Danny. "We have our mission. And we don't have enough force to stop this."

Melissa knew he was right—and she had said that, and felt it, and did feel it.

But these were real people getting killed.

"Sudan First will retaliate," said Nuri. "Once they hear what's up. Both sides go after soft targets first. They're basically cowards."

Melissa thought of the clinic. It was an obvious and easy target.

She went over to the tent where they were making coffee, remembering the women and their children there, the people she'd treated before the shooting victims came. Her mind conflated the two, imagining the children shot up, the women bleeding from bullet wounds.

She had to do something.

DANNY WATCHED AS THE PICKUPS RETREATED BACK toward the residential area of the city where the Meurtre Musique supporters lived. Their grass huts would be easy targets for retaliation. Didn't they realize that?

Most likely they did. But just as likely they felt they had to avenge the earlier shooting, and would have to fight it out.

It was senseless, but there was nothing he could do about it. The question was whether it would interfere with his mission—random bullets flying in the air weren't going to make things easier.

On the other hand, all the gunfire would make a perfect cover for a raid. No one would notice if he went in.

"Thirsty, Colonel?" asked Melissa, walking over to him with a cup of coffee.

"Sure."

She gave him the cup. "How do you take it?"

"Black's good."

"I want to borrow one of the motorcycles to get into town," she said, sipping her own. "I need to be there in an hour, just at dawn."

"What?"

"The clinic," she told him. "I need to get back."

"It's not a good idea to go there," said Danny. "There's going to be a lot more fighting."

"I think that's why I should go."

Danny stared at her. She was like his wife more than just physically; he couldn't quite figure out what she was thinking.

"We put you in as a spy yesterday," he told her. "That made sense. Now, though, we have all our gear here—we don't need someone on the ground."

"You'd be amazed at what these people tell me."

"Like what?" said Nuri skeptically.

"I found that first house."

"So did we," answered Nuri.

"I'm going, Colonel," she said, turning back to him. "I'll go if I have to walk."

"Let's talk about it in private," said Danny.

THE NIGHT SUDDENLY SEEMED INCREDIBLY COLD, AND Melissa wished she'd taken a sweater. She and Danny walked away from the tent area, moving along the hardscrabble field. The remains of a stone foundation sat overgrown by weeds; with a little imagination, Melissa could picture a prosperous native farm.

"You can't go back in there," said Danny as they walked. "You'll be a target."

"No more than anyone else."

"I can't let you. It doesn't serve any purpose."

"It does serve a purpose." She felt she owed Bloom, who had helped her, and now would be a target. But at the same time, Melissa also thought that being there might allow her to get Li Han— he might come right to her. But she hesitated telling Danny all of this—her emotions and her sense of duty were all confused. "I can gather intelligence. I can find out what's really going on."

"We can drop bugs in there. There's no need to risk your life."

"Eavesdropping gear just tells you what people say. It can't steer conversations. It can't tease information out."

"You want to go in to help these people," said Danny.

"I'll help them because it will help me. But that's not why I'm going in. Li Han may come to them. I'll be able to get him."

"That's not going to happen," said Danny.

"Whatever. I'm not going to argue. You may be in charge of Whiplash, but you're not in charge of me."

"You need sleep," he told her, staring at her face. "You're tired."

He had strong eyes. He was a strong, powerfully built man. Yet there was care and concern in his voice. Softness.

"I want to get Bloom out," she told him. "She helped me. She was an MI6 agent. Now she'll be in danger."

"She's a spy?"

"No. She was. She got out and became a nurse. But she helped me find the house. With what's going on, she'll be targeted."

"I don't think so."

"Honestly, Colonel, there is nothing you can do."

Danny stared at her for a few moments more. Melissa suddenly felt weak—it must be fatigue, she thought, or perhaps hunger: it had been a while since she'd eaten.

Danny clamped his lips tight together.

"I can't stop you," he said finally.

"No, you can't."

"First sign of trouble, you get the hell out of there."

"No shit," she said.

4

CIA Headquarters

JONATHON REID STEPPED INTO THE ELEVATOR IN THE lobby of the CIA headquarters building and pressed the button to go up to his office. He hadn't had much sleep—after returning from the White House he'd lain in bed, eyes open, for hours.

A parade of past problems marched across the ceiling. Reid had participated in a number of operations and projects during his career that could be questioned on any number of grounds. He could think of two that were frankly illegal. In both cases he was operating under the explicit orders of the director of covert operations. And in both cases he felt that what he did was completely justified by the circumstances, that not only America but the world benefited by what he did.

But not everyone might agree. He imagined

that if he were the case officer here, if he were on the ground in Africa, or even further up in the chain of command, he would feel completely justified by the goal. Li Han was a clear danger to America. He was not a "mere" sociopath or killer. He possessed technical skills difficult for terrorists to obtain, and he was willing to share that skill with them for what in real terms was a ridiculously cheap price. He was, in a military sense, a force multiplier, someone who could influence the outcome of a battle and even a war.

The U.S. and the world were in a war, a seemingly endless conflict against evil. Li Han clearly deserved to die.

Given that, was the process leading to that end result important?

Under most circumstances he would have answered no. As far as he was concerned, dotting a few legal i's and crossing the bureaucratic t's was just bs, busy work for lawyers and administrators who justified their federal sinecures by pontificating and procrastinating while the real work and risks were going on thousands of miles away.

But Raven required a more nuanced view. Li Han deserved to die, but should the Agency be the one making that judgment?

And should they alone decide what to risk in carrying out that judgment?

Raven wasn't a simple weapon, like a new sniper rifle or even a spy plane. It was more along the lines of the atomic bomb: once perfected, it was a game changer with implications far, far beyond its use to take down a single target.

It was Lee Harvey Oswald all over again.

Of course, he was assuming the President didn't know. Perhaps she *did* know. Perhaps she had played him for a fool.

Or simply felt that he didn't need to know.

Maybe his problem was simply jealousy. Maybe the real story was this: Jonathon Reid couldn't stand being out of the loop. Even now, far removed from his days as a cowboy field officer, he went off half cocked and red-assed, laying waste to all before him.

He knew it wasn't true. And yet some might see it that way.

Inside his office, Reid sat down and looked at Danny Freah's most recent updates on the Whiplash operation. The involvement of the Russian agent alarmed him. He quickly brought himself up to date on the Russians and their various operations in Africa. It wasn't clear whether they were trying to make a new push onto the continent, perhaps to be part of future mineral extraction operations, or were simply on the lookout for new clients for their weapons. Either theory made sense, and in any event neither changed the situation.

It was inconceivable that they had caught wind of Raven and knew it would be tested there.

Or was it?

Even though it appeared that Whiplash had things under control at the moment, Edmund had to be informed about the Russian. Reid took a quick run through the overnight briefing, making sure there wasn't anything major he had to be aware of, then called up to the director's office.

"Mr. Reid, the director is out of communication at the moment," said his secretary. "I'll put you through to Mr. Conklin."

Out of communication? That was a new one on Reid.

Conklin came on the line. He was Edmund's chief of staff, an assistant. Reid rarely if ever dealt with him.

So it begins, he thought.

"Jonathon, what can we do for you?" asked Conklin.

"I need to speak to Herman."

"I'm afraid that's going to be difficult to arrange for a while."

"This is critical."

"I'm sure. But—"

"Why would it be difficult to arrange? Is Herman all right?"

"The director is fine."

"It has to do with Raven," said Reid, unsure whether Conklin would even know what that was.

Apparently he did. "You should talk to Reg on that."

Reginald Harker: Special Deputy for Covert Operations, head of the Raven project, probably the idiot behind the whole screwed-up situation in the first place.

Not the person Reid wanted to speak to.

"This is really a matter for Herman," he said. "It's critically important."

"Reg is the person to speak to," said Conklin.

"I'll do that. But inform Herman as well."

"I will pass a note to Mr. Edmund at my earliest opportunity."

Reid hung up. He started to dial Edmund's private phone, then stopped.

How paranoid should he be? The system would record the fact that he had made the call; the internal lines could also be monitored.

Should he worry about that?

What if it wasn't a coincidence that the Russians were there? What if someone inside had tipped them off?

But who?

Reid debated with himself, but in the end decided that paranoia had its uses. He left his office, left the campus, and drove to a mall a few miles away. After making sure he wasn't being followed, he took a lap through the building, found a drugstore and bought a prepaid phone. Then he walked through a large sporting goods store to the far entrance to a parking lot. He went outside and after once again making sure he wasn't being followed, used the phone to call Edmund's private phone.

He went straight to voice mail.

"We need to talk ASAP," he said.

Reid hung up, then made a call with his encrypted satellite phone. When he got voice mail again, he hung up. After sending a text through the secure system—it took forever to hunt and peck the letters—he set the ringers on both his phone and the cell to maximum and went back inside. He pretended to be interested in the tread-mills and T-shirts before leaving.

On the way back to the campus, he called Bre-anna, this time with an encrypted phone. She an-swered on the second ring.

"Have you seen the overnight update?" he asked.

"Yes, of course."

"We can't let the Russians get ahold of this. If a handoff is made to the Russian, they must take him out," said Reid. "There should be no ques-tion."

"All right. We'll need a finding."

"I'll take care of that," said Reid.

"Did you speak to the President?" Breanna asked.

"We had a brief session," he said.

"Anything I should know?"

Reid spent a long moment thinking of what to say before answering.

"There's nothing that came out that affects us directly," he said finally.

"Jonathon—is there anything else I can do? Should I come back to D.C.?"

"No, I think I have it under control," he said finally. "Stay in touch. Keep your phone handy."

"You sound tired," she added just before he was about to hang up.

"Well, I guess I am," he told her before ending the call.

"YOU'RE TRYING TO TRUMP THIS UP INTO SOMETHING," charged Harker when Reid met him in his office.

He picked up the coffee cup on his desk, brought it about halfway to his mouth, then in a sudden fit of anger smacked it onto the desktop, splattering some of the liquid. "You want to create a scandal. There's nothing here, Reid. Nothing."

"I'm not creating a scandal," replied Reid. "I'm simply doing my job."

"Which is what?"

"Getting Raven back. Keeping it from our enemies."

"I know you're angling for the DIA slot," said Harker. "It's not going to work. Everybody can see through the games you're playing."

Reid said nothing. Denying interest in the job—which he had absolutely no intention of taking—would only be interpreted as a lie. In fact, everything he said would be interpreted through Harker's twisted lens. It was pointless to even talk.

"I only came to you because I'm having trouble speaking to Edmund." Reid rose. "And I'm concerned about the Russians."

"Herm doesn't speak to traitors."

Reid stared at Harker. The man's face was beet red.

"This isn't a question of loyalty to the Agency," he said.

"Get out of my office," said Harker.

"Gladly."

5

Duka

MELISSA WATCHED MARIE BLOOM SURVEY THE RECEP-
tion room, her hands on her hips. The clinic director turned and looked at her with a worried
expression.

"Ordinarily, this room would be full," she said.
"But maybe we should count our blessings."

"Yes," said Melissa softly.

They had seen only a small handful of patients
since opening at dawn. Now it was past noon.

Bloom sat down on the couch that faced the
door. Her face was drawn. "Did you bring these
troubles?"

"No," said Melissa.

"Did the man you're hunting for?"

"I don't know. I don't think so."

"Do you know what's going on?"

"One of the people from Sudan First fired on
the leader of Meurtre Musique."

"I know that. What's *really* going on?"

"That's all that I know."

"The problem with you people . . ."

Bloom let her voice trail off, not bothering to
finish the sentence.

"I'll leave if you want," said Melissa finally. "I'm
only here to help. That's the only reason."

"How could I ever believe that?"

The door opened. Melissa felt her body jerk-
ing back, automatically preparing to be on the
defensive.

A pregnant woman came into the room. In her arms she had a two-year-old boy. The child was listless, clearly sick.

Melissa looked over at Bloom. She had a shell-shocked expression.

"I'll take this one," said Melissa, going over to the woman.

She held out her arms. The mother glanced at Bloom, but gave the child over willingly. She said something in African, explaining what was wrong. Melissa could tell just by holding the baby that he had a fever.

"Come," said Melissa in English. "Inside."

The woman followed her into the far examining room.

It was an infection, some sort of virus or bacteria causing the fever. Beyond that it was impossible to diagnose, at least for her. The fever was 102.4; high, yet not so high that it would be alarming in a child. There were no rashes or other outward signs of the problem; no injuries, no insect bites. The child seemed to be breathing normally. Its pulse was a little slow, but even that was not particularly abnormal, especially given its overall listless state.

Melissa poured some bottled water on a cloth and rubbed the baby down.

"To cool him off a little," she said, first in English, then in slower and less steady Arabic. She got a dropper and carefully measured out a dose of acetaminophen. Gesturing, she made the woman understand that she was to give it to the baby. The mother hesitated, then finally agreed.

As she handed over the medicine, Melissa realized that the woman was running a fever herself. She took her thermometer—an electronic one that got its readings from the inner ear—and held it in place while the woman struggled to get her baby to swallow the medicine.

Her fever was 102.8. More serious in an adult.

And what about her baby? The woman looked to be at least eight months pregnant, if not nine.

Melissa took the stethoscope.

"I need to hear your heart," she said.

She gestured for the woman to take off her long, flowing top. Unsure whether she truly didn't understand or just didn't want to be examined, Melissa told her that she was concerned about the baby.

"You have a fever," she said.

The woman said something and gestured toward the young child on the examining table, who was looking at them with big eyes.

Realizing she was getting nowhere, Melissa went out to the waiting area to get Bloom to help.

Bloom had nodded off. Melissa bent down to wake her. As she did, the pregnant woman came out from the back, carrying her child.

"Wait," said Melissa, trying to stop her. "Wait!"

"What's wrong?" asked Bloom, jumping up from the couch.

"She's sick. Her baby may have a fever, too."

Bloom spoke in rapid Arabic. The woman answered in her own tongue. Whatever it was she said, Bloom frowned. She answered, speaking less surely. The woman waved her hand and went to the door.

"You have to tell her," said Melissa.

"I can't stop her," said Bloom as the woman left.

"We could at least give her acetaminophen, something for the fever."

"She won't take it," said Bloom. "It'd be a waste."

"But—"

"If we push too hard, they won't come back. They have to deal with us at their own pace."

"If she's sick, the baby may die."

"We can't force her to get better."

Melissa wanted to argue more—they could have at least made a better argument, at least explained what the dangers were. But her satellite phone rang.

"I—I have to take this," she said, starting for the door. "I'll be right back."

Thinking it was Danny calling to tell her what was going on, she hit the Talk button as she went through the door.

"Yes?" she asked.

"Melissa, what's the situation?" asked Reginald Harker.

"Hold on, Reg. Let me get somewhere I can talk."

She walked outside, continuing a little way down the road. The harsh sun hurt her eyes. There was no one outside, and the nearby houses, which yesterday had been teeming with people, seemed deserted. Otherwise, the day seemed perfect, no sign of conflict anywhere.

"I'm here," she told Harker.

"What's going on with Mao Man?" he asked.

"We have him tracked to a house on the north-eastern side of town."

"What about the UAV?"

"We think it's nearby."

"Think?"

"We're not entirely sure." His abrupt tone pissed her off. Try doing this yourself, she thought.

"When will you be sure?"

"I don't know. There's a Russian who's trying to buy it—"

"Do *not* let the Russian get it."

"No shit."

"Mao Man has to be terminated. Take down the Russian, too. Take down the whole damn village—what the hell are you waiting for?"

"Reg—"

"I'm serious, Melissa. Why do you think I sent you there? What the hell did we invest in your training for?"

"I have no idea," she told him stonily.

"Don't let these Whiplash people run the show. They have their own agenda. Tell them to stop pussyfooting around and get the damn thing done."

"Fuck yourself," she said. But he'd already hung up.

Melissa pushed the phone back into the pocket of her baggy pants. She was so angry she didn't want to go back into the clinic; she needed to walk off some of her emotion. She clenched her hands into fists and began to walk.

She'd gone only fifty yards or so when she heard

trucks in the distance. The sound was faint, the vehicles far off, but instinctively she knew it was trouble.

6

Washington, D.C.

ZEN SAT IN THE HOSPITAL WAITING AREA, TAPPING HIS fingers against the arms of his wheelchair. Not since he ran for the Senate had he felt such a combination of anticipation and anxiety. Not that he'd cared about the outcome—he would have been just as content retiring from politics as a two-term congressman and getting a job in the private sector. In some ways he'd have been happier, since few jobs had such a demand on anyone's time.

The door opened. Dr. Esrang walked in, alone.

"Doc, how are we doin'?" asked Zen.

"Hard to say," said Esrang. "Brain activity is normal. For him. Physically, no problems. Mood—well, that's always the question, isn't it?"

"Once around the block and back inside," said Zen.

"You're not actually—"

"Figure of speech, Doc," said Zen.

"Yes, of course. All right. We're ready."

"I think it's going to work," said Zen.

Esrang started for the door, then stopped. "Jeff, let me say something, if you don't mind."

"Shoot."

"There may be setbacks."

"I understand."

"If you're serious, we have to keep at it. If this doesn't go well, then we try something else. All right?"

"Absolutely," said Zen.

"We keep at it." Esrang went in then. Pep talks were out of character for the doctor; maybe it was a good omen.

Stoner emerged a few minutes later, flanked by a female nurse who was nearly as big and broad-shouldered as the two male attendants/body-guards waiting for him. Esrang trailed them, a concerned expression on his face.

Just a damn walk in the sunshine, Zen thought. But it was the first time Stoner would be allowed into the unfenced public area outside.

A baby step, but an important one.

"Hey, Mark," said Zen. "I was thinking we'd get outside a bit today and walk around. I'm feeling a bit frisky. What do you say?"

Stoner turned toward him but said nothing. His face was blank.

"Good," said Zen, as enthusiastic as if Stoner had agreed. "Let's go."

He began wheeling toward the exit. Stoner and the nurse followed. Dr. Esrang stayed back.

"Did you catch the game last night?" Zen asked. "Nationals took the Mets with a homer in the bottom of the ninth."

"Good."

It wasn't much of a response, but Zen felt vindicated. He rolled slowly down the corridor, pacing himself just ahead of his companion. Jason Black, his aide, was standing there waiting. Jason pushed open the door and held it as the small entourage exited the building. Zen took the lead, rolling along the cement path toward a small picnic area.

"Good view, huh?" Zen wheeled to a stop.

"Of garbage cans," said Stoner.

It seemed like a non sequitur, just a random comment. Then Zen realized Stoner was looking at the back of a building some hundred yards away.

"Can you see them?" he asked. "How many?"

"Eighteen."

"What about the flowers?" asked Zen, pointing to the nearby flower bed.

Stoner looked, then turned to him. "Yeah?"

"Bree likes flowers," said Zen, searching for something to say. "Teri, too. My daughter. Teri. You have to meet her."

Stoner didn't reply.

"Good day for baseball," said Zen.

Stoner remained silent. Zen tried to get a conversation going, talking about baseball and football, and even the cute nurse who passed on an adjacent path. Stoner had apparently decided he wasn't going to talk anymore, and said nothing else. After they'd been out for about fifteen minutes, Dr. Esrang came over, looking at his watch.

"I'm afraid it's time for Mr. Stoner's physical therapy," he said loudly. "If that's OK, Senator."

"It's OK with me," said Zen. "Assuming Mark feels like sweating a bit."

Stoner turned toward the building and began walking. Zen wheeled himself forward to catch up with him.

"Maybe we'll take in some baseball, huh?" he asked. "If you're up to it."

Stoner stopped. "Baseball would be good."

"Even if it's the Nats?" joked Zen.

Stoner stared at him.

"Their record is—well, they are in last place," admitted Zen. "So, it may be a tough game to sit through."

"Baseball is good," said Stoner.

"THAT WENT VERY WELL," ESRANG TOLD ZEN AFTER Stoner had returned inside. "Very well."

"You think so?"

"He talked to you. He said a lot more to you than he's said to anyone."

"He said three or four sentences. Then he just shut down."

"It's what he didn't do that's important," said Esrang. "No rage, no attempt to run away. I think he's slowly coming back to his old self."

"Maybe."

"I would say he might be able to go to a ball game, as long you're under escort," said Esrang.

Zen was surprised, but he wasn't about to disagree. "I'll set something up. You coming?"

"Absolutely . . . The Nationals will win, right?"

Zen laughed. He'd started to wheel into the building when he heard Jason Black clearing his throat behind him.

"Excuse me, Doc. We'll find our own way out." Zen turned back to his aide. "What's up?"

"Steph needs to talk to you," said Jason. "Like as soon as you can."

Zen pulled his BlackBerry from his pocket. There were half a dozen text messages, including two from Stephanie Delanie—Steph—his chief legislative aide. The Senate Intelligence Committee had scheduled an emergency session for eleven o'clock—they'd just make it if they left right now.

"Grab the van, Jay," said Zen. "I'll meet you out front."

"What's up?"

"Just the usual Senate bs," said Zen.

7

Southern Sudan

TWICE AMARA CAME TO CHECKPOINTS MANNED BY GOVernment soldiers, and twice he drove through them, slowing then gunning the engine, keeping his head down. He'd learned long ago that most times the soldiers wouldn't risk trying to actually stop a pickup, knowing they faced the worst consequences if they succeeded in killing the driver: whatever band he belonged to would seek vengeance immediately. The Brothers were especially vicious, killing not only the soldiers but any relatives they could find. It was an effective policy.

Besides, the soldiers were more interested in bribes than checking for contraband. Their army salary, low to begin with, was routinely siphoned off by higher-ups, leaving the privates and corporals in the field to supplement it or starve. Amara knew this from his older cousin, who had been conscripted at twelve and gone on to a varied career in the service until dying in a shoot-out with the Brothers at sixteen. By then his cousin was a sergeant, battle-tested and the most cynical man Amara knew, a hollow-eyed killer who hated the army and admired the Brothers, though eventually they would be the death of him. He had urged Amara to avoid the army, and warned him twice when bands were coming to "recruit" boys from his village—"recruit" being the government word for kidnap.

His cousin's influence had led him to the Brothers. Amara lacked the deep religious conviction many of the Brothers and especially their leaders held. He joined for survival, and during his first action against a rival group, found he liked the adventure. His intelligence had been recognized and he was sent to a number of schools, not just for fighting, but for math and languages as well.

He liked math, geometry especially. His teachers told how it had been invented by followers of the one true God as a method of appreciating God's handiwork in the world. To Amara, the beauty was in the interlocking theorems and proofs, the way one formula fed to another and then another, lines and angles connecting in a grid work that explained the entire world. He sensed that computer language held some of the same attractions, and his one regret in killing Li Han was that the Asian had not taught him more about how it worked before he died.

Amara's promise was so great that he had won the ultimate prize: an education in America. Handed documents, he was sent to a U.S. college in the Midwest to study engineering. He was in well over his head, simply unprepared for the culture shock of the Western country. He was not a failure—with effort and struggle he had managed C's in most of his classes, after dropping those he knew he would fail. But within two years the Brothers recalled him, saying they had other jobs. Someday, he told himself, he would return, only this time better prepared.

The black finger of an oil-drilling rig poked over the horizon, telling Amara he was nearing his destination. He slowed, scanning both sides of the road. Here the checkpoints had to be taken more seriously; they would be manned by the Brothers rather than soldiers, and anyone who didn't stop would be targeted by an RPG.

He found the turnoff to the hills, then lowered his speed to a crawl as he went up the twisted road. Moving too fast was an invitation to be shot: the guards had standing orders to fire on anything suspicious, and they were far more likely to be praised for caution than scolded for killing a Brother who had imprudently alarmed them.

Amara spotted a man moving by the side of the trail. He slowed to a stop, and shouted, *"As-Salamu Alaikum wa Rahmatullahi wa Barakatuhu."*

The shadow moved toward him. Two others appeared on the other side of the trail. Then two more behind him. Amara was surrounded by sentries, all of them four or five years younger than himself. They were jumpy and nervous; he put both his hands on the open window of the car, trying with his body language to put them at ease.

"I am Amara of Yujst," he said in Arabic, naming the town he had taken as his battle name. "I have completed my mission."

"What mission was that?" snapped the tall man he'd first seen. He was not necessarily the oldest of the group—he had only the outlines of a beard—but he was clearly in charge.

"The mission that I have been appointed. It is of no concern to you."

"You will tell me or you will not pass."

"Are you ready for Paradise, Brother?" said Amara.

The question caught the tall one by surprise, and he was silent for a moment.

"One of you will ride with me," Amara continued. "You will come into camp. The rest will stay here and guard the pass."

"What gives you the right to make orders?" said the tall one, finding his voice.

"I told you who I am, and why I am here. I need nothing else."

"Two of us will come," said the tall one, trying to save face with the others.

Amara might have challenged this, but decided he didn't want to waste time. "Move, then."

The tall one got into the cab; another man climbed into the truck bed, squatting on the tarp. They drove through two more switchbacks, watched by guards crouching near the rocks. As Amara turned the corner of the last curve, he spotted a small fire flickering in a barrel ahead. Men were gathered around it, warming themselves. The stripped shell of a bus stood behind them, crossway across the path. Amara slowed even further, easing toward the roadblock in an almost dead crawl.

The man in the back of the truck yelled at the sentries near the fire, telling them to move quickly because an important Brother had arrived on a mission. Even so, they moved in slow motion over to the bus. The vehicle had been stripped of its engine and much of its interior, its only function now to slow a determined enemy. The men put their shoulders and backs to the front and pushed, working the bus backward into a slot in the rocks. They held it there as Amara went past, then slowly eased it back in place.

Amara pulled the truck to the side of a small parking area just inside the perimeter. Vehicles were not allowed any farther; the way was blocked by large boulders, protection against vehicle bombs. He took the laptop from beneath the seat and got out of the truck.

"You will guard the contents below the canvas

with your life," he told the two men who'd accompanied him. "If they are even touched, you will be hanged, then fed to the jackals."

Even the tall sentry had no answer for that.

Amara turned and held his hands out.

"You will search me, then take me to Brother Assad," he told the approaching guards. "And be quick."

8

Duka

LESS THAN THREE MINUTES AFTER MELISSA RAN BACK inside the clinic, bullets crashed through the windows. By then she and Bloom had barricaded themselves inside one of the examining rooms with the patients who'd been inside.

Melissa hunkered down behind the desk they'd pushed against the door as a truck drove past outside. There were shouts and a fresh hail of bullets. She reached down and rolled up her pant leg, retrieving her 9mm Glock from its holster.

"That's not going to do much," said Bloom, a few feet away. Two patients, a mother and four-year-old daughter, were huddled next to her. The other patients, both teenage women, both pregnant, were at the far end of the room, crouched down behind the overturned examining table.

"It's better than nothing," said Melissa.

She took out her sat phone, forgotten in the rush for cover. There were two missed calls. Before she could page into the directory, the phone rang. She answered quickly.

"What the hell are you doing in that building?" demanded Danny. "Why wasn't your phone on?"

"It was on," she told him. "The volume on the ringer was down. I couldn't hear."

A round of bullets blew through the building. Two or three whipped overhead. One of the women screamed. Another was crying.

"What's your situation?" asked Danny.

"We have four patients in here, three women and a child. What's going on outside?"

"They're shooting up the town," said Danny. "Where in the building are you? I can't get a good read."

"The back examining room."

"Stay there. One of the trucks is coming back."

There was fresh gunfire at front. This time, though, none of the bullets was directed at the clinic. The Sudan First gunmen were driving through the area, firing indiscriminately.

"All right," said Danny. "They're moving south. Are you all right?"

"So far."

"We're coming for you. Is there a basement?"

"No." She'd already decided this was the safest room in the building.

"Don't do anything until you hear my voice."

"Sure," she told him.

* * *

DANNY CLOSED THE CONNECTION.

"She's nothing but trouble," said Nuri. "I told you. And this Bloom. If she's really a washed out MI6 agent—"

"Not now, Nuri," snapped Danny. "Boston, Flash, you're with me."

Danny left the tent, trying to control his anger as he strode toward the Mercedes. The truth was, Nuri was right—even if he should've kept his mouth shut about it.

Boston and Flash hustled behind him, humping two ammo-laden rucks apiece. Beside their SCAR assault rifles, Boston had an M-48 squad-level machine gun.

They piled into the car. Danny started the engine and was about to pull away when Nuri grabbed the back door.

"I thought you were staying," Danny said.

"We better hurry—there are two dozen men coming by foot from the Sudan First camp."

9

Southern Sudan

AMARA'S ESCORTS EYED THE LAPTOP NERVOUSLY. THE case was more than large enough to hold a charge of plastic explosive powerful enough to take out a good portion of the small cluster of buildings that served as the nerve center of the camp.

He'd shown them that it worked; beyond that, Amara could offer no other assurance. He held it under his arm and walked with them to the small hut where Assad lived and worked.

Assad had served an apprenticeship in Iraq and was one of the older members of the Brotherhood, respected for his experience, though not completely trusted by all because he had been born in Egypt. He and Amara had not been particularly close before this assignment, and in fact Amara suspected that Assad was not the one who chose him.

Assad's cousin Sayr served as his aide and bodyguard. He was standing outside the house, and put up his hand as Amara approached.

"You're back," said Sayr. "You've taken your time."

"I drove night and day," answered Amara. "And ran two blockades."

Sayr pointed to the laptop. "That is not allowed in the hut."

"This is why I came," said Amara, holding it out.

"It's not allowed inside. I'll take it."

Amara hesitated, but turned it over. There was no alternative.

"Be careful," he said. "It has a program on it that's important. Do not even turn it on."

Sayr frowned at him. Amara wondered if he even knew what a program was—unlike his cousin, Sayr was not particularly bright.

One of his escorts knocked, then opened the

door to the small building. Assad sat in the middle of the floor on a rug. There were pillows nearby, but no other furniture.

"I have returned, Brother," Amara said, stepping inside. "I have eliminated the Asian as directed and returned with the computer and the guidance system."

Assad nodded. He stared blankly at the rug, seemingly in prayer, though it was not the time to pray. Finally he looked up and gestured for Amara to sit.

"The Asian is dead?" Assad asked.

"As you directed."

"He was an evil man," said Assad. "But a useful one."

The door opened. Sayr entered and walked over to his cousin, stooping down and whispering in his ear. As he straightened, he shot Amara a look of disdain.

"Very good," said Assad, his gaze remaining on Amara. "Fetch us some tea."

Sayr gave Amara another frown, then left.

"How strong is your belief?" asked Assad. "If it were necessary to sacrifice yourself, could you do it?"

A shudder ran through Amara's body. A true believer was supposed to be prepared to sacrifice himself for jihad, accepting death willingly for the glory of the Almighty. But it was a complicated proposition. It was one thing to be willing to die in battle, and quite another to accept what Assad seemed to be asking: deliberately sacrificing himself.

The Brothers did not as a general rule use suicide bombers to advance their agenda. They were considered unreliable. But there were always exceptions.

Amara hoped he wasn't to be one.

"Could you become a martyr?" repeated Assad.

"Of course," said Amara, knowing this was the only answer he could give, even if it did not come from his heart.

"You hesitate."

"I . . . only question my worthiness."

Assad smiled but said nothing. Sayr returned with a small teapot and two cups. He carefully wiped Assad's and set it down before him. He was much less careful with Amara's; liquid dripped from the cup.

"He doesn't like me," said Amara when Sayr had left. "But I have done nothing to him."

"You've taken his place on an important mission to America," said Assad.

"I have?"

"We have been asked by friends to help a project they have undertaken. One of our Brothers is in the Satan capital. He needs some technical assistance, and equipment. We think you can help him."

"What sort of help do you mean?" asked Amara, unsure if the question was meant literally or was a more subtle way of asking if he would be willing to become a martyr.

He certainly hoped it was the former.

"Drink your tea," said Assad, nodding, "and I will instruct you."

10

Duka

THEY WERE STILL ABOUT TWO MILES FROM THE CITY when MY-PID told Danny that the trucks blasting the area occupied by Meurtre Musique had met up with the men on foot.

"Where are they headed?" Danny asked the system.

"Insufficient data."

"They're kind of aimless," said Nuri, watching on his control display. "They're just intent shooting up whatever they can. There's a group of men in Meurtre Musique's area. Looks like they're planning a counterattack."

"We'll go north and come back around from that end."

"Don't get too close to the house where Li Han is," said Nuri. "We don't want to spook him."

"We're the last thing he's going to worry about," said Danny.

He pressed the accelerator to the floor, speeding down the road. There was gunfire in the distance.

I shouldn't have let her go, he thought. He'd put the whole mission in jeopardy.

Why had he given in? The argument that he couldn't stop her didn't hold water.

It was because she was pretty, he realized, and he liked her.

What a fool he was.

* * *

DESPITE THE FACT THAT DANNY HAD TOLD HER NOT TO leave the building, Melissa asked Bloom if there wasn't a safer place in the vicinity. The clinic, she reasoned, was the largest building in the area, and a ready target for anyone who didn't like Meurtre Musique.

"There are the huts," said Bloom. She was shaking. "The walls are mud."

"It still might be better than staying here," Melissa told her. She pulled the desk back from the door.

"What are you doing?"

"I'm going to scout the front."

"What if they're nearby? Don't go."

"Are you OK?"

"Of course not."

Melissa looked into the older woman's eyes. She saw fear there for the first time. She hadn't completely believed the story about Bloom leaving MI6; she thought there was a good chance that she was in fact still an agent under deep cover. But the look in the nurse's eyes told her it was true.

Or close: maybe she hadn't quit. Maybe they had eased her out because she wasn't strong enough.

"They're not nearby," Melissa told her.

Bloom nodded reluctantly.

Melissa scrambled across the hall to a room with a window looking toward the road. There was no one outside.

"Marie, come on!" she yelled. "Let's get out of here."

* * *

"They're moving out of the building," said Nuri. "Shit. Why the hell can't that bitch just do as she's told?"

Danny felt a swell of anger—not at Melissa, but at Nuri, for calling her a bitch. "She's just trying to do her job," he said tightly.

"Bullshit. Her job was getting Li Han. She's not even doing that. She's screwing everything up. Typical Agency prima frickin' donna."

Boston reached across from the passenger seat and tapped Danny on the knee. Danny glanced over. Boston had his game face on, a look that said he shouldn't waste his brain on trivia.

Right as usual, thought Danny.

"Give me directions to Agency officer Ilse," Danny told MY-PID. "Avoid contact. Avoid the warehouse area."

"Proceed forward one hundred yards." MY-PID began a terse set of directions that took them over the old railroad tracks, skirting the warehouse area they'd raided. Then the system had Danny turn right and go up a hill; they passed a run of circular huts, each smaller than the next.

A red ball erupted in the city center.

"Mortars!" said Nuri.

"Colonel, these huts are filled with soldiers," said Flash. "I just saw two guys in a doorway with guns."

"Yeah, all right," said Danny.

A second later something tinged on the fender.

"They're shooting at us," Flash said calmly.

* * *

MELISSA HEARD THE EXPLOSIONS IN THE DISTANCE AS she helped the woman and child into the front room.

"Come on," she said in English, scooping up the little girl. The mother grabbed her arm and together they ran out of the clinic, hurrying across the road into the empty field.

"Stay here," said Melissa after they had gone about twenty yards. She handed the little girl over to her mother. "Here. OK?" She gestured with her hands. "Here."

"Stay. Yes," said the woman.

Melissa raced back across the street. She heard automatic rifle fire not far away.

One of the pregnant women appeared in the doorway, holding her belly. Melissa worried that she was about to give birth.

"Here. Quickly," said Melissa, grabbing her arm. "Marie? Marie!"

"We're coming," said Bloom inside.

Melissa started walking the pregnant woman across the street. The woman was gasping for air, clutching her stomach.

"It's OK," said Melissa. "Relax. Relax." A stupid thing to say, she realized, even under much better circumstances.

She steered her toward the other woman and her child. The tall grass made it harder for the pregnant woman to move; it seemed to take forever to get there.

"We have to go farther back from the road," said Melissa. "Back in that direction—on the other side of those bushes." She turned and saw Bloom and the other woman just reaching the field. "Come on," she said, reaching down and scooping up the little girl. "Let's go."

A high-pitched whistle pierced the air. A dull thump followed, and the ground shook with an explosion. The girl screamed in her arms.

"Come on!" yelled Melissa. "Come on. They're shelling us."

DANNY JERKED THE WHEEL HARD, TRYING TO STAY WITH the road as it swerved between a pair of native huts. Shells fell fifty or sixty yards to his left, and there was sporadic gunfire from some of the houses nearby.

"We're about a half mile away," said Boston calmly. He pointed to Danny's left. "They're on the other side of that field."

"That's where they're shelling," said Nuri behind him.

Danny gave his phone to Boston. "Get Melissa on the line and stay with her," he told him.

The Osprey was barely five miles away. He could call it in if he needed to.

And what then? He'd have to hit Li Han right away, then go for the Russian.

He didn't have all his gear yet, and their presence would be obvious. But better to blow their cover and accomplish the mission than keep their cover and fail.

The road bucked with a pair of fresh explosions. The mortar shells were coming closer.

"There's your turn," said Boston, pointing ahead.

Danny started to slow.

"Duck!" yelled Boston.

The roof of the Mercedes seemed to explode. Someone was firing at them from the hut near the intersection.

"Shit on this," said Boston, leaning out the window and returning fire.

Danny swerved hard, fishtailing onto the new road in a hail of gunfire. The car lurched to the right as he pushed hard against the wheel, trying to keep moving in a straight line.

"Our tires are shot out," he yelled. "Hang on!"

MELISSA STRUGGLED TO KEEP THE PREGNANT WOMAN moving. The mortar shells were landing harmlessly in a wide, rocky ravine no closer than a hundred yards away. But she knew that at any moment the men firing them would adjust their aim.

Bloom and the woman she was helping caught up.

"There's another farm there—see the building?" said Bloom, nodding ahead. The building was up a gentle slope about two hundred yards away.

"OK," said Melissa. It was a destination, at least. She glanced to her right, making sure the woman with the child was coming.

A few seconds later she saw something moving through the field on the left. She thought at first it was an animal, a horse or even a zebra. Then she realized it was men—three of them, rushing down in the direction of the clinic.

Bloom started to yell and wave her hand.

"No, no," hissed Melissa. "We can't trust them."

"They're with Gerard," said Bloom. "They'll help."

"How do you know?"

"I'm sure of it."

"You don't know!"

Melissa grabbed her as she started to wave. But whoever they were, or whatever side they were on, the men didn't stop, or even seem to notice; they kept running in the direction of the building. The mortars had ceased firing, but there was another ominous sound in the distance—the trucks were returning.

Suddenly, the woman Melissa was helping screamed in agony and stopped moving. She bent her head and shoulders down, caught in the midst of a convulsive contraction.

Melissa dropped to her knee and looked at her face. The woman gasped for air, closed her eyes, then moaned with a fresh contraction.

Less than thirty seconds had passed between them.

"Marie! Marie!" yelled Melissa. "She's having the baby now! Right here! Help!"

Washington, D.C.

D.C. TRAFFIC WAS SURPRISINGLY LIGHT, AND ZEN MANaged to make it to the Intelligence Committee meeting a few minutes early. He quickly wished he hadn't: Senator Uriah Ernst hailed him in the hallway outside the room and immediately began haranguing him.

"What exactly is the administration up to, Zen?" said Ernst. "What the hell is your President doing?"

"Probably nothing good," laughed Zen.

"Don't try and snow me. I know you're on her side these days."

"I don't really know what we're talking about," said Zen.

"I'll bet. You've never heard of Raven?"

Zen shook his head.

"It's an assassination program—or so I understand."

"New one on me."

"I'm getting to the bottom of this," said Ernst. He shook his head and went into the hearing room.

Ned Barrington, the committee chairman, met Zen just inside the door. "Got a moment?"

Zen nodded and wheeled himself over to the corner.

"Ernst says the CIA is running an assassination program outside of the oversight procedure," said

Barrington. "He thinks the President set it up to circumvent us and the law."

"I don't know anything about it," said Zen. "This isn't one of the 6-9 programs?"

"No. Not at all. Supposedly, anyway. I don't even know if it exists," admitted Barrington. "I wouldn't believe anything based on Ernst's rantings."

The 6-9 programs were targeted "actions"— the word assassination was carefully avoided— directed at terrorists who were deemed a threat to the U.S. Similar to other programs conducted by earlier administrations, 6-9 was tightly controlled, with targets approved according to a strict set of standards. As it happened, Zen had argued that the standards were too restrictive; they required two different sets of legal review, and many inside the CIA, which administered the program, felt they were too time-consuming.

"Your wife's not involved in any of this, is she?" Barrington asked.

"I haven't a clue," said Zen truthfully.

"I hope not, for her sake."

A few minutes later Zen found himself trying to clamp his mouth shut as the meeting began with a blistering diatribe from Ernst. He claimed that the President had circumvented the constitution by authorizing assassinations of "who knows who."

"She's leading us into World War Three. That's where we're going," declared Ernst.

"With all due respect, Senator," said Zen fi-

nally, "how exactly do you see this leading to
World War Three?"

"The government cannot have a policy of ex-
terminating its enemies. Especially when they are
heads of state."

"This program is directed at heads of state?"
said Zen.

"That's what I've heard. Raven is a sign of an
Agency and an administration run amok."

Barrington tapped his gavel. Zen suspected
that Ernst was simply ramping up the charges so
the committee would vote to investigate. For all
Ernst knew, there might not even be a Raven program—or a rumor. He'd used the tactic before.

Unfortunately, he was a senior member of the
Senate, an important fund-raiser for the other
side, and a frequent talk show guest. He couldn't
simply be ignored.

"The senator from Tennessee has a point," said
one of Ernst's fellow party members, Ted Green.
"We should get Edmund up here and find out
what the hell is going on."

"And the National Security director," said
Ernst.

"Why not ask the President herself?" said Zen
sarcastically.

"If she'd take my phone calls, I would."

"All right, all right," said Barrington. "We'll
have Edmund come in."

12

Duka

DANNY MANAGED TO KEEP THE CAR ON THE ROAD AS both tires on the passenger side blew out. He rode the rims for a few hundred yards, wrangling it more or less into a straight line, before the back of the vehicle lifted with an explosion. Someone in the shacks behind them had fired a rocket-propelled grenade; fortunately, it hit the road far enough behind them that most of the blast and shrapnel scattered harmlessly. But the shock threw the car out of Danny's control, pushing it into a ditch.

"Everybody out!" he yelled.

They flew through the doors a few seconds ahead of the next grenade, which turned the Mercedes into a fireball. Danny could feel the heat as he scrambled through the field, trying to find cover. Nuri was on his left, Boston and Flash somewhere behind them.

It took him a few moments to orient himself. He checked his rifle—locked and loaded—then reached for his ear set, which had fallen a few feet away.

Boston and Flash were calling for him.

"I'm here," he told them. "Forty yards south of the car. Nuri's near me," he added. Nuri was hunched over the control unit for the MY-PID a few yards away.

"I see ya," said Boston. "Ya got three tangos coming down the road on your right as you look back at the vehicle. We have shots. What do you want to do?"

Once slang for terrorist, "tango" had become a generic word for any hostile.

"You have them?" Danny asked. "Take 'em."

Two quick bursts and all three fell dead.

Danny crawled over to Nuri.

"Our missing CIA officer and the women are in a field over that little ridge," said Nuri, pointing. "On the other side of this farm building. MY-PID says one of the women is in labor."

"Labor?"

"The trucks are moving up from that direction, and there are men on foot coming straight up this way. We're in the middle of deep shit, Colonel."

"You're a master of the obvious, Nuri," said Danny, starting down in Melissa's direction.

THE BABY WAS DEFINITELY COMING. ITS MOTHER SQUAT-ted in the field, bent low but still on her feet. Melissa, on her knees, cradled the woman's head as Bloom worked on the other end, clearing the brush down and rolling the mother-to-be's dress back so she could see what was going on.

"Crowning!" said Bloom. Her voice was stead-ier than before, braver, as if by attending to the woman she was finally able to push away her fear.

Melissa's training for birth consisted of a single twenty minute lecture with a quick simulation in-volving a plastic doll. She held her breath as the woman pushed in response to another strong con-traction.

"Almost, almost!" said Bloom. She switched to

Nubian, pleading with the woman to push. The woman was beyond instructions, acting instinctually; her body tensed, and Melissa gripped her, knowing she was about to convulse.

The outside world had slipped away. If there was gunfire, if the mortar shells were still falling, Melissa heard none of it. She was oblivious to everything except the pregnant woman's body as it pushed a new life into the world.

The mother fell back against Melissa. Bloom held up the bloody, gasping infant.

"I need a knife!" she said.

"I don't have one."

"Here!" yelled a voice in the field a few yards away. "I'm coming!"

It was Danny Freah.

13

Duka

MILOS KIMKO LOWERED THE FIELD GLASSES AND RUBBED his forehead.

"Very good, these mortars, no?" said Girma. "You see how we crush our enemies."

"These were your allies, weren't they?"

Girma waved his hand. He was still in the middle of a khat jag; Kimko doubted he had slept in the past forty-eight hours.

There were at least three firefights in the city, two on either end of the main street and another up in the area where most of the Meur-tse Meur-tskk followers lived. Kimko hoped Li Han was hunkered down well.

"By tonight we will own Duka," said Girma proudly. "And from here, we make our mark—all of Sudan."

"You're not to target any building near the railroad tracks and the old warehouse, you understand?" snapped Kimko. "Or you will get no more weapons."

"You give me orders, Russian?"

Girma's eyes flashed. For once Kimko forgot himself. Seized by his own anger, he balled his hand into a fist. Only at the last moment was he able to hold back—there were too many of Girma's followers nearby.

"I need what the Chinaman has if I am to get you more weapons," said Kimko. "If it is destroyed, I will have a very hard time."

Girma frowned, but turned and said something to the men working the mortars.

Be patient, Kimko told himself. *Once you have the UAV, you can leave. Take it back to Moscow personally—the hell with the expert Moscow is sending, the hell with the SVR, the hell with everyone but yourself.*

"I need a jeep," he told Girma.

"Where are you going?" yelled Girma. "Are you trying to betray us?" He grabbed the pistol at his belt.

"Don't be a fool," said Kimko. "My country

wants the aircraft. I have to meet the Chinaman. It's almost dusk."

Girma pointed the pistol. Kimko, his own weapon holstered, felt the strength drain from his arms. But he knew that the best way to deal with Girma was to remain defiant and bold; these Africans hated weakness.

"Shoot me and you'll never get another bullet," he told him Girma. "My employers will come and wipe you out."

Girma frowned. Slowly, he put his thumb on the hammer of the pistol and released it.

"You are lucky I like you," he said.

14

Duka

DANNY FOLDED THE UMBILICAL CORD AGAINST THE EDGE of his combat knife and pushed hard, slicing clean through. The baby seemed pale but breathing.

The shelling had stopped, but there was still plenty of gunfire in the distance. A black swirl of smoke rose from the center of the city.

"They're fighting on both ends of town," said Nuri. "Sudan First has some men and trucks moving up the road in that direction. The last of the Meurtre Musique men will be down there in a few minutes. Our best bet is that way," he added, pointing northeast.

"Any action where Li Han is?" asked Danny.

"Not even a guard posted," said Nuri. "Two brothers are in a building about a quarter mile closer to the village."

"What are they doing?"

"They're inside. Maybe they're sleeping."

"They sleep through this shit?" said Boston.

"They've probably slept through worse," said Nuri. "They're two miles out of town," he added. "As far as they're concerned, the fighting might as well be in L.A."

"What about the building where he was yesterday?" asked Danny.

"The two brothers that went back are still inside. The trucks are around back."

Danny rubbed his chin.

"Whatcha thinkin'?" asked Boston.

"I'm thinking we hit that building first," said Danny. "It's close enough to the fighting that they'll be distracted. We take out the trucks, get in there, see what's what. Then we go and get Li Han."

"When are we doing this?" Nuri asked.

"It'll be dark in an hour," said Boston.

"You think we should wait?" asked Nuri.

"That's not what I'm saying," said Boston. "But the Osprey is an easy target in the day—if it comes down now, they can hit it with RPGs, let alone a missile."

"We'll take the women someplace safer," said Danny. "We'll have the Osprey come in when it's dark, if we can wait that long. They pick us up, and we'll go directly to the raid."

"What do we do about the women?" asked Nuri.

"We'll take them with us. Evac them as soon as we get a chance."

"All right," said Nuri. "Fighting's going to stoke up in a few minutes. The two sides are just about close enough to see each other."

"COME ON," DANNY TOLD MELISSA.

"What are we doing?"

"We're going to get out of this mess—the forces are moving together across the way in a field about a half mile from here. One or both of them will probably try flanking in this direction. We want to be out of here."

"Then what?"

"My Osprey will come in and pick us up. Depending on the circumstances, we'll have it evac the civilians as well. I just don't know where to put them."

"All right."

Danny smirked at her.

"What?" she said.

"You're approving my decision."

"Yes."

"I'm glad you like it."

"Colonel, I keep telling you—this is my operation. You're just helping."

"Keep telling yourself that. Sooner or later you'll believe it."

* * *

Boston eyed the woman who'd just given birth.

"I don't know, Colonel. Moving her. I don't know."

"We don't have a stretcher," said Danny, "and we're not leaving her."

"I can carry her, that's not the problem," Boston told him. "But I don't know about moving her. She's lost a ton of blood."

"She'll lose a hell of a lot more if they put a bullet through her," snapped Nuri.

That settled it for Boston. "Boost her on my back and tell her to hang on."

Nuri and Danny helped her onto Boston's back as gently as they could. The woman was exhausted and barely conscious. Boston grabbed her forearms to hold her in place.

Flash, meanwhile, had doffed his armored vest and pulled off his shirt to wrap the child. Bloom put the baby into the shirt and tied off the bottom, swaddling it, then snugging it against her chest. She folded her torso over the infant, protecting it as much as possible.

The baby boy's round eyes looked at the world with unabashed inquisitiveness, undoubtedly wondering what the hell he had just descended into.

Flash started to put his armored vest on Bloom.

"No," Danny told him. "You have a point. You need the vest."

"She's got the kid."

"They won't be in the line of fire. Don't be a hero."

Slowly, the small group began moving through

the field, Flash at the front, Danny at the rear, Boston, Nuri, and the women in the middle. Melissa had the toddler in her arms; the two other patients who'd been in the clinic flanked her, each holding onto the back of her shirt.

As they crossed the road, they heard grenades and gunfire from the direction they'd come from.

"Keep moving," said Nuri. He repeated it in Arabic and then the local language, helped by MY-PID. "Get across the road and move west."

15

Washington, D.C.

WHEN CHRISTINE MARY TODD WAS ELECTED PRESIdent, the pundits and chattering class had declared that her main attention would be on domestic affairs, issues like unemployment, health care, and education. She'd expected as much herself. Having spent years focusing on the world's problems, the time seemed ripe for the U.S. to turn its attention homeward. There was an enormous amount of work to be done in the country. America was recovering from a deep recession, and while the war on terror seemed never-ending, it had been wrestled into a manageable if still tricky state—or so it appeared from a distance.

But since she'd been in office, Todd had found

that more than sixty percent of her time and an outsized amount of her energy were spent on international affairs. China and Iran were openly hostile, North Korea threatened war with the U.S. as well as South Korea, the Germans were making noises about rearming in the face of a rising Russian defense budget, and the war on terror grew more intricate every day.

At the same time, the tools Todd had to deal with these problems were unwieldy. They also came with complications of their own, the latest being the CIA and its clandestine Raven program.

It wasn't clear when rumors of the program's existence had first begun circulating, much less where they originated. But literally within hours of her ordering Edmund to tell her everything he knew about it, word of its existence seemed to have reached every corner of the D.C. establishment.

That word, of course, was wildly inflated and focused on the sensational; the rumors had the U.S. attempting to assassinate world leaders and even using the program domestically. The lack of hard data encouraged the wildest speculation and attracted the most diverse political agendas possible. The fact that the computer software at the heart of the program wasn't mentioned was hardly reassuring. It wasn't surprising that as soon as word reached the Senate Intelligence Committee, they voted to call Edmund in.

"I don't think everyone in Washington has heard." National Security Advisor Dr. Michael Blitz shifted uneasily in the chair in Todd's working office, a small former cloakroom next to the cabinet room in the West Wing. The President liked to work there, like most of her predecessors, reserving the Oval Office for meeting visitors and ceremonial occasions. "I think what we have here are a set of older rumors being given some fresh wind. I would bet that someone on Edmund's staff gave the information to Ernst. Once he got it . . ."

Blitz made a fluttering motion with his hand, mimicking a bird taking flight. "That will just make things worse."

Todd pushed herself up out of her chair. She'd never liked sitting for very long, and this job required a lot of it.

"You can't let him testify before Congress," said Blitz. "Not until the weapon is recovered. Assuming what Reid told you is true."

"I realize that." Blitz's mention of Reid bothered her—she was hoping to somehow protect him as the source of her information. But she'd had to tell Blitz where she'd gotten the assessment of Raven in the first place, otherwise he wouldn't have taken it as seriously as he should.

If it were up to her, she'd let the committee roast Edmund for having gone ahead with the program without proper authorization. In fact, she was planning to fire him over this—as soon as Raven was safely in hand.

But in the meantime she couldn't take the chance of word getting out and the terrorists in Africa discovering exactly how potent the weapon was. In theory, Edmund *might* be able to limit his testimony artfully enough so the real purpose and value of Raven would remain hidden. But she wasn't willing to take that risk.

"Very possibly this weapon isn't as effective as anyone believes," said Blitz. "You know how these things go. The contractors pump them up—"

"We can't really take that chance." Todd paced around the very small office, literally moving only a few feet each way. Finally she sat back in her seat. "I can't have him testify until Raven is recovered. His schedule will have to be full for a few days, that's all."

"That will get them talking all the more," said William Bozzone, her politcal advisor. Bozzone was a lawyer and former congressman who held the official title of Counsel to the President, but was well known in Washington as her personal ward healer.

"I understand."

"There's another problem, you know," added Blitz. "Senator Stockard. Maybe you should brief him before his wife does."

Todd frowned. Zen was an ally on some matters and an antagonist on others. The fact that his wife headed the Office of Special Technology worked in Todd's favor, to an extent, even if he abstained from matters relating to it. Still, he could be a potent critic, all the more so because he knew what he was talking about, unlike people like Ernst.

"I don't think there'll be any pillow talk," said Todd.

Blitz raised an eyebrow in disbelief.

"I don't." The president liked Breanna Stockard; she reminded her of herself twenty years before.

"Irregardless, you want to keep him on your side," said Bozzone.

"I can't tell one person on the committee and not the others," said Todd. "Even Zen. I know he'll be discreet, but even so—you see how far this has gone already."

Todd folded her arms. The committee had voted to ask Edmund to appear *immediately*. Washington's definition of "immediately" was a lot looser than most; even so, she doubted she could delay Edmund's appearance for more than two or three days without some political ramifications—and undoubtedly a new round of rumors. Reid had assured her that Whiplash was moving ahead with the recovery operation, and expected to have the UAV in hand by the end of the day. But she didn't want any word of the weapon's potency reaching the committee—or more specifically, Ernst and his rumor mill—until after it was back in the U.S., which would add another twenty-four hours.

Two days. Surely that was understandable.

"His calendar is going to have to be full," Todd said finally. "And I'll find something for him to do for the next day. Then he can go before them. If I haven't fired him by then."

"They may subpoena him. Cause a big stir."

"We'll quash it."

"Ernst would love that," said Bozzone. A subpoena would only be for show—but in Washington, the show was as important, if not more so, than the substance.

"Too bad Raven didn't target him," said Blitz.

"Don't even joke," said Todd.

16

Duka

NURI LED THEM TO A GROUP OF DILAPIDATED BRICK buildings tucked into the side of a rolling hill. Even though they didn't stop, it took nearly forty minutes to get there, weaving across the fields and down a pair of narrow, crooked paths. The fighting remained behind them. While the sun had pushed below the horizon, a glow could be seen from the center of town; MY-PID said much of it was on fire.

The only good news was that neither Li Han nor his people had moved since the battle had begun. Hera, in charge of the assault team waiting with the Osprey, reported that they were ready to move whenever Danny gave the order.

Even though MY-PID declared the cluster of buildings clear, Danny decided he wasn't going to take any chances with the women and the children. He had Flash run ahead and make sure there were no lookouts hiding in the brush. Then he went to check the buildings.

There wasn't much left of four of the five. Their roofs were collapsed, and in one case two sides had been completely removed, the clay bricks salvaged for some other project in town. Hiding in the ruins would be better than nothing—but only just.

The fifth building was two stories tall, with a large, boarded-up window on the second floor facing the direction of the railroad tracks. The door at the front was boarded as well; there were no other openings.

The wood blocking the door was nailed tight. Flash took his knife and began prying out nails, sliding the blade in and then working the edge near the hilt under the heads until he could get them with his fingers. Getting the first board was slow, tedious work, but once it was off, he found he could pry out the board directly below it, and then the next, making a space large enough to crawl through. Flash hit a button on his uniform sleeve, activating an LED flashlight sewn into his cuff.

"Looks clear," he told Danny from inside.

Dropping to his knees, he pulled down the visor on his helmet and slipped into the building. Danny turned around, making sure no one was following them.

"Jesus," Flash muttered over the radio.

"What's up?" said Danny.

"Looks like a torture chamber in here. Damn."

"What?"

"Take a look."

Danny slipped his visor down as Flash shared

his image over the Whiplash circuit. A small window opened in the lower left-hand corner of Danny's screen. Instantly it filled with images from Flash's helmet infrared sensor, giving him a hazy view of the interior of the building.

There were rings in the walls. Chains hung from various points, including two beams that ran across the ceiling.

"Is the place clear?" Danny asked.

"Of people, yeah," said Flash. "Probably filled with ghosts. There's a trench in the floor, and a drain. Shit."

"It's a slaughterhouse," Danny told him. "For animals. Food."

"Oh."

Flash swept the interior. Besides the large main room, there was a corridor and a set of smaller rooms on the west side of the building. All were empty.

Danny signaled to the others to come up. In the failing daylight they seemed to take forever.

"Let's get them inside the building," Danny told Nuri. "Get them safe and figure out what we're going to do."

"They don't want to go inside," said Melissa.

"What?"

"Marie says they think it's unclean. It was a slaughterhouse."

"Tell them it's the only safe place for them."

"They want to go back to their homes."

"No way," said Danny. "There's fighting all through the city."

Melissa nodded and went over to talk to Bloom.

The two women huddled with the patients they'd rescued from the clinic for several minutes, trying to persuade them that the building was the only safe place for them.

Danny looked at the overhead images of the city. Much of the downtown was either on fire or destroyed. There was a running gun battle in the cluster of huts at the western end of Duka. The two sides were slowly being drawn to each other, converging in the residential area. There must have been at least a hundred dead by now; he avoided asking MY-PID for an estimate.

THE PREGNANT WOMAN WAS IN SHOCK, STARING BLANKLY into the distance while clutching her baby. Melissa didn't entirely understand what the other two women were telling Bloom—the slaughter- house was unclean or haunted or both—but the gist of it was obvious: they weren't going inside the building under any circumstances, including gunpoint.

"They won't go inside," Bloom told her. "They just won't. It's taboo. They want to go back to their families."

"It's impossible. The city's in flames."

Bloom argued with the women some more, but it was no use.

"They want to go back and get their families," added Bloom. "They're insisting."

"They'll be killed," said Melissa.

"I'm trying to tell them that. I suggested a camp—they won't even go there."

Melissa gave up.

"I can't get them to budge," she told Danny. "They want to go back to their houses. Despite everything."

"Look, we're just going to leave them here," he told her. "There's a jeep heading for the building where Li Han was holed up. The Russian's in it. We have to go."

"All right."

"You can stay with them if you want, but—"

"I'm not staying," she told him. "I've helped them as much as I can. Now I have to take care of business."

"Osprey will be here in two minutes." Danny spun around. "Nuri! Take my rifle. You and Boston stay with the women. We're going to go get the Russian at their meeting place."

17

Duka

THE CITY WAS A BLOODY, THIRD WORLD DISASTER, THE two rebel groups savaging it as they tried to get at each other. There would be no winners here, only survivors who'd be left to crawl through the rubble, and probably ultimately abandon it.

Kimko hated them all, including and especially Girma, who sat behind him in the open-top jeep, AK-47 in his hands, bouncing up and down on the seat with khat-fueled excitement and adrenaline. There seemed to be no getting rid of him.

They were nearly to the warehouse when Girma leaned forward and yelled instructions to the driver. He immediately slammed on the brakes and began making a U-turn.

"Where are we going?" Kimko demanded.

"Ha-ha, we have blown up Gerard's house," said Girma, holding up a two-way radio. "I want to see it burn. I have heard on my radio."

"I need to be at my meeting."

Girma frowned. "First we see the house."

"Damn it, Girma, I need to get there!"

Girma's frown morphed into something more threatening. "I am in charge," he said. "You are a salesman. We will go where I want. Then you can get your trinket."

Kimko cursed to himself. These people were animals. Worse.

They veered through the city square where Girma had started the war the day before. The pavilion lay in a pile of rubble. The buildings on either side had been gutted by fire; there were pockmarks in the facade. Across the way, the clinic that Girma's people had run was now destroyed; part of its front wall lay scattered along the road. But that didn't stop the wounded from gathering there; two aides were ministering to them, overseen by a pair of fourteen- or fifteen-year-olds with Kalashnikovs.

Small fires were burning everywhere. The air smelled like burnt grass and acrid dust, mixed with cordite and the scent of burning metal. A pack of dogs ran down the street, dragging some-thing between them.

A corpse.

They swung west, moving into a district of tra-ditional round huts with their cone-shaped roofs. It was here that most of the tribesmen belonging to Meur-tse Meur-tskk lived. Bodies were scat-tered in the yards. The majority were women and children. Dead animals lay along and in the road; the driver made no effort to avoid most of them, simply speeding over the remains.

Girma, meanwhile, chewed his khat leaves.

Two men with guns stood in the street ahead, waving their arms as the jeep approached. Kimko put his hand on his holster, ready to pull the pistol out if needed.

Girma stood up, holding onto the roll bar. He raised his rifle and fired a burst in greeting.

The men ran to him, jabbering. Girma leaned forward and pointed the driver to the right.

"Too many enemies down road," he told Kimko. "We'll see them later. Dead."

18

Duka

WITH THE RUSSIAN HEADING TO THE WEST OF THE CITY rather than Li Han's house to the north, Danny decided not to commit his small force or risk the aircraft getting close to the fighting yet. He told the pilots to hold back; in the meantime he and the others would proceed to the stationmaster building and set up an ambush.

"I want to hold the Osprey off as long as I can," he told Melissa. "It's a straight shot for us through that field and then up the hill and over. Flash and I can get there pretty fast. Can you keep up?"

"I can keep up."

Danny led the way at a strong trot. The circuitry in the night vision screen on his helmet could turn the dull dusk as bright as day if he wanted, but Danny found that too distracting: it looked so real that it was hard to remember it was just being synthesized by the sensors; in his opinion, that made it easier to subconsciously miss something. So he stayed with traditional night vision mode, which made it clear that he wasn't seeing the entire picture; the difference could be critical.

When they reached a narrow dirt road on the other side of the field, Danny picked up his pace, sprinting about thirty yards to a stream that emptied into a small pond near the railroad tracks about a quarter mile away. The streambed was rocky, and he had to pick his way, glancing back every so often to check on Melissa behind him. Her breathing was labored but she was keeping pace.

"Subject jeep has stopped in residential area," declared MY-PID.

"Why?" asked Danny.

"Insufficient data, operand uncertain," said the Voice, getting technical on him.

"Display jeep video feed in lower screen one," said Danny.

The image from the Global Hawk popped into the lower-left-hand side of his visor. It was grainy, magnified beyond its optimum size. Danny couldn't make out much more than an indiscriminate crowd.

He slowed, then stopped so he could focus on the image. He was worried that Li Han was there.

"Subject identified as Milos Kimko—confirm he's at the jeep site," Danny told MY-PID.

"Confirmed." A box appeared around the figure in the passenger seat of the jeep.

"Is Li Han there? Subject code-named Mao Man—is he at the jeep site?"

"Negative."

"Confidence level?"

"Confidence level 98.3 percent," said the computer tartly.

"Where is he?"

The building two miles east of town was highlighted.

"Confidence level?"

"Confidence level 98.2 percent," snapped the computer.

MELISSA SAW DANNY STOP A FEW YARDS AHEAD. EVEN though she was straining, she waited until she caught up to him before slowing. She huffed for a few moments, trying to get her breath back.

"I thought you'd tire eventually," she said to him.

He turned toward her. With the shield on his helmet down he looked like a space traveler.

"What's that?" he asked, pushing the shield up. "You're tired?"

"Just checking to make sure we got the right place."

"Do you always run to your targets?" Melissa asked. The front of her thighs were suddenly stiff. She pumped them slowly, knowing she had to keep them loose.

"If necessary." Danny gave her a tight yet disarming smile. "Once we bring the Osprey in, the Russian will know something's going on. If word gets to Li Han, we'll spook him."

"I see."

"There are two possible buildings," he told her. "We're not sure which one they meant, but they're close to each other. We'll check them out, then set up an ambush. Ready?"

Not really, she thought, but there was no way she would admit it.

DANNY SET OUT AGAIN, THIS TIME AT AN EASIER PACE. They crossed the stream and trotted down in the direction of the abandoned warehouse area.

The two buildings MY-PID had marked as the possible meeting place were located right next to the tracks. One was small and squat, little more than a locker. The other, about thirty yards away, was a three-story shell, a ruin that towered over everything around it.

Danny slowed to a stop about two hundred yards from the building. The back of the house where Li Han had been when they left the bug was to his right, nearly a quarter mile away. The warehouse they had raided was in the complex, a half mile to the east, directly on his left as he looked at the three-story building.

"What do you think, Colonel?" asked Flash. "We close enough?"

"Big one first," said Danny, magnifying the image the helmet was projecting. If people were around, they were well hidden. "We check them, bug them, then swing around to the other side and wait. This way, when the Osprey comes in, we'll have the far side covered."

Danny lifted the visor and looked at Flash. The trooper nodded. Melissa was a few feet away, hands on her knees, trying to catch her breath.

"You all right?" Danny asked.

She held up a hand, waving at him.

"Does that mean yes or no?" he asked, coming over.

"I'm good," she gasped. "You set a pretty quick pace."

"I like to run, I guess."

"So do I." She looked up and smiled. "At least I thought I did."

"Can you breathe?"

"I can breathe," she snapped.

"Come on around this way. We're going to check the buildings. If they're empty, we're going to bug them, and then duck back to a spot over there where we can cover them both."

"What if they're not empty?"

"Then we'll deal with it."

19

Duka

THE BODY THEY DRAGGED THROUGH THE YARD OF THE house and into the dirt road was barely recognizable as a human being. It had been battered and its clothes almost completely torn off, except for the shoes. As Kimko approached, it looked more like a collection of meat held together in a mesh sack.

Remarkably, the man was still alive. He writhed and jerked, arms flailing. Kimko watched as the men pulling him let go, ducking away as if afraid of his blows.

Two men nearby held torches; they threw a yellow hue around the semicircle of tormentors and victim. Half a dozen Sudan First soldiers stood in a loose circle watching the man as Girma walked over and laid his boot into his midsection. He placed it there gently at first, letting it rest easily on the man, who paused his writhing to stare up at him. Girma grinned, then stomped. The man curled around the blow, gasping.

Kimko saw the man's face clearly as he turned in his direction. It was Gerard.

A shudder of revulsion ran through Kimko. If

the man had any true courage, he would have died fighting rather than letting himself be captured and humiliated.

Animals.

"How great are you now, Gerard?" yelled Girma. "Now that your bodyguards and lackeys are gone? Where is your haughty manner?"

Girma kicked him in the head. Blood spurted onto Kimko's boot. This enraged him; he stepped back, than lowered his AK-47 and fired point-blank into his enemy's skull. The men nearby shielded their faces against the bits of flesh and blood that splattered toward them.

"Let the dogs have his body!" yelled Girma. He fired into the dead man's midsection to emphasize his point.

A woman screamed inside the hut on the other side of the road. Gunfire quickly followed. Kimko turned in time to see three soldiers, none older than fifteen, emerge from the hut. It took absolutely no imagination to realize what they had done.

"We are in control!" yelled Girma, clapping Kimko on the back. "Come! We will go and get your airplane. You are our hero. You have made all of this possible, with your weapons."

20

Duka

THEY WENT TO THE SMALLER BUILDING FIRST. EVEN AT A trot, Melissa found it hard to keep up with Danny and Flash. They were dressed in full combat gear, helmets, vests, and heavy boots, along with their guns and assorted equipment, and yet they moved like cheetahs, leaping forward. She quickened her pace, then dropped belatedly as they hit the dirt.

"What?" she said, but either they didn't hear or simply ignored her, rising and moving in opposite directions to flank the concrete structure. Unsure what to do, Melissa decided to follow Danny; she half crawled, half ran in an arc behind him.

"Clear," hissed Danny when she caught up to him.

At first she thought he was giving her some sort of command, but then realized he was telling Flash over the radio that there was no one on his side.

"Come on," he told her. "Let's have a look. I want to plant a bug inside."

The only opening was a steel door, secured by a combination lock. Danny took out a small key gun—a lock-picking device that offered various small picks to work keyed locks.

"I hate picking locks," he said.

"Here, let me see," she told him.

Melissa took the small device—folded, it was about the size of a pocketknife—and worked the main lock on the door, clicking the tumblers quickly. But the combination lock was wedged in a way that prevented her from seeing the back. She twirled the dial a few times, then tried a popular combination, passing thirty-six, then coming back to twelve, then coming back as she gently applied pressure, hoping to find the last number.

She didn't. The lock remained fastened.

"You're going to have to remember some numbers for me," she told Danny.

Holding the lock in her left hand, she put her right ring and middle fingers through the lock and began turning the dial gently back and forth, feeling for the gates. She ended with ten numbers, separated by four digits.

"What are you going to do? Try every combination?" asked Danny.

She wasn't, just the most likely ones, which on that sort of lock were almost always the solutions. She went slowly at first, then fell into a rhythm. She got it on the fourth try.

"Here you go," she told Danny, slipping the lock off its hasp.

He creaked the door open, dropped to his knees and peered inside.

"Forget it," he said. "Inside's filled with junk. They're not meeting here."

THEY WERE HALFWAY TO THE SECOND BUILDING WHEN MY-PID told Danny that the Russian had just gotten into his vehicle.

"They're on their way," Danny told Flash over

the radio. "Drop back and cover me. I'll get some bugs down."

"Yeah, roger."

Danny turned back to Melissa, who was huffing next to him as he ran.

"They're coming," he told her. "I want you to hide over there."

He pointed to the ditch across the road. It was about thirty yards from the building.

"What are you going to do?"

"I'll get a bug in and get out."

"Is Li Han coming?"

"He hasn't made a move yet that we've seen. Stay back," Danny added. "If you see anyone coming, just keep your head down. We'll take care of it."

He didn't wait for her to answer, sprinting toward the building. Much of the roof had fallen in, and the UAV's infrared camera could give MY-PID a fairly clear view into about two-thirds of the interior. There was also no door, and hence no lock. Danny stepped over a small pile of rubble into the ground floor and scanned the interior. An old desk sat to his left, surrounded by bricks and the debris. The two floors above looked like the broken teeth of a sawed-off comb, jagged and leaning down. He hopped onto the desk, reaching up to the remains of the floor above, and placed a bug there.

"Subject is estimated to be two minutes away," warned MY-PID.

Danny jumped back down. As he turned to go, he realized he'd left two large boot prints on the top of the desk. He swept the top with his hand,

but that only made things look even stranger—
now the desktop was the only thing in the place
not covered with dust.

Not sure what else to do, he reached his hands
under and pulled the desk up onto its back, removing the top from sight. Then he spread bricks
and some large beams over the area.

"Subject is thirty seconds away," warned the
computer.

"What happened to my two minutes?" he demanded.

MY-PID took the question seriously and asked
him to rephrase.

Danny bolted to the door. He sprinted toward
the spot where he'd left Melissa, bounding in with
a head-first dive.

"Here he comes," said Flash.

"Any sign of Li Han?"

"Negative."

21

Duka

Kɪᴍᴋᴏ ɢᴏᴛ ᴏᴜᴛ ᴏғ ᴛʜᴇ ᴊᴇᴇᴘ ᴀɴᴅ ᴡᴀʟᴋᴇᴅ ᴏᴠᴇʀ ᴛᴏ ᴛʜᴇ
building, trying to get as much distance between
himself and Girma as possible. He needed a plan
to get away from him. The odds of that happen-

ing peacefully shrank exponentially with each khat leaf Girma stuffed into his mouth.

The sun had gone down about a half hour before. Li Han was undoubtedly waiting somewhere nearby, watching. Hopefully he wouldn't be spooked by Girma and his men.

Maybe he'd kill the bastard. Now there was a possibility, Kimko thought. Maybe he could work that into the deal.

The building was a wreck, though at least this one couldn't be blamed on Girma. Kimko took a small LED flashlight from his pocket and shone it around the place. There was a battered desk and a massive pile of debris, and nothing else.

The hell with the UAV, he decided. He was getting out of Africa as soon as possible. He'd walk if he had to.

"Where is your man!" shouted Girma, back near the truck.

Kimko could shoot the bastard himself—but could he take the bodyguards as well?

Girma walked through the door. "Where is he?" demanded the African. His AK-47 was slung under his shoulder, his hand near the trigger.

"He's late," said Kimko.

"Ha! You see—you cannot trust these people. Chinese."

"He's working with the Brothers," said Kimko.

"Ha, the Brotherhood are cowards. You see, none of these people have the strength of Girma. Girma is a lion!"

Girma is an asshole, thought Kimko.

"How long do you wait?" Girma asked.

"I don't know."

"You don't wait!" shouted Girma. "You go to see him."

"I don't know where he is."

Girma smiled. "You are with the lion now. Come."

22

Duka

THE WOMEN HAD SETTLED INTO A KIND OF SEMICOMA-tose state of shock, huddled together next to the ruined outbuilding on the slaughterhouse property. Gunfire continued sporadically in the city, stoking up for a few minutes, then dying down, like a fitful whale surfacing for a romp before heading back to the depths. Nuri knew from MY-PID that the Sudan First army was routing Meurtre Musique. It was a murderous fight, with the defeated shown no mercy; both sides simply gunned down anyone who attempted to surrender, women and children included.

"Looks like some of them are headed in our direction," he told Boston. "Can we call in the Osprey?"

"They ain't gonna make it," said Boston. "They're waiting for Li Han to show up at the meeting. Colonel Freah wants the MV-22 to stay away until they make the attack. Might spook him."

Naturally, thought Nuri. It was the right decision, but it didn't make things easier for them.

"What do you think we should do?" he asked.

"I say we cross out of this field and head north," said Boston. "We get into the brush, hide there. Sitting here makes no sense. The tangos are more than likely to come up and look in the building. I know I would."

"You think we can get them moving?"

"We can always carry them," said Boston. "I'll scout down to the road and come back. Be ready."

Nuri got up and went to the nurse, Bloom. She was holding the baby in her arms, swinging him gently back and forth. The baby's mother was passed out next to her, slumped backward against the side of the building.

"We have to move," he said. "The troops are coming this way."

"They're exhausted," said Bloom.

"We *have* to move."

"I can't."

"We have to." Nuri looked at her. "You're with MI6?"

She shook her head. "I was. I quit."

"Well don't quit now." He reached down and helped her up. Then he looked at the woman who'd given birth. Her mouth gaped open; Nuri wasn't even sure she was still alive until he bent close and heard her breathing.

There was no way she was moving on her own.

He dropped to his knee and shifted his shoulder so he could lift her in a fireman's carry. He rose with a grunt, stumbling back a step, not quite balanced. Then he started to move toward the road.

There was a low whistle in the air behind him.

Shit, he thought as the mortar shells began to land near the main building.

23

Duka

"WHERE'S THE RUSSIAN GOING?" FLASH ASKED DANNY over the radio as their subjects got back into the jeep.

"Damned if I know."

"They didn't take anything."

"Yeah, I know. Stand by."

Danny had MY-PID replay the translated conversation. It sounded as if the African Kimko was with knew where Li Han was.

"What's going on?" asked Melissa.

"They didn't want to wait for Li Han," Danny told her. "I think they're going to find him."

"Shouldn't we go there?"

"Let's let them get there first," said Danny. "If I bring the Osprey in, Li Han may run."

"It would be easier to talk to you if you didn't

have the helmet on," Melissa said. "At least flip the shield up."

"I'm watching them," he told her.

"Oh."

He flipped the shield up anyway. "I'm not trying to be rude."

"I know. I just—I'm not familiar with your gadgets."

MY-PID told Danny the car was stopping at the house where they had placed the initial bug. He flipped down the screen again and watched the UAV feed as the men went to the door. The African who'd been talking to the Russian took the lead. Their two escorts fanned out around them. There was a flash, then they entered the building.

"Shit," said Danny. "Whiplash team—Osprey, get to that building! Flash, let's go."

He turned and started to run. Melissa climbed out of the ditch and sprinted just behind him.

"What?" she gasped between breaths. "What's going on?"

"Looks like they're trying to get a discount on the price," said Danny.

KIMKO GRIPPED HIS PISTOL AS GIRMA LEAPT FROM THE jeep, gun blazing. The gunfire had actually started from the house, but that was immaterial— the whole thing was bollocks.

Damn, damn, damn.

Kimko started toward the front door, then realized that was exactly the last place he wanted to be. Even if he managed to get the UAV now,

Girma was sure to shoot him. He was just too unstable.

If he was going to get out, he was going to get out now.

Without the UAV?

Without the UAV. But with his life.

"I'll cover the back," he yelled, bolting from the front of the house.

DANNY WAS ABOUT FIFTY YARDS FROM THE BACK OF THE house when the Osprey swept in, pivoting around to the street side and depositing the team. The Russian's people had gone through the door; there was gunfire inside the building, a metal staccato of Kalashnikov rifles.

"Left!" Danny yelled to Flash. "Take the left."

"Subject running eastward," warned MY-PID.

"Zoom."

The system ID'ed the figure as the Russian. He was about sixty yards from the house, running toward the warehouses.

"Was he inside the building?" Danny asked MY-PID.

"Negative."

"What does he have with him?"

"One handgun, unidentified."

"Radio?"

"Uncertain. No transmissions."

"Track him. Stay on him."

"Tracking."

Danny decided they could ignore the Russian for now; obviously he'd panicked.

"Osprey, take out all the vehicles around the target house," he radioed. "Team, stand back."

The chain gun under the MV-22's nose began to revolve. A spray of black and red began to spit from the mouth of the 30mm twin cannons, chewing the vehicles into pieces with the staccato jabs of a boxer hitting a speed bag. The quick and brutal rhythm eliminated the jeep and the two white pickups parked at the side.

Suddenly the Osprey jerked hard on its wing, fire igniting behind it—flares.

Someone inside the house had fired a missile.

24

Duka

THE WOMAN NURI CARRIED SEEMED TO GAIN TEN POUNDS with every step. She was slung over his shoulders and inert, like a sack of rapidly hardening cement. His pace slowed as he ran down the hill toward the road, and even the inspiration provided by the mortar shells that were starting to fall in the field near the house began to wane. He squeezed the woman's legs tighter as the shaking ground caused him to lose his balance. He caught himself, only to jab his left foot into a hole a moment later. He tumbled forward, trying to send his free shoulder to the ground first and avoid crashing onto the woman.

The next thing he knew, he was in Boston's arms. The trooper broke their fall and set them on the ground.

"Damn, you're heavy," he told Nuri.

"Thanks."

Boston scooped up the woman and hurried across the nearby road. Nuri followed, out of breath. It was now dark, and in the uneven field Nuri tripped again and fell flat on his face. As he rose, he heard machine gun fire back near the slaughterhouse.

By the time he reached the others, Boston had organized them into a little clump behind some brush at the edge of a thick layer of woods.

"Osprey will be here soon," said Boston. "They just went in."

"Good," said Nuri, getting his breath.

The women clustered around Bloom, hugging her for warmth or perhaps protection.

"Shit," said Boston, looking back toward the slaughterhouse.

"They're coming down toward the road," he said. "They must have seen us."

One of the small buildings near the slaughterhouse erupted in fire. The red light silhouetted three figures with guns coming down the side of the hill.

"We can get deeper into the woods," suggested Nuri.

"Don't want to get too deep," said Boston. "Who knows what the hell's in there?"

"Whatever it is, it's better than what's in front of us."

"I'm going to draw them away." Boston got to his feet.

"Wait!"

"Don't worry. Take them into the woods. I'll get them from the side. When the Osprey is clear, I'll hear and come back."

"Boston! Hey! Stop."

But Boston was gone.

25

Duka

THE OSPREY PIROUETTED IN THE SKY, ITS PROPELLERS straining. In level flight it was at least twice as fast as the average helicopter and considerably stronger. But in a hover it was not much more maneuverable than the average Blackhawk, and a somewhat bigger target.

The Stinger that had been launched at it sniffed its decoy flares, homing in on them rather than the baffled exhaust from the MV-22's engines. It quickly realized it had been duped and exploded, spraying the air with shrapnel. Fortunately, the Osprey pilots were able to get the aircraft far enough away from the warhead so the hot metal fragments completely missed.

But they had a much more difficult time with the simpler rocket-propelled grenade, launched from a different window. Aimed by sight, it was fired as the MV-22 swung away from the Stinger, and by luck or well-trained design, it crossed the path the aircraft was taking. It struck the fuselage a glancing blow. The effect was not unlike what would have happened had the shell hit a caged armor arrangement, greatly decreasing the weapon's impact. Nonetheless, it sent pieces of metal through the side of the aircraft and one of the propellers.

The MV-22 shuddered abruptly, a frightened horse trying to buck its rider at the sight of a rattlesnake. The two pilots settled her quickly, easing off the stricken engine and trimming their controls to compensate. They edged the aircraft into a wide bank as gently as they could, then found a place to land in a field opposite the railroad tracks, about eight hundred yards away.

In the few seconds it took for the Osprey to right herself, Danny located the room the missiles had been fired from. Hopes of recovering the Raven without damage were no longer operative; he pumped a grenade into the launcher attached to his SCAR, took aim, and fired the 40mm shell into the house.

There was a low thud as it exploded. The corner of the building imploded, crumbling in on itself.

"Osprey, what's your status?" said Danny as the dust settled.

"We're intact, Colonel. We're on the ground. We have problems with one engine."

"Can you fly?"

"We're checking the systems. We should be able to, but I don't know what our payload will be. I'm just not sure yet, Colonel."

"Roger that. Keep me informed."

My fault for letting them get too damn close, Danny thought.

"Colonel, doesn't look like we have any more resistance," said Sugar. She was on the other side of the building. "No more activity. No gunfire."

"Hold your positions," he answered.

Whether he'd been too aggressive in bringing the Osprey up close, Danny now reacted by being cautious, having MY-PID analyze the situation before proceeding. The computer assessed at fifteen percent the likelihood that some of the gunmen inside were still alive and able to fight. It based this assessment on an elaborate algorithm, the sum not only of what it had seen of the battle to this point but of hundreds of other firefights whose data had been entered into its memory.

But what did fifteen percent really mean? Danny didn't know. In truth, he wasn't comfortable with using the system in that way to help him make combat decisions, which was why he hadn't bothered to ask for the assessment earlier.

It was better just to go with your gut.

"All right, team up," he barked. "Shug, you know how this is done. Anything moves, nail it down. With *prejudice*."

Sugar quickly organized a small group to enter the building. Rather than going through the front door, they blew a hole in the side, tossed grenades in for good measure, then entered in undertaker mode: anything that was alive wouldn't be when they were done.

Danny watched the building anxiously for signs that it might collapse.

"Secure," said Sugar finally. "We have seven individuals, all dead, on the main floor. Checking the rest."

"Seven?" It was several more than MY-PID had predicted.

"There's a basement, Colonel. Looks like they might have been sleeping or hiding down there."

"Roger that." He flipped up his shield. Melissa was standing nearby, looking at him.

"Nothing so far," he told her.

"I want to go in."

"I don't know if it's safe."

"If it's safe for them, it's safe for me. This is my deal."

"All right."

"Where's Li Han inside?"

"He's still back at the other house." MY-PID had the other building under surveillance; no one had moved inside.

"Don't you think that's strange? He missed an appointment here," added Melissa. "With all the fighting? He's still just sitting there?"

"You've been watching him, you tell me. You say he's patient—he sat in a cave for weeks."

"True."

The damage to the Osprey upset Danny's plan to hit the house immediately after taking this one.

He needed to get over there fast, but they didn't have transportation.

"Boston, you on the circuit?" he asked.

Boston didn't answer right away. Danny had MY-PID zoom the Global Hawk image onto his location. He was surprised to see that Nuri and Boston had split up—Nuri was across the street, and Boston was in the field.

Then he saw why.

"Busy at the moment, Colonel," answered Boston. "How long before that Osprey gets here?"

"We have a problem with the bird," said Danny. "What are you dealing with?"

"Dozen tangos in the weeds. I have it under control."

There was a burst of gunfire.

"We'll be there as soon as we can," Danny told him.

MELISSA STEPPED THROUGH THE HOLE IN THE SIDE OF the building, then moved to the side, trying to get her eyes to adjust. It was dark outside but even darker in here; she saw absolutely nothing.

One of the Whiplash people loomed in front of her, the black combat gear making him blend into the background.

Her blend into the background. It was Sugar.

"Ms. Ilse?"

"Yes. Are any of the people in the house Mao Man—Li Han, the Chinese agent?"

"No Asians. All African. There's gear and what looks like the UAV in the basement," said Sugar. "Can you come this way?"

"OK."

"Uh, you can't really see, can you?"

"No."

Sugar reached to her sleeve and flipped on a light. An LED beacon was sewn into the cuff. "Better?"

"Much," said Melissa. She followed the trooper to a door near the front of the house and descended a set of steps. There was a body halfway down, riddled with bullets. The blood on the steps below was still wet.

Melissa scooped up the AK-47 at the bottom of the stairs.

"This way," said Sugar, leading her to the side.

The Raven UAV sat in the middle of the basement. It was missing a wing and part of the tail section. Part of the fuselage had been disassembled, and the cover for the computer area was missing as well. Melissa rushed over to it, sliding to her knees to examine it like a child rushing to open presents on Christmas.

The computer was missing.

Shit. Damn.

She looked up at Sugar.

"We need to search the basement and the rest of the house for circuitry, memory boards," she told her. "Anything that looks like a computer."

26

Duka

WHEN NURI HEARD THE GUNFIRE IN THE FIELD, HE glanced at the women. They stared at him blankly, sharing the frozen expression of people resigned to a terrible fate. Even Bloom seemed to have given up. Her lips were moving rapidly though no sound came from her mouth.

She was praying, he realized.

Only the newborn seemed to have any spirit left—his eyes darted around, still in wonder at the wide world around him.

No way was he going to get them to move.

"All right, I need you to stay here," he told Bloom. "Whatever happens, stay hidden. You understand? Do you understand?"

She didn't answer.

"Hey!" Nuri started to shout, then realized that wasn't wise. The result was a loud hiss, foreign even to him. He grabbed Bloom's arm and shook her. "Do you hear me? You're going to stay. All of you."

"We stay," she repeated.

Nuri took his Beretta from its holster. "Use this if you need it," he told her.

She stared at it.

"If you need it," he told her, pushing it at her.

What he meant was—kill yourself and the women so you don't have to suffer if the bastards get past us. But he couldn't say that.

Bloom remained frozen.

"It's here," he told her, putting it down. "I'll be back. Watch them."

Nuri pushed into a crouch, then scooted to his right, deciding he would take the bastards in the field from the side opposite Boston, catching them in a cross fire. Unlike Boston, he didn't have a combat helmet, which meant he didn't have night vision. But he didn't mind it: he could see the outlines of the field and where the enemy was, and he could move without the claustrophobic sense helmets always gave him.

"Boston, I'm going behind them," he said over the team radio circuit.

"Move the women back."

"They ain't movin'. You keep these guys' attention, I'll nail them from behind."

Nuri scuttled along the edge of the woods, his enemy to his left. He wasn't exactly sure how much room to give them before turning. He simply ran for a few seconds, glanced to see where the gun flashes were, then ran a little more. Finally he threw himself down and began crawling in the field.

The Sudan First fighters were clustered near the dirt road where they'd crossed, scattered in a staggered line about four men deep. They'd only had rudimentary training. Besides being packed relatively closely and not recognizing that they were opposed by a single man, they fired wildly, wasting bullets and not coming close to their target.

Three of them, apparently having lost their nerve, began crawling to the west, moving perpendicular to Nuri as he came down the hill. Trying to get away, they were inadvertently coming toward him.

Nuri raised his rifle. He leaned his head over, peering through the scope. But he couldn't see the image. He raised his head, checking to make sure the caps were off—they certainly were, and the scope was on and operating. But for some reason his eyes just wouldn't focus. He moved his head back and forth, still trying to see through the damn thing, his nerves starting to rise.

I need to shoot these bastards now!

Finally he decided they were so close he didn't need the scope. He started to pull his head back— and of course that was when the image appeared in front of his eye.

The men were low to the ground, moving on their haunches. He raised his shoulder slightly, bringing the crosshair level with the chest of the first man in the group. Slowly, he swung to the left, praying he wouldn't lose the image.

He tightened his finger against the trigger. The SCAR was a light gun, and for Nuri it always seemed to jump to the right. His plan was to take advantage of that—he'd move in that direction, left to right, taking all three if he could.

His target rose, full in the crosshairs.

The gun gave a light, rapid burp as he pressed the trigger. He swept it right, then brought it back, pumping bullets into the tangos. All three were now on the ground, though he couldn't tell if he'd hit them or they simply flattened at the sound of bullets crashing nearby.

"Grenade!" yelled Boston over the radio.

Nuri turned to look in Boston's direction, hoping his friend would be able to avoid the explosion. Belatedly, he realized that Boston was warning him that *he'd* fired. He ducked as the shell exploded less than forty yards away, back near the larger clump of tangos.

A collective scream followed the bang, one of the wounded men screeching in pain. Nuri turned his attention back to the men in front of him, sighting the prone bodies through his scope. One moved. He fired, but the gun jerked against his shoulder, the bullets flying too high. He leaned back left, fired again. The bodies jerked with the impact of the bullets.

Nuri jumped up and began running toward them. He reached them in a few quick strides, his thighs straining. They lay a few feet from each other, guns on the ground. Dropping to his knees, he grabbed the weapons and tossed them into the field.

Gunfire stoked up again near the road.

"Boston—what's going on?"

"I got three or four more still moving, right by the road. You see them?"

Nuri got to one knee and peered through the weapon's sight. Once again he had an almost impossible time sighting.

Jesus, I'm going blind out here.

Finally he saw them. He loosed a stream of bullets, then saw a glowing tracer flick from his barrel—he'd reached the end of the magazine.

He slammed the box out and around, using the

spare—the team rifles had their mags doubled up so they were easy to change. He fired another burst, then rose to a crouch and began going down the hill.

"What do you think? What do you think?" he asked Boston.

"Yeah, they're down. Hold your position. I want to make sure no one's moving up on the left from the buildings."

Nuri dropped back to one knee. He looked down at the scope and saw it was flickering—it wasn't his eyes; there was something wrong with the optics or circuit.

Somehow, that failed to reassure him.

A dark veil hung close to the ground. He took the scope and found that the image held steady if he kept his hand on the top. He scanned the field. The men closest to him were dead or dying. Nothing else moved.

"All right," said Boston. "We're clear here. You see me? I'm on the road."

Boston rose and waved his arm.

"I see you."

"I'm going to check these bodies here. Then I'm coming up in your direction. You're covering me."

"Right. My scope's screwed up."

"What?"

"Aw nothing. I'm good." Nuri rose. His legs had stiffened and his arm had tensed so long that it felt almost numb. He swung his upper body back and forth slowly, trying to loosen the muscles.

His eye caught something moving in the area

where the grenade had exploded. He froze, staring at it.

Nothing.

Nuri started walking in that direction, moving slowly. The men there must be dead, he knew, yet he was filled with nervous energy, anticipation.

Fear. That was what he was filled with. He was so tired he was starting to be afraid of things.

He stopped about ten yards from the closest dead body.

All dead. Nothing to worry about. Once again he scanned the field, left to right, then back, slowly. He could hear his heart pounding in his chest.

And something else. Something pushing against the tall grass.

He turned in its direction and started to raise his rifle so he could use the scope. A shadow rose near the road.

"Watch out!" he yelled.

In the same moment he lowered the barrel of his rifle and fired a burst, short of the shadow. Without thinking he raised his left arm slightly and fired another burst, this one dead on.

There was a scream. Boston, on the other side of the road, fired as well.

"You OK?" he asked Boston.

"I'm good, I'm good. We get him?"

"Yeah, he's done."

Nuri took a long, deep breath, then tried not to breathe at all, listening.

"Not bad work for a spy," said Boston when he came close. "Back to the women?"

They found them exactly where Nuri had left them. The pistol was still on the ground, a few feet from Bloom.

27

Duka

KIMKO RAN UNTIL HIS LUNGS FELT LIKE RED HOT IRON burning through his chest. Explosions, gunfire, the Osprey—he was running from the Apocalypse, the Horsemen determined to drag him to hell. Finally his legs gave out: he tumbled forward in a heap, collapsing in the front yard of a native hut.

He had no energy, no will to live. The damp ground swallowed him; the night soaked into his pores.

At some point he realized the gunfire had stopped.

I must go, he told himself, *before they come for me.* And so he began to crawl, tentatively at first, then more steadily.

Escape.

Finally, Kimko climbed to his feet and began walking. He took stock as he walked, figuring out where he was—east of the city, in the scrub hills that rose into mountains. He tried to make sense of what had happened: the Americans had intervened in the small war, surely to get their UAV back.

He tried to think of what to do. He couldn't go back to the Sudan First camp, clearly, and to go back to the city was death. But by the same token, he couldn't survive out here by himself. Even if the Americans didn't hunt him down and the two different factions left him alone, the wilderness was not a place for a man with only a pistol.

It would take at least a day on foot to reach another settlement; it could easily take longer if he got confused.

What was he to eat? Or drink—he craved vodka, and would gladly now have drunk a liter without stopping, without even thinking.

He had his sat phone. He could call his supervisors for help.

It meant admitting that he had failed. It also wouldn't guarantee help would be sent. On the contrary, further failure might be viewed in the harshest possible light. They might leave him to rot.

He needed to think of a better plan.

28

Duka

DANNY'S FIRST PRIORITY WAS THE OSPREY. THE AIRcraft could take off with one engine, the pilots assured him, but it would be slow and its lifting ability would be limited; better to wait while they assessed the damage to the propeller and the engine, which they believed might be easily repaired. Though dubious, Danny agreed. He assigned Hera and two troopers to help and maintain a perimeter.

The next problem was to retrieve the UAV Sugar had found in the building. The aircraft was light, but Danny didn't want to waste time or manpower carrying it to the Osprey. Instead, he told Sugar and two other troopers to leave it in the basement with charges in case it had to be destroyed; in the meantime they would guard the house.

That left two problems: Li Han and the Russian.

According to MY-PID and Danny's own review of the surveillance footage from their UAVs, the Russian had run off without taking anything. He was armed with only a handgun. They had a good view of where the Russian was, about a mile and half to the east. He was on foot, with no one nearby; Danny decided they could leave him for now and concentrate on Li Han.

Which meant getting across town. That was more a problem of distance than resistance: the fight had devolved into a raucous pillaging of the Meurtre Musique area, with about a dozen Sudan First members setting random fires and massacring any civilians who hadn't fled into the fields and jungle to the west.

Danny mapped a path to Li Han's hideout that would skirt the troubled area. It was about three miles by foot.

"Anybody with a gun gets in our way, take them down," he told his small group as they set out.

"I'd like to just shoot them all," said Melissa.

"Yeah, me too," he muttered, then he added more loudly, "Let's stay focused."

They'd gone about a half mile when MY-PID reported a pair of pickups heading in their direction.

"Here come our taxis," said Danny. He divided the group, splitting them along the road.

"Flash, you have the second truck; I have the first," he said. "Shorty, if we don't get the drivers, the trucks stop no matter what."

"Gotcha."

"WHO YOU GOING WITH?" DANNY ASKED MELISSA.

She hesitated, then ran after Flash.

By now her body had been bruised and strained to a point beyond exhaustion. Her mind seemed to have sunk into a place below her head somewhere, as if her body were a tower where it could roam freely. The gunshots, the explosions, the Osprey rotors—all of the miscellaneous loud noises had hardened her eardrums and encased her head in a shell.

Melissa copied the team as they took positions, sliding down on one knee like the others. At the last moment her trail foot snagged and she tumbled sideways, rolling awkwardly. She stayed down for a moment, dizzy and embarrassed. Finally, she tucked her elbow against the ground and levered up just in time to hear a gun burst nearby. There was another pop, then silence.

Unsure what was going on, Melissa craned her neck and saw that everyone was moving. She pushed to her knees, then hopped up and ran with the rest.

DANNY TOOK A POSITION A SHORT DISTANCE FROM THE road, visor up, sighting through his scope as the two trucks barreled toward them. The drivers appeared to be either drunk or having some sort of contest; they veered back and forth, the one in the front not letting the other pass. He zeroed in on the driver, pacing his weave.

"Mine," he said, and fired. The bullet slammed into the driver's forehead, killing him instantly. The pickup veered to the right; the vehicle behind it rammed into the rear, twisting and then stopping itself, the driver shot through the temple by Flash.

The rest of the team opened fire then, downing the five men packed into the rear of the trucks. The gunfight was over before any of the tangos had a chance to pick up their weapons.

"Let's get the vehicles," said Danny, starting to run.

29

Ronald Reagan Airport
Washington, D.C.

ZEN ROLLED HIS WHEELCHAIR FORWARD AS SOON AS HE saw Breanna walking toward the baggage area. It felt good to see her—all these years, and there was still a twinge of excitement after a long separation.

"Hey, if it isn't the lonesome traveler," he said loudly, getting her attention despite the crowd.

"Zen—what are you doing here?"

"I was looking for somebody to have a scandalous affair with."

"Tired of being a senator?" She leaned down and kissed him.

"Actually, I think it would help my career."

"Teri?" she said, asking about their daughter.

"I sold her to the nuns."

"Stop," she said, swatting at him playfully.

"Misses her mother terribly. I guess my cooking just isn't good enough for her."

"I'll bet. And how are you?"

"Trying to duck the latest tempest in a teapot—there's your bag."

Breanna grabbed it off the carousel, and with a well-practiced flick of her wrist, extended the handle.

"Jay's in a no-parking zone out front," said Zen, spinning around to lead the way.

"Just because you have government plates doesn't mean you can park where you like," scolded Breanna playfully.

"Sure it does."

She laughed. "So what controversy are you ducking?"

"Some big blowup about a CIA program. Something called Raven. Ernst has a bug up his ass about it."

Breanna was silent. Zen glanced up at her. Her face had suddenly gone white.

"Bree?"

"Where did you park?"

"Is there something I should know about?" said Zen. "Do you have something to do with Raven?"

"Why?"

Crap, he thought. Breanna had to be the worst liar in the world.

"Bree—"

"Maybe I'll grab a cab and head straight for the office," said his wife.

"Whoa, hold on." He grabbed the bag handle— it was the only thing he could reach as she started to pull away. "Truce, OK? No work discussion. None."

"I have to get to the office."

"We'll drop you off."

"That might not look right."

"Breanna, what's going on?"

They were stopped right in front of the doors. People swerved around them, a little more indulgent than they might have been as one of the obstacles was in a wheelchair.

"Jeff, I can't discuss it. You know."

"Come here," he told her, motioning with his head to the side. "Come on."

She went over, clearly reluctant.

"Listen," he started, "just to fill you in—Ernst has heard all sorts of rumors about this CIA program. Supposedly it's some sort of unauthorized assassination deal. You know Ernst, you give him a whiff of something to bash Ol' Battle-axe with and he's off to the races."

Ol' Battle-axe was one of Zen's nicknames for the President. It was considerably more benign than many of his others.

"If you're involved in this," he added, "you really oughta tell me."

"Raven is not an Office of Special Technology project."

"You're lawyering up."

"Jeff—don't push me."

Zen put his elbow on the chair rail and leaned his forehead down. When he had urged her to take her job—and he *had* urged her—he promised they would keep their private lives separate.

It was the sort of promise that always came back to kick him in the butt, time after time.

"I'm not going to push you," he said. "Let's grab something to eat. Just you and me."

"I have to get back to the office," she said, pushing away.

"I'm glad you're back!" he said as she went off.

The sentiment was sincere, but so were the curses under his breath as he wheeled around and headed for his van.

30

Duka

THERE WERE NO PARALLEL ROADS TO THE HIGHWAY leading out of town, and the hills would make it hard to flank the house quickly. Danny decided it would be best to race past the house to the south where some of the brothers were and go directly to Li Han's. MY-PID would track Li Han if he escaped; his lack of a vehicle meant he couldn't get very far.

There was gunfire from the lower house as they passed, but neither of the trucks was struck. Two troopers jumped from the back as they passed, securing the road in case the men there decided to interfere. The rest of the team sped on to the target.

By now Danny had a bad feeling about the house and Li Han. MY-PID was powerful but not infallible. He hypothesized that there might be a tunnel deep enough and long enough for the bastard to have escaped.

No one fired as they pulled up and surrounded the place. They blew out the front door and went in with flash-bangs and guns ready.

Li Han was lying exactly in the middle of the floor, dead. The flight computer and missing circuitry for the Raven was nowhere to be found.

"Looks like somebody did your work for you," Danny told Melissa when she rushed in.

BLOWBACK

———

1

Room 4, CIA Campus

BREANNA ARRIVED AT ROOM 4 JUST IN TIME FOR THE tail end of Danny's update. He was speaking from inside a truck as he drove to the Osprey; his face, projected by a camera embedded in his helmet, looked worn. His voice was hoarse. The fighting in the city had died down, even the victors decimated and exhausted.

"I never asked MY-PID to analyze whether Li Han was dead or not," Danny said. "The computer just responded to my questions. I should have."

"Would it have changed anything, Danny?" asked Breanna. "If you knew he was dead earlier?"

"I don't know," he said.

They hadn't seen him killed, and the slow loss of temperature over time was hard to detect through the thick thatch of the roof. But Breanna knew that Danny would in fact blame himself for missing what he considered a key piece of information.

"That may be one area to improve MY-PID's programming," she said. "Having some sort of prompt if a subject is dead or wounded."

"Yeah."

"How bad is the damage to the aircraft?" Breanna asked. "Can you evacuate?"

"The backup Osprey just refueled in Ethiopia and is en route," said Danny. "The crew says they can get Whiplash One airborne if necessary. They've been talking to Chief Parsons."

"Good," said Breanna. Parsons, a former maintainer and chief master sergeant at Dreamland, was her personal assistant, a troubleshooter for all things mechanical.

Danny believed that they had enough weapons and ammunition to hold off anything the locals could throw at them over the next twenty-four to forty-eight hours, which would give them more than ample time to figure out what to do about the damaged MV-22.

The real problem was finding Raven's guidance system. While they had to recheck all the places they had raided and get the Russian, Danny believed that the most promising theory was that one of Li Han's guards had taken it. That would explain why he had been shot.

"If it is in the Brothers camp, can you get in there and search?"

"I need to study the place," said Danny. "We won't be able to just go up and knock on the door."

They spent a few minutes discussing logistical matters, Breanna making sure they were well supplied. If they did hit the camp, Danny wanted some equipment from the States as well as more personnel.

"All right. Get some sleep," she told him when they were ready to sign off.

"When I get a chance," said Danny. He tried to smile, but it only made him look more tired.

"I FELT I HAD TO INFORM THE PRESIDENT," REID TOLD Breanna. "There was no other choice."

"I know."

"The rumors may have come from her staff, but more likely they came from the Agency."

"Why would Edmund leak it?"

"I doubt it was him. Not everyone in the organization appreciates his leadership." Reid paused. Anyone in a position of authority anywhere in government had many enemies. "He hasn't been particularly forthcoming with me."

Reid reiterated what Rubeo had told him, and what he had heard about the software. But the lack of information from Edmund was frustrating; he simply didn't know how dangerous Raven was.

"In theory," he told Breanna, "Rubeo believes it could take over any sort of computing device, adapting and changing itself to fit the medium. But how far along they are in actual fact and practice, I simply don't know."

Breanna pushed the hair at the side of her head back, running her fingers across her ear. The gesture reminded Reid of his wife when she was younger.

"Did you tell Danny this?" she asked.

"I haven't shared Dr. Rubeo's assessment, no. There's no need, operationally. Clearly, he knows it's not just a board of transistors, based on our concern. I don't know how much the CIA officer on the ground has told him. Or what she even knows, for that matter."

"Could she be in the dark as well?" Breanna asked.

"Hard to say."

"Why in God's name—"

"They probably felt that, because it was Africa, there was no risk. That would be a common perception."

"Misperception," said Breanna.

"Yes."

The Agency was famous for such misperceptions, thought Reid—always underestimating the enemy. That was the cause of most intelligence failures, wasn't it? Lack of imagination, lack of crediting the enemy with as much if not more foresight than you had? That was the story of Pearl Harbor, of the Russian H-bomb, of 9/11—of failure after failure, and not just by the U.S.

"The political controversy adds another dimension," continued Reid. "They have even more incentive to clam up. I wouldn't be surprised if they thought we leaked it."

Breanna frowned.

"It's going to cause trouble with your husband," added Reid. "I'm sorry for that."

"We'll deal with it." Breanna straightened and rose from the table. "Which one of us will tell the President that we have the UAV but not the computer?"

"I think we should both make the call."

2

Duka

IN THE END, IT WAS MOMENTUM RATHER THAN LOGIC OR threats that got the women moving—Nuri and Boston pulled each to their feet and nudged them in the right direction, simply refusing to take no or inaction as an answer. They shuffled rather than walked, but it was progress nonetheless. Nuri took the infant from Bloom, hunching his body over it to keep it warm. It was sleeping, its thumb in its mouth.

Boston led the way around the outskirts of the woods, hiking toward the north-south highway that ran through the city to the south. There was still a glow from the center of town; the air smelled of burnt wood and grass. Sudan First appeared to have wiped out Meurtre Musique, but the rebels had lost so many people that in all likelihood the city would eventually be abandoned.

They were just in sight of the picket Danny had set up around the fallen plane when the backup Osprey arrived. It came in from the north, having taken a wide circle around the city to avoid any possible enemies. The aircraft swung down to the ground ahead, barely a shadow in the night.

"Why'd you bring the women?" asked Danny as the small group staggered into the makeshift camp.

"I didn't know what else to do with them," said Nuri.

"They can't stay with us."

"I know, but we can get them to a refugee camp or something."

"Where?"

"I don't know." Nuri turned to find Bloom. She was walking with the woman who'd given birth, moving mechanically.

"We're going to take you to a camp," he said. "Where would be the best place?"

Instead of answering, Bloom reached her hands out to take the baby.

"A camp," said Nuri, reluctantly turning him over. "Where would the best one be?"

"Maybe you should ask which is the least worst," said Melissa. "I'll talk to her."

"It's all right. I have it under control," said Nuri.

"She's not talking to you."

"She's not going to talk to you either."

But Bloom did, haltingly and in a faraway voice. She suggested a place called Camp Feroq, which was run by her relief organization a hundred miles southwest.

"I never heard of it," said Nuri.

"I'm sure we can find it."

Nuri found himself arguing against it, though he wasn't exactly sure why. He told Melissa that they should be relocated somewhere nearby, which would make it possible for them to eventually return. Yet he knew that wasn't logical at all.

"You just suggested they go to a camp themselves," said Danny.

"Most of them are hellholes," answered Nuri.

But he knew Danny was right, and he let the matter drop.

As far as Danny was concerned, his mission was to retrieve every bit of the UAV, and so he wasn't surprised that Reid and Breanna told him that the control unit had to be recovered. But the fact that Breanna was suggesting an attack into the Sudan Brotherhood camp put the matter into an entirely different category.

Before he dealt with that, he needed to finish the search and pick up the Russian.

Given the fact that Nuri could speak Russian, it made sense that he come on the mission, which would be launched from the backup Osprey. Melissa wanted to go as well. Danny told her flatly he didn't want her help.

"I know what the flight computer looks like," she argued. "You need somebody along who can identify it."

"It's a frickin' computer," snapped Nuri. "How hard is that to figure out?"

"The Osprey's going to be pretty packed with the combat team," said Danny diplomatically. "We have to make a couple of drops and then move in. It's a coordination thing. Why don't you watch after the women and help Boston make a plan to research the first building we hit and the area near it. This is just a pickup job. We've all practiced this a million times."

She finally agreed. Aboard the aircraft, Nuri asked Danny why he was being so nice to her.

"I'm not being nice to her."

"She's been lying to us the whole time," said Nuri, standing over him as the aircraft spun toward the hills.

"When has she lied?"

"She hasn't told us the whole story," said Nuri. "She's trying to save her ass and take the credit for getting all the pieces back."

"I don't know about that."

"Don't let these Agency types bulldoze you. They're sweeter than crap to your face, then you find out they've been knifing you in the back."

"Sometimes you act like you got a stick up your ass," Danny told him. "Other times it's a two by four."

The pilot announced they were five minutes from the first insertion.

EXHAUSTED, KIMKO LAY ON THE GROUND, HALFWAY BE-tween sleep and consciousness. His mind threw thoughts out in odd patterns, numbers mixing with ideas, old memories filtering into what he saw around himself in the jungle.

Most of all he wanted vodka.

Kimko thought about letting go and falling asleep. But it would be the same as accepting failure, and that he could not do. So after a long time on the ground he took a deep, slow breath and struggled to his feet.

There were noises around him—wind rushing by. He turned quickly, sure he was being followed by some animal, but nothing appeared.

No, he was alone, very alone, lost in the middle

of Africa and sure to die here, thirsty and tired, a spy, unknown and unloved.

His mind wandered even as he tried to focus on the jungle before him. He saw his ex-wife and spit at her.

He looked down at the ground, looking for the path.

When he looked up, a man in a black battle dress was standing before him.

Kimko turned. There were two more. He was surrounded.

Not by soldiers, by aliens.

A short, youthful man with wide shoulders appeared behind them. He spoke Russian. He was a human.

"Where is the control unit for the UAV?" asked the man. "The flight computer. What did you do with it?"

"What are you talking about?" asked Kimko.

The man raised his pistol and held it in his face.

"Tell me," said the man.

Kimko jerked away, but one of the aliens grabbed him by the shoulder. The grip was intense. It drained all of his strength away.

"Where is the control unit?" demanded the short man, pointing the gun directly at his forehead.

"I have no idea—"

The gun went off. The bullet flew by his head.

Am I dead?

I'm dead.

No, no, it's an old trick. Intimidation. I've done this myself. I've done this.

It's a trick.

"You are coming with us," said the man.

Was he dead? Had Girma the idiot shot him after all?

Kimko started to struggle. This *was* real, though it didn't make any sense—he pushed and threw his fists.

"You're not taking me alive!" he yelled.

But as the words escaped his mouth, he smelled something sweet in his nose. Something was poking his back, poking him in a million places.

Sleep, said a voice inside his brain. *Sleep.*

Milos Kimko collapsed to the ground, already starting to snore.

"SOUNDS LIKE HE'S GOT A BREATHING PROBLEM," Danny said.

"He's OK," said Sugar, checking him over. "That Demerol will keep him out for a while."

"Nolan, you and Shorty see if you can backtrack the trail he came up through. See if he threw anything away," said Danny. MY-PID had already looked at the video feeds, but Danny wanted it checked anyway. "Work your way back to the city. We'll hook up with you."

The two men set out. The rest of the team fanned out nearby, checking to see if Kimko had hidden or dropped anything nearby.

"Searching's a waste of time," said Nuri. "He never got it. I'm beginning to think they never had a control unit in the first place."

"They needed something to fly the plane," said Danny.

"Maybe Melissa took it and she's been lying all this time."

"What do you have against her?"

"I told you, Danny, she's a bad seed."

Danny shook his head.

"I want to take him to Ethiopia and question him," said Nuri.

"That's fine."

"We'll know what he knows in a few hours. But best bet now is probably the Brother who killed Li Han. That's who we need to find."

3

Jomo Kenyatta International Airport
Nairobi, Kenya

AMARA TOOK HIS SHOES OFF AND PLACED THEM IN THE plastic tub. He put his backpack into a second tub, then pushed them together toward the X-ray machine. He felt as if everyone in the airport was looking at him, though he knew that couldn't be the case. He'd already gotten through two different security checks; this was the last before the gate.

With the tubs moving on the conveyor belt, Amara stepped over to the metal detector frame. A portly woman in a military-style uniform held out a blue-gloved hand to stop him from proceeding.

Heart racing, he saw the light on the nearby X-ray machine blinking red.

Don't panic! Don't run!

He looked back the officer. She was motioning him forward.

He stepped through, half expecting the alarm to sound, though he had no metal in his pockets, no explosives, no knives, no weapons. His clothes had been carefully laundered before he was driven to the airport.

Clear. He was clear. On his way to America.

He started to look for his shoes. But the woman with the blue gloves took hold of his arm.

"Sir, step this way," said the woman in English.

Startled, Amara wasn't sure what to say.

"Please," she said, pointing to the side. "Step over there."

Two other officers, both men, came over behind her. Amara stepped to the side, as she had asked. His throat started to constrict. He wasn't afraid—he'd never been a coward—but it seemed unfair to be stopped so early in his mission.

"Please open your bag," said an officer on the other side of the conveyor belt. He spoke English in an accent so thick and foreign that Amara had to puzzle out what he said, and only understood because he was pointing.

He tried to apologize for his hesitation. He'd been told repeatedly to be nice to the guards; it would make them much more cooperative. "I didn't, uh—"

"Open the bag, sir."

Amara reached to the zipper and pushed it

down. He had only a shirt and a book here, as instructed.

"You have a laptop?" said the man.

God, the laptop. He'd forgotten to take it out of the compartment so they could look at it specially.

What a fool! The simplest thing! And now trapped!

"I do, oh I do, I forgot—" he said.

"Could you turn it on, please?" said the officer.

Amara pulled the laptop out and fumbled with it as he reached for the power button. In the meantime, another officer came up behind the first and whispered something in his ear, pointing behind them. They turned around to watch someone else in line.

The computer took forever to boot up. The screen blinked—the hard drive failed the self-test. He had to press F1 to proceed. He did so quickly; the computer proceeded with its start-up.

The security officer who'd had him take out the laptop called over to the woman with the gloves. Then he turned and went with the other man to check on the person he'd pointed out. Momentarily confused, Amara focused on the laptop, waiting patiently for its desktop to appear.

"What else do you have in the bag?" asked the woman officer.

"My shirt, my uh—some paper," he said.

"In this compartment." She reached in and pulled out the power cord and mouse.

"To make it work without the battery," he said.

"Yes, yes, of course. Very good. You must remove laptops separately from now on."

"I'm sorry. I—I forgot."

"Go. You may go."

Amara hastily put everything back in the bag, then went to find his shoes.

He was through. Next stop, America.

4

Washington, D.C.

PRESIDENT TODD STARED AT THE WORN SURFACE ON her desk, her eyes absorbing the varied scars and lines. The desk was her own personal piece of furniture, one of the few pieces she brought to the White House. She'd always found a certain mental comfort in familiar physical objects; the small, solid desk reminded her of her many past struggles, not only hers but those of her father and grandfather, both of whom had been small town doctors in what seemed a different America now. Many a patient's life was saved at this desk, she believed; if wood could be said to have a soul, this one's must surely be a powerful force for good.

She needed some of its strength now. The day's developments had not been good.

There was a knock on the door to her small office.

"Come," she said.

David Greenwich, her chief of staff, poked his head in.

"Mr. Reid and Ms. Stockard have arrived, ma'am," he said. "Everyone else is in the cabinet room, waiting for you."

"Very good, David."

"You have that dinner with Kurgan and some of the New York crew this evening."

"I won't forget."

"We could cancel."

"Oh, stop, David," she said, rising. "You're mothering me."

"Just looking out for you. I know how much you're going to enjoy that one," he added sarcastically.

"I assure you I'm fine. And tell my husband that as well."

"He didn't say anything."

"I'll bet."

Todd smiled to herself as she left the office. All of these men, fussing over her—it could easily go to her head if she let it.

Then again, reality was always waiting to give her a good kick in the gut if she got too full of herself.

It was giving her a double job today.

BREANNA TOOK A SEAT AT THE LONG TABLE, MAKING SURE she was between Edmund and Reid. Edmund had brought Reginald Harker with him, along with another man, Gar Pilpon. Pilpon, about forty, had extremely white hair and a set of thick, trifocal glasses that made his eyes look almost psychedelic. His pupils were red, or at least appeared to be red in the light of the cabinet room where they were meeting.

President Todd's National Security Advisor, Dr. Michael Blitz, sat at the other end of the table opposite Edmund. Next to him was the President's political advisor, William Bozzone. If the request to brief her in person hadn't been unusual enough, Bozzone's presence signaled that what seemed a routine matter a few days before had blossomed into a full-blown crisis.

"Very good of you all to come on short notice," said the President as she entered. "Don't get up gentlemen. Breanna, I'm glad you could make it. How's your daughter?"

"Very good, Ms. President."

Todd's smile disappeared as she sat down. That was her style: right to business.

"So, as I understand it, we have everything but the computer that runs the aircraft," she said, looking around the table. "Am I correct?"

"That is right," said Breanna.

"And we know where it is?" Todd turned to Edmund.

"My person on the scene is continuing to search."

"I was under the impression that Whiplash had been called in to supervise the recovery," said Todd sharply. Clearly, she was not happy with him or his Agency. She turned back to Breanna. "Am I right?"

"Yes. We recovered the aircraft in a building that was being used by the target of the assassination program. We subsequently found his body on the other side of the city. He apparently was killed by a member of the Muslim separatist group he was helping. We think the killer took the control unit. That's one of our theories, at least."

"How many theories do you have?" asked Blitz. "Jonathon?"

"We are pursuing several," said Reid dryly. They had agreed he would speak sparingly.

"How long before we recover the rest of the aircraft?"

"I can't give an estimate," said Breanna.

"Do they know what they have?" Blitz asked.

Edmund answered before Breanna could.

"The Raven control unit looks exactly like other UAV control units," he said. "It would be impossible for them to know."

"It actually looks quite different," said Reid sharply. "And of course, the programming inside it is very different."

Breanna gave him a slight tap with her foot under the table. He was doing exactly what he had sworn he wouldn't do.

"These Africans are primitive," said Harker. "That's one of the reasons the region was chosen in the first place. They have no idea."

"If they have no idea," said Todd, "then why did they take the control unit?"

"American technology can always be sold. They'd sell a toaster if we dropped one there."

"We have to assume that they *can* figure it out," said Blitz. "Eventually. We need to get the unit back."

"I agree with that," said Edmund.

The President turned toward Breanna and Reid. "You're confident that you can get it?"

"We're reasonably sure," said Breanna. "But it would be foolish to make guarantees. We don't even have all the technical data on the flight computer. We've made our own assessments based on what its capacity is supposed to be, but quite honestly, the amount of information—"

"I'm sorry, I'm not following this," said Bozzone, speaking for the first time. "Are you saying you don't know what you're looking for?"

"We haven't been given a picture of it, let alone the technical details," said Breanna.

"We didn't see that as operationally necessary," said Edmund. The tone of his voice made it clear he would have thrown a brick at Breanna if he had one.

"This doesn't sound like a lot of cooperation," said Bozzone. "At a time when everyone in the administration should be working together. How do you expect them to do their job if you're not helping them?"

"There's a certain amount of need to know—"

"Let's cut to the quick here," said the President. "Herman, you will cooperate. You will give Ms. Stockard and Mr. Reid *whatever* information they require. Is that understood?"

"Yes."

"Now—this computer. How dangerous exactly is it?" asked the President.

"It has—unique capacities," said Edmund.

"It's essentially a virus that, once programmed to kill someone, will not stop trying to do just that," said Reid. Breanna didn't bother kicking him—she would have said the same thing.

Edmund was being almost criminally evasive. "It's very dangerous. If it's released into the wild, so to speak—"

"Well, um, characterizing it as an, um, virus, that is not highly accurate," said Pilpon. "It is, um, simply a set of instructions, carefully controlled. It has been hobbled—"

"But isn't it true that the basic program is designed to adapt to its environment?" asked Reid.

"Yes."

"Which means the program can go into any computer it's hooked into—and by computer, I mean processing chip."

"Well, not um, exactly. It couldn't go into the chip in your car, for example. There are a large number—"

"If I had access to it, I could certainly figure out how to get it into another computer, couldn't I?" asked Reid.

"I don't know about that. The circumstances would be difficult."

"Do the Africans who took the computer know this or not?" asked the President.

"We don't believe so," said Edmund.

"If they have it, it's just a bunch of circuits to them," insisted Harker. "It's a toaster."

The President frowned. "Mr. Edmund, I understand Congress wants to talk to you about Raven."

"The Intelligence Committee has requested a briefing," said Edmund.

Breanna expected a long discussion to follow. Instead, the President rose.

"You will not speak to them until we have recovered this unit," she told him sternly. "Is that clear?"

"Very."

"William, work out the details. Executive privilege, whatever road we have to take. Stall, then bring out the heavy guns. Breanna, Jonathon, please bring this to a successful conclusion quickly. Get it back. I'm sorry, I have to leave, I have other commitments. Thank you all for your time."

5

Duka

THEY WERE IN THE SLOG PART OF THE MISSION—PAST the high excitement of combat, with a lot of work to be done, yet without the adrenaline.

A potentially dangerous time, when fatigue and boredom conspired to make even the most dedicated soldier cut corners.

Danny switched around the assignments to make sure the people searching the buildings had not been involved in the first searches. He personally checked on the different teams, riding back and forth in one of the captured pickups with Melissa. The city had fallen into a stupor, dead and wounded lying near sleeping, exhausted fighters.

"We should do something about that," said Melissa after they passed a pair of rebels lying by the road. MY-PID, analyzing their body heat, reported that they were dead.

"Like what?" said Danny.

"Bury them, at least. I don't know." She shifted uncomfortably in the pickup. The seat belts had been cut away; neither could belt themselves in against the pothole-induced bumps and lurches. "I feel like we should do more."

She was quiet for a while, then, without prompting, volunteered that she had been scared.

"It wasn't the shooting," she said. "It was the baby. I—I didn't know what to do."

"Bloom was there."

"She was. She was panicking about everything except the baby. For me it was the other way around."

"Everybody has a breaking point," said Danny.

"I didn't break. I might have. I could see it."

"True," said Danny.

"I didn't think about them as people when I got here. But now, I see them and I think, oh my God . . ."

Melissa trailed off, silent. Danny wanted to say something but wasn't exactly sure what.

"Maybe you realized why we fight," he said finally, still unsure that he had the right words.

They continued in silence toward the warehouse they had hit the first night. Hera and one of the new Whiplash troopers, Shorty, were standing outside, waiting. They'd just finished searching it, with no sign of any of the missing UAV components. Hera and Shorty had also checked on two small buildings nearby, both deserted. Neither appeared to have been even entered by anyone for months if not years.

"Sorry," Hera told him. She and Shorty got in the back.

"I shouldn't have let the Osprey get hit," Danny told Melissa as they drove back toward their camp.

"How is that your fault?"

"I could have kept it back."

"Would it have been as effective?"

It was a good and obvious question, and one he wasn't entirely sure how to answer. There was always a balance between taking action and being safe.

"I don't know," he said finally. "But I guess I feel I should have told them to be more careful."

"If someone told you that, would it have made any difference?"

"Probably not," conceded Danny.

"I don't see how you're supposed to be perfect— doesn't every plan get changed once the battle starts, or something like that?"

"Something like that." Danny smiled. It was odd how suddenly he felt so comfortable talking to her.

6

CIA Headquarters Campus

JONATHON REID WAS ABOUT TO OPEN HIS CAR DOOR IN the Langley parking lot when a black government limo pulled up behind him. Reid knew exactly who it was, and could have guessed more or less accurately what was going to be said. He wanted to be anywhere but here, but there was no way to escape. He sighed to himself, then turned to face Herman Edmund as the rear window rolled down.

"Jonathon, come in here a moment, would you?" said Edmund.

"I'm actually late for an appointment," said Reid.

"It'll keep."

Reluctantly, Reid walked over to the far side of the car and got in the back, next to the CIA director. There was a partition between the driver and the backseat; it was closed.

"Why are you doing this?" demanded Edmund. "I thought we were friends."

"This isn't personal," said Reid. "There's nothing personal involved."

"You were trying to make me look bad with the President."

"Herm, that's not true. I barely spoke."

"Your tone was atrocious. Raven is an important project," continued Edmund. "It was started two directors ago. It wasn't my idea."

"I'm sure it's important."

"So why are you sabotaging it? What if I were I to do the same with Whiplash?"

"I don't see that as a parallel situation in any way," said Reid.

"No, of course you wouldn't."

"You do oversee Whiplash, the Agency component at least."

"Oh come on, Jon. Everyone knows it's your baby. You got it assembled, you got the funding, you convinced Magnus and the others in DoD to go along. It's your baby. If anyone were to look at it cross-eyed, you'd scream."

"The way Raven was deployed was not characteristic of your best decisions," said Reid. He consciously picked his words, making the stiffest choices. Distance would be useful. This wasn't a personal matter, and Edmund shouldn't see it that way.

"Deploying the weapon without extensive testing and safeguards was ill-advised," Reid continued. "You were almost guaranteed that something would go wrong."

"You have no idea of the safeguards we employed," said Edmund. "Or how much testing it's undergone. Sooner or later it has to be used. That's the real test. This—This was just a bizarre set of circumstances. The Predator caused the accident. It was part of the safeguards and it bit us in the butt—if we hadn't had it with the flight, we wouldn't be here talking."

"It's a powerful weapon," said Reid.

"So powerful it should be under your control. Is that it?"

"Not necessarily, no."

"But if it were a Whiplash project, that would be all right. If your private army had it, then nothing could ever go wrong."

"Whiplash is just our—is just *the* action arm of the Joint Technology Task Force, of Room 4," said Reid. "Nothing more."

"No, 'our' is the key word there." Edmund had a smug expression on his face, strangely triumphant, as if Reid had proven his point. "I want you to think of what you're doing to the Agency here, Jonathon. I know you're jealous of me. But think of the Agency. The institution. Our oaths. Our history. You're going to drag the Agency through the mud. Again. You. Both of us swore we would never let that happen. I'm just surprised that you went back on that. I expected a lot more from you."

"I'm not involved in the politics at all."

"Oh come on. You didn't tell Ernst?"

"Absolutely not."

"I know you're the one who went to the President, Jonathon. What did you do? Use Breanna Stockard? Did she tell her husband? Was he the one who tipped off Ernst? I know he has his own agendas. I don't buy all that hero crap."

"Breanna did not tell either her husband, or Ernst. I have no idea who tipped off the senator. Most likely it was someone on your staff."

"Now you're getting ridiculous." Edmund's face reddened. "Get out, Jonathon. We're done."

"Herm—"

"Out of my car. I can't fire you, obviously, but I can tell you that our friendship is done. I've been too trusting of people. Ironic for a spy, isn't it?"

7

John F. Kennedy International Airport
New York City

AMARA WALKED INTO THE DIMLY LIT HALL TRYING TO GET his bearings after the long airplane flight. He'd been to America before, but that experience didn't help him now. He knew he had nothing to fear—and yet he had everything to fear. The customs agent sat in a small booth similar to a toll collector's. The man frowned as Amara handed over his passport.

"Why are you here?" the agent demanded.

"Vay-Vacation."

"What's a vay-vacation?"

The agent's hostility made it easier somehow.

"I am here to visit my aunt and uncle," said Amara. "I have their address."

The official frowned and began examining his passport. "You've been in America before."

"Yes, sir. I have been to school here."

"You are thinking of getting a job."

"It's very difficult to get a job," said Amara. This

was his first answer that hadn't been rehearsed. But it didn't need to be. "I am helping my country build itself. There is much to be done."

"That makes sense." No longer interested in him, the agent flipped the passport pages back and forth, then stamped his book. "Be careful," he said as he handed it back.

Be careful of what? Amara thought, shouldering his backpack out to the luggage claim area.

A half-dozen men in dark suits were standing near the doors, holding cards with handwritten names. He glanced at them. The terminal building felt a little unbalanced, as if the floor were tilted. He went to the carousel, watching the luggage move around. Three-fourths of the bags were black, and at least half of those looked like his. Amara eyed them nervously, twice examining a suitcase before realizing it wasn't his.

Finally, with the crowd around him thinning, he found his bag. He pulled it off the belt and turned to leave.

"Amara, my cousin," said a man on his right. "We are glad you are here."

His voice was extremely soft—so low, in fact, that Amara nearly didn't hear him. The tone belied the words: rather than being a warm greeting, it sounded cold and impersonal.

Which, of course, it was.

"My uncle," said Amara, trying not to let the words sound like a question.

"This way. We'll take a cab," said the man, who had tan skin, but lighter than his. If he'd had to guess, he would have said he was Egyptian or Palestinian. He took Amara's bag and led him to the large doors at the front of the terminal. "Is your backpack heavy?"

"I have it."

Amara remained on his guard as he was led to a cab parked at the curb.

He knew little of the project, beyond the fact that the Brothers were cooperating with others, presumably in exchange for money.

Amara wasn't sure if the taxi driver, who looked Palestinian, was part of the network. He knew better than to say anything that would give himself away. And as his guide was silent, he thought it best for him to remain so as well.

The city sprawled on both sides of them as they drove toward Manhattan. The rows of houses seemed endless. Tall buildings rose in the distance. It had been nearly three years since he'd been in New York. The city had seemed like a vast temptation, a fascinating place filled with many sweets, a decadent paradise. Or hell, depending on one's point of view.

"First time in New York?" asked his "uncle."

It was a dumb question, thought Amara—his "uncle" should know the answer.

"I have been here before," he said.

"A grand city for a young man like yourself."

Amara turned to the window, staring at the old bridge they were crossing. When he first came to New York, he was surprised to find so many *old* things: he'd assumed the name was literal. And there was a great deal of dirt and grime, so much so that it reminded him of Cairo. But a few days in Manhattan and he stopped noticing such things.

They drove through the heart of the city, weaving through thick morning traffic. Finally, they pulled up to a curb.

"Come now," said his uncle.

Amara got out of the car and waited as the other man retrieved his bag. The driver closed the trunk, nodded, then left.

They descended a long flight of stairs to Penn Station. Two National Guardsmen in battle dress were standing against the wall, M4s ready.

Amara wondered if they had ever used them in battle. Neither man had the hard glance that he associated with tested warriors.

His uncle led him down the long hall of shops, past stores and stalls. Amara's nose was assaulted from every direction; his stomach began to call for food.

They stopped in a crowd of people. His uncle turned toward a large board with the names and numbers of trains.

"We're just in time," he told Amara, reaching into his pocket. "Here is your ticket. Your track is at the end of the hall. Take the elevator on the right. Number twelve. Go."

Amara made his way to the train, an Amtrak Acela bound for Washington, D.C. He settled into a seat and tried to relax as the train pulled out of the station, running through the long tunnel to New Jersey. Within a half hour he had dozed off, exhausted by the travel.

* * *

He saw Li Han's face in his dreams. It was exactly as he had seen him in Sudan: a mixture of sneering and respect, kindness mixed with disdain.

In the dream, Li Han began lecturing him about how to fly the UAV. Amara tried to pay attention, but there was one major distraction—the hole in the middle of Li Han's skull where he'd shot him.

Somewhere in Delaware a conductor shook Amara awake.

"Did you have to get off at this next stop?" asked the man.

Amara jerked upright in his seat. He looked around—he wasn't sure where he was.

"Do you have your ticket?" asked the conductor.

Amara pulled it from his pocket.

"Oh, I'm sorry," said the conductor, examining it. "You're Union Station. All the way in D.C. I apologize. I must have gotten you confused with someone else."

He handed the ticket back. As he took it, Amara realized that he'd been given two tickets.

A message.

He glanced up at the man. He was almost white: Iranian, Amara would guess, or perhaps Iraqi.

There was a phone number on the second ticket. Amara understood he was to call that number when he arrived at Union Station. He tucked it into his pocket, then leaned against the side of the train, hoping to fall back asleep.

8

Sudan Base 1
Five miles southwest of Duka

MELISSA PULLED OUT HER SATELLITE PHONE AS SOON AS the repaired Osprey reached the new operating base Danny had set up southwest of Duka. She was well overdue to check in.

It was still early. Harker might be sleeping.

It would serve him right.

"What?" her boss said gruffly, answering the phone.

"This is Ilse. The flight computer is not in Duka."

"No kidding."

"Our best bet is that it's south in the mountains, with the Sudan Brotherhood. One of their members left the city, probably after killing Mao Man."

"You told me that yesterday, Melissa. This is old information."

"We need permission to search the camp. Can we?"

"That's not up to me. You're *sure* it's not in Duka?"

"We've looked everywhere, believe me."

"And it wasn't at the crash site?"

"God, what do you think? I'm a fool? You do."

"You have to watch these Whiplash people," said Harker. "They're trying to screw us."

"How so?"

"There's all sorts of political bullshit back here. You're sure it's not in Duka?"

"I'm sure."

"Did you personally check every one of the hiding places? Or did Whiplash?"

"Personally?"

"You heard me. Did you?"

Screw you, thought Melissa, hanging up.

DANNY PATTED THE REPAIRED ENGINE COVER OF THE Osprey. Dented and crumpled, the skin looked like a piece of paper that had been wadded up and then pressed flat. But it was tougher than it looked—the whole aircraft was. Despite its shaky early history, the Osprey had proved its worth in countless high-risk situations, and not just for Whiplash.

"She's good for another ten thousand miles," said one of the pilots, admiring the aircraft from the other side of the wing. "I was thinking maybe I'd dent up the other engine housing so they look like a matched set."

"Probably not a good idea," laughed Danny. He pointed to the crew chief and the two maintainers who'd been flown in to help put the aircraft back together. "Those guys might give you grief."

Pretending to notice them for the first time, the pilot spread out his arms and bowed to them. It was a joke, of course, but it reminded Danny of a truism he'd learned back at Dreamland—you did not want to mess with the men and women who maintained the aircraft.

Nor underestimate them. These aircraft sergeants—both were men, and both tech sergeants—had been personally selected by Chief

Master Sergeant Al "Greasy Hands" Parsons, who, though retired, arguably knew more about every operational aircraft in the Air Force inventory than any man or computer. Parsons was always going on about how good a job his people and the Air Force technical grunts in general were; it would have been bragging if it weren't true.

"Colonel, this aircraft will take you to hell and back," said one of the sergeants. "But I have to say, sir, your choice in pilots leaves quite a bit to be desired."

Even the pilot laughed.

Danny walked over to the combination mess/command tent, thinking this might be a good moment to catch a brief nap.

Melissa met him just inside. Her eyelids drooped; she had what looked like thick welts under both eyes.

"When are you going to the Brotherhood camp?" she asked.

"I don't know for certain that we are," said Danny. "But it'll be tonight at the earliest."

"I'm going with you."

"All right."

"You're agreeing?"

"Yeah. I need all the help I can get."

"Oh." Her body seemed to deflate. Danny sensed that she had been prepared to argue with him. But he saw no reason to keep her away; she'd proven herself. And it was at least still partly her mission. "Good."

"The Sudanese army is escorting a bunch of

ambulances and relief workers to Duka," he told her. "They should be there inside an hour."

"Oh?"

"Your friend Bloom arranged it. She's going with them. She is a spy, huh?"

"Used to be."

Danny nodded.

"You oughta get some rest," he told her.

"Yeah," she said. "I should."

9

Ethiopia

MILOS KIMKO WOKE ON THE COT, HIS HEAD POUNDING as if he had a hangover. He had no idea where he was, but he could tell from just the smell that he wasn't in Sudan anymore. The aroma in his nose was less meaty, drier.

He forced his eyes to focus. He was in a canvas tent. He started to get up, only to find that his hands and legs were shackled together.

"You're awake," said a voice in Russian behind him.

Kimko leaned over on the cot. A man dressed in a pair of nondescript green fatigues stood near the flap door. There was another man with a rifle behind him.

"What?" said Kimko.

"Do you prefer English or Russian?" asked the man, still in Russian. He was short, though he had a muscular build.

"Your Russian is atrocious," snapped Kimko. It was an exaggeration—the words were certainly right if a little formal, though his pronunciation could use a little work. But Kimko did not want to give the man the satisfaction.

"English is fine for me," said the man. "What did you do with the UAV?"

"I have no idea what you're talking about."

"Of course you do."

"Who are you?"

"It's not important who I am. Where is the UAV? Did Li Han give it to you?"

"Li Han. Who is Li Han? I don't know him. Who are you? Why have you taken me here? You're an American—I can tell from your accent. Are you CIA? Who are you?"

"It's who you are that's important. You're a Russian gun dealer, violating UN sanctions. You're a criminal."

"I'm not a criminal."

"Do you really think the SVG is going to get you off, Milos? The reality is, they washed their hands of you years ago. When you first turned up with a drinking problem. And when your boss wanted to screw your wife."

Kimko couldn't help but be surprised by the amount of information the man knew. He tried to make his face neutral but it was too late.

"Of course I know," said the other man. "I know everything about you. You were on the scrap heap before they brought you out for this assignment. You thought you hit rock bottom, but it's amazing how much further you had to fall." The man reached into his pocket and took out a small, airplane-size bottle of vodka. "This will make you feel a lot better."

Kimko started to reach for the bottle, forgetting the chains. The man laughed at him and shook his head.

"Where is the UAV?"

Kimko lowered his head, trying to regroup. He had to do better—if he was going to survive, he had to do better.

But he wanted that vodka. The American was taunting him. He knew every weakness.

He had to do better.

He slapped the bottle away. But the man, lightning fast, grabbed it before it fell.

"Good reflexes," said Kimko.

"Thank you."

"Tell me your name," Kimko said. "Tell me your name, so I know who I'm talking with."

"John. You can call me John. Where is the UAV?"

"In the city somewhere." Kimko raised his head. "He said he had it and would show me a picture."

"You'll have to do better than that," said Nuri. He pocketed the vodka bottle. "I'll be back."

OUTSIDE THE HUT, NURI HAD MY-PID REPLAY THE conversation. Analyzing the voice patterns, it judged that the Russian had been telling the truth.

He was weak, though. He truly wanted a drink. With a little effort and patience, Nuri knew he could undoubtedly elicit a great deal of information, everything the Russians were trying to do in Africa.

But he didn't care about any of that. He needed to know where the Raven flight computer was—and that seemed to be the one thing Kimko couldn't tell him.

Surely he knew something. The only question was, how much vodka would it take to find out?

The little bottle Nuri had shown Kimko was his entire stock. It had been in his luggage, a souvenir from his flight from Europe to Egypt that he'd pocketed and then forgotten. It was barely a shot's worth.

Damn good thing he'd caught it in midair. Try it a hundred times and he'd never do it again.

"Get him some food," Nuri told one of the guards. "Don't talk to him at all. I'm going to go for a walk and clear my head. I'll be back."

10

Washington, D.C.

IT WAS NOT EASY TO FIND A PAY PHONE. AND WHEN Amara finally did find one and dialed the number, he went straight to voice mail.

Flustered, he hung up. He had no idea what to do or where to go. He'd never even been in Washington, D.C., before.

He had a cell phone but was sternly warned to use it only once, and that was to call and say he had arrived at his final destination. Using it for any other purpose was beyond question. He was sure to be punished for doing so; he guessed the punishment would be death.

Amara walked around the train station, trying to decide what to do. He would have to find a place to stay. That part was relatively easy, even though he had limited funds. The question would be what to do next.

The bookstore had a stand with small magazines listing inexpensive hotels. He studied it, then found the taxi stand. But as he queued up for the line, he saw from the magazine ad that he could get there from the Metro. That would be cheaper.

Back inside, he passed the phone booth and decided to try calling his contact one last time.

A male voice answered on the second ring.

"Yes?"

"This is Amara from the old country," he said. "I've come looking for my cousin."

There was no answer. Fearing a trap or perhaps a simple mistake with the number, Amara was just about to slap the phone down when the man said, "Go to the Air and Space Museum. Wait outside."

"What train do I take?" asked Amara. But the man had already hung up.

Amara found his way to the Metro and bought a fare card. He could feel the others staring at him as he wheeled his suitcase down to the tracks. But there were other travelers with cases as well.

Someone bumped into him from behind. Amara jerked back.

"I'm sorry," said a white girl, about nineteen or twenty. She had a stud below her lip. She put her hand up to reassure him. "I didn't see you there."

"I, uh . . ." Amara's throat was suddenly very dry. He searched his brain for something to say in English. "I . . . wonder which way."

"What way?" She gave him a bemused smile.

"I have to meet someone in front of the Air and Space Museum. Is hard to get to? From here?"

The girl led him back over to a map of the subway system, explaining how he would have to go. She smelled like flowers, Amara thought. American girls always did.

SOME FORTY MINUTES LATER, AMARA PACED IN FRONT of the museum, trying to look inconspicuous.

He froze as he saw a police car pass by.

It's all been a trap, he thought. An elaborate hoax to get me to America. They'll throw me in Guantánamo and torture me there for life.

"Cousin," said a deep voice as a hand clapped him on the shoulder from behind.

Amara, startled, spun around. A short, light-skinned man with an extremely scraggly beard stood behind him. It was difficult to correlate the voice with the man—he was diminutive, barely the size of a thirteen-year-old boy.

"How is my uncle and aunt?" asked the man. His English had a Pakistani accent.

"I'm good—they're good," said Amara, trying to pull himself back together.

The little man rolled his eyes.

"Come on," he said under his breath. "Crap."

He took Amara's rolling suitcase and began leading him down the block.

"Call me Ken," said the man after they had gone several blocks. "I will call you Al."

"Al," said Amara.

"Nothing else. You have a cell phone."

"No," said Amara.

"Good. Anyone give you anything in New York?"

"No."

"Good."

Ken continued walking. They had left the Mall area and were now on a residential street.

"This is my car," said Ken, pointing with a key fob to a battered Impala and opening the trunk. "Get in."

Amara did as he was told. Ken didn't speak again for nearly a half hour. By then they were pulling down the back alley of a row of dilapidated town houses.

"Wait while I undo the fence," said Ken, throwing the car into park. He got out, undid three locks with different keys, then unwrapped the chain that held the fence together. Amara glanced up. There was barbed wire at the top of the fence line.

Car parked and gate relocked, Ken led Amara down a short flight of concrete steps to a steel door. Two more keys. They entered a tiny hallway.

Once again Ken had to unlock a door guarded by several locks, one of them a combination. They stepped into a dark basement.

"This way," said Ken after relocking and bolting the door behind them.

"You have cat eyes," said Amara, trying to follow in the pitch-black.

"Don't trip," said Ken.

Amara managed to follow him across the darkened room to a set of stairs leading up. If there was a light, Ken didn't bother using it, leading him up to the first floor of the house, where once more they went through the ritual of locks.

"The bathroom's in the back," said Ken, leading him into the apartment. "Go through the kitchen, take a right. You can put your things in the bedroom on the left. Don't touch anything."

Amara took his things into the room, then went to the bathroom, keeping the laptop bag with him. The room was small and narrow, and smelled of ammonia. The overhead light was extremely bright, and the porcelain, though old, glistened. The taps worked separately; it took a bit of juggling to get his hands washed at a comfortable temperature.

Ken was waiting for him in the kitchen. He had a metal pot on the stove for coffee.

"So you're the help they sent," said Ken skeptically. "What's your specialty?"

"I don't have a specialty."

Ken frowned. "What did they tell you?"

"Nothing. I brought a program that will help you."

"In the bag? Let's see it?"

Amara removed the computer from the back-pack and turned it on. Ken turned his attention to the old-fashioned coffee percolator he'd put on the stove. Brown water blipped up into a tiny glass dome at the top. He adjusted the flame, bending down so close to it that Amara thought he would burn his nose if not his entire face. The pot vibrated on the stove, the liquid percolating inside.

"The people who sent you are ignorant," said Ken. He practically spat. "They're all idiots. They're not much better than the ones we're fighting against. In some ways, they're worse. Do you even pray?"

The question caught Amara by surprise.

"I pray," he said.

Ken pulled the percolator off the stove and poured a bit of coffee into a white mug sitting on the sink counter. Satisfied after examining it, he filled the cup, got another from the washboard, and filled that. He returned the pot to the stove. Only then did he turn off the gas. The flame descended back into the burner with a loud *pouff*.

The entire kitchen smelled like coffee. Amara felt his senses sharpening.

"Here," said Ken roughly, setting down the cup. "You'll probably want sugar." He pointed to a small covered bowl in the middle of the table. "The spoons are in the drawer behind you."

Amara tried two spoonfuls of sugar, then added a third and finally a fourth. Ken drank his plain.

"Let me see the computer," said Ken.

Amara pushed it over. The control program

had started on its own, columns of figures filling the screen.

"This is supposed to help me?" said Ken. "How?"

"It's a control unit," snapped Amara, no longer able to hide his resentment at being treated like a fool. "It controlled an American UAV. Target data is entered on the screen, and then the aircraft knew what to do."

"Useless," said Ken. He pushed the keys, paging the screen up and down. "I asked them for a Predator control unit. I was ready to adapt that. I was assured that it could be obtained from the Sudan. And yet this is what they give me? I can't use this to fly a plane. Where are the controls? Why are we even working with Africans? They are imbeciles."

"The man who examined this was Chinese," said Amara. "He was a genius. He said it controlled an aircraft more powerful than a Predator. He knew what he was talking about."

"Where is he?"

"He's dead," said Amara. Then he added, with a touch of cruelty that he hoped would set Ken back a notch, "I killed him."

"Then he couldn't have been much of a genius," answered Ken, not intimidated.

11

Washington, D.C. suburbs

Breanna felt a pang of anxiety as she pulled into her driveway and saw Zen's van. She hadn't seen her husband since their meeting at the airport the day before. She'd managed to get home after him the night before, and leave before he got up— not that she'd been avoiding him exactly, but the timing was extremely convenient. They hadn't even texted during the day.

Breanna took her keys from the ignition, opened her pocketbook, then decided that her lipstick needed to be fixed.

That done, she got out of the car, walking slowly to the door. Her daughter Teri met her there, practically tackling her.

"We're glad your home," said the third-grader after accepting two kisses, one for each cheek. "Dad and I cooked!"

"He did?"

Zen's culinary prowess consisted of speed dialing the local pizza joint and hitting the button to talk at the McDonald's drive-in.

"Lasagna," said Zen from inside. "And it's just ready."

"Eating early?" said Breanna.

"Baseball game."

"Oh."

"Problem?" asked Zen.

"I have a meeting tonight."

"I thought you might. Caroline is in the den, doing her homework."

"She gave us some hints on cooking," whispered Teri.

"You weren't going to tell," said Zen, mock scolding his daughter. He pretended to chase after her as she ran off laughing.

"She's in a good mood," said Breanna.

"Glad to see you home. As am I."

Zen spun around and went back to the kitchen. Their stove was regular height, which limited his access to the front burners only. He had a small pot of sauce there; to check it, he removed it from the burner and held it over his lap to stir. It wasn't the safest arrangement, but Breanna had learned long ago not to say anything.

He put it back and opened the oven.

"*Mmmm-mmmm.* I think it's ready," he said, wheeling around to the refrigerator.

"Jeff, about yesterday . . ."

"Apologizing for not playing hooky?"

"I shouldn't have run out like that. I know."

"That's OK. It at least got me prepared for your stonewalling the committee."

"Excuse me?"

"Word is, my favorite President told the CIA director to inspect military bases in Alaska for the next three weeks. His schedule is full."

"I doubt anything like that happened."

"It's all right. At least I know where to deliver your subpoena."

"Jeff, you're not going to subpoena me."

"Why not?"

"Because I have no involvement—"

She stopped short. She meant that she had no involvement in the original Raven program, not in recovering it. But she realized now that she looked foolish—and like a liar.

"I was joking," he said, though his voice was suddenly very serious.

"I know."

"Don't forget who you are," he added.

"I do know who I am."

"Yeah. So do I."

"What's that mean?" She pressed her lips together, angry—not at him, but at herself for lying.

"Dinner's ready," said Zen loudly. He took a thick towel from the center island and put it on his lap, then pulled the lasagna from the oven. "Come and get it!" he yelled, wheeling himself toward the table.

ZEN ATE QUICKLY. HE WAS RUNNING A LITTLE LATE; ordinarily he would have caught something at the park, but he'd wanted to make sure he stayed and talked to Breanna.

It hadn't gone quite as well as he planned, but at least the ice had been broken. Somewhat.

Hopefully this was just bs and would blow over quickly.

In the meantime, he was looking forward to the game. He drove over to his district office and picked up a friend, Simeon Bautista, a former SEAL who occasionally did some bodyguard work for him. Then he went over to the hospital, where Stoner and Dr. Esrang were waiting inside the lobby.

"Mark, Doc, hey guys," said Zen, wheeling over to them with a flourish. "This is my buddy Simeon—he watches over me sometimes to make sure I don't get into a fight with Dodger fans." Zen winked at Stoner, who simply stared back. Esrang nodded. Zen saw the two hospital security people eyeing them nervously. "We ready?"

"I think we're good," said Esrang, leading the way to the van.

Truth be told, Zen would have preferred that the psychiatrist stayed home. It wasn't that he was in the way, or even a particularly bad companion. But it added a therapeutic flavor to the outing that made things less comfortable than he wanted. It was bad enough that the doctor had insisted on a bodyguard. Simeon at least was low key and affable, though not overly talkative—a perfect combination, Zen thought. The problem was, if Stoner really went on a rampage, it would take a dozen Simeons and an M1A1 tank to subdue him.

The traffic was light and they made it to the game with nearly a half hour to spare. It was a sparse crowd, even though they were playing the Dodgers. In fact, a good portion of the crowd seemed to be L.A. transplants, with more than a spattering of Dodger blue around them.

"Want something to eat, Mark?" Zen asked. "Hot dog?"

"Hot dog?"

Zen took the question as a yes. "One or two?"

Stoner held up his hand, showing two fingers.

This was really a good idea, thought Zen, call-ing the vendor over.

THERE WERE THOUSANDS OF FACES, EACH ONE POTEN-tially a threat.

Stoner looked at each one, studying them. The habit was ingrained, part of him, who he was.

There was another part, too. Deeper maybe.

He continued looking, memorizing each face. He hadn't seen any of them before.

"Here." Zen handed him the hot dogs.

A hot dog. Frankfurter. Red Hot.

Had he had these? They seemed familiar.

He had. He liked them. It was a long time ago. Before.

"You want mustard or ketchup?" said Zen.

"Ketchup?" asked Stoner.

"Ketchup!" yelled Zen to the man pulling the food from the box.

This was all familiar. The man with the box, with the hot dogs—did he have a gun?

Stoner braced, his body ready to react. His muscles tightened, his breathing became almost shallow.

The man took something from his pocket.

Tiny packets of ketchup, which Stoner knew he would do. Somehow, he knew. The pattern was familiar, yet new.

He began to eat.

"Good?" asked Zen.

"Different," said Stoner.

"Better than hospital food, huh?"

"I don't know."

Zen laughed.

"The food isn't bad," said Stoner.

"Honest?"

He turned to Zen, pondering why he would ask that question. As he did, his eye caught something moving above. He cringed, right arm flying up.

"What?" asked Zen.

A small aircraft circled above. Stoner focused on it. It had a camera in the nose, two small engines, no pilot. A UAV drone.

"It's a police department UAV," said Zen.

"It's watching us."

"Not us, the stadium. Checking out the crowd for security," explained Zen. "All right?"

Stoner looked at it, watching the pattern it made. He focused his eyes on the camera. It scanned the crowd, moving back and forth, back and forth.

"What do you see?" Zen asked.

"There's a camera in the nose, inside the dome."

"You can see that in the dark?"

"Of course."

"Like Superman—X-ray eyes."

The first doctors had called him Superman. He knew that wasn't true—he was more like a freak, a robot created from human flesh, created to do some bastard's dirty work.

A robot like the plane?

He glanced back toward the sky, watching it circle.

"All right," he said finally. He turned to Zen. "When does this ball game begin?"

"Five minutes," said Zen, rising. "Right after the National Anthem."

12

Southeast Washington, D.C.

AMARA SAT IN THE KITCHEN WHILE KEN WORKED OVER the laptop, studying the program for hours, punching keys and mumbling to himself. He put his face right next to the screen as he worked, his nose nearly touching it. Amara wondered if he would be sucked inside if he hit the wrong key.

"I see," said Ken finally.

He rose and picked up the laptop. Unplugging it but keeping it on and open, he walked back toward the stairs. Amara followed him down into the darkness.

Ken flipped a light switch at the bottom of the stairs. The basement flooded with light so strong Amara's eyes stung. He shaded them as he trailed Ken over toward an ancient, round oil burner. There was a door just beyond it, secured with a padlock and a chain. Ken undid the locks, then pulled open the door and stepped into a primitive wine cellar. Shelves lined the left wall; two large wooden barrels sat on pedestals just beyond them. Dust and spiderwebs were everywhere.

A sheet of heavy, clear plastic hung from the ceiling just past the second barrel. Ken pulled at the sheet, revealing a seam. Amara followed him through, passing into a twenty-by-thirty-foot work space lined with gleaming new toolboxes, a large workbench, and commercial steel shelving. There were a number of high- and low-tech tools—a pair of computers, an oscilloscope, a metal drill press. In the middle of the floor sat a small UAV, engines fore and aft on the fuselage, wings detached from its body and standing upright against the bare cinder-block wall.

Ken knelt down and opened the laptop, staring at the screen before pushing it to one side. He rose and went to the workbench.

"I need solder," he said, rummaging through a set of trays.

These were the first words Ken had spoken to him in hours, and they filled Amara with an almost giddy enthusiasm.

"So the program will help you," said Amara.

"Can I trust you to buy solder? Do you know what it is?"

"Of course," said Amara.

"It's too late to get it now," said Ken, his voice scolding, as if it were Amara's idea in the first place. "Get us something to eat. Buy a pizza and bring it here. There's a store on the corner."

"Pizza?"

"You know what pizza is, don't you?"

"I know what pizza is."

"Go. Lock the front door behind you. Ring the bell twice, wait, then once and twice more. If you don't follow that pattern, I won't let you in."

DESPITE HIS JET LAG AND THE WAY HE HAD BEEN TREATED, Amara felt a burst of energy after he locked the front door and trotted down the steps. He walked with a brisk, almost jogging pace for about half the block, pushed along by a sense of mission—not the pizza, but of doing something useful.

Amara did not, in his heart, hate America or Americans. On the contrary, he liked much about the country where he had studied. And he had found that most Americans he came in contact with were helpful and even on occasion kind.

The fact that he'd been sent on a mission that would hurt Americans did not, somehow, connect with that feeling. It existed in an entirely different realm. He didn't have to rationalize that Americans were fighting against what the Brotherhood stood for; he simply saw his mission separate from his experiences with and feelings for real Americans. He was like a professional sports player who could play ferociously against another team, and yet at the end of it think nothing of shaking and even hugging his opponents.

The heat in the pizza parlor was overwhelming. It was moist and pungent, an oregano-scented sauna.

"Hey," said the man behind the counter. He was a white man with a child's face and a belly two sizes too large for the rest of his body. "Help ya?"

"Pizza. To go."

"Cheese?"

It had been quite a while since Amara had eaten pizza. But the safest answer was yes.

"Yes," he told the man.

"Large or small?"

"Large," said Amara, guessing.

"What da ya want wid that?" said the man, punching a cash register. "Soda?"

"Uh, yes."

The man pointed to a trio of coolers at the side.

There were a variety of sodas and other drinks; the last was filled with beers.

He took a water for Ken—he couldn't imagine he would drink anything else—then, giving in to temptation, pulled open the beer cooler and took a Coors.

"Gotta drink the beer here," said the man behind the counter.

Amara didn't understand.

"I can only sell it to serve," said the man. "OK? So if you want it . . ."

He shrugged, as if his meaning was obvious.

"OK," said Amara. "I'll drink here."

Just as well—Ken might take the ban on alcohol far more seriously than he did.

"Thirteen fifty," said the man, ringing up the bill. "Pizza'll be done twelve minutes."

Amara fished into his pocket and pulled out two twenties. He handed one to the man, took his change, then sat down with his beer.

It tasted like water with algae in it. But he drank it anyway. He didn't realize he was gulping until he was more than halfway through.

Two teenage girls came in, texting on their cell phones as they walked to the counter. Amara remembered that he hadn't called to say he had arrived.

He got up, leaving the drink, and went outside.

His finger paused over the quick-dial combination.

Two rings, then he went directly to voice mail.

"I am here. It is very hopeful," he said in Arabic. After he hung up, he turned quickly to make sure he hadn't been overheard. Using Arabic had been a mistake—he should have made the call in English.

It was nothing to worry about now. Amara went back inside to wait for his pizza and finish his beer.

13

Ethiopia

NURI WATCHED THE SKY, WAITING AS THE SHADOW DE-scended. By the time he could make out the parachute, the SEAL harnessed into it was only a few feet from the ground. The sailor walked into his landing, then began gathering his chute. He had it squared away by the time Nuri arrived.

"Hey, Navy," said Nuri.

"You're Jupiter?" answered the SEAL.

"Yeah." Nuri thought the code word was funny, and gave a little self-deprecating laugh.

The man retrieved a small ballistics case from his kit. "Here you go."

"Thanks. The command post is that large building up there on the left," said Nuri. "Someone'll find you food and arrange for a pickup."

"Thank you, sir."

Nuri started away.

"Tell me, if you don't mind—what exactly is it

that I just brought you? They rushed me special here from Italy and flew me on my jetliner. I never seen such a fuss."

"Bottle of vodka," said Nuri.

THE RUSSIAN WAS JUST FINISHING HIS DINNER WHEN Nuri entered the tent. A small card table had been placed in the middle. The guards had removed his hand restraints, but were watching him carefully from the side.

"You can wait outside," Nuri told them. He put down the case and pulled out the empty chair.

"How was dinner?" he asked Kimko in English.

"All right."

"You prefer English or Russian?"

"Your Russian is horrible."

"Ready to talk?"

"I have said everything necessary to say."

"I think you have a lot to say."

Kimko smiled and shook his head. "Nuri, you are young yet. You do not know how this game is played."

"No?"

Kimko laughed. "You waste your time. You are Mr. Nice Guy. Before, when you threaten me with the gun—that was more effective. Then you feed me. Mistake. You should make me wait. Hunger pains do much."

Nuri reached down and opened the case. He removed the two glasses from the cushioned interior and set them down. Then he took the bottle of vodka and opened it.

Kimko said nothing.

"I know all about you, Milos. You have no secrets."

Nuri put a finger's worth of the liquid into the one closest to him. MY-PID was recording the session through a video bug planted in the far corner of the walls near the ceiling; it analyzed the Russian's facial features and what physiological data it could deduce about how he was reacting to Nuri's interrogation tactics. It gave Nuri a running update on the data as it watched.

But he didn't need MY-PID to tell him that Kimko really wanted the vodka.

Nuri picked up the glass and swirled it: it was all very dramatic and over the top, but he had a captive audience, and hamming it up only helped.

"I know you work for SVG," he told Kimko. "I know who your supervisors are. I know every stop in your career. I know how you got shafted. Because your boss wanted to sleep with your wife. It was an injustice. They screwed you. You should be a supervisor by now. Or a rich man. A very rich man."

Nuri took a small sip from the glass. He *hated* vodka.

"I can help you," he continued. "With my help, you can get out of Africa. I can help get you promoted. I can make you rich. And most of all, I can help you get revenge."

Kimko's pupils dilated ever so slightly; Nuri didn't need MY-PID's nudge to tell him he had just scored big. He paused, hoping Kimko would talk, but he didn't.

"You can talk to me, and I can help you a lot," said Nuri. "You don't like being assigned to Africa. That's clear. I can give you information that will get you out. And no one will know where it came from. Except you and me."

"You are more clever than I thought."

"No. I just have all the cards. But I can share." Nuri gestured at the bottle. "Why not use them to get yourself out of this shit hole."

"It is a shit hole," agreed Kimko.

"Talk to me about the UAV. Who else knows about it? Who wants it?"

"You claim to know everything and you don't know that?"

As an intelligence agent, Kimko presumably knew the basic interrogation technique called for starting with questions one knew the answer to, so the subject's truthfulness could be tested. He was parrying, trying on his side of the table to determine what Nuri really knew.

Nuri changed direction.

"Tell me about Li Han. Why would SVG want to deal with him? The man is a criminal. Despicable. A sociopath."

"We all have our faults," said Kimko dryly.

"What's yours?" Nuri took another sip from the glass.

"I have many, many faults," said Kimko, casting his eyes downward.

"I can help you get out of here," said Nuri. "You don't want to be here. It's a rat hole."

"You're here."

"Oh, I get to leave." Nuri laughed. "They just

sent me back for you. Who are you selling to? Sudan First? They're psychotic."

Kimko shook his head.

Nuri tried a different tack. "Who do you think was your competition to buy the UAV?" he asked. "Was it the Iranian?"

The suggestion of the third party—who of course didn't exist—took Kimko by surprise, and it took him a moment to recover his stony face.

"You were my competition, I would suppose," he told Nuri, leaning back. The shift in posture told MY-PID—and Nuri—that he was unsure of himself.

"You didn't know about the Iranian?" Nuri asked. "So you don't know why he was here?"

Kimko waved his hand.

"You're not telling me an Iranian smoked you, are you?" asked Nuri. "You didn't know he was with Girma? Are you kidding? Was your boss right—are you washed up?"

Kimko's eyes flashed with anger. For a moment Nuri thought he would grab and fling the vodka bottle. He'd already decided that he would let him do that, let the bottle break—the smell would only make Kimko more desperate once he calmed down.

But Kimko didn't. He hunched his shoulders together, physically pulling himself back under control.

"You're a salesman," said Nuri. "Why would you want to buy the UAV?"

"Who says that I am buying this thing?"

"Come on. You were prepared to deal. But how did you know what you were buying?"

"I was not going to deal. No buying."

"Li Han isn't a buyer. He's a seller. And a worker bee for whatever slimeball will stick a few million dollars into his account. Right? I'm surprised you would deal with him," added Nuri. "Considering that he helped the Chechens."

Kimko raised his head.

"You didn't know? You guys don't know that?" said Nuri. This part was easy—he wasn't lying.

"You're a liar. You don't know nothing. You're a child."

"In 2012—the bomb in the Moscow Star Theater. Used an explosive initiated from a cell phone. That's common. There was wire in the bomb with lettering. You traced it to Hong Kong. Our friend was there a few weeks before the bomb was built. There's other evidence," added Nuri, who had gotten all the background from MY-PID and its search of the files and data on Li Han. "Maybe I'll give it to you, if it will help. Of course, if your boss knew that you were dealing with someone who helped the Chechens— that probably wouldn't be a good thing. I guess it would depend on how the information came out. Who shaped it. We call that a slant in America."

"I had no deal," said Kimko harshly. "I despise the man."

"Feelings and business are two different things," said Nuri. He rose, leaving the bottle and glasses on the table. "I'll be right back."

* * *

KIMKO STARED AT THE VODKA.

He was beyond starved for a drink.

But if he reached for that bottle—where would it take him?

He knew nothing of value. His contacts among the Africans were probably well known by this Nuri. As for the UAV, he had already told him everything he knew.

Yet the American wanted more. Logically, that must mean they had not recovered it.

He couldn't help them on that score either.

So really, as far as his duty was concerned, there was nothing preventing him from taking the bottle. There was nothing he could say that Moscow could object to.

But that was the rub—Moscow wouldn't believe he'd said nothing now. And clearly this Nuri had some sort of evidence to ruin him. True or concocted, it wouldn't matter.

He lowered his head to his hands.

One drink. One drink.

The smell of the vodka Nuri had poured in the glass permeated the tent. There was no way to resist.

He pulled the glass over. Before he knew that he had lifted it, he'd drained it. His lips burned, his throat.

He put the glass back on the table, defeated.

"YOU CAN HAVE MORE," NURI TOLD KIMKO, STANDING behind the chair. He felt bad for the Russian; he looked as if he had collapsed.

"I can't help you," said Kimko, his voice sub-
dued. "I had few arrangements. The Brothers have
established supply lines with the Middle East, al
Qaeda. We can't compete. They're friendly, of
course, but they don't buy. They get everything
they need from bin Laden's successors. I knew
nothing about the Iranians. I assume it's their
Revolutionary Guard, but I know nothing."

"Tell me who you saw in Duka."

"First—I was supposed to call someone yesterday. I lost my phone. I need to call him. If I don't,
Moscow will know I'm missing."

"Who?"

"He's insignificant."

Nuri reached down and picked up the bottle.
He filled the glass.

"Come on," said Nuri. "We have to help each
other here."

"He's an expert in UAVs. He needed to inspect
the aircraft. They were sending him to find me. I
need to talk to him. Or they'll think I defected."

"We don't want that," said Nuri.

THE ENTIRE CONVERSATION LASTED NO MORE THAN
sixty seconds.

"There was fighting in the city," Kimko said as
soon as the other line was opened. "I've had to
take shelter in Malan. The UAV must have been
destroyed. I'm sorry that I didn't meet you."

"I heard of your troubles and made other arrangements," said the voice on the other end,
before hanging up.

A few seconds later MY-PID supplied the location of the other phone. It was in southeastern Sudan—the site of the Brothers of Sudan main camp, to be exact.

14

Washington, D.C.

CHRISTINE MARY TODD TOOK A LAST SPOONFUL OF soup and got up from the table.

"Working tonight?" said her husband. "I thought you had the evening off?"

She made a face at him.

"Tomorrow?" he asked.

Todd sighed.

"I was thinking we could sneak over to the stadium tomorrow night," said her husband. "We haven't used the box all year."

"Daniel, we were at a game two weeks ago."

"Oh. But that doesn't count—you brought the House Speaker with you. And you know what I think of him."

"Your opinion is undoubtedly higher than mine," said the President.

Her husband smiled. It was true.

"I don't know," she told him. "This thing with Ernst."

"Oh, don't let it bother you." He reached out

and touched her hand. "Take a little time off. We'll have fun."

"The Nats always lose when I'm there."

"Because you don't cheer enough."

"Well, I don't know. We'll see."

"No, you'll *try*."

"That's the same thing."

"No, it's not."

"All right." She patted his shoulder. "I will *try*."

"Video in bed?" he told her. "*Saving Private Ryan*?"

"I don't know if you should wait up."

"If I don't fall asleep."

"We've watched that video three times in the last two months."

"Good movie."

"Yes, but—"

"Oh, all right," he said, overstating his concession. "We'll watch *The Golden Heiress*."

She had been wanting to see that one for weeks. Obviously, he'd gotten the video already; he was just teasing her. She gave him a kiss.

"Thank you, Daniel. You know I love you."

"And I love you," he said, reaching up to kiss her back.

HER HUSBAND'S GENTLE TEASING PUT HER IN A GOOD mood, but it didn't last as far as the West Wing, where she was holding an emergency meeting on the Raven situation. The CIA director's refusal to hop immediately over to the Hill and sing for his supper had predictable results—there were all sorts of rumors now about what he might be hiding.

All of them wrong, fortunately.

The one thing everyone got right was the supposition that Edmund's stonewalling was coming at the President's behest. Which naturally directed all of the vitriol in her direction.

Todd spotted her chief of staff David Greenwich rocking back and forth on his feet as she approached the cabinet room. On good days he hummed a little song to himself while he waited. On bad days he hummed louder.

The walls were practically vibrating with his off-key rendition of "Dancing in the Streets." She assumed the selection was purposely ironic.

"All present and accounted for," said Greenwich, spotting her. Besides everyone who had been at the meeting the day before, Todd had added Secretary of State Alistair Newhaven. He had brought along the Undersecretary of State for Counter-Terrorism, Kevin McCloud, and a staff member who was an expert on the Sudan.

"Edmund looks like he's wearing a bulletproof vest," added Greenwich.

"I hope you're joking."

"I am. But he does look quite a bit worse for wear. The others, so-so."

Todd let him open the door for her. She glanced at her Secret Service shadow, so unobtrusive she almost forgot he was there, then went in.

"Very good, I'm sorry I'm late," she said. "No gentlemen, don't stand. Thank you for the thought."

She pulled out her own seat and sat.

"All right. Where are we?"

Breanna Stockard gave a summary of the search so far. There was nothing new on the Raven, but there was one ominous development.

"A Russian operative arrived at the Sudan Brotherhood camp in southeastern Sudan a few hours ago," said Breanna. "We believe he may be there to obtain the flight control portion of the aircraft. In fact, we have pretty good evidence that that is the case. Circumstantial."

"Are you sure?" said Edmund. He apparently hadn't been briefed.

"I literally heard about this in the car as I pulled up," said Breanna. "We're still checking everything out. The operative was headed for Duka, made some sort of contact the NSA picked up, and then drove to the Brotherhood instead. He's an expert in UAVs. But we don't know for certain that the aircraft is actually at the camp."

"We have to act on this," said Edmund.

"Assuming it's real," said Harker. His tone was odd—somewhere between genuine concern and sarcasm. Todd couldn't tell which he intended.

"What do you propose?" she asked.

"That we go into the camp," said Breanna. "We send Whiplash in. We get the computer. If it's there."

"Do we have a plan?"

"It's being developed. They'll be ready to move at nightfall."

"You're proposing an attack on the Sudan Brotherhood?" asked Secretary of State Newhaven.

"Yes," said Breanna.

"It's a completely domestic organization," said Newhaven. "They don't even have connections with al Qaeda."

"That's not entirely correct," said Edmund. "They have gotten support from them. Arms and money. Even with bin Laden dead, the group is strong in Africa."

Newhaven turned to his expert, who, while admitting that the two groups were sympathetic to each other, said there was no hard evidence of anything more than that. The CIA and State Department experts then proceeded to bat around definitions and nuances.

Todd glanced over at Jonathon Reid. Her old friend was silent, his eyes nearly closed. She knew the whole Raven affair disturbed him greatly; it was certainly costing him friends inside the Agency.

"Jonathon, what are you thinking?" she asked finally.

"I think whether there's a connection there or not, there's simply no choice," Reid said. "This weapon is too dangerous to chance it falling into other hands. We need it back."

"I agree." She turned back to the others. "I think the evidence is clear. They have contact and support from al Qaeda. If they've gotten support from al Qaeda, then they're allies of al Qaeda. If they are allies with our enemies, they are our enemies. The fact that our action will inadvertently assist the Sudanese government is unfortunate, but in the end, coincidental. And acceptable. We will strike them and retrieve whatever we find at the camp."

* * *

NURI'S CALL FROM ETHIOPIA WITH THE NEW INFORMA-
tion had caught Breanna off-guard; she hadn't
had enough time to properly process it, barely
discussing it even with Reid before the meeting.
Striking the camp seemed like a no-brainer, an
obvious decision. But as she sat across from the
President and listened to the objections from the
State Department experts, she realized the implications were enormous. The U.S. would in effect
be taking sides with the Sudanese government
against its rebels—but the U.S. did not support
the Sudanese government in the least. On the
contrary, there was more than ample proof that
the government itself had ties with al Qaeda. If
anyone should be attacked, it was them.

Even assuming Raven was there and the attack
went well, there were sure to be unforeseen diplo-
matic consequences, especially since the Russian
agent would presumably have to be killed.

"Why kill him?" asked Harker.

Edmund frowned but said nothing. It was Reid
who explained.

"Risking a witness, even one who never actually
got Raven in his hands, would be foolish."

Was the weapon worth risking war over, asked
the Undersecretary of State. Especially with Russia?

It was a philosophical question, since no one
felt it would get that far. But Breanna had her own
answer: it might very well be. Based on the information the CIA had reluctantly turned over,
Ray Rubeo thought the program was every bit as
dangerous as Reid had feared.

Though Rubeo being Rubeo, he had added a host of caveats to his assessment, starting with the obvious fact that he hadn't inspected the actual software, just some of the technical descriptions.

The real villain was Harker, who'd decided to test the weapon without getting approval from anyone, except Edmund—or she *assumed* it was Edmund's doing. You couldn't actually tell in Washington. Edmund was generally defending his underling, or at least deflecting most of the flack. But that didn't make him guilty—the President was going to be taking the flack for the tiff with the Intelligence Committee, and she certainly hadn't approved the program.

Or had she?

Washington could be a maze of mirrors, each corridor a twisted path leading to a dead end.

Were Edmund and Harker so wrong to test the weapon there? Whiplash, and Dreamland before it, had tested a legion of cutting-edge weaponry in dangerous situations. They'd lost their share of them as well.

Breanna heard her father's voice in her head:

We didn't spend all this money making these damn things to keep them on the shelf. We have to use them. We lose them, that's the breaks. That's the price of playing the game.

"Swift action is what we need," said Bozzone, the President's personal counsel. "With the weapon secured, Director Edmund could go before the committee and tell them what happened."

"More or less," said Blitz. "More less than more."

Under other circumstances, the line would have generated a laugh or two, or at least a nervous chuckle. Today it didn't.

"We say Raven was a secret UAV project being tested in the Sudan," said Bozzone. "It crashed. We have it back."

"This is where we were yesterday," said Blitz, referring to a private debate. "Once we start talking about it, they'll ask why it's special, they'll ask about the assassination program, they'll ask a dozen questions that he can't answer truthfully, or at least not fully."

"And as I said yesterday, the best approach is simply to tell the whole story," said Bozzone. "As long as the unit is back, there's no problem. Even Ernst will keep that a secret. And if he doesn't—well so what? As long as we have the UAV, then we're the only ones who can deploy it."

"Acknowledging the existence of a weapon can have bad consequences," said Reid.

"Gentlemen, thank you," said Todd, cutting them off. "We'll make the decision on what will be disclosed when it needs to be made." She looked around the table, then fixed her eyes on Breanna. "In the meantime, Ms. Stockard, Mr. Reid—have Whiplash recover the missing components. At all costs."

15

Duka

Danny drifted between consciousness and sleep. He'd learned long ago to take advantage of the lulls to grab some rest—ten minutes here, a half hour there. They weren't exactly power naps, but they were better than fighting the fatigue full-on. Tiny sips of energy.

Random thoughts shot through his semiconscious mind. Who cared about the damn flight computer anyway? Couldn't they just get the hell back home?

He saw his ex-wife in their bedroom. It seemed so warm.

She morphed into Melissa. That was better—much, much better.

His ear set blared with an incoming call on the Whiplash circuit. He jerked back in the seat where he'd dozed off, pulling his mind back to full consciousness. The tent was empty.

"This is Freah."

"Danny, this is Bree. Can you talk?"

"Yes, go ahead."

"You're authorized to strike the Brotherhood. You are to secure the control unit to the UAV."

"All right. Can I use the Marines?"

A small contingent of Marines had been detailed to provide security at the Ethiopia base at the start of the deployment, but Danny had left them on their assault ship in the Gulf of Aden, deciding he didn't need them.

"Yes. Draw whatever you need. But—you need to attack as quickly as possible."

"It won't be until dark. There are a lot of people in that camp, Bree. In the area of two hundred fighters."

"Tonight, then. The Russian UAV expert is in the camp. He can't get out."

She didn't say "killed," but that's what she meant. That actually made things a lot easier.

"All right," said Danny. "We'll be ready. One thing, Bree . . ."

"Yes?"

"You might think about bombing the camp if it's that critical."

"We did think about it," she told him. "There are too many caves to guarantee success. I know you'll do your best."

16

Washington, D.C.

THE NATIONALS PUT ON A HITTING DISPLAY IN THE bottom of the sixth, batting around for seven runs and sending the L.A. fans scurrying for the exits. Even the outs were loud—the last drove the Dodger right fielder against the fence, where he managed to hold on despite taking a wicked shot to the back.

"That had to hurt, huh?" said Zen.

"Not much," said Stoner.

"Not for you, maybe."

"What do you mean?"

"Just—you have a high pain threshold." Zen wasn't sure that Stoner fully appreciated how much stronger he had been made by the operations and drugs.

"Oh."

The Nats brought in a rookie to mop up in the eighth inning. Zen noticed that Stoner tracked each ball as carefully as if he were a scientist trying to prove some new theory of motion.

"The ball drops six to eight inches as it reaches the plate," said Stoner after the second strikeout.

"He's got a hell of a curve, huh?"

"It spins differently than the others."

"Can you pick that out?" asked the psychiatrist.

"Thirty-two revolutions per second," said Stoner.

"Thirty-two?" asked Zen.

"On average."

"You counted?"

"Yes."

Zen leaned down to look past Stoner at Dr. Esrang. The psychiatrist nodded.

"That's pretty good eyesight, Mark."

The rookie struck out the side. Zen took out his phone and did a Google search—it turned out the average curveball rotated in the area of twenty-five to thirty times per second.

The kid would be someone to watch.

When the game ended, Stoner was silent all the way out.

"This was good," he told Zen as they got into the van. "Can we do it again?"

"Sure," said Zen. "Any time you like."

"Tomorrow. I would like tomorrow."

"Well—maybe. I have to check my calendar." He glanced back toward the doctor, who was nodding vigorously. "I may be able to."

"Good," answered Stoner. "Very good."

17

Southeast Washington, D.C.

AFTER HE'D MANAGED TO STEAL THE POLICE UAV FROM the company that manufactured it, Ken's initial plan was to develop an automated control unit that would fly the aircraft into a hard target—the White House, preferably.

His al Qaeda contacts had obtained the explosives and then promised additional assistance. Amara apparently was that help.

While it was clear to Ken that Amara could offer no real assistance, the program he had brought with him seemed to be exactly what he was trying to write on his own—except it was considerably more sophisticated.

And yet, in some ways, simpler. It was certainly a control system, though it didn't work like any conventional control system he was familiar with.

The program was divided into a number of modules. The largest and most complicated seemed to involve learning routines. This section had a series of overrides, and was related to an interface that allowed for the control of an aircraft, though it was much more rudimentary than what Ken had seen in either the Israeli or the German UAV systems he was familiar with.

More interesting was the section whose internal comments made it clear that it was meant for targeting. The section had inputs for GPS data, which Ken expected. But it also wanted physical data on the target itself. There were several pictures of an Asian man that filled the variables.

Those seemed easy to replace; there was a screen that controlled this, which Ken had been able to access upstairs.

Connected to the UAV's own control section, Amara's program seemed to have a life of its own. It had certainly taken over all of the laptop's resources—the machine's hard drive whirled and buzzed, presumably as different parts of the program ran their operations.

But what were they, exactly? The laptop had a set of diagnostic tools that were clearly top notch, but they couldn't keep up with the program.

Did it matter? Could he just give it a target and launch it?

He'd been working on this for months now, and part of him didn't want to stop. That was the scientist, not the warrior in him, as his teachers would have said.

The warrior knew he must strike soon. His al Qaeda contact had warned that the police were searching for the UAV and might close in. And perhaps they'd done so already—he had not heard from his contact in over a week.

Ken left the laptop as its program ran and went upstairs for a break. Amara had gone up to bed a few hours before; he could hear him snoring from the kitchen.

Searching the African's things took no time at all. Of course he didn't have a weapon. He had little money. He didn't even have a phone.

Worthless. But at least he wasn't an assassin.

Back in the kitchen, Ken made a fresh pot of coffee. The percolator had been a revelation: he loved the slightly burnt, metal-tinged taste the old-fashioned pot gave the liquid.

Just as the liquid began to darken in the top globe, he realized it was nearly midnight—time to check the bulletin board where his contact left messages. He signed on through an anonymous server and went to the assigned chat board. It changed every twenty-four hours; tonight it was a site that gave help to homeowners looking for information about air conditioners.

He started scrolling through the messages. They were inane, asking about BTUs and cooling capacity, and how well sealed a duct should be.

Then suddenly he noticed one had been left by CTW119.

Or as it should be read: 9/11 WTC.

He called the message up:

YOU HAVE EVERYTHING YOU NEED TO BUY
YOUR SYSTEM. DO SO QUICKLY! TODAY IF
POSSIBLE.

To a casual browser it was nothing more than a
hackneyed advertising slogan left by a salesman.

To Ken, it was a command that he must strike
as soon as possible.

He took his coffee and went back down to work.

18

Washington, D.C. suburbs

ZEN WAS MILDLY SURPRISED THAT BREANNA'S CAR
wasn't in the garage when he came home. Inside,
he found Caroline dozing in front of the televi-
sion. She woke when he flipped the set off.

"Your aunt call?" he asked.

"No, Uncle Jeff. She didn't."

"I thought she'd be back by now."

"It's OK. Teri was a doll. I'm going to tuck into
bed."

"All right. See you in the A.M."

Zen went into the kitchen and got himself a
beer. The question of whether to wait up for Breanna was moot—he heard the garage door open
between his second and third swigs.

"Hey there, lonesome traveler," he said as she came through the door.

"Jeff, you're still up?"

"Just got in from the game," he told her. "Mark did great."

"Oh—oh, yeah. How is he?"

"He's doing better. I think a lot better." Zen watched her put down her pocketbook and rub her eyes. "Long day?"

"Tomorrow's going to be worse."

"Want to tell me what's up?"

The pained expression on her face told him the answer long before her words did.

"I can't."

"This have anything to do with Raven?" he asked.

"Jeff, don't go there," she said harshly. "That's out of bounds."

"Hey, don't yell at me," he said, a little louder than he intended.

"You're the one yelling."

"Listen, Bree—"

"Our deal was, we don't bring work home." She grabbed her pocketbook and began stalking down the hall. "That was our deal."

"Wait a second." He reached for her, but she was just far enough from him, and just quick enough, to elude his grasp. "Breanna. *Breanna Stockard.*"

She slammed the door to their bedroom.

Zen put down his beer and rolled his wheelchair down the hall after her. The door was locked.

"Hey, come on," he said calmly. "Open the door."

There was no answer.

"Breanna." He struggled to keep his voice down. Caroline was on the other side of the house, but Teri's room was right next door. And in any event, the house wasn't *that* big. "Listen—I argued against the subpoena."

The door flew open.

"What subpoena?" demanded Breanna.

"The one the committee chairman is going to issue tomorrow."

"That's bullshit. You can't subpoena the executive branch. You're just doing it for publicity."

"I'm not doing anything for publicity. I voted against it."

Breanna started to close the door, but this time Zen was too quick—he rolled forward just enough to block it. She pushed for a moment, then let go.

"Hey, why are you mad at me?" he asked.

"I'm not."

"Well you're doing a pretty damn good imitation. Look at this—you made me spill my beer."

Breanna scowled, then went into the bathroom. She closed the door; it wasn't quite a slam, but it wasn't gentle either.

Zen wheeled himself over.

"You know, we really shouldn't fight about this," he said. "Unless there's a really good reason. A *really* good reason."

He heard the shower go on. Zen took a sip of his beer. He tried not to reach the obvious conclusion from Breanna's anger: Ernst was right and something seriously illegal *was* going on.

The next few days were not going to be pleasant. His responsibility as a senator meant he could not sit by blindly and twiddle his thumbs while the administration did whatever the hell it was they were doing.

Todd must have really screwed up this time.

"I'm gonna check the sports scores and finish my beer in the den," he told the closed door. "When I come back, truce. No work discussion, no nothing. Promise?"

There was no answer.

"Good enough for me," he said, wheeling back toward the living room.

19

Southeast Washington, D.C.

AMARA WOKE IN THE MIDDLE OF THE NIGHT, HIS INTERnal clock stuck somewhere between Africa and America.

He could smell Ken's coffee. The burnt liquid permeated the air, its caffeine tickling his nose and throat.

Something about the man scared him. Physically, he was nothing, a weakling. But there was something in his gaze that made him very scary, as scary as any of the blank-eyed teenagers stoned out on khat and the other drugs the warlords sometimes used to encourage their men. Even spookier was the fact that he was smart, smarter even than the Asian, Li Han.

Lying in bed, Amara thought of his earlier time in America. The country was not the great enemy that the followers of al Qaeda claimed. It was a strange and bizarre place, a country of heathens and devils, certainly, but also one where a man might be free of his past.

Lying in bed, he recalled his days as a student. Most of the teachers he had were arrogant jerks, prejudiced against him because he was African and a Muslim. Yet a few had tried to encourage him. He thought about one, a black man who taught history, who invited him into his home around Christmas.

Christmas. The ultimate Christian holiday. It should have been abhorrent, and in fact Amara had only accepted out of loneliness. But the man and his wife—they had no children—were so low key about it, so matter of fact, and above all so kind, that he had begun asking questions. He was impressed by their answers.

"A day not to be selfish," said the professor. "That's the best way to sum it up for someone who's not Christian."

"And by not being selfish, to save yourself for eternity," added his wife.

The idea was foreign to Amara. Not the element of religion—he certainly believed in an afterlife. But it seemed strange that one could guarantee a place there simply by helping others.

The other person who had been nice was a Jew. He didn't know this at first. The man was his math professor. He'd found Amara sitting alone in the college café one lunchtime and asked to sit down. This became a habit through the semester. Only after a few weeks did it dawn on Amara that the man was Jewish. The man never talked about religion or asked about Amara's, but comments he had made about one of the holidays made it clear enough.

At the end of the semester, grades faltering, Amara was in danger of flunking out. The professor helped him find free tutoring, aiding him with his English, his main barrier. He also loaned him money, and would have helped him find a job if Amara had stayed for the summer.

What if those men were killed by the weapon Ken was constructing? How would he feel?

Were they soldiers, too, as the Brothers' allies claimed?

What of their relatives, their wives?

It was OK to kill an enemy tribe in revenge. But where was the revenge here? His people had not been harmed.

It was not murder when it was jihad. But was it jihad to kill a man who believed his greatest achievement was to help someone?

The apartment was cold. Amara shifted around under the thin blanket, trying to keep warm. He drifted in and out of sleep. He tried to push his memories away. At one point he saw Li Han in the house, laughing at him. He turned over, realized he'd been dreaming.

There was a shadow in the room, standing over him.

Ken.

He bent down and moved his arm swiftly.

"You have served your purpose," said Ken.

Something flew across Amara's throat. He started to protest, to speak, but his mouth wouldn't respond. It was full of liquid, salty liquid—blood.

He gasped, then began to cough. The shadow disappeared, then the room, then thought.

All was warm; finally, all was warm.

UNEXPECTED
CONSEQUENCES

———

1

Southeastern Sudan

AT PRECISELY 1303 THE CELL PHONE TOWERS THAT provided southeastern Sudan with its characteristically spotty reception had a power failure. This was not unprecedented; the system had crashed three times in the past two months alone. There were few calls on the network in the area to begin with; not only was the service considered extremely unreliable, but it was also commonly assumed—incorrectly, as it happened—that the government monitored all calls through the cell tower.

Somewhat less usual, there was a malfunction at the same time involving the satellite telephone network most convenient and popular in the area. Anyone on a call inside a hundred-square-mile circle—there were about two dozen—heard a bit of static, then had their conversation fade in and out before completely dying. A few seconds later full service was restored; it was somewhat unusual, but not entirely inexplicable—sunspots, bizarre electrical fluctuations, even strange weather patterns were randomly but plausibly blamed by the few people who happened to be inconvenienced.

The fact that both events occurred simultaneously was not, of course, an accident. The power disruption at the cell towers was accomplished by explosive charges, which wiped out the transformers at two key stations. Had it been detected, the evidence would have pointed to a rebel group, of which there were many operating in the Sudan: the explosive was manufactured in an Eastern European country known for its easy exportation policies. The men seen in the vicinity were driving a four-door white pickup common to many groups. The men, all three of whom were black, wore anonymous brown fatigues that had their origins in China—another common quality among the ragtag groups that vied for control in this corner of the country.

The men were actually two Marines selected personally by the third man, Sergeant Ben "Boston" Rockland, from the two Marine platoons assigned to the Whiplash operation and rushed to Ethiopia only two hours before.

Blowing up the transformer was a rather crude and old school approach to killing communications. While effective, it stood in sharp contrast to what happened to the satellite communications, also perpetrated by Whiplash. This was actually accomplished by a high-altitude balloon and a UAV only a bit larger than the average buzzard. Indeed, the UAV looked very much like a buzzard from the distance; one had to get relatively close to see the net antenna that trailed from the wings or the stubby protuberances from the bottom. These antennas allowed the unmanned aircraft to intercept and redirect satellite signals emanating from the ground to the Whiplash satellite system. This redirection brought the ground half of these transmissions to MY-PID, where they could be altered as well as modified; the system could allow normal communications to proceed through an antenna in the small balloon, or route them to human operators located at an NSA facility in Maryland to conduct the calls.

In effect, no one in this small corner of the world could call home without MY-PID's permission, and even then it might not be home they talked to at all.

Thus was the Brothers camp isolated from the rest of the world.

DANNY FREAH, EN ROUTE SOUTH IN THE REPAIRED Osprey, worried that the disruption of telephone service would tip off the people inside the camp that they were about to be attacked. He wasn't as much worried about them increasing their defenses as the possibility that they would begin leaving the camp. While he had the road under surveillance, dealing with a mass exodus would have been nearly impossible.

MY-PID now estimated there were nearly 400 people inside the camp, though only 250 to 300 were likely to be fighters. At the moment, Danny had only twenty people to stop them, counting

Melissa. The roads were mined and the ridges surrounding it could be blown up to stop an exodus, but it would be extremely messy.

His force would be augmented at nightfall by four Whiplashers arriving with more equipment from the States, the two platoons of Marines he'd been assigned, and the SEAL who had parachuted in with Nuri's vodka. The SEAL was so eager for action when he saw the Marines arriving that Nuri told Danny he'd probably be shot if Danny didn't give the OK.

"And I doubt I'll get the gun out of my holster before he draws his," Nuri had added.

Pitting a force seventy-odd strong against three hundred made for almost suicidal odds in a traditional military situation. But this wasn't going to be a traditional military situation. Not only were the core fighters highly trained, but Danny had formulated a plan to use Whiplash's nonhuman assets to balance the odds.

Primary reconnaissance was being provided by a Global Observer, a long-winged spy plane that could cover a vast swath of northeastern Africa from high altitude. With wings as long as a 747, the odd-looking, push-propeller plane was fueled by hydrogen cells that allowed it to stay airborne for weeks at a time. Her long wings and spindly body mounted an array of video and infrared cameras that covered the entire compound. With backup from the Global Hawk that had been circling over Duka, MY-PID had a comprehensive image of the enemy camp. The computer could selectively zoom in on any spot in the entire area.

The images would be fed not just to Danny and everyone else on the Whiplash team, but to the Marine commanders via their standard "tough-book" laptops.

Spread out over almost a mile in the mountains, the Brothers' stronghold looked something like a pair of sunny-side-up eggs with slightly separated yolks and a misshapen and large white ring. The defenses were situated in a way to protect against an outside attack—from the ground.

The "yolks" were clusters of clay and stone buildings that were like miniature citadels, about a half mile apart. Analyzing intelligence data relating to the terrorist organization, MY-PID had decided the cluster to the northeast was the most likely command post; most radio transmissions seemed to have originated from that area, and the satellite images showed more human traffic there.

Studying the same data, Danny concluded the opposite. The Brothers were undoubtedly aware that they were being monitored, if only by the Sudanese authorities; they would do everything in their power to throw them off. So he decided his first attack would be aimed at what was supposedly the less important "yolk," with action at the other cluster intended simply to hold the enemy in place.

At first, anyway.

Danny rendezvoused with the Marine commanders in an abandoned oil field about ten miles north of the Brothers' camp fifteen minutes after communications had been cut. The small village near the field was abandoned about a year before, after the wells went dry; they had polluted the groundwater long before that, making the place virtually uninhabitable by anyone who didn't have a reason to be there.

Nuri and Hera, who would liaison with the Marine platoons, came as well, as did Melissa and Flash, who was filling in for Boston as Danny's chief enlisted officer.

Danny arrived a few minutes early, and was on the ground waiting when the Marine Osprey skimmed in over the flat terrain, flying so low its wheels could have touched the ground had they been extended. The aircraft maneuvered so it was behind a set of derelict derricks, then landed neatly thirty yards from the Whiplash bird.

"Colonel Freah, helluvapleashuretameetya," said the first man off the helicopter, Captain Joey Pierce. The officer in charge of the two platoons, Pierce had a Midwest accent but ran his words together quicker than someone from New York; Danny, whose ex-wife had come from New York, had trouble parsing the syllables into actual sentences.

It took him about ten minutes to sketch out the basic plan, emphasizing that the situation would be fluid from its inception.

"My people will hit the interior of the compound at 2300," Danny told the captain. "We need you to tie down the main part of the Brothers' force with an attack in this area here, and a feint at the main gate first." He pointed to two areas on the southern side of the camp. "We need them to think that the main attack is occurring there. Once they're committed to defending that area, we'll come in."

"Won't they just reverse course and attack you?" asked Pierce.

"They won't be able to," said Danny.

"Colonel, with all due respect." Pierce pointed to the map. "Looks pretty open to me."

"It won't be," said Danny. "And whatever your forces do, absolutely do not pursue them inside the camp. For your own protection."

"Our protection?"

Danny nodded solemnly. "We'll hook into your communications just prior to the assault. Flash has a rundown on the emergency procedures, and what we'll do if there's a hurry-up—if things happen before the planned assault time."

Danny glanced at Nuri when Flash had finished.

"Did you want to add anything?" he asked the CIA officer.

"Just that Colonel Freah isn't kidding when he says don't pursue," said Nuri.

HERA FELT THE SLIGHTEST TWINGE OF JEALOUSY AS SHE caught the CIA officer Melissa Ilse glancing at Danny. There was something about the way she looked at him that bothered her. She felt almost protective of the colonel.

"What look are you talking about?" Nuri asked her as they trotted toward the Marine Osprey to head back to the platoon staging area. Since MY-PID wasn't available to the Marines, Nuri and Hera would stay with them during the assault.

"Just a look," said Hera.

"Danny would never ever hook up with her," said Nuri flatly. "Ilse is bad news. No way."

Men, thought Hera. Always clueless.

2

Washington, D.C. suburbs

BREANNA TOOK ONE LAST LOOK AT HER DAUGHTER sleeping in the bed, then gently closed the door and slipped down the hallway.

It was just past 5:00 A.M.; even her early rising husband wouldn't be out of bed for another twenty minutes or so.

She grabbed the coffeepot and filled her steel insulated commuting cup. Then she went out to her car in the garage as quietly as possible, opened the door and headed for work.

If everything went well in Africa, the controversy would more or less blow over. Edmund could go before the Intelligence Committee and explain that Raven had crashed and had then been recovered.

He'd be out of a job shortly thereafter, but that wasn't her concern.

The question was, what would happen to Raven?

As Breanna saw it, there were two possibilities:

it could be abandoned, or it could be handed over to the Office of Special Technology.

Surely it wouldn't be abandoned.

She cleared security at the main gate of the CIA headquarters complex, then drove to a lot about two hundred years from the Room 4 building. The building itself had no parking, even though there was ample room around it; it was one more way of confusing the ever more invasive satellite eyes and other data gatherers employed.

Downstairs, Breanna was surprised by the smell of strong coffee. Only one person made the coffee so strong that it could be smelled outside the electrostatic walls: Ray Rubeo.

Sure enough, she found the scientist himself sitting at the table in their main conference room with Jonathon Reid.

"Ray, what a surprise," she said.

Rubeo accepted a peck on the cheek with his customary stiffness. "I thought I might be useful," he said.

"Ray has been examining the Raven software," said Reid. "Which our colleagues so reluctantly made available. I didn't think you would mind."

"No, it's all right."

"It is an extremely powerful core, with a great number of flaws," said Rubeo. "One of which is the fact that they're using a temporary interface."

Rubeo waved his hand over the table and tapped down with his right thumb. This opened a panel on the wall at the far side of the room, changing the wall surface into a projection screen.

"Coding display one," Rubeo told the computer.

A slide appeared. It was a "dump" of computer code.

"It was written in C++," said Rubeo. "Inexplicably."

"The point being that anyone can interpret it," said Reid.

"Yes," said Rubeo, drawing out the word.

Not anyone, thought Breanna—she certainly couldn't. But the point was, anyone with a reasonable knowledge of programming could.

"I would guess that they did this for two reasons," said Rubeo. "The first being that they didn't want to risk the actual program. This is somewhat isolated from the core modules that make up the actual Raven program. The second is that they did it for expediency; this part of the program was developed very quickly. I would guess within a matter of weeks. Perhaps even less."

"Why so fast?" Breanna asked.

Rubeo touched his earlobe, where he had a gold post earring. It was an old habit, usually signaling he wanted to make some difficult pronouncement.

"Politics," suggested Reid before Rubeo could speak. "The timing suggests that Reginald Harker was interested in becoming head of the DIA. If he had successfully taken out a high priority target like Li Han, he would have had an excellent leg up."

"Harker broke the law and risked a top secret development program so he could get a better job?" said Breanna.

Reid didn't answer.

"Using this command module may have been

seen as a safeguard," said Rubeo. "It certainly isn't as robust and manageable as I would imagine a mature interface is. Still, the core program must be recovered. If the Russian operative is able to make it from the camp—"

"He won't," said Breanna.

3

Washington, D.C. suburbs

ZEN WOKE EVEN GRUMPIER THAN USUAL, SURPRISED and yet not surprised that Breanna had already slipped out to work.

At least the coffee was still warm. He bustled about, getting Teri breakfast, then shaving and dressing himself. He left Caroline sleeping in the guest room and headed out, Teri riding shotgun in the backseat. After dropping her off at school, he swung over and picked up his aide, Jay, then went to the hospital, where Stoner was already in physical therapy when he arrived.

"Did you sleep at all?" Zen asked, wheeling himself into the exercise room.

"I'm good."

Stoner pushed a set of free weights over his chest. He was lifting five hundred pounds, by Zen's reckoning, and didn't seem to be straining.

"Are we going to the game tonight?" asked

Stoner. His tone was genuinely enthusiastic—the first time Zen remembered him sounding that way since he'd been rescued.

"Yeah, if you want."

"I do."

Zen watched Stoner pump the weights. He reached twenty, then put the weights down easily on the stands.

"I wish I could do it that easy," said Zen.

"Then you'd have to take the whole package. Headaches, not really knowing who you are. Not trusting your body."

"I know a little bit about that."

Stoner nodded.

"The doctor says some of what they did to me might help you," said Stoner.

"Me?"

"Is that why you're hanging around?"

"You mean my legs?"

"Exactly."

The enthusiasm had been replaced by something else—anger.

"No," said Zen. "I've been down that road. A lot. They've done a lot of things trying to help me to walk again. None of them worked, Mark. This is what I am. This where I am. It's just the way it is."

"That's too bad," said Stoner.

The silence was more awkward than even Stoner's question.

"I come to see you because we're friends," said Zen, trying to fill it. "You saved Breanna, remember?"

"Yeah," he said after a very long pause. Zen wondered if he really did.

"And we were friends before," said Zen. "Remember that?"

"Vaguely," said Stoner.

"And . . ." Zen hesitated. "I was . . . sorry I couldn't protect you and the others in that helicopter. I always felt . . . as if I should have done something more. I should have gone against orders and figured something out. Whatever. Something . . ."

Stoner looked at him for what seemed an eternity. "It's OK," he said finally. "I understand."

Then he went back to pumping more iron. Zen glanced at his watch. He had to leave.

"I'll see you tonight," he said.

"I'll be ready."

HE DID REMEMBER. EVERYTHING.

Mark Stoner sat on the edge of the weight bench, thinking about dying, remembering how it had all happened.

It wasn't Zen's fault at all. Zen wasn't anywhere near at the time. Even if he had been, there was no guarantee he could have done anything. None.

He himself had accepted the risks. That was the nature of the job.

Zen had risked his life to get him back here alive. They were more than even, the way those things worked.

It was good to have a friend.

He rose and took two more plates from the rack, slipping them on the bar one at a time.

It would be good to go to the game. Baseball was a good thing.

Even if the hot dogs gave him heartburn.

4

Southeastern Sudan

THE BROTHERS WERE CALLED TO PRAYER AS THE SUN set, joining Muslims around the world in turning toward Mecca to fulfill the requirements of their faith.

Just as the prayer was ending, a trio of small rockets arced over the advanced lookout posts and struck the guard posts at the main entrance. A split second later a half-dozen more struck the gutted bus used as the gate, obliterating it.

The rockets looked like Russian-made Grads. Which they were. Mostly.

Ordinary Grads were extremely simple weapons, mass-produced and exported around the word, including to Hezbollah, which used them against Israel. As originally designed, they sat in a tube and were fired. In the original version, the tubes were massed together and mounted on the back of a truck.

These three rockets were fired from tubes on the ground. But their rear sections included stabilizers and steering gear that made them considerably more accurate than the originals. The mechanisms were interlaced with explosives, which meant they disintegrated when they landed.

The real alteration was in the nose, where the explosive used an aluminum alloy mixed with a more common plastic explosive base to produce an explosive power some eleven times more destructive than the original warheads.

A tenth missile—this one unguided—flew a few feet farther, landing harmlessly on the roadway behind the post. The charge in it was stock, or at least appeared so. It failed to ignite properly, fuming but not exploding. This in fact was its intent: evidence for anyone who had a chance to see it that the attack had been launched by a rival group.

A dozen men died instantly. The other fighters in the camp reacted with indignation, grabbing their rifles and rushing to defend the camp and avenge the insult to their beliefs. They were met with a hail of gunfire from the Marines, who had spent the past two hours creeping up the hills into position. At roughly the same moment, another dozen rockets were fired at two sniper posts and four gun positions overlooking the camp. The sniper positions were essentially depressions in the rocks, and firing so many missiles at them was arguably overkill; the resulting explosions caused small landslides, not only obliterating the men there but turning the positions into exposed ravines that could no longer be used for defense.

Even as the dust from the rocket strikes was settling, the first mortar shells began raining down on the positions. These were standard-issue, Marine Corps high explosive M720 rounds, armed with M734 Multioption fuses set for near surface burst—not fancy, especially compared to the weapons Whiplash was deploying, but extremely effective. Fired from a range of roughly 3,000 meters, the rounds exploded behind the first wave of enemy troops, then walked inward toward the defenses, in effect sweeping the enemy toward the front line.

Danny had a bird's-eye view of the explosions as they rocked the southern side of the camp. He and the rest of the Whiplash team had jumped from the back of an Osprey moments before the first rockets were launched. All were wearing glide suits, which allowed them to guide their free fall into precise routes specified by the GPS module in their smart helmets.

In contrast to the noisy action at the "front" of the camp, the Whiplash team's descent was entirely silent and, in the dark, practically invisible.

"Target area," Danny told the helmet. The view changed to a square roughly fifty by twenty meters at the eastern end of the cluster he was assaulting. A red box appeared around two shadows at the left side of the box—armed men who might present trouble. They had just manned a bunkered security post.

"ICS, target and eliminate enemy in designated box A3," Danny said, this time talking through MY-PID to the integrated combat system aboard the AB-2C that had joined Whiplash for the operation.

The AB-2C was a specially modified version of the B-2A, prepared under Office of Special Technology supervision as part of the Air Force program to investigate replacements for the AC-130. The AB-2C was essentially just a test bed for the weapon system; it was very likely that the final design would be completely automated. But in the meantime, the two men and one woman aboard as crew relished the chance to show what they and their aircraft could do.

Unlike her conventional gunship forebears, the modified stealth bomber carried no howitzers or cannons. Instead, there were two laser weapons in what had been the Spirit's bomb bay. Descendants of the Firestrike weapon first developed by Northrop Grumman, the lasers were capable of sending a directed beam of just over 100 kW into a target.

The forward laser of the AB-2C burned holes in the skulls of the two mujahideen manning the post in a matter of milliseconds. The crew then sought other targets, concentrating first on the prepositioned machine guns, cooking off their ammunition so they couldn't be used against the Marines.

Meanwhile, Danny did one last check of the target area and the descending squad before manually deploying his parachute. Though not absolutely necessary, the chute allowed for a softer, surer landing—and not coincidentally, was a hell of a lot easier on his knees.

"I'm in," said Sugar, landing just to his left on the roof of the building in the center of the targeted compound.

Danny touched down a few seconds later. He quick-released his chute gear and sprinted toward the rooftop defense position. Sugar had already secured it, ramming what looked like a small stopper in the mouth of the machine gun in place there.

"Fire in the hole!" she yelled, somewhat dramatically.

Danny turned away as the charge in the stopper ignited. The blast ripped back the barrel of the gun, rendering it impotent. The sound was lost in the crescendo of the attack near the front gate.

"Let's go inside," said Danny as the other two members of his fire team reached the roof.

MELISSA WAS THROWN AGAINST HER RESTRAINTS AS the Osprey pitched hard to get on a new course, avoiding the MC-17 swooping in low over the compound. As the black cargo aircraft came in, two large containers trundled down the interior rail system to the rear bay doors. The large rectangular boxes looked like smaller versions of the shipping containers that carried so much freight around the world. Long droguelike parachutes deployed as the boxes left the aircraft, slowing their descent just enough to allow the cushioned bottoms to properly absorb the blow from the fall.

The flat screen at the forward station in the Osprey's hold received input from the MC-17's target-drop system; it declared the boxes had hit exactly 13 and 27 centimeters from their "optimum" positions.

"Good enough for government work," joked the crew chief, watching over Melissa's shoulder.

As they hit the ground near the larger citadel, the sides of the large crates unfolded, revealing a quartet of TinkerToy-like objects on a platform. These odd contraptions, known to the Whiplash team simply as Bots, could be configured for a variety of tasks. The eight that had just landed were all equipped with M-134 Gatling guns, essentially the same weapons fired by a door gunner in a helicopter or a crewman on a riverine boat. Moving on tanklike treads, the bots fanned out around the larger of the two central compounds, taking up predesignated positions.

As the last bot reached its destination, all eight began to fire, peppering the exterior of the half-dozen buildings with a barrage of gunfire for exactly twenty-two seconds. As the last bullet hit, a dozen small munitions, launched from the "arms" of the Osprey Melissa was riding in, struck their targets, removing the roofs from the buildings.

Melissa jerked up as the crew chief tapped her on the shoulder.

"Be ready to land in zero-five," said the chief.

She gave him a thumbs-up, then keyed the screen to show the area Danny was attacking to the northwest.

DANNY CAME IN THROUGH THE DOOR AS THE FLASH-bang grenades exploded, his visor automatically adjusting for the burst of light. Something moved on his left; he turned and tapped his trigger, killing a Brother gunman instantly. This was a "full prejudice" mission—no holds barred. The rules of engagement allowed anyone inside to be shot. Everyone in the compound had already declared themselves a member of the Sudan Brotherhood, and the unit's alignment with al Qaeda made them a legitimate enemy of the United States.

The team moved through the room quickly, reaching the exterior hallway. The next two rooms were unoccupied—the walls were so thin they could see the heat signatures on their helmet screens—and they reached the hallway in seconds.

"Fire in the hole!" yelled Nolan.

Standing at the head of the stairs, the trooper dropped a frag grenade down. As soon as it exploded, the team descended to the first floor of the two-story building. Nolan stayed on the steps while the rest raced to check the rooms.

The walls were either thicker or insulated, and they could no longer count on their infrared images or MY-PID's interpretation. They swept each room methodically, hitting them with grenades and then coming in. Each room looked like a classroom, with a small desk and a number of chairs—a finishing school for terror.

When the last room had been cleared without finding anyone, Danny checked in with the team that had landed on the building at the diagonal corner from them.

"Flash, what's your situation?"

"Building cleared. Twelve enemies encountered, twelve down."

"Move on."

"Moving."

"Got all the action over there," quipped Nolan. "I picked the wrong team."

Floor cleared, Danny was about to move on to the next building when he heard a shout from Sugar in the back room. He ran over in time to see her pulling a desk away from the side. She kicked the corner of the carpet behind it, revealing a metal trapdoor on the floor.

"Used a string to close it," she told him. "Squeezed past the desk."

Danny covered her while she opened it, revealing an unlit staircase.

"Drop a grenade," he told her.

She did.

"Goes down pretty far," she told him after it exploded. "Then in that direction, to the north."

"We'll have to come back and check it," he told her. "Help me with the desk."

They turned the desk on its side and slid it over the hole. Then Danny posted a pair of small video cams, one on the desk and the other at the side of the room, and had MY-PID monitor them for any movement. He also added a pair of charges near the hole so they could blow up anyone trying to escape by remote control.

MY-PID had apparently not discerned the tunnel because of the building structure and angle, which either by design or accident obscured the image on standard radar techniques. The computer calculated—with a 43.5 percent certainty, an admission that it was just guessing—that the tunnel was connected to a mine shaft some two hundred yards away, which had been seen by the radar.

"Target the mine shaft opening," Danny told the Ospreys. "See if you can bomb it closed."

In the meantime, the rest of Danny's team cleared the second building, a one-story structure where three fighters attempted to hold out. Armed with AK-47s, all three were quickly overcome.

"Running out of buildings," said Flash, reporting that his team had cleared its next objective.

"Keep moving," barked Danny.

NURI DUCKED AS A SUDDEN BURST OF GUNFIRE bounced through the rocks just to his right. The bullets themselves were well off the mark, but they shattered the nearby rock outcropping, sending a fusillade of chips showering in every direction. Several hit his helmet so hard that he fell down. He had an instant headache—but it was far better than what might have occurred had he not given in to Pierce's "extremelystrongpersonalrecommendation, sir!" that he don a Marine helmet to go with his Whiplash-issued armored vest.

Shaking the blow off, Nuri rose in time to see the Marines he'd been with pump several grenades into the position behind the flattened bus. One of the grenades hit a small store of ammo. This resulted in a cascade of shrapnel even larger than the one that had engulfed him, but it didn't stop the Brothers who were several yards behind the position from firing.

The Marines countered with a heavy dose of lead from their M-16A4s. Nuri added some rounds from his own SCAR, then saw two of the enemy soldiers running down the hillside on his left. As he swung around to fire, one of the men dropped straight back, taken down by a Marine sniper.

The other tossed a grenade, big and fat, directly at him.

AS THE REST OF HIS TEAM HEADED TO TAKE DOWN THEIR third and final building, Danny diverted to check on the "spikes" that had been launched and planted just after the start of the mission.

The "spikes"—they had no official name beyond a series of letters and numbers—were a quartet of long metal tubes that were literally rocketed into the ground after being launched from the MC-17. After insertion, a network of small wires shot from the bodies of the spikes, creating a field of electric current—a virtual electric fence, or for the more sci-fi oriented, a force field. Anyone attempting to run through the area protected by the spikes would receive a massive jolt of electricity, roughly the equivalent of three hits from a commercial grade Taser.

The system wasn't foolproof. A very determined enemy willing to sacrifice a few men could conceivably force his way through. And an enemy that knew what he was dealing with could punch a hole through the defenses by destroying two of the spikes. But in the dark, a confused and unsophisticated enemy would be surprised and stunned by the force of the blow: as evidenced by the two twitching men lying on the other side of the fence Danny saw as he approached.

With the assurance that the spikes were working, he took a quick detour to his left, running in the direction of the citadel cluster where the bots had landed. Here another set of spikes had embedded themselves between the closest ring of defenders and the buildings. Covering a wider ground, the spikes were backed by two of the bots. At least a half-dozen bodies lay on the other side of the virtual fence; from where Danny was, it was impossible to see if they were dead or merely stunned by the shock.

The bots had the buildings under siege. A violent firefight flared at the southeastern corner. Danny considered calling in another round of mini-JDAMs to subdue the resistance, but decided not to—too much damage and they'd never be able to recover the missing UAV parts if they were inside.

By the time he returned to the buildings he'd attacked, both teams were engaged in a gun battle with several Brothers around the last unsearched building.

"I figure this much resistance, it's a good bet what we want is inside," said Flash, who was huddled behind the corner of the building across the way. "What do you want to do?"

"Put some grenades through the window," said Danny. "Lives are more important."

Strictly speaking, that wasn't true—everyone on Whiplash was expendable, and they knew it—but Flash complied. He loaded a round into the snap-on launcher beneath his SCAR's gun barrel, sighted on the window the Brothers were firing from, and pulled the trigger.

An ordinary grenade fired by a skilled fighter would have a fair chance of getting through the window, but even a novice could have succeeded with Flash's setup. The grenade was a guided munition, designed to follow the beam projected by the laser at the top of Flash's gun. The round flew through the window and exploded inside, instantly killing all three fighters.

The gun battle continued. There were four men up on the roof of the building. Two had machine guns, and with constant fire they were able to keep the team at bay. Flash had sent two troopers around the side, and he was reluctant to fire any grenades near them, fearing they would be crushed by the wall if it collapsed. Their positions were marked out on his screen by MY-PID, which kept track of the members by reading the location of the transponders in bracelets each wore.

Danny finally decided the best solution was to call in a laser strike.

"Team, stand by," he told the others before connecting with the laser plane.

"Alert," said MY-PID, interrupting his transmission. "Four subjects are exiting from Mine Entrance X-ray Dog one five."

The attack by the minibombs had failed to close the entrance. Danny told the laser ship to stand by, then called up to the Osprey, where his four-member team of reserves, including Melissa, were waiting for their part in the assault.

"We have a slight change in plans," he told them. "We have people coming out of the mine."

"We're just talking about it now," said Shorty, handling the team communications. "We'll get them."

"Melissa, are you all right with this?" Danny.

"I'm anxious to get going."

"Roger that. Whiplash Six out."

NURI CURSED AS THE GRENADE EXPLODED A FEW YARDS away. By then he was facedown in the dirt, the rest of his body hunched flat. The concussion slammed him flat so hard he blanked out. He came to a moment later, feeling as if the back of his skull had been blown straight off. But only his helmet had been forced away, the chin strap sheared off.

He'd also lost his right earplug. He fished around for it—the plug had his radio headset embedded in it—but couldn't find the wire. It had been severed in the explosion.

Amazing I wasn't hit, he said to himself.

He glanced at his right arm and realized that wasn't true—blood was running down the front of his bicep, soaking into the skin.

Shit.

"Sir! Sir! You OK?" yelled a corpsman, running to his position.

Nuri flexed his fingers.

"I'm OK," he told him. "Help some of those guys."

"Where?"

Nuri looked in the direction of the Marines

who'd been with him earlier, expecting to see them lying on the ground. Instead, they were charging the gate position.

"I'm fine," he yelled to the corpsman, hustling after them.

MELISSA GRIPPED THE ASSAULT RIFLE AND TRIED TO steady her breathing as the Osprey sailed toward the hill where the men were escaping from the mine. Despite her best efforts, she was hyperventilating, gulping huge wads of air into her lungs.

The aircraft began to stutter. Melissa looked up, worried that they were about to go down.

"They're firing rounds to try and stop them," explained Shorty. "The pilots will herd them into a corner, assuming they don't kill them. Be ready."

"I'm ready," she yelled. "I'm as ready as ready."

DANNY TURNED THE CORNER JUST BEHIND FLASH AS THE laser took out the last of the gunmen on the roof. Already Sugar and one of the other troopers were at the door; within seconds there was a double explosion inside—a pair of grenades tossed by the two Whiplashers. Smoke rose from the building, and then the wall at the corner of the house furled downward, collapsing from the force of the blast.

"Shug!" yelled Danny.

"I'm OK, Colonel. We're here. All present and accounted for."

The team pushed into the house, moving quickly through the first floor. The only people they found were dead—a dozen fighters, all with weapons either in their hands or nearby.

Danny had concluded by now that either his guess on where the UAV parts would be found was wrong and they were in the second cluster of buildings, or they had never been in the camp to begin with. The search of the second floor, which had suffered considerable damage and was missing half its roof, seemed to confirm that, though they did retrieve a desktop computer from one of the rooms where the wall had partially collapsed.

"Sugar, secure the computer CPU with the drive and everything," said Danny. "Everybody else, we'll form up outside and take the other cluster."

Danny did a quick review of the situation. The men who'd come out of the mine shaft were being pursued by the team in the Osprey; MY-PID could track them relatively easily now and they wouldn't get far. The defenses at the southern wall of the compound had been almost completely neutralized. Upward of four dozen individuals were hunkered down in the huts and tents scattered on the northwestern side of the compound; they showed no inclination to join the fighting. MY-PID's analysis showed these were mostly women.

But resistance at the last citadel remained strong. Apparently realizing the bots wouldn't go inside the buildings, the men in the outer ring of houses had spread out, firing intermittently and quickly retreating. This made it more difficult for the robots to concentrate their fire. While the guns did a reasonable job of chewing into the outer walls, the Brothers had begun firing from well inside and in some cases behind the buildings.

Danny had the laser pick off anyone who was uncovered. Then he called over to the Marine captain to get him to move his mortars so they could target the complex.

"I don't want them to fire unless I give the order," Danny told Pierce. "But it may come to that."

"Will do—we have a couple of hard knots of resistance on the western and eastern ends," reported the captain. "We'll keep them engaged." His voice calmed somewhat under fire—truly something you'd only find in a Marine.

Danny circled around toward the north side of the second compound. Flash had repositioned the bots to support their assault. He released two to go back and cover the approach from the gate area, in case the Brothers there tried rallying and ran through the spikes. And he detailed one to accompany them inside the buildings, giving them extra firepower if necessary.

Flash looked up as Danny came around the corner to join the small group. "We're ready," said Flash.

"Textbook," said Danny, raising his hand and waving them to start.

THE MARINES CLEARED THE GATE POSITIONS AND RAN toward the charred remains of the bus. Nuri realized they weren't going to stop.

"Wait!" Nuri yelled. "No! *No!*"

He couldn't tell if the Marines heard him or not. Between his headache and unbalanced hearing, the entire world seemed off-kilter, a crazy quilt of explosions and gunfire.

"Stop, damn it! Stop!"

There were some barks over the radio net— garbled communications that literally sounded like dogs yapping. Nuri sprinted over two dead bodies and caught up to the Marines as they broke past the rocks on the other side of the bus. One of them looked back, but if he saw him, he obviously thought he was urging them on—they continued running, clearing the second set of defenses and the bodies clustered there.

Screaming at the top of his lungs, Nuri tried to warn them about the spikes. There were several bodies near the invisible fence, Brothers who'd been knocked out by the voltage or possibly shot in the cross fire. The Marines seemed intent on getting beyond them before they stopped running.

Nearly out of breath, Nuri was about to give up—the hell with the damn jerks if they couldn't obey an order not to attack past a certain line. The spikes would teach them a thing or two about being overaggressive.

Then he saw one of the bots trundling up in their direction.

With a stream of curses, he plunged ahead, lunging toward the first man in the group. He leapt up, throwing himself into the middle of the knot as they reached the fence line. Alerted by the bracelet on his wrist, the bot halted its targeting sequence, fearing friendly fire.

Unfortunately, Nuri's momentum took him and the Marine he landed on full force into the virtual fence. His head felt as if it had exploded, then went numb. Every joint in his body vibrated.

He fell to the ground, head still within the field, writhing in pain. He tried to push himself back but could not. His legs and arms flopping helplessly up and down, he tried to talk but could not.

Because the fence was nonlethal, MY-PID's safety protocols did not allow it to turn the device on or off. It did, however, send an alert to Danny, who dropped back from his assault team and ran down to the fence line. By the time he got in range to see what was happening, the Marines had found their own solution—they pulverized the two devices closest to Nuri, destroying the current.

Not knowing exactly what had happened, Danny assumed Nuri had somehow forgotten about the device. Shaking his head, he told the corpsman to see to him and other two men who'd been paralyzed, then had the rest of the Marines follow him.

5

Washington, D.C.

"COME TO ORDER! COME TO ORDER!" DEMANDED SENator Barrington, the Intelligence Committee chairman.

Ernst practically foamed at the mouth, but he did stop speaking.

"Now," said Barrington, slamming his gavel down once more for good measure, "we will have a vote on the motion to hold the CIA director in contempt of this committee—"

"And the President," said Ernst.

"We will *not* subpoena the President."

"The President is the one we need to hear from. We should subpoena *her*. Drag her in here in chains, if necessary."

Zen had had enough.

"Why do you keep hammering on that?" he said. "What the hell good is it going to do?"

"We have to go on record—"

"Gentlemen!" Barrington once more handled the gavel with feeling. Zen wondered if his arm was becoming numb. "You will address the chair. Senator Stockard, you have the floor."

Zen cleared his throat. "Everyone knows that the administration and I have not always agreed on everything. In this case, however, I think we should give them the benefit of the doubt— temporarily. If we vote to send a subpoena, it's going to get ridiculous headlines and be blown up by the media," continued Zen. He knew that was actually Ernst's goal, but hoped the rest of his colleagues would listen to reason. "This whole thing is going to become a political football that has nothing to do with the Agency or Raven, whatever it is."

"As if you don't know," said Ernst.

Zen ignored him. "Mr. Chairman, if our goal here is actually to *get* information, rather than

embarrassing the administration and maybe interfering with the country's pursuit—"

"What pursuit?" yelled Ernst.

Barrington pounded on the table.

"I move to end discussion and vote," said Zen,
realizing it was hopeless.

The motion carried quickly, the senators anxious to get out of the chamber. Zen was the only
one opposed.

6

Southeastern Sudan

DANNY RAN THROUGH THE RUBBLE OF THE RUINED
one-story building, leaping across the battered
stones just in time to join the team assaulting
the second house. By now the gunfire had nearly
stopped, with only a few gunmen at the far western stretch of the camp defenses continuing to
fire. But MY-PID detected heat signatures inside
several of the buildings in the last citadel, and
the crazy-quilt nature of the complex meant they
had to move slowly. The computer tagged and
followed each individual enemy as best it could,
feeding a raw tally to Danny upon request—it
knew of at least five individuals inside the building they were going into, and at least two more in

the adjacent one, which shared a wall and almost certainly a doorway.

They found the first two individuals bleeding out in the hallway, gut-shot by earlier fire. Neither had long to live; the team members pulled away their weapons, trussed their arms for safety, then carried them outside the building. Danny watched as the two men laid one of the enemy soldiers down gently.

The gesture struck him as odd and yet touching at the same time—the gravely wounded enemies had been trying to kill the Whiplash troopers just a few minutes ago, and were now being treated with a remarkable and even incongruent sense of dignity and care. In his experience, the acid of battle usually eroded any impulse toward caring for an enemy; he had seen many men simply kill people terminally wounded as they passed. He wondered if either trooper could have explained what they did. Most likely they would have said only that they were getting the men out of the way, and would have been at a loss to say why they hadn't simply dumped them on the ground. It was all unconscious action, an expression of how they lived rather than how they thought.

Danny caught up with the team clearing the last room in the building. The procedure was repetitive to the point of being industrial: mechanical gestures with their hands, a sweep of eyes, the call of "Clear."

"Room is clear!" yelled Flash.

An explosion shook the building. MY-PID immediately warned that the right side of the structure appeared ready to collapse.

"Back up! Back up!" yelled Danny, who couldn't see what was happening in the room.

There was gunfire, then another explosion. Danny grabbed hold of the trooper in front of him and pulled him back.

"Out! Out!" he yelled, and then stepped up to the next man, pulling him back, and then the next.

The floor rumbled. Flash and Nolan appeared in front of him, backing their way out.

"Let's go! Let's go!" yelled Danny as the building began to fall around them.

The dust blocked his helmet's infrared vision, shrouding him in darkness. He put his hand out and touched the back of one of his troopers—it was impossible to tell at the moment which—and nudged him, moving with him as the wall to the right sheared downward. Something hit Danny in the back and he tumbled forward, bowling the other man over. He pushed up, throwing off a beam, then realized he was outside. The upper floor of the building had almost literally disintegrated, spewing its remains in the air. The assault team began sounding off; MY-PID reported that all were accounted for.

The Marines who'd come up with Danny from the front gate began helping clear the debris. The air around them was still clouded with dust, but the far side of the citadel was clear enough for both the bots and the laser ship above to make out a dozen targets trying to escape. Within moments the twelve were dead.

MY-PID reported that it could not find any heat signatures within the building complex.

"There were computers and metal in that room," Flash told Danny, pointing to the collapsed debris. "I think the aircraft were in there."

"Let's get digging."

"THEY'RE PUTTING UP THEIR HANDS," SAID SHORTY. "They want to surrender."

Melissa looked at the screen. There were four men, one of whom was almost certainly the Russian—MY-PID identified him as clean-shaven and wearing western clothes.

He had a duffel bag.

"Cease fire," said Shorty over the Osprey radio, though the pilots already had. "What do you think, ma'am?"

Her orders were to recover the UAV brain intact if possible. That potentially conflicted with what Danny had told her—they would kill the Russian.

Which took precedence?

Did it matter? She couldn't kill the man in cold blood. Not even Danny would have done that.

The Russian would be valuable—they could get a lot of intelligence out of him if he really was an expert.

"Let's get down there and take them," she told the trooper.

THE MC-17 SWOOPED DOWN OVER THE CAMP AND dropped its third and last container into the area just south of the cluster of buildings. This one contained two bots, which were somewhat larger than the others. They looked like downsized construction vehicles: one had a clamshell, the other a crane arm with various attachments.

Unlike the gun bots, which were powered by small hydrogen fuel cells, these ran on turbo diesel engines. They lacked innate intelligence; team members controlled them via a set of remote controls. While more powerful, they were not much different than the devices used back home at small construction sites to handle jobs where traditional-sized earthmovers and cranes were either overkill or too big to fit on a work site.

Two troopers checked them out, started them up, then walked them over toward Danny and Flash, who were already pulling some of the debris away.

It took about ten minutes before they could see the outline of the room. In fact there was an aircraft there—MY-PID ID'ed the wing of a Predator. With a little more digging, Danny could make out other parts of the aircraft and a tabletop with diagnostic tools.

He suddenly got a strange feeling—not so much a premonition as déjà vu.

"Everybody back!" he yelled. "Back!"

Flash looked up at him. "Boss?"

"Back!" Danny demanded. "Controllers, you too."

After the team retreated to the outskirts of the ruins, Danny changed the video feed in his screen to the crane's.

"I can pull the wing straight up, Colonel," said the man operating the bot.

"Go for it."

Danny watched as the crane's claws grasped the wing and pulled upward. There was a flash. An explosion shook the ruins, bringing down the parts of the building that hadn't fallen earlier.

"How'd you know?" asked Flash as the dust settled.

"It looked familiar," said Danny.

MELISSA WENT OUT LAST, TROTTING BEHIND THE WHIP-lash team members as they surrounded the four men. The vest and helmet she'd donned were heavy and foreign; while the team members compared them favorably to the traditional body armor, they felt constricting to her. Sweat poured down her temples, and her arms were awash with it.

"Put down any weapons," Melissa said in Arabic.

When no one moved, she realized she'd forgotten to switch her com system into loudspeaker mode. Her mind blanked and she couldn't remember how to do it. Finally, Melissa flipped up her visor and yelled the words.

The men held their arms out to their sides.

"Separate!" she ordered. "Move apart or we will fire."

They slowly began stepping aside. Two of the team members walked toward the man farthest to the right. The Osprey circled ahead, the thump of its rotors vibrating against the hard ground and nearby hills. Melissa felt her heart racing and tried to calm it.

Suddenly, one of the men began running toward her.

Why? she wondered.

Then she knew.

"*Bomb!*"

DANNY SAW THE FLASH IN HIS VISOR SCREEN AS HE switched back to check on the escapees.

All he saw was white in the center of black. It seemed like forever before the camera on the Osprey supplying the feed readjusted.

There was a team member down.

Melissa.

"What the hell is going on?" he demanded. "Shorty? Shorty!"

"We have one man down," said the trooper. "Another minor injury. All of the prisoners are dead."

"What the hell happened?" demanded Danny.

"He had a vest, and explosives in a knapsack. We have high-tech parts in a bag."

"What's Melissa's status?"

"Breathing. Losing a lot of blood."

"Evac her the hell out of there."

"We're working on it, Colonel. We're working on it."

7

Room 4

JONATHON REID PUSHED HIS CHAIR AWAY FROM THE
table and rose. He felt as if he'd taken a breath of
fresh air for the first time in weeks.

"The electronics match," he said. "We've got it.
Thank God."

"I'm always amazed at how much God is blamed
for what humans do," said Ray Rubeo.

Reid stifled a smirk. He hadn't known the scientist even believed in God.

"They'll all be back in Ethiopia inside an hour,"
Breanna said. "Three wounded, including the
CIA officer. Light casualties, considering."

Reid nodded. It was an absurdly low casualty
rate, given what had been at stake.

There was a certain poetic justice in the fact
that the person who'd been most seriously
wounded was the one attached to the program. It
was an extremely uncharitable thought. Yet that's
what he felt.

He also felt it would have been far more satisfy-
ing if it was Harker who'd been wounded.

"Ilse has lost a lot of blood," said Breanna, who
as usual seemed to be reading his mind. "But her
vitals are stable. She took some shrapnel in the
face. That's probably the most serious. The cut in
her neck didn't reach the artery. I'm pretty sure
she'll live."

Reid nodded. The other two injuries were Marines. Both were bullet wounds, one in the arm and one in the leg.

"As soon as all our people are out, the Tomahawks will finish off the camp buildings," said Breanna. "It'll be wiped out completely."

"Do you want to tell the President, or should I?"

"You go ahead," she said. "I'll stay here until they're all on the ground."

Walking to his office, Reid realized that, if he wished, he could hint that the Russian involvement in the entire affair seemed less than coincidental. It could easily be made to seem part of a conspiracy to purposely "lose" American technology, without actually appearing criminal about it. A case could easily be constructed that pointed the finger at Harker.

Easily.

But Reid would not do that. He knew the facts. And even though he wished Harker ill, he would not bend the truth to harm him.

It occurred to Reid as he sat down at his desk that Harker might actually be in line to take over Edmund's job. If that were the case . . .

No, Reid told himself, *I must act responsibly.* No conspiracy theories, no hints, just the facts.

He picked up the phone and called the White House.

"YOU'RE AWFUL QUIET," BREANNA SAID TO RUBEO AS they watched the first Osprey take off.

"Yes," he said, in his long drawn-out way.

"Is there a problem?" she asked.

"We have the hardware," said Rubeo.

"And?"

"One never knows."

8

Ethiopia

DANNY HOPPED OUT OF THE OSPREY AS IT SETTLED down, sprinting toward the building that had been turned into a temporary clinic. Two Navy doctors and a small team of corpsmen were flown in prior to the strike to tend to the wounded.

A corpsman met him at the door.

"How are my people?" asked Danny, stepping into the large room.

"All stable, Colonel. We're just getting ready to evac to Germany."

Four stretchers and a host of medical equipment were spread out in the room. One of the patients was sitting on a chair, arm in a sling. Another was sitting up on his bed. The medical people were clustered around the third, lying prone on the table.

"How's Melissa?" asked Danny.

"Serious but stable," said one of the doctors near her. He came over to Danny. "She'll make it. Your people did excellent work. Excellent."

"Can she talk?"

The doctor grimaced. "She's unconscious. Her face is fairly bashed up. She'll need plastic surgery. Maybe a lot."

Danny walked over to the stretcher. Melissa's face was bundled in bandages.

Her face. Her beautiful face.

"Transport is ready!" yelled the corpsman. "They're waiting for us!"

"Let's move it!" said the doctor.

Danny stepped back and watched as they took her and the others out.

"Don't let her die, God," he prayed quietly. "And let her be the person she was before all of this."

9

The White House

CHRISTINE MARY TODD TOOK THE NEWS LIKE SHE TOOK most news—calmly, without noticeable emotion. She thanked Jonathon Reid, not only for helping make the mission a success, but for having had the fortitude to bring the matter to her attention despite what she guessed was considerable personal anguish and, undoubtedly, backlash from the intelligence community.

She hung up the phone, then called Blitz and Bozzone in to see her.

Waiting for them, she took a sip of tea—lukewarm, but welcome nonetheless—and tried to stretch her legs in the small office. The Intelligence Committee vote was deeply unfortunate; it made it difficult for her to send Edmund over to talk to them without seeming to give in. The political nuances of weakening her image could easily come back to haunt her in the future.

But now that Raven was safely in their hands, she had no problem giving the committee the information. In fact, handled properly, it could help fend off another episode like this one.

How exactly could she deal with this?

Perhaps she could persuade the committee to pull back on the subpoena. But they seemed to be in no mood to do so, not given the vote. Only Zen Stockard had stood against them.

She went back to the phone. "Give me Senator Stockard's office."

Bozzone came in while she was waiting on the phone. Todd motioned for him to sit down.

Zen's appointment secretary said he was on the Senate floor, which made it impossible to talk to him immediately.

"I'd like to speak with him personally," Todd told her. "When do you think he would have a hole in his schedule?"

"For you, he would always be available, Ms. President. But um, uh—"

An idea occurred to her.

"Does he still go to the Nationals baseball games?"

"Yes, ma'am. As a matter of fact, he's planning on going this evening, I happen to know."

Todd winked at Bozzone. "Ask if he'd like a better seat."

10

Room 4

WITH THE TEAM BACK SAFELY, MY-PID WENT TO WORK filling in the background and details. It examined the data gathered during the raid, including the cell and satellite phones that had been collected. The computer attempted to find and connect information relating to the phones— where they'd been bought, how they were paid for, etc.—with a vast data bank. The first wave of queries established that the phones were all somewhat ordinary, purchased in Europe at various times. The second found a number of other phones that were undoubtedly purchased at the same time—their sim cards were part of a series that would have been included in a large batch of purchases. The next round of queries and links discovered that, for the most part, the phones had been used in Africa and the Middle East— Egypt especially.

The computer traced the line of money that

paid for the phones back to al Qaeda. It was a thin, tenuous line, but a line nonetheless.

There was an incredible amount of data, most of which seemed trivial and only distantly related. The only thing that really stood out was the fact that a cell phone purchased by the same credit card that had bought a number of others at the camp had been used the night before in Washington, D.C.

"That's more than a little interesting," said Breanna.

"Hmmm," said Reid, looking over the results.

An hour later Reid and Breanna sat together in the back of a Chevy Impala. Up front, the head of the FBI task force on domestic terrorism waited with them as a Bureau emergency response team and officers from the Washington, D.C., SWAT unit prepared to go into a house near where the call had been made. The decision to ask for a search warrant had come after the discovery of the cell phone led to a scouring of phone records that discovered a link between the number that had been called and a landline in one of the apartments on the street itself.

The link was tenuous—the number the cell phone had called had been used several months before to call a number in Pakistan used by a known Muslim radical; that radical, in turn, had called another number, which had called the D.C. apartment. But that information led to data about the man who had rented the apartment, a supposedly Egyptian student who, it turned out, was not registered as a student in American immigration records.

This did not make him a member of al Qaeda. Nor could it be assumed that the man had failed to register as the law required: Mistakes in the records were very common, as the FBI supervisor explained.

But it did have to be checked out.

They weren't taking it lightly. The SWAT team alone had two dozen men on the scene. And that didn't count the ordinary policemen blocking the street and helping cover the rear alleyway.

The FBI supervisor, Bob Randolph, was an affable Boston area native who'd relocated to D.C. some years before. Breanna had met him once or twice at government conferences, but had never had more than a brief conversation with him.

"Lovely area," he said, glancing at the graffiti scrawled on the wall of the garage across from them. Next to the building, several garbage cans overflowed with refuse.

"It'll be quiet tonight," said Reid dryly.

Randolph gave a polite little laugh. Then he put his hand to his ear.

"Here we go. They're going in," he said.

Breanna folded her arms against her chest, waiting. She thought of her fight with Zen—not a fight so much as a disagreement, and not so much a disagreement exactly as just uncomfortableness. She'd been forced into a role she didn't want to be in, opposing him.

He always seemed to take it all in stride. Why couldn't she?

"They're inside," said Randolph. He leaned toward the driver. "Let's move up."

Breanna jerked her head as a bomb squad truck raced past them to the front of the building.

"Are there explosives?" she asked.

"Just a precaution," said Randolph. "They're just securing the place now. We have to, you know, anticipate."

They pulled up at the end of the block. The adjoining houses had been evacuated; Breanna could see small knots of people on the other side herded behind a pair of police sawhorses, one of which was just now being put in place.

"News media will get a hold of it soon," said Randolph. "Hold on."

He pressed his hand to his ear.

"We have a dead body inside," he said. "And traces of explosives in the basement."

"If nothing else," said Reid, "it would appear we've got a story for the press."

11

Washington, D.C.

KEN GLANCED TO HIS LEFT AND RIGHT AS HE OPENED the car trunk. He'd found it necessary to steal the car to get here easily; the trade-off was paranoia that someone would spot it and know it was stolen. As highly unlikely as that might be, he couldn't get the thought out of his mind.

The trunk smelled of fuel. No wonder: the can he'd packed had tipped over while he drove, sending the liquid all over. But no harm done: There was still plenty left.

He took the small robot airplane from the rear of the trunk. Cradling the two wings under his right hand and holding the body in his left, he managed to push the trunk lid back down. Then he walked up the short flight of steps from the schoolyard to the back of the building.

The athletic field was empty. It was starting to get dark. He was two hours behind schedule; he'd planned to launch much closer to five but had last minute problems loading the program into the plane. He was sure it was going to work—sure that the guidance system knew it was supposed to target Christine Mary Todd, the Satans' President, and knew that her primary location was the White House, which was just over the next hill about three-quarters of a mile away. He'd entered the information about the President— in fact, nearly everything he could find on the Internet about her personal habits, her vehicles, her aides, the Secret Service—everything. He'd found several human interest stories and entered them as well. The program interface had taken it eagerly.

Whether it would actually *work*—whether his guesses about the software program were correct—that was impossible to tell.

The bomb he had embedded in the fuselage of

the aircraft would definitely go off, of that he was certain.

He assembled the wings. The UAV was a simple and ingenious aircraft, a perfect weapon. Anyone who saw it in the air would believe it was a police monitoring device. The camera was still attached, in fact—it had to be, as it helped guide the aircraft.

Wings attached, Ken stood back and pressed the ignition on the controller to start the plane.

The engine started right up. He turned, wondering if he heard someone coming up behind him.

There was no one there. By the time he turned back around, the aircraft was racing across the field, bouncing as it became airborne.

It seemed to have a mind of its own, as if anxious to complete its mission.

Go! he thought. Go!

It did—for about sixty seconds. Then suddenly it veered to the right, zooming high into the clouds.

Ken stared in disbelief. Not only was it going off course, but it was flying away from the city.

He was a failure.

Angrily, he slammed the knapsack that contained the laptop to the ground and kicked it several times, even jumping on it in his anger. Finally he got control of himself. He had to dispose of the thing; it was evidence.

He'd find another way to strike. For now, he had to follow through on his plan to escape.

Ten minutes later, crossing the bridge on Route 1, the smell of the fuel in the trunk gave him an idea: he should stop and throw the car into reverse, cause an explosion that would at least kill someone.

But he wasn't a martyr at heart. His death had to mean something. And it wouldn't. Not yet.

He crossed the bridge and found a place to park. Then he walked back down to the river and with a heave tossed the knapsack and laptop into the water.

When he was sure it had sank, he turned and began walking in the direction of the Pentagon Metro stop. Before the night was through, he'd be on an Amtrak heading for Florida.

After that, who knew?

12

Nationals Park

"RADIO SAYS YOU CREATED QUITE A TRAFFIC JAM ON THE way over," said Zen, wheeling past the Secret Service agent to greet the President as she arrived at the game.

"Getting through Washington by street is always fun," she told him, leaning down to kiss him on the cheek. "If it wouldn't have caused such a fuss, I would have come by helicopter."

"Given the pitchers tonight, you may want to leave by one," said Zen. "And soon."

"Oh come on."

Zen nodded at the President's husband, who, though not as hardy a fan of the Nationals as Zen had become, was nonetheless a fellow sufferer.

"Who are your friends?" asked the President, gesturing to the small entourage Zen had left back by the entrance to the President's suite.

"A very good friend of mine, Mark Stoner," Zen told her. "He was a CIA officer—"

"Oh, that's the man who tried to kill you," said Todd. "And you saved his life."

"He was sick."

"I know the history well," said Todd. She had sent Zen to the meeting where he had inadvertently become Stoner's target. "Is he OK?"

"He's still recovering. He has a long way to go. He's with one of his doctors, and my bodyguard. Baseball seems to be helping bring him back."

"I'd like to meet him." The President glanced at the head of her security detail. "OK?"

"I think it would be fine," said Zen.

The Secret Service agents were wary, but the head of the detail nodded. Zen wheeled back a bit.

"Hey Mark, Doc, come on. Simeon—you too."

The men, along with two more Secret Service escorts, came into the suite box. Just then, the National Anthem began.

"I'm afraid you'll have to excuse me a moment, gentlemen," said the President. "I always sing with the anthem. I hope my voice won't offend you."

STONER GAZED AROUND THE BOX, TAKING IT ALL IN. The President and her entourage were behind a thick plate of bulletproof glass, looking out at the stadium. There were two rows of seats in front of the box; these belonged to the suite and were unoccupied, except for two Secret Service agents who surveyed the crowd. Zen had hinted they might be able to sit there during the game; the view was actually not as good as from his seats, he claimed, but there would be free waiter service.

Stoner's gaze moved out beyond the windows. There was another police UAV above the stadium, flying over the area where the parking garage was. It circled the stadium, its wing dipping erratically.

It looked like the one from the night before. And yet, as he studied it, he noticed several differences. Its nose was bigger than the other one. It was flying differently—the other had orbited endlessly; this one weaved, as if looking for something specific.

Stoner took a step forward, then another.

The aircraft turned. It was coming for them.

No . . .

Yes.

He leapt forward. One of the Secret Service agents put a hand up to stop him. Stoner tossed him aside, then jumped up and grabbed his fingers into the wooden panel of the ceiling, using them to swing his feet up against the glass. It broke with a splatter and he sailed into the seats overlooking the ball field. He tried to roll onto his side as he flew but couldn't quite make it; his elbow smacked hard against one of the seat backs.

It hurt. That was a new sensation.

Stoner rose, saw the aircraft, and leapt straight out at it, his bionically enhanced legs giving him the leverage of an Olympic pole vaulter.

He caught the wing of the aircraft with his right hand, pushing it as violently as he could before falling straight down into a black, black hole.

13

Nationals Park

ZEN GASPED AS THE AIR IN FRONT OF THE SUITE ERUPTED in fire. Something burst in his face. He and his wheelchair flew backward against the wall. The next thing he knew he was on the ground in the dark. Something was on top of him. It was a piece of the ceiling. He pushed it off, then levered himself upright in time to see two Secret Service agents with drawn Uzis pulling the President from the suite.

"What the hell!" yelled Zen.

Someone grabbed him and jerked him up.

"What the hell is going on!" he yelled, taking a swing with his elbow.

He and the man who had picked him up fell down.

"Sir, we're with the President," yelled another man. "We're taking you to safety. Just come!"

Someone else was yelling, "Go, go, go!"

Zen was picked up again. This time he didn't fight.

Two and a half minutes later he was deposited in the back of a black SUV. President Todd was next to him.

"Are you OK, Jeff?" she asked.

"I—I guess so."

"There was a bomb in a plane," Todd told him. "They're just getting the details now. I have to go back to the White House."

"My friends—"

"They're upstairs."

"I want to stay with them."

"Jeff, this is very serious."

"I have to stay with them," insisted Zen.

Todd rapped on the window separating her from the front.

"Let the senator out. He wants to be with his friends."

"Ma'am—"

"Considering that one of them just saved my life," she said, "it's the least we can do."

BY THE TIME ZEN REACHED STONER, HE HAD BEEN loaded onto a stretcher and was being taken out onto the field where a medevac helicopter was waiting. One of the attendants who had worked on him after he fell into the crowd looked at Zen and shook his head.

"Is he dead?" Zen asked.

"Which one?"

"The guy who fell from the box up there," said Zen, pointing.

"No, sir. But I don't think he's going to make it."

Zen turned his head as the helicopter lifted off with Stoner inside.

"He will," Zen said. "I've seen him die before."

14

Washington, D.C. suburbs

BREANNA RAN TO THE DOOR AS ZEN'S VAN PULLED UP. She hesitated, unsuccessfully trying to stop her tears before opening the door.

"Hey," he said as he wheeled toward her. "What's up?"

"Oh my God, Zen, how can you be so goddamn cool?" She ran out and threw her arms around his chest. Her sobs erupted into a body-shaking tremor.

"Hey, I'm OK," he protested. "Hardly even a scratch. I was more worried about my wheelchair."

"Jeff, Jeff," she said, over and over again. "God. My God."

"Hey guys!" Zen waved.

Breanna turned around to see Teri and Caroline in the doorway. Two local policemen and the department chief loomed behind them; the chief had taken it upon himself to come over to protect them.

"I don't know what all the fuss is," he said as

the girls ran to him. "But I'm not proud—I'll take kisses."

When she managed to calm down, Breanna asked what had happened.

"I'll give you a rundown as I change," Zen told her, glancing at Teri—an indication he didn't want her to hear all of the details. "But I gotta go over to the hospital. Mark's there."

"Mark?"

"Stoner. He saved the President's life."

None of that had been in the media reports.

"Is he OK?" Breanna asked.

Zen glanced at Teri again.

"I gotta go. Help me change, OK?"

Breanna suppressed a shudder, then followed her husband into the house.

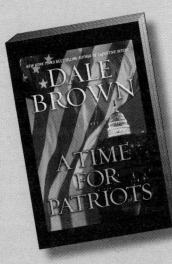